WIND SONG

WIND SONG

Unity Hall

HEADLINE

First published in 1992
by HEADLINE BOOK PUBLISHING PLC

10 9 8 7 6 5 4 3 2 1

British Library Cataloguing in Publication Data

Hall, Unity
Wind song.
I. Title
823.914 [F]

ISBN 0-7472-0446-2

Typeset by Medcalf Type Ltd, Bicester, Oxon

Printed and bound in Great Britain by
Richard Clay Ltd, Bungay, Suffolk

HEADLINE BOOK PUBLISHING PLC
Headline House
79 Great Titchfield Street
London W1P 7FN

For
Judy Chilcote –
special agent

PART I

Chapter One

The small, barefooted figure in rough, torn breeches and full-sleeved dirty shirt was no lad. Had Matthew Oliver approved of a wager he would have risked a golden sovereign on it. The shackled ankles were too slight, there was a narrowness to the hips and the unmistakable suggestion of curves under the loose, concealing shirt. It was his fancy that if the brimmed hat the figure wore was pulled away from the half-hidden face a tumble of curls would descend. Black curls? He stroked his small, pointed beard thoughtfully. No, maybe russet curls.

The girl, for he had convinced himself that this was indeed a girl, stood quietly between the two lads to whom she was shackled hand and foot. They were placed slightly apart from the fifty or so other men who, similarly chained, had just been unloaded from the *Indeavour* and into the open space that was used for slave-trading in the ramshackle town. The girl's companions stood close to her, their attitude protective; a pair of ill-sorted guardians. One was a huge fellow, bare of foot, head and chest. With clinical interest, Matthew noted that before the ten-week voyage from Bristol, the boy, who was perhaps seventeen, would have been in fine physical condition. Now his muscles hung slack from his upper arms like those of an ageing woman and his bones outlined his rib cage. But then Captain West was not renowned for the generous feeding or treatment of his cargoes.

Perhaps because he was so small, the other lad appeared younger. He barely topped the girl, but there was an alert and wiry look to him. Below a shock of bright red hair, dark brown eyes raked his surroundings, taking in the clumsily paved space in which he stood, the watching crowds and, in particular, the block. It was from this that Captain West would auction these newly arrived slaves on behalf of Sir William Stapleton, the Captain General and Chief in Command of the Leeward Islands.

'To them that hath shall be given,' Matthew muttered to himself as Nathaniel West, whose rolling walk resembled that of the old tubs he coaxed across the Atlantic, moved to confer with his sailors. Assessing their share of the booty, Matthew surmised. Each shackled man waiting in the caressing sun of a January morning on the island of St Christopher would fetch Sir William (a man already devilish wealthy) between 20 to 25 sovereigns, depending on his health and size. Of that money, the crew would take a share.

3

Two ungodly emotions had driven the God-fearing Matthew Oliver to ride down into Old Road Town from Windsong, his sugar plantation below the mountains. Curiosity and envy. The curiosity, admittedly tinged with dismay, had been to see these slaves arrive on the island. It was an unusual occurrence since the men were both white and British. The authorities called them criminals, convicted of sedition, and declared that their due punishment was ten years' unpaid labour for the planters of the West Indies. The authorities added piously that the traitors were fortunate to be alive; many of their fellows had died at the gallows.

Matthew's envy was for Sir William Stapleton who had now controlled the Leeward Islands for thirteen years. It was a post that Matthew coveted. He had settled on the island as a young man nearly twenty-eight years before in 1657 and as a colonial administrator had been instrumental in its growth. He had received little financial reward. The post should have been his. But Sir William Stapleton, a good servant of His Majesty King James, had been awarded the islands, and now two hundred of these sturdy British yeoman and seemingly one girl, to do with as he wished. Stapleton would keep what men he needed to work on his own plantations on the neighbouring island of Nevis and sell the others.

Matthew dragged his eyes from the maid in man's clothing, a sight he found peculiarly exciting, and looked around him. The sky was brilliant blue with small scudding clouds agitated by the trade winds which absentmindedly ruffled the palms and the violet and aquamarine sweep of the Caribbean Sea. A pair of brown pelicans plunged breathtakingly from a great height, diving for their breakfast. Behind, tree-clad, conical green mountains rose leisurely into the blue above. 'But man is vile,' said Matthew to himself as he looked again at the scene before him.

The slave market was an ant heap of prisoners, black slaves attending their wealthy masters or overseers who had come to buy or to gape, half-drunk sailors celebrating the end of the voyage, mulattos and whites from the town who were present out of the same curiosity that had drawn Matthew. The atmosphere was oddly quiet. The everyday shouts and hollers were missing as if the audience, repressed by the sight of their own kind in such a plight, felt it wrong to create a din. Even the noisy French, come from Basse-Terre, the capital of their portion of the island, suppressed their voices and their gestures. But nothing could suppress the smells of fish, rank meat, horses and their dung, rotting seaweed, all levened by the sweeter scents that the winds wafted from the mountains above. But stronger than all the normal smells of island life was the stench from half-hundred unwashed bodies, bodies no doubt suffering from the flux. The awful sickly odour, like a good soup gone bad, contracted the nostrils as these dispirited and near-to-death white men stood in chains, weary from the horrors of the journey, uncertain of their fate.

It was wrong to sell men, thought Matthew, who knew and regretted that he could not run his wife's huge plantation without slaves. But

4

they were black slaves. There was *some* difference, he assured himself. White men should not be sold.

He had no intention of buying any of these and lining Sir William's pockets even further, but the little group of three young people and in particular the girl excited his curiosity.

He dug his knees into his horse's side and urged the mare gently through the crowd, trying to hold his breath as he neared the sick aroma of the prisoners. As he came within speaking distance of the three, he covered his mouth with his handkerchief, reined in and sat looking down at them. The two lads closed round the maid. The bigger boy glared; the younger and smaller smiled ingratiatingly.

Matthew leaned and with his whip touched the girl on the shoulder. 'Tell me, my dear,' he said gently, 'why does a young maid masquerade as a lad?'

'He is no maid,' the biggest boy growled.

Matthew resisted the temptation to tip off the girl's hat with the end of his whip. Instead he raised his eyebrows quizzically.

The red-head, undoubtedly the quicker and smarter, accepted that the game was up. 'We dressed her in my garb for her safety, sir. Against the sailors on the voyage,' he said, ignoring a scowl from his fellow.

Matthew laughed. 'You might as well wrap a diamond in cheesecloth to hide its glitter.'

The big lad held up a fist like a fair-sized ham constrained in chains, and said gruffly, 'This was a better guardian in the end.'

Matthew could believe it. 'And why is she here?' he asked.

The girl lifted her head and extraordinary green eyes stared up at him. Underneath were black smudges of fatigue and grimy, rounded cheeks, but the eyes were clear as a washed windowpane, still untouched by life's sorrows, candid and full of truth. He felt the most extraordinary sensation, part lust and part pity. The pity overwhelmed the shaming lust and he was left with an urgent need to give her the gift of his protection; to rescue her from whatever unpleasant fate lay before her.

'They say I am a traitor, sir.'

She was no more than fifteen, of that he was certain, and the West Country was in her voice, reminding him of his youth.

'And are you so?'

She shook her head indignantly. 'No, sir. I did nought but help embroider a banner.'

Embroider a banner? He did not understand, but this was no time for explanations.

'And your companions?'

'I am her brother,' the big lad said.

'And we are all cousins, sir,' said the red-head. 'Ben Clode, at your service.' He attempted a courtly bow, rattling his chains and dragging the tall lad forward with him.

Matthew removed the handkerchief from his face and smiled. They stared up at him hopefully.

5

'And your name, mistress?'

'I am Amelia Quick,' the girl said, and made a credible curtsey before pulling herself to stand tall as her height would allow. 'And this is my brother, Zachary Quick.'

Zachary, too, attempted a bow and Matthew sat regarding them, stroking his beard as he always did in times of perplexity. They were of good family, he was certain. The name Quick nudged at forgotten corners of his memory.

'There was a Quick family at Upottery. Quick Manor—'

'Ours,' said Zachary. 'Our home,' and added bitterly, 'until three month ago. Now the property of the Popish King.'

Ah! This one did preach sedition, but then Matthew himself cared little for the idea of a Popish king on the throne of England and cared less for good West Country folk sold into slavery for their opinions. Nevertheless he put his fingers to his lips.

'Hush,' he warned, 'or your troubles will be graver.'

The girl's limpid eyes were on him, her tongue, small and pink, crept nervously to lick her soft, full, lower lip, and the unbidden lust stirred again. Matthew was convinced that she wanted his help but was too proud to ask.

He made his decision. He would not leave this exquisite waif to be prodded and inspected by the lecherous hands of the overseers who waited for the auction to begin. Without speaking he turned his impatient horse and rode to where Captain West stood. He and West were old adversaries. The sea captain's life, ferrying slaves, had brutalised the man but there was some decency left in him somewhere.

'The three young ones,' he began.

West, barrel belly thrust forward, looked up at him. 'With the maid?'

Matthew nodded.

'She's untouched. I saw to it. Nought but a child.' His voice was unctuous.

And you expect a better price for it, Matthew thought as he said, 'I will buy all three.'

A venal gleam lit the captain's eye. 'All three?'

'Seventy sovereigns.' Matthew's voice was firm. He anticipated the captain's protest that it was not enough. 'Plus twenty for your own pocket,' he added, low-voiced, 'which shall be a small and private matter between you and me.'

The captain nodded a cynical turn to the corners of his mouth. 'The lad's fists are like a leg-o'-mutton, sir,' he warned.

Matthew took his meaning. West believed he was after the virgin. He wanted to refute the insinuation but decided it was beneath his dignity. Besides, he realised with the same dismay that always struck him in these matters, it could have been the truth.

'Unshackle them,' he said coldly. 'There is nowhere now for them to run. Tell Beauboy to take them to Windsong. The money will be with you by noon.'

6

'Aye aye, sir.' Nathaniel West mockingly touched his forelock and grinned knowingly as Matthew turned his horse to ride away. As he left he was aware of the suggestive laughter of the crew.

Amelia felt the cold chill of a new despair as the elderly man turned and rode away from them without a word. She had been certain he would do something for them, but it seemed he had simply lost interest. Zach should not have mentioned the Popish King. Perhaps the man was a Catholic himself.

She watched as he rode towards the fat captain and some conversation took place. Then, with the captain nodding like a puppet, the man rode away again to be followed by a burst of raucous laughter from the sailors on the dock.

'What will happen now?' she whispered to her companions.

'We are to be sold, like so many head of cattle,' Ben said. 'I imagine we will be made to stand on that block there so all can judge our worth.'

Amelia shuddered. 'It's too like the dock again.'

'Take heart,' Ben said. 'It's just a block. There's no Judge Jeffreys and no gallows hung above it. Ten years' servitude, that's all we must face. Ten years.'

'We shall be old when we are free again,' Zach said, his voice gloomy.

'Not too old. And remember, we live when others died.'

'Perhaps death would have been better than this dishonour.'

'No,' Amelia told her brother firmly. 'Life is better. Do not speak so, Zach.'

She was afraid but would not let it show; besides, hope was prickling her thumbs. She felt a conviction that this place could not be all evil. When they had been brought up on deck that morning the island appeared a paradise. The sun so warm, and yet not burning, the sea so pretty, breaking on wide dark beaches, mysterious and strange after the red sands of Devon she had known all her life. She found the tall, bare-trunked trees alien but somehow graceful, while the sweeping green fields stretching up to deeper green mountains refreshed a mind and body that had suffered hunger, heat, terror and personal degradation for the past ten weeks.

Yet here in the marketplace she was afraid again. She knew black people existed but had never in her life seen one, and the black faces with their wide nostrils and thick lips alarmed her by their strangeness. But these men were quiet. She could read nothing in their passivity. It was the white men, who walked among the prisoners, prodding and poking at their muscles, who seemed cruel and brutish.

A burly sailor with a black beard was moving towards them leading a rough wooden cart drawn by a dispirited sway-backed horse. A huge black man was driving. Ben and Zach moved protectively closer to Amelia as they neared.

'Put your fists away, my lad,' the sailor said, flashing a gap-toothed grin at Zachary. 'You're on your way.'

On their way where? The fear of the unknown created a knot in Amelia's hungry stomach.

'To where?' asked the irrepressible Ben.

'You'll see.'

The sailor had produced a key and was busy unlocking their shackles. All three stood dazed as the chains fell away, rubbing at their raw and bleeding wrists, attempting to bring back life into suddenly freed hands and feet.

The sailor ordered them into the cart and the black driver's face showed comical alarm. His eyes were round as a bull's-eye in his face and the dark pupils rolled in neat circles.

'I'm not takin' 'em if they be free to run and I be blamed,' he protested.

'Orders,' said the sailor. 'From the captain. Unless you want your black hide whipped, you'd better obey 'em.'

'I just a' soon get my hide whipped as get myself kilt.'

'You'll get kilt anyway if you don't do as you're told, Beauboy,' the sailor said with surprising good humour. 'Besides, where they got to run to? How they going to run on them ankles? What strength they got in them arms to hurt a great black monkey like you?'

He spoke with truth. Free as she was, Amelia felt that she could have climbed Glastonbury Tor in the time it took to get into the cart. Her ankles and wrists bled, oozing pus, and wobbled as if the bones had been extracted.

Grumbling to himself, the driver gave the horse a stiff lick with his whip.

'Don' you forget. I got this,' he said, turning to face his passengers and waving the whip threateningly.

Amelia caught the whiff of his fear. She had been astonished enough when the huge mouth had opened and the man spoke English in what was an oddly high voice for such a large fellow. But that he should be frightened of them seemed inconceivable.

'Please do not be afraid of us, sir,' she said, speaking slow so that he would understand. 'You shall not need your whip in defence against us.' And she put out her hand and laid it on the man's bare arm.

He looked at the whiteness of her hand against the darkness of his skin, stared into her face and shook his head. She was aware she had bewildered him, but she did not understand why. She withdrew her hand and he seemed more at ease.

'Where do you take us, sir?' she asked.

This made him shake his head again. 'Windsong,' he said as gruffly as the high timbre of his voice would allow.

'Windsong.' She repeated the word. 'Is it far?'

'Not far.'

He did not seem to want to talk. He turned a back like an oak on them as if they were not present.

'We must have been purchased,' Ben commented. 'By that fellow maybe, the one on the horse who spoke to us. I saw him speaking to the captain.'

Amelia shut her eyes tight and said a quick little prayer that it was indeed him who had bought them. She had liked the man's smile and the squirrel look of the flesh round tired grey eyes. She believed him to be kind.

None of them spoke again as the cart rumbled and bounced over a rough track that led like a tunnel through a forest of tall, yellow-green, waving shoots. The wind rustled and ruffled whatever crop this was and caused it to creak like an old door in need of oil.

'Please, sir,' Amelia said to the driver, tapping him gently on the shoulder. 'What is this?' She pointed to the greenery that enclosed them.

He looked surprised at the question. 'You don' know?' She shook her head. 'Uhh!' he said wondering at such ignorance. 'It be sugar cane.'

'It's pretty.'

'Pretty!' He laughed and scratched his head with the end of the whip. 'You gonna find out soon 'nuff 'bout sugar cane. It don' be pretty when you in the middle there acuttin' at it.'

'Is that what we must do?' Ben asked.

Beauboy turned to look at them consideringly. 'Maybe not you, you be too small, too weak. Not the missie. Dust in there choke her in no time. But you,' he stabbed a black finger at Zach, 'big lad like you, you be cutting it soon, sure 'nuff, and it hard.'

They looked at the green forest with new eyes and none spoke.

Beyond the sugar cane the land began to rise into a forest of a different kind. Huge, thick-leaved, leathery trees lined the track, hanging heavy with strange fruits, and bright, exotic flowers brightened the way. Amelia caught a glimpse of yellow and red birds, more brilliant than any Devon knew, that darted and swooped in the foliage. Then the path widened and the flora became a cultivated border of great beauty. Round a bend a house appeared at the end of a long drive edged with exceedingly tall palm trees. It was a three-storey Jacobean manor house in grey stone and as well-kept as any grand house in Britain but it looked somehow grim and cold in this tropical setting. Blind, unwelcoming windows stared at them and nothing moved.

'That be Windsong,' Beauboy volunteered now he was in sight of safety.

'Is that where we are going?' Ben asked.

Beauboy turned and his mouth split into a smile like a pumpkin cut for Halloween. 'That's where you all goin',' he said nodding slowly, 'and that's a real bad place for the likes of you.'

'Why?' asked Amelia. Although the house looked unexpectedly English she felt instinctively that it was an unhappy place. She was sure that bad things could happen there.

Beauboy chuckled and said once again, 'You'll find out, sure 'nuff, just like the rest of us had to.'

*   *   *

9

Matthew Oliver had been feverishly working out what he would say to his wife as he rode back to Windsong. They had no need of more slaves and the question of where these three young people would be housed occupied his mind. He feared they would be put in with the blacks. There was nowhere else for them to go unless he could persuade his wife to use the house attics but she had always refused to have slaves sleeping under her roof for fear of being murdered in her bed. The fact that these people were white might change her mind. He had bought them on impulse, unable to bear the thought of harm coming to the girl, as it surely would elsewhere, and now he must explain his action. Matthew was prone, and always had been, to impulsive, generous gestures; gestures that rarely pleased his dominant wife.

Elizabeth Oliver had been born on St Kitt's and had never left it. It was her family who had built Windsong, first on the profits of tobacco back in the days of the early settlers and then, when they discovered that they could not compete against the quality of the tobacco grown in the American colonies, on the rich rewards of sugar. An only child, she had inherited the property and, though he despised himself for having done it, Matthew had married her more for her fortune than for her face. It was a narrow face, with nostrils so tight and a nose so pointed that it was hard to imagine how she breathed. Elizabeth's attitudes were as narrow as her features and as spiky as her bones. Yet she dressed extravagantly in a manner that belied her views and she wallowed in rich pomp and ceremony. Her home was as overdressed as she was herself. In private, she leaned towards the Church of Rome but it would have been social death to admit such a bias in a society where Catholics, mostly Irish, had no more standing than blacks.

Elizabeth, like most other whites on the island, loathed and feared the slaves. She also loathed the Irish, conveniently separating the race from their religion. This prejudice caused problems. The laws of the West Indies said that planters must employ a certain number of white servants, so that the ratio of blacks to whites on the islands remained a stable ten to one. Most white servants were Irish and Elizabeth refused to hire them. She also disliked paying wages, however small the sum was.

It had been a marriage in name only for many years. They had produced two children – first a boy, Justinian, whom Matthew had hoped would console him for the sterility of his marriage. But Justinian, now eighteen, was a whining fop with a taste for more ale than was good for him. And Charlotte, though charmingly pretty, lacked any other charm and was totally under the thumb of her mother. After Charlotte's birth, Elizabeth bore two stillborn babies and in fear of her life refused to lie with her husband again. He was forty-five now and celibate. Years before, he had taken his pick of women slaves who could not refuse to comply with his more extravagant and shameful needs. Then out of disgust with himself and a great effort of will the importunate urges had been curbed. Now he found more comfort from his Bible than the soft parts of women.

He went to the back of the house where he knew that Elizabeth would be seated on the shady veranda which he had had added to the house as a concession to the climate. She would be working at her embroidery. A creature of habit, she placed herself here every morning, the wild garden before her and beyond the unexplored cloud-capped middle range of the mountains.

'Where have you been?' she asked accusingly and with no word of greeting as he appeared. 'You rose early.'

'Yes, my love,' he said, handing his hat and whip to her black maid and gesturing for the girl to be gone. 'I have a surprise for you.' He had long ago discovered that it was simpler to placate her than to protest.

'A surprise?'

He sat down in the chair beside her and stretched out his booted legs. 'I know, my sweet, how much you dislike having slaves about you . . .'

'Indeed,' she said petulantly, 'ungrateful, treacherous and greedy as they are, but what else is one to do in this God forsaken island?'

'But what if you had a white maid for yourself and Charlotte and a white valet for Justinian?'

She pursed her lips and frowned. 'We cannot afford to pay for our help, husband,' she said severely. 'Not with the greedy bellies of more than a hundred slaves to fill.'

'We would not have to pay a penny.'

'I will not have Irish in the house.'

'Not Irish. Good English West Country folk from near to my own home. I purchased them this morning from the *Indeavour*. A girl, no more than fifteen, you can train to your ways—'

'From the *Indeavour*? Are they not those who marched against the King? The traitors allotted to Sir William?'

'These are too young to have had any real part in it. The two fine lads—'

'Two!'

'One such a great lumping yokel that he can work with the field slaves.' Matthew hastily abandoned Zachary in favour of rescuing Amelia from the field work which would take her far from the house. 'And the other, small and quick, who can be Justinian's personal man. They are ours for ten years. And for once we will be nearly within the law for our quota of whites.'

Elizabeth took a great quivering, disapproving breath, gathering her nostrils into a pleat.

'More mouths to feed, and to have put good money into Sir William's pocket is a disgrace,' she said reproachfully. 'How much did you pay?'

The one thing on which Matthew and his wife, who yearned to be Lady Oliver, were in total agreement was that Sir William had usurped Matthew's true place.

'Elizabeth, Elizabeth, you do not enquire the price of a gift.' He made his voice jocular, but she would find out anyway. Since he had resigned his post as a colonial administrator when Sir William came to the islands

11

he was totally dependent on the estate, as she was for ever reminding him. And she scrutinised every penny that came to and left Windsong, sitting at Pottle the old bookkeeper's side to make sure that not so much as a farthing went astray.

'A gift from whom?' Her pale blue eyes glinted suspicion.

'From your loving husband.' He rose to his feet and bowed.

She sniffed to let him know that she was aware she received no gifts that did not come indirectly from her own purse.

'Bring these traitors to me,' she demanded.

'Indeed, dearest. But traitors they are not. Of that I can assure you.'

'In that case why are they here?' she asked with irritating logic.

'They will explain.'

'I do not listen to explanations from slaves and common criminals,' she said icily.

He thought it best to say no more, bowed again even deeper and kissed her hand. He took his leave, a mental picture of the girl's soft, untried face in his head, and reflected not for the first time that when a man married for money he worked considerably harder than if he had not.

As the cart lumbered up the drive, Amelia saw that the elderly man from the slave market was standing on the flight of grey stone steps in front of the great double doors of the house.

'It *is* him,' she whispered.

Zach was silent but Ben looked as if he would have rubbed his hands if it were not so painful to do so.

'Good,' he whispered back.

'I don't like it,' Zach muttered. 'I don't like it at all.'

'We have to bear it,' Amelia said firmly. She loved her brother dearly – he and Ben were all she had in the world – but he was suspicious and pessimistic by nature. He had always been the despair of his tutors. Perhaps because he was inarticulate he could be aggressive to the point of violence. But never with her.

She took his hand and tried to console him by reminding him that at least all three of them were still together and not alone.

'But for how long?' he muttered.

Beauboy was about to drive round to the back of the house when the man on the steps called him to bring the cart up to the front steps.

Grumbling to himself, the black man changed direction and stopped where the man stood. He motioned for them to leave the cart. 'I wish to speak to you,' he said.

He came down to the path and walked a few paces ahead of them to stand under a tree with thick succulent leaves which made a perfect umbrella of shade in the noon heat. Anxious and still unsteady on their feet, they followed him.

Amelia thought he looked uneasy. He had lost the air of considering calm with which he had regarded them in the marketplace. He also looked older now he was bare-headed. His fair wig was too youthful for the thin features beneath and the deep lines of suffering under his eyes showed clearly without his broad, plumed hat to shield his face.

'I am Matthew Oliver and I will do the best for you that I can,' he began in a conspiratorial manner. 'You understand I am a Devon man myself. I do not care to see my fellow countrymen in these straits and at so young an age. That is why I have brought you here. Now you will meet my wife, Mistress Oliver. But there must be no seditious talk before her; no harsh words about the King. You must remember that you are to be her servants and behave accordingly or she will not tolerate you in her home.' He mopped briefly at his forehead. He sounded almost as if he were pleading. 'Be obedient, respectful, accept and understand your position.'

'What is our position, sir?' Amelia asked.

'If my wife agrees, you are to be maidservant to her and our daughter.'

'And Ben and my brother?'

'That is for my wife to decide. Now you will follow me.'

He was afraid of his wife, Amelia realised as they trooped through the house at a speed which left no time for anything more than an impression of great riches. She whispered to Zach warningly, 'Best do as he says.'

'Yes,' said Ben, rolling his eyes, 'we must accept our position.'

Zach merely grunted.

At the back of the house they were led on to a long wooden floor with a wooden roof open in front to the garden. Amelia had never seen a structure like it but it was a cool and pleasant place to be. Some distance beyond the colourful garden were several thatched buildings made from roughly-cut logs which Amelia guessed were the stables. On the covered area sat a bone-thin woman wearing a vulgarly vivid red dress with a large white collar. Her fair hair fluffed over her forehead and down the sides of her face and was held in a knot behind. She sat very upright, her entire bearing autocratic, and yet this was no true lady, Amelia was sure of it.

'Mistress wife,' Matthew Oliver said, 'these are your new servants.'

The woman fixed them, particularly Amelia, with suspicious eyes.

'Step forward, girl,' she commanded with an imperious wave of her hand.

Amelia did as she was told and, hiding her resentment at the woman's tone, swept a deep curtsy.

'Take off your hat.'

Amelia removed it. She could not know that the sight of her hair, carelessly hacked by Zach to masculine length while they waited in Taunton Jail for transportation to the West Indies, caused Matthew a pang of pity.

'Why are you garbed in men's clothing?'

'To keep my virtue on the passage here, lady,' Amelia said, eyes cast down. 'I was afraid of the lusts of the sailors.'

Amelia had been born resourceful and intelligent, but the last few

13

months of her short life had bred in her an added quick cunning and a determination to survive. She realised that their immediate future was in the hands of this woman and that she must be won over if they were not to find themselves in worse conditions. At least the woman's downtrodden husband seemed to be an ally, though she suspected he had little power in his own home. As young as she was, Amelia was also aware of the attraction that she had for men. She had early recognised a look in lads' eyes that she believed meant she could do with them what she wished. That look had been in Master Oliver's eyes. She knew that during the ten weeks of horror on the *Indeavour* it was not only Zach's fists that had kept her safe, but her own look of innocent entreaty that said without words, 'Help me, cherish me'; a look that could move most men but achieved little with women.

'The girl is virtuous,' Matthew said quickly.

'I should trust so. But does she have knowledge of the duties of a lady's maid?'

'Oh, but yes, your ladyship, I do,' Amelia lied, thinking that awarding the woman an improvement in rank could do no harm.

'What age are you?'

'Near to sixteen, your ladyship.'

'And by whom have you been employed?'

She could sense that the woman did not believe her and also that Zach, the proud son of a gentleman father, was beginning to burst with indignation. She threw him a warning look.

'The headmistress of an academy for young ladies in Taunton, your ladyship,' Amelia improvised, her eyes fixed firmly on the wooden floor. 'A Frenchwoman and most particular about how things were done. Ben Clode, my cousin here, was valet to her husband, and my brother, Zachary, his groom.'

Zach could barely restrain his anger listening to this demotion of their position in life, but Ben bowed low from the waist and said, 'Your servant, your ladyship.'

'We have no need of a groom,' said Matthew's wife dismissively to Zach. 'I have no doubt that our overseer can make use of you in the fields. You,' she stabbed a finger at Ben, 'will be valet to my son, and you, young woman, will take care of the needs of my daughter and me.'

'It will be a great pleasure, your ladyship.' Amelia curtsied again, a mocking curtsy that caused her new mistress to give her a sharp look.

She turned to her husband. 'Get Jake to put them in quarters,' she instructed him.

'In the house?' Matthew asked tentatively.

She looked at him as if he were insane. 'The house! Indeed not. The slave quarters.'

'But, my dearest—'

'They are slaves, are they not?' she snapped. 'You have paid good money for them. Put them where they belong.' Three times she jerked

14

her bony chin into her neck, agreeing with herself, before shouting surprisingly loudly, 'Truly. Come here.'

A young black girl, her head swathed in a brightly coloured bandana, appeared from the house.

'Yes, ma'am?'

'Take these new slaves down to the kitchen and keep them there until Jake arrives. And send someone to fetch him.'

'Yes, ma'am,' said the girl. She beckoned to be followed and set off down the length of the wooden platform, a high rounded bottom swaying under the cheap fabric of her long skirt. She led them through another door and into a kitchen that was uncomfortably hot from a huge fire, in front of which a spit turned. Amelia was surprised to find that except for the fact that the kitchen's inhabitants were black it was little different from any in England. A dark-skinned boy sat on a high stool near the window and a huge black woman whose great breasts met her vast stomach stood holding a basting spoon, staring at them.

'Who these, Truly?' she asked.

'Mistress say new slaves, Mama,' the black girl said laconically.

The woman's black face showed astonishment. 'But they be white.'

'She say new slaves.' Truly sounded indifferent. 'And you better git Joshua,' she said to the boy. 'Overseer's comin'.'

'I don' never seen a white slave,' the woman said. She moved forward cautiously, as if to inspect them closer. She stared into Amelia's face and Amelia, fascinated by this first close sight of someone so different in colour, stared back. The woman's skin was not truly black, more like pitted old mahogany. Near to her white teeth her large, purplish lips became a deep pink. Her nose was twice as wide as Mistress Oliver's and all the better for it. Her dark brown eyes were round with small red lights flashing in them, encircled by short spiky eyelashes like the hair on a brush. The coarse black hair on her head was plaited flat to her head in a manner that must have taken many hours to achieve. She seemed very old to Amelia and as if she was sad and suffering, but there was something about the face that fascinated.

'Why you staring at Bella, gal?' the woman asked.

The question took Amelia by surprise. She had not been aware of staring.

'I've never seen anyone black close up before,' she blurted out. 'Except Beauboy.'

'Oh, him.' Bella sniffed. 'White folk call him Beauboy 'cause he be so ugly. You think I be ugly?'

'Oh no.' Amelia was not being polite. This woman was different but definitely not ugly. Understanding that Amelia had spoken honestly, Bella smiled broadly and the sadness in her face was wiped away.

'Everyone else white think I be ugly.' She put her hands on her broad hips and cocked her head to one side. 'What age you?'

'Fifteen. Nearly sixteen.'

15

The woman nodded. 'Just 'bout the same age as they brought me here. You not go'n like it, white gal.' And Amelia picked up the note of barely suppressed satisfaction in her voice.

Bella moved to inspect Ben and Zachary who fidgeted under her searching gaze. Truly, as dark and glossy as her mother, stood watching, her arms folded. The boy had left his stool and was moving towards the door. He turned to stare at Amelia as if he recognised her and to her astonishment the familiar look was in his eyes. How on earth could she attract him, she wondered, when to him her skin must look raw? Fascinated, she stared back. He was different in appearance from the two women; his lighter skin was the shade of polished oak, his nose less broad at the nostrils, his lips generous but redder and his hair wild about a well-shaped head. Will Shakespeare's Othello must have looked like this, she thought.

'I'm goin', Mama,' he called as he slipped out of the door, a big, powerfully built lad of perhaps seventeen, bare-footed and in ragged clothes. Amelia watched him leave, wondering how a brother and sister could be so physically different.

Bella returned to her cooking, her daughter followed the boy, and the three young people waited in anxious silence until a white man who was no doubt the overseer, came into the kitchen, followed by a gargantuan black man. Amelia disliked the overseer on sight. He was tall with beefy shoulders topped by a small head with coarse features. His pale blue eyes glared through his own lank yellow hair and he held a long, heavy whip in a way that suggested he enjoyed using it. It took him little time to dispose of them. Zach was sent off to the cane fields with the black man where he was to be quartered with the field slaves. Amelia and Ben were to live with the house slaves in the log cabins that she had believed to be stables.

It was amazing how quickly it was possible to adapt, she thought after a fortnight of sleeping on straw and covered only by a torn sheet, thrown out from the big house as being beyond repair. She had been given similar clothing to that of the other women slaves: a cheap coarse linen skirt and bodice with a bandana which she chose to wear as a shawl. The slaves' quarters were naked of furniture with merely an open fire and chimney on which to cook the food they grew themselves in a small patch of land near the cabin. They ate off cracked and chipped crockery, throw-outs from the house. Bella and other house slaves slept on the ground floor. Amelia was above, up a ladder and through a hole in the ceiling, with the young ones – Ben, Truly and Joshua and some smaller children who had their duties but were the only ones with a modicum of freedom.

Her own duties were not so much arduous as tedious and unpleasant. She had to be at the house by daybreak to prepare Mistress Oliver's breakfast and then that of her daughter Charlotte. The rest of the day she was at their beck and call, washing and pressing their clothing, making repairs, curling their hair, heating water and helping them with their toilette as well as bringing them what food and drink they required. She emptied their chamber pots and the most intimate details of their lives were left to her to clean up. Her day's work was finished when they went to bed not long after sundown. She tried to be submissive, to hide her superior education and background, but blood would out, and Elizabeth resented her.

Amelia's duties had previously been performed by Truly, who was now relegated to housework and kitchen duties. Truly called her 'white gal' contemptuously and would not speak to her, which meant there was no one Amelia could ask for advice as to how the work should be done. In fact, though she was aware of Joshua's eyes on her all the time, none of the slaves ever spoke to either her or Ben. His duties appeared to be much the same as hers, except that he acted as groom as well. After a week of this, his bright spirit seemed quenched. He was silent and seemed ashamed in some way that Amelia could not understand. They barely spoke to each other in the smoky, foetid darkness of the cabin. Both desperately sought sleep as an escape from a life for which they were not prepared. The food they were given was inadequate, mushy vegetables and some vile-tasting fish neither of which they recognised or liked. And all the while Amelia worried about Zachary. She and Ben were not permitted near the field slaves' quarters. It was a life of deprivation with no conversation, no books, no love or companionship. Nightly she fought despair.

Amelia detested her mistress and seemed unable to hide her feelings. There was little to choose between Elizabeth Oliver and her daughter, Charlotte. The girl was a month or so younger than Amelia and though a prettier, softer seeming version of her mother, she was spoilt and selfish. Both women cuffed their new maid freely if she did not please them. Elizabeth was the more spiteful and ready with her slaps and pinches, for ever snarling that the French mistress must have been a simpleton if she had been pleased with Amelia as a maid.

It was twenty days after their arrival on the island when Amelia dropped and broke Elizabeth Oliver's glass powder bowl, spreading a white dust around the bedchamber. Her furious mistress, who seemed to have been waiting for just such an opportunity, accused her of wilful clumsiness and ordered her three strokes of the whip so that she would learn to be more careful. The leering Jake lingeringly stripped her in the compound where the slaves gathered after the day's work was done and tied her arms up over the low branches of a tree. He then wielded the whip with brisk efficiency. The pain was indescribable but the nakedness was worse. Somehow Amelia stopped herself from crying out in front of an audience of sullen slaves who had been gathered to watch her being made an example of. Her nails bit into her clasped hands, her back ran blood, as did her lips where she bit them. But she did not cry. Not until her nakedness was again covered and she was back in the cabin.

17

'If you been black you'd 'ave got ten strokes,' Bella said, but there was a note of sympathy in her voice. She bathed the weals, as she had already silently bathed Amelia's slowly healing wrists and ankles.

'Then I'm glad I'm not black,' Amelia said through gritted teeth.

'So you should be, gal,' Bella said angrily. 'But you tell me how you white mama let you be here, way from you home.'

'I have no mama,' said Amelia, wincing as Bella gently dabbed at her back. 'She died when I was six.'

Bella's hand stilled. 'Then we both motherless chil'en,' she said, her voice sad. 'My mama got kilt when they brung me here. I happy she not here but I miss her real bad, even now. And it near 'nuff eighteen years.'

They were in the downstairs room of the cabin where a little light still came through the door. Ben had already gone upstairs to his straw pallet. He had come home that evening white-faced and distressed, not wanting to speak. Amelia could not tell if his distress was for her or for himself and she did not have the energy to ask. Her optimism was dimmed. This life could not go on, she told herself. Ten years. It was impossible.

Joshua had been sitting at the door of the cabin, his back to his mother and Amelia, as if he could not bear to watch.

'Mama,' he said quietly. 'Master's coming.'

Bella stiffened. 'Now what he want?' she said. 'He not been here for many a year but he want something, that for sure. And it not go'n be me takin' his fancy after all this time.' She made a pouncing movement towards her daughter. 'Truly, you get you'self out of here and quick.' She turned to Amelia. 'Maybe it you he after,' she said maliciously. 'And white gal, you go'n have to do what he wants, just like we has to.'

Amelia stared at the black woman. 'What must I do?'

'Open yo' legs for him, that what you do,' she said. 'It a slave's duty, gal. All part of the work. Used to be me he come here for fucking when I 'bout your age. Now it your turn.'

The unashamed note of satisfaction in her voice cut Amelia to the quick.

Matthew was beside himself. He had come home from an afternoon meeting with the vicar of St Thomas's in Middle Island to find his wife smug and self-satisfied sitting in the drawing room.

'Ah, there you are,' she said. 'Again you manage to be away when I need you.'

'My dear, I apologise. What was it that I could have done for you?'

'The girl Amelia has broken my powder bowl. The one we had especially sent out from England.'

'Your powder bowl?' He could not picture any powder bowl.

'Yes. Just wilful carelessness. She had to be punished. She is far too

18

hoity-toity. She acts as if she is superior to me – have you not noticed? In your absence I ordered that Jake give her three lashes.'

He felt his throat close. He was sure the blood had drained from his face. For the past three weeks he had thought of nothing but the girl and her wonderful green eyes and how he could best protect her so that, in gratitude, she would freely give herself to him. Already he had failed. He had watched her surreptitiously as she went about her duties, longing to talk to her, longing to know her better. Had his wife noticed? Was she aware of his obsession and was that the reason for such cruelty?

'Three lashes.' Matthew's voice came out as a croak.

'I know it was not enough, but I was merciful. I ordered that the house slaves should watch. The sight might make them less greedy and careless. It rather killed two birds with one stone, I thought, and besides,' she added carelessly, 'I never cared much for that powder bowl.'

He wanted to strangle the smug woman sitting there in a yellow gown that turned her complexion the same bilious colour. She was gloating. He hated her. He had always hated her, he realised. But she was his wife and without her he was nothing.

'Do you approve?' she was asking. 'Was it sufficient?'

He swallowed and, hating himself as much as he hated her, said, 'I think your decision was absolutely right, my dear. I'm only sorry that I was not here to take the burden from your shoulders.'

Somehow he got through supper. He excused himself, saying that he wanted some fresh air. He asked if she would join him for a turn in the garden, knowing she would not. In the quiet kitchen he lit a lantern and set off towards the slave quarters. He hesitated outside the largest of the cabins.

'Amelia?' he called tentatively.

There was silence, and then her voice said wearily, 'I'm here.'

He ducked his head and came into the rancid room. He held the lantern high and looked around, relieved to see no one else was about.

'Where are the others?'

'Gone upstairs.'

'You are alone?'

'Yes.' She sat motionless, but her voice sounded apprehensive.

He was silent. Then he said, 'I must talk to you, but the smell in here is insupportable. We will go outside.'

'If you wish.'

'You can walk?' He knew he sounded anxious.

She shot him a resentful look and rose to her feet. He could see how she was careful not to stand straight and stretch the torn skin on her back. She followed him out and he walked ahead of her towards the garden where a wooden seat had been placed under an angel trumpet tree. A sweet, sensuous night-time scent came from the long, white flowers and a soft wind sighed in the branches. He motioned for her to sit and settled himself beside her, placing the lantern on the ground.

'Are you all right?' he asked, his voice low.

He could see the weary nod of her silhouetted head.

'My wife told me she had been obliged to have you whipped. I was in town. I had no idea—'

'He took my clothes,' she interrupted bitterly, 'and let all watch.'

He winced. He could smell blood. 'I'm sorry.'

'Your sorrow does not heal my hurt and my shame.'

Without looking at her he said, 'I cannot bear to think of you unclothed before the slaves and whipped, but there is little I can do. This plantation is the property of my wife.'

'I had understood that,' she said and he could hear the contempt in her tone.

'But worse would have happened to you at another plantation.'

'What could be worse?' Her voice was full of suppressed anger. He was aware she should not be speaking to him like this as if she was an equal but he did not care.

'Many things.' He thought of her being raped by the odious Jake who would have done it without hesitation had she been a field slave. Or left to the attentions of the field slaves who would enjoy taking a white girl after years of helplessly watching their women used by white men. He was disgusted with himself when the very thought brought to life those long-dormant desires that had tormented him in his youth.

'What do you want from me?' she asked.

'Only to talk.'

'Ah.' She sighed. 'Nothing more?'

Much more, he thought, but repeated, 'Nothing more.'

They were silent and then he said, 'I still do not understand what brought you here.'

'The rebellion of course,' she said, almost dismissively. 'My school in Taunton had embroidered a banner for the Duke of Monmouth to present to him when he landed to fight against the King. They said those of us who had worked on the banner had committed treason. We were all flung into Taunton jail. Some of us died from the pox. Others were fined and the money given to the Queen's ladies-in-waiting. There was no money for my fine since papa was dead – killed at Sedgemoor and his estates confiscated. Judge Jeffreys sentenced me to transportation with Zach and Ben. They had sheltered the rebels at our manor and were lucky not to have been hung, drawn and quartered. Papa believed that Monmouth had a right to the throne—'

'That is not true,' Matthew interrupted. 'As the illegitimate son of the King, Monmouth had no divine right of kingship.'

'Papa said Monmouth was the firstborn of the King, and a Protestant. But it doesn't matter any more. Monmouth is dead, headless at the Tower, Papa lies buried somewhere on Sedgemoor and King James sits safe on his throne.'

'I am sorry about your father,' he said.

'My papa was a gentleman,' Amelia said, her voice fierce. I'm glad he is dead. It would break his heart to see the circumstances in which Zach and I find ourselves. Maid to your wife! Your wife is not fit to polish my father's hunting boots.'

'Shush!' he said, wanting to be angry and terrified someone would overhear. 'You must not speak thus.'

'Why not?' she said coldly. 'Will you have me stripped and whipped again for my impertinence?'

'Never. Listen, Amelia,' his voice was urgent, 'if you can praise my wife and daughter, make them feel they are important, defer to them, stroke them as if with butter, your life will be easier. If you are clever with them, you can do as you will. You are educated—'

'I am,' she said proudly, 'and the lack of books in this life is almost the worst deprivation.'

'I will bring you books, but you must not let the slaves see them. It is forbidden for the slaves to read.'

'Indeed,' she said indignantly. 'Why?'

'White people on these islands are afraid that one day the slaves will rise up against them. Religion is forbidden them in case they learn from the scriptures that all men are equal. They are held in their place by brutality, fear and ignorance.'

'By people like you.'

'By people like me,' he said quietly, remembering with shame his own cruelties in the past. 'I am not proud of what happens at Windsong. But it is the system and I am one of the few who sees that it is wrong. Most see the blacks as animals.'

She was silent. Then she said, 'I do not understand how people can be so cruel. Black people are no different to us. I live with them. I know they feel hunger, love and fear. They bleed, too. I have seen the scars on their backs, scars that I will no doubt carry. They have pride and they suffer.'

'As you suffer.' He beat his fist into his palm. 'Amelia, I will try to protect you, but I beg you to tread softly with my womenfolk. It is the best advice I can give you to keep you from further harm. I know. It is the path that I have been forced to follow myself.' He had moved to hold her by the shoulders and he felt her wince as he turned her body towards him. The urge to kiss her was irresistible, the knowledge that none would gainsay him if he took her for himself had made him erect, but her tiny gasp of pain sobered his desires.

'I will leave you to sleep,' he said, forcing himself to draw away from her. He stumbled to his feet, and taking the lantern to guide him, full of bitter thoughts, made his way through the star-strung night and the chirruping of a million insects to his lonely bed.

Amelia returned to the cabin and pulled herself painfully up the ladder to the upper floor, stopping every few steps to let pain subside. She did not know whether to be disappointed or relieved that Matthew Oliver had done nothing but talk. Unlike many other girls of her age, she had

21

no experience of men, but the concept of sex and what it entailed was no mystery to her. If he had taken her, he might have made her his mistress and her life would have improved. She knew that mistresses at court in London held favoured positions but was astute enough to realise that Matthew was too afraid of his wife to create any such situation. It was a pity she could not marry him. He was old, but he was kind and anything would be better than the life she was leading.

She thought with envy of her classmates back home who were already safely married. Once there had been a betrothal between her and the eminently suitable young son of an earl. They were to have married on her fourteenth birthday but it had all come to nought when the earl's family had learned of her father's dangerous pro-Monmouth sympathies. She had not minded. She had no feeling for the lad and did not want to leave her Devon home for life in London, but it would have been a million times better than this. She sighed. It was no use dwelling on the past.

It was tensely still and silent in the blackness upstairs. There were no night sounds of little grunts, snores, and the soft moans of misery that normally filled the dark nights in the slave cabin, only the shrill din of the insects outside. It was as if the room itself was holding its breath.

'You all right, gal?' Bella's voice whispered through the velvet black as Amelia groped her way to her place.

'Yes,' she whispered back.

A rustle ran through the room as if everyone had been afraid to move before.

'What he want?' It was Truly speaking.

Amelia hesitated. Both Bella and Truly's voices sounded softer, friendlier than she had ever heard them before. If she said that Matthew had not touched her and done nothing but tell her how to deal with his wife, they would think it just another example of the cruel differences between white and black.

'I don't want to talk about it,' she said.

She heard a woman's sigh and a whimpering groan that seemed to come from Ben.

'Now you one of us, gal,' Bella told her softly. 'You no different in no way. You a *real* slave.'

Again there were sounds of movement. Amelia's eyes were becoming accustomed to the darkness. She saw that Bella, Truly and Joshua had raised themselves and were sitting with their backs to the wall. Ben lay inert, while the smaller children turned over to sleep.

'What I don' understand is why you white folk here anyway?' Bella pondered in the blackness.

Amelia thought of the difficulties of explaining the politics of far-away England to these untutored people. 'It's a long story,' she said.

'We likes stories,' Joshua told her.

Amelia was silent, gathering her words, remembering how long ago, when she was small, her mother had told her stories using the simplest of words. 'I'll try to explain,' she finally said, 'but perhaps you won't understand.' She heard Bella's exasperated snort, and realising she was offended said quickly, 'In my country, England, which is far over the seas, we once had a great, good King.'

'We got kings in my country,' Bella interrupted truculently, 'and our country be far over the seas, too.'

'This King was called Charles II, and his firstborn son he called the Duke of Monmouth, but the mother of the baby was not his Queen.'

'The Queen she sure 'nuff be mad.' Bella sounded shocked. 'That man be made leave our tribe in my country. That a very bad thing havin' baby by 'nother woman.'

'The Queen was very unhappy,' Amelia agreed. 'The poor lady wanted to have babies, but they always died.'

'Just like ordin'ry folk,' said Bella. 'That happen to me so many times I almost lost count.'

'So when good King Charles died not very long ago, his brother, James, became our King because Charles had no son by the Queen to take his place. But the people were unhappy because' – She hesitated. Religious differences were difficult to explain to people who were not permitted any religion at all. How could she possibly explain the schism between Catholicism and Protestantism? But surely her audience had their own African gods? The mistress at her school had said all primitive people had gods. 'The new King did not believe in the same gods as the people of the land,' she continued. 'So when Charles's firstborn came back from over the seas to try to take the throne, many of the people fought for him. But he lost the battle.' She stopped then and dropping her voice low added, 'And the King ordered that the Duke of Monmouth's head be cut off and placed on a pole outside one of the King's houses for all to see.'

There was gasp and then a respectful silence at this dramatic conclusion.

'That other King's gods be bigger, stronger gods?' Bella eventually suggested.

Amelia could not quite bring herself to agree to that. 'Perhaps,' she said. 'But my papa was one of those who died fighting for the King's son. Ben and my brother and I were sent here as a punishment. We must slave as you slave for ten years.'

'But we,' Truly pointed out, 'slave until we die.'

Bella took no notice of her daughter's bitter interjection. Amelia was aware of the huge woman's bulk gently swaying backwards and forwards. 'It strange,' Bella was saying as if speaking to herself. 'It another tribe, with different gods, who got me here, just like you. They fight our tribe, they kill our King, and they sell us to white men. They brung me and my papa and my mama here, but Papa, he die on that terrible ship. He clean jumped over the edge and into the sea rather than be captive. My mama got kilt of a fever and they left me all 'lone for bad things to happen. It were a sailor who did to me what the master did to you tonight. That sailor he hurt me real bad. He take me on the deck and he fuck me till I lose my senses and he go on fuckin' me though I like near to death. Near every night he do it till I hate him so bad I want kill him like he killin' me.' She sighed and added, 'But he give me Joshua, so I guess maybe it worth it.'

So Joshua was half-white. Amelia felt overwhelmed with the injustice of it all. 'We are all in the same situation,' she said passionately. 'We must be friends and help each other.'

'I don' know how be friends with a white person,' Bella said doubtfully. 'I never met one I rightly cared for.'

'Mama, she's right,' Joshua said. 'She not just white. She a slave, like us.'

Bella considered. 'What you think, Truly?'

Amelia felt rather than saw the shrug in the darkness.

'Jus' as you likes, Mama,' Truly said, her voice indifferent. 'She sure one of us now.'

24

Chapter Two

'For wither thou goest, I will go; and where thou lodgest, I will lodge: thy people shall be my people, and thy God my God: Where thou diest, will I die, and there will I be buried: the Lord do so to me, and more also, if ought but death part thee and me.'

As Joshua read out loud his finger went laboriously over the page of the Bible. Truly listened intently. When he had finished the passage, he passed the book to his sister whose turn it was to read out loud.

Matthew had kept his word. He furtively sought Amelia out to enquire of her health almost every other day and he contrived to pass her a Bible, a copy of the works of Will Shakespeare and a slim volume of poetry. These she kept hidden under the straw of her pallet and on Sundays, the one day in which the slaves were permitted a little free time, she would find a corner and settle herself down to read.

It was Joshua who showed the first curiosity and asked her to read to him. She had tried Shakespeare first, but found that he understood little of it. The simple Old Testament Bible stories were better and easier to explain and gradually Truly crept to listen as well. From there it seemed logical to teach them to read for themselves.

It was surprisingly simple. They were eager to learn, though many words had to be explained since their vocabulary was meagre. Amelia took to squirrelling the ends of candles from the house so they could read in the cabin at night. She also gathered scraps of writing material, and tiny amounts of ink and discarded quills and began teaching them to write their own names. It gave her pleasure to defy the slave masters' rules, though she knew that it would be a great deal more than three strokes of the whip if she was caught trying to educate black slaves. Bella, Truly and Joshua knew it too and the risks that she took on their behalf helped wipe away any suspicion and resentment.

By the time she had been at Windsong for six months the little black family had accepted her completely and their companionship raised the quality of her life. She had steeled herself to take Matthew's advice and discovered there was no compliment, however extravagant or ridiculous, that was not accepted and preened over by Elizabeth. Amelia managed to suppress the naturally superior manner that her previous life had bred in her and became as ingratiating as most black slaves, appreciating that they behaved so in order that life might become easier.

25

And with them, in the safety of the cabin, she joined in the mocking of their masters and mistresses.

Elizabeth Oliver now declared herself well satisfied with her white slave, constantly remarking that it was the whipping that had created the change in attitude.

Amelia told herself ruefully that maybe it was.

She had been intent on personal survival, but gradually, as her position became more secure, she began to worry again about Ben and Zach.

Ben's behaviour was strange. He rarely spoke to her. It was as if he was avoiding her, and she found his reticence deeply hurtful. She felt completely isolated from her own kin. His tasks took him away from the house more than hers did. Justinian, wearing his finest clothes, liked to go to the taverns in French Basse-Terre where the slaves whispered he consorted with low life. Ben must accompany him, and when his master, who could not hold his ale, was dead drunk, it was Ben's task to bundle him on to his horse and bring him home. Often it was well past ten o'clock and the other inhabitants of the cabin were fast asleep when Ben returned. He looked ill all the time. She knew there was something badly wrong, but he would not confide in her. He would not even speak to her, and she could not understand why. Of Zach there was no word. The field slaves were not permitted near the house; like all the plantation owners, the Olivers lived in ill-concealed terror of the pent-up strength and resentment of these people they regarded as so many pieces of property. The slaves had no rights and were treated as nothing more than potential criminals who might steal, rape and murder, as indeed they might, given the opportunity. Elizabeth considered them animals and was for ever complaining that they died, and how dare they after she had paid good money for them.

But proximity had made Amelia close to these alien people, snatched from their homeland as she had been. She was beginning to understand, almost admire, them. They were cunning. They stole when they safely could. They bore bitter hatred for their masters which they carefully concealed. Some were masters at the dangerous art of dumb insolence. But they had their own code of stringent morals. The memory of their own language was fading, yet some remembered how things had been done in Africa. She learnt that they came from a simple but structured society. There was no lack of intelligence, stifled though it was, and she admired the way they had adapted to their situation. Most of them appeared like the willow, bending to the will of the whites and yet retaining, oak-like, their own strength; they were even able to be happy when they were together. She was not displeased that they now saw her as one of them.

She knew that many died. 'Them field slaves is lucky if they don' die after three years,' Bella told her. In Europe there was an insatiable appetite for sugar which created a constant demand for labour in the sugar islands of the Caribbean. The slave-bearing ships from Liverpool and Bristol, via Africa, still sailed in to sell what of their human cargo survived the hellish crossing and sailed back with sugar in their well-scrubbed and vinegar-purified holds.

The planters were rich and greedy for goods and there was much trade in the luxuries that Europe could provide. The slaves were allowed one new set of clothes each year, but their mistresses were totally preoccupied with their wardrobes; they had little else to interest them. Amelia still could find no warmth in her heart for Elizabeth but perhaps because they were so much of an age she and Charlotte had struck up a curious relationship where sometimes it seemed more as if Amelia was the mistress and Charlotte the maid.

Charlotte was poorly educated and resented it. She had always wanted to be sent back to England, but her mother would not countenance it for reasons of expense. Charlotte had a vision of England as a kind of paradise, she saw herself at court, imagined that given the opportunity she would marry well, perhaps even to someone with a title. She was a pretty girl with a full, discontented mouth, who could sigh and be full of woe one moment and happy and laughing the next. She had her beaux, mostly from the military who were quartered on the island, for white women were in short supply in the Caribbean, but none of the men who courted her was as wealthy as her family, and she and her mother dreamed of better things.

'Tell me of London,' she would demand of Amelia as her hair was dressed.

Amelia, who knew little of London herself, fed Charlotte's fantasies and assured her that most certainly she would be a grand success should she ever make her appearance at court.

'The ladies of London are in no way as comely as you,' she assured her, and for all she knew it might well be true.

'I long to be elegant,' Charlotte would sigh. 'My, you are nought but a maid and yet you speak French.'

'Ah, well, it is only because my mistress was French,' Amelia consoled her, not adding that it was a different kind of mistress, a headmistress, who had insisted that nothing else was spoken at the school.

'You could go to Basse-Terre for me. You could pretend to be French,' Charlotte suggested. 'There is a seamstress there who makes the most divine clothes, but Papa says that Basse-Terre is not safe for the English. The French permitted only Papists to colonise their lands overseas so the Irish have settled there with them and the Irish have no love for us either. But Basse-Terre is so much livelier than Old Road Town and Justinian goes there all the time. It is most unjust that I am not permitted. But you could go for me. There is a much wider choice of furbelows than here. I wonder if Papa would give you a *laissez passer* to go on my behalf.'

No slave could leave his area of work without a pass that stated he had permission to be elsewhere. In Amelia's opinion it was most unlikely that Matthew Oliver would refuse the pass if she herself were to ask for it. She could see his eyes mooning after her as she moved around

27

the house. He was for ever making some excuse to stop her and speak to her in urgent little bursts while his glance ran around like a squirrel in a cage to make sure he was not being observed.

He gave her the pass and the visits to Basse-Terre became a regular occurrence. The town was situated on a long beach of dark volcanic sand and its roughly paved narrow streets were lined with well-built thatched brick or stone houses. There were taverns full of drunken sailors, tea houses, a milliner's shop and other stores where goods from both France and Holland were on sale. Basse-Terre had a good selection of household goods, fine wines and luxurious fabrics. Amelia used to tell herself that maybe London had no better to offer. Beauboy would drive her in the old wagon from Windsong, and once in the streets, away from the stifling plantation, Amelia felt a sense of freedom. She would purchase ribbons, feathers, buttons and fine lace for Charlotte as quickly as possible so that she had time to herself to wander and explore.

The free time was a luxury. She sometimes sat on the seashore where she never tired of watching the pelicans dive for their dinner and observing the prowling flight of the huge, sinister frigate birds. To sit by the sea on this distant shore reminded her of her home. Great schooners and men o' war sailed in to shelter in the roadstead formed by the hills. Most brought in goods or fresh cargoes of slaves. Amelia could not see a slave ship without a shudder. She never went near the slave market, but liked to explore the narrow streets of the town which had a fine town hall, a graceful Catholic church and a Jesuit college.

It was in the slum area of Irishtown that she met Molly McGuire. She had noticed the Columbus Tavern, a well-kept building on Connell Street, and out of curiosity had peeped in one day. A small but sturdy middle-aged white woman stood behind the long wooden bar and the place was full of swaggering sailors who made lewd gestures to her to enter. She hurried on her way.

But one morning in June her mistresses were to spend the day with the Ramillies family at Macabees, a plantation situated further down the island. Amelia was not required to accompany them and Charlotte had said that if she wished she could spend the morning in Basse-Terre, providing she checked to see what the French milliner had that was new and brought back detailed descriptions. After the visit to the milliner, Amelia was walking down Connell Street when she was stopped by the sound of a woman's shrill voice coming from the Columbus Tavern. Curious, she pushed open the tavern door. The white woman she had seen behind the bar was beating the head of a sailor with a battered pewter tankard. The sailor was so drunk he could hardly stand on his feet. No one else was in the tavern, it was still too early.

'Touch me, would you, you murdering swine,' the woman was screaming. 'Rob me, would you, you thieving wretch! You'll rue the day you met Molly McGuire.'

Drunk or not, the sailor, big and bearded, was more than a match for the screaming, furious woman. Two huge hands fastened round her throat, and slowly the shouts were silenced. The sailor had his back to Amelia but from her place in the doorway she could see the woman's face begin to turn purple, heard the choking gasps. The man appeared to be chuckling to himself as he lifted the woman from the ground and deliberately squeezed tighter. Amelia realised that unless she did something, and quickly, the woman was going to die. The only possible weapon in the bare room was a heavy wooden bucket full of dirty water standing on the wooden floor. She grabbed it and, two-handed, threw the water over the sailor and his victim. Then, holding the empty bucket by its wooden handle and swinging it with all her weight behind it, she hit him with all the force she could muster on the back of his head.

The iron rings that held the wood in place connected with his skull to dramatic effect. He let go of the woman's throat and slowly and silently, like a felled oak, slid to the ground. At the same time the momentum of the heavy bucket toppled Amelia to the ground beside him.

'Holy mother!' the woman croaked, her hand clutching her throat. 'Where did you come from?'

'Outside,' Amelia said with perfect logic as she scrambled to her feet.

'And just in time for me.' Molly McGuire gave the sailor's collapsed body a hefty kick in the ribs, bent to remove his knife from his belt, and tottered towards the bar where she pulled a bottle down from the shelf and, taking a rummer, filled it. She took a long swig, coughed, and then, eyebrows raised, handed the glass towards Amelia.

'What is it?' Amelia asked.

'Good cognac.'

Amelia shook her head. She felt surprisingly pleased with herself. The justified violence seemed to have released something in her. She too gave the sailor a quick kick in the ribs. Molly McGuire was leaning against the bar getting her breath back, her throat showing distinct red finger marks. Her greying hair was dressed in a style more suited to a woman of lesser years. She wore a heavy sacking apron over what had once been an elegant gown and Amelia judged it was now used for work. She had a round, wrinkled face and very bright blue eyes which were scrutinising Amelia with unabashed curiosity.

'Why are you dressed like a slave?' she finally enquired when she had had another swig of the cognac.

'Because that's what I am.'

'Bondswoman?'

'Ten years.'

The woman nodded knowingly. 'I heard tell there was a girl on the *Indeavour*. You are she?' Amelia nodded. 'What's your name?'

'Amelia Quick.'

'You speak like a lady. Are you certain that you don't wish a touch of cognac?'

And she, Amelia thought, sounded Irish.

29

She shook her head at the cognac.

'You're Molly McGuire,' she said.

The woman laughed a surprisingly light and girlish laugh. 'Now how is it that you are knowing my name?'

'You were shouting that he would rue the day he met Molly McGuire.'

'Was I indeed? When the thieving bastard crept up behind me I was so fashed I have no recollection of what I said or did. 'Twas lucky for me you were passing or I would have been in another world – and it would not have been heavenly paradise, not with the life I've had to lead. It seems that I am owing you my life and maybe my immortal soul since you have permitted me time to repent my sins. I thank you with all my heart.'

Amelia was embarrassed. The woman's speech was curiously out of date, over-flowery for the times. She murmured something deprecating and, changing the subject asked, 'Is this your tavern?'

'It is. And I myself once a bondswoman, though long ago now.'

Amelia was astonished. 'You were a bondswoman?'

'I was. Thirty-five years ago now, me and me mother, now long dead, God rest her soul. I was sent here when just a slip of a girl like yourself. They sent me to Macabees.'

'I'm at Windsong.'

'Then you're fortunate. Macabees is hell on earth.'

Amelia could not contain her curiosity. 'Why did they send you?'

'My mother and I had committed the dreadful crimes of being hungry, of being without work and of being without money. Oliver Cromwell, God rot him, sent us here with many others from holy Ireland to slave for the plantation owners, just as you slave now. But it passes. All changes.'

Amelia had no ambition to own a tavern but the thought that it was possible to achieve some kind of success after life as a bondswoman filled her with hope.

'How long did you slave?' she asked.

'Nigh on twelve years.'

'And how did you become a tavernkeeper?'

Molly McGuire folded her arms across her square frame and pursed her lips. 'Hard work,' she said briefly.

Amelia wanted to ask more, but something in the woman's stance told her questions would not be welcome.

The man on the floor was stirring. Molly gave him another contemptuous kick. 'I'll be off to find the constabulary,' she said, 'and you had better be on your way, Amelia Quick. If he comes to and puts you and the bucket and the pain in his thick head together, it could well be my turn to rescue you.'

Molly became a friend. Amelia visited her briefly whenever she was in Basse-Terre. Together they talked of the horrors of the crossing to this new land. At Windsong she and Bella talked, too. All three women had experienced the misery of the appalling heat, of lying like a parcel on a shelf night and day, unable to sit up, steaming, stinking. Bella and Amelia understood what it was to be shackled hand and foot (that Molly had escaped) and to lie in your own filth and that of others for ten long weeks below the decks while some around you, struggling for breath in the suffocating heat, gave up and died. The heat was so intense that the sailors refused to go below. Vicious rats preyed on the prisoners. Amelia, Molly and Bella remembered it all well. It was a nightmare that did not fade and the shared experience created a sisterhood that transcended both colour and religion.

Amelia's sixteenth birthday passed without being marked. She forgot the date until it had come and gone, but she was no longer lonely. Joshua became her shadow, and her friend as well as her pupil. Both he and Truly tried to copy the way she spoke, always reverting to their own people's patois in the cabin and in front of their masters. Amelia was comfortable with them both but happier in Joshua's company. She liked the way he looked. He was, she thought, wonderfully handsome and she could not imagine that he could find pleasure in her pale skin that turned so red in the endless sunshine and was constantly covered in red bites and stings from a myriad of unknown insects.

He looked subtly different from his own people but was not treated as an outcast by them. There were now too many slaves with white blood for that, but he was not as close to his mother as Truly was.

'She called Truly 'cause she truly mine,' Bella had explained. 'When they brung me here there was a man from my village and I love him and he love me. We made Truly between us two. She black like me and him. But she and Joshua the only babies I ever did get to keep. The others they all die. Even the master's they die, but he don' care. He glad and I be glad too, because they only be more slaves for that skinny wife o' his if they live.'

'What happened to your man?' Amelia asked.

'He die, too. He just pine away and go remembering home far away where he be free. Only the strong live here, gal. Still, we lucky. We house slaves. Them field slaves, they don' live too long.'

And Amelia feared again for Zach.

She told herself at first that Joshua was a substitute in her life for her brother. She helped him with his patch of land behind the cabin where he grew vegetables to help supplement their dreary diet. He kept a few chickens which scratched around in the rich soil, and every now and then, if one of the hens went broody and there were new chicks, one of others would be killed for the pot. Sometimes when her mistresses were napping in the heat of the afternoon, she would help him with his work in the main gardens, remembering how she had once enjoyed pottering in the gardens of Quick Manor helping the gardeners, and she described to him what her life had once been.

'You have slaves in England?' he asked her one day as he hoed between the rows of sweet corn.

31

'Gracious, no!' she said. 'We had servants. People we paid to work for us.'

'Black folk?'

'No, white.'

'White people did the hard work? Not just the bookkeeping?'

'Yes. There are no black people in my country. No slaves.'

He shook his head, astonished. 'Then I don' understand why we be slaves here.'

'Neither do I,' she told him.

They worked in silence for a while.

She was thinking of Zach when she spoke again. 'Why do they let you stay here?' she asked him. Joshua was as big and strong as her brother. 'Why don't they send you to the fields?'

'Because my father was a white man,' he said abruptly. 'Some folk hate me for that.'

'I see.'

'He was a bad white man like all the others.'

She hesitated. 'Not all white people are bad, Joshua,' she said. 'Perhaps you have a white grandmother or uncles who are good people and you are of their blood, too.'

'I wish I was white,' he said fiercely. 'If I was white then I be free.'

'Perhaps,' she said, adding, with wisdom beyond her years, 'but there are many kinds of slavery, Joshua, even in a white world.'

'And if I be white, it could be different 'tween you and me,' he went on doggedly.

'We are the people we are,' she said, deliberately misunderstanding, for the look was in his eyes again and the look from him stirred something inside her that she had never felt before. She felt shy and excited, hot and cold, sobered and elated all at the same time. 'We are friends and there is no difference between us.'

He looked at her and suddenly smiled a smile of surprising beauty. 'Oh, there be differences between us,' he said cheerfully and looked straight at the region where her full breasts swelled the cheap linen of her blouse. She felt herself turn scarlet as her eyes involuntarily went to where she saw a sudden, unaccustomed swell at the apex of his breeches.

Confused, she bent to grub in the rich soil. 'Gracious,' she said, 'don't the weeds grow fast!'

The small exchange altered things between them. The careless friendship vanished. She found herself aware of him in a different way. His presence made her slightly breathless and brought about curious tingly, warm feelings that she could not ignore. And there was a heat to his brown eyes when he looked at her. She was careful to keep well away from him in the darkness of the cabin though she did not quite understand why.

The following week, in the hot humidity of a July Sunday while the Olivers were at church, she was sitting in her usual place just where the garden became wilder, under the shade of a vast red-leaved tree. She had chosen to read Othello but her mind was wandering. The Bible was ready at her side for when Joshua and Truly came for their secret lessons. But only Joshua came.

She could tell he had been under the yard pump, sloshing cold water over himself. His shirt clung wet to his torso, and his hair was flat upon his head.

'Where's Truly?' she asked, looking up as he neared.

'Not coming. Not yet. She asked if you hide the book under some leaves for her. She want to read for herself.'

'Oh?'

He did not elaborate. He merely bent to take her hand and pull her gently to her feet. 'Come,' he said.

She did not protest. His hand felt rough in hers as if she could feel every callous his work in the gardens had put there.

'Where are we going?' she asked.

'To walk.'

The penalties for leaving the plantation or for straying where they were not permitted were severe, but on Sundays there were few supervisors about. And besides, the gardens around the house were enormous, running eventually into a wild piece of forest where she had never been.

It was there that he was taking her.

'I show you somewhere pretty. Pretty as you be.'

She was flattered, but nervous about entering the forest. She knew there were snakes there, but with a stick in his hand to brush away the thick undergrowth, he strode ahead confidently leading the way until they came to a rough manmade path which gradually widened as it went slightly downhill and deeper into the trees where big rusty red and tiny yellow butterflies danced. Quite suddenly the trees thinned at an open glade where the grass was as green as Devon grass and where a small stream tinkled into a large pool.

He stopped. 'See,' he said. 'This my secret place. No one but me know about it. No one but me ever come here. I hid the way in, then make the path to get here.'

She was delighted. The air struck cool, there was the gentle sound of running water, the sky above was pale blue and even the trees looked less carnivorous, friendlier.

'Oh, Joshua,' she said clasping her hands in delight. 'It's just like home. It's just like England.'

He was equally delighted by her reaction, and they stood smiling at each other, both a little embarrassed. Then she ran towards the pool and looked down into it. It was clear and sparkling, a few lazy fish darting above small pebbles where the shadows were. At the edge it was shallow, but she could see that the gravelly bottom sloped away abruptly.

'We have so many streams and pools like this on Dartmoor,' she said, excited. 'Zach used to fish . . .'

'Sometimes I thought to catch the fish to eat, but I didn't want to hurt anything,' he said. 'I felt' – he struggled to express himself, 'I must leave it like it be. Or something bad happen.'

She understood exactly what he meant. The kind of life they led created unreasonable superstitions.

'Do you go in the water?' she asked.

'Yes. But it be too deep for you. I can stand but it be over your head.'

'But I can swim,' she said.

'Swim?'

'I'll show you.'

Having said it, she hesitated. Should she go into the water in her clothing? There was nothing underneath her skirt and top.

'Turn your back,' she told him. Obediently he did as he was told. She quickly pulled off her garments and tiptoed into the water, loving the feel of the water on her bare legs. She walked, with little gasps against the cold, until her breasts were covered. 'Now you can turn round,' she called, falling on her stomach to hide her breasts and gently moving her arms to stay afloat. 'Come in, it's wonderful.'

It was his turn to hesitate.

'I'll shut my eyes,' she promised, but she only veiled them and watched as he stripped off breeches and shirt. His body was powerful, muscled, just like Zach's had been when they swam together, still untried children before their lives changed so dramatically. But Joshua's skin was shining brown and seemed to attract the sun. Light bounced off him in gleaming spirals. He looked like some ancient god; a brown Pan perhaps with his curly, springing hair. He ran towards the water and came in splashing and laughing as the water deepened, jumping up and down until his shoulders were covered.

'It feel good,' he shouted like a schoolboy.

'Very good,' she agreed.

He was close to where she floated when he suddenly stood still and very slowly stretched out his arms as if under some compulsion. He placed his hands on her shoulders and pulled her towards him, her body floating behind. Then he freed one hand to stroke her face.

'It feel the same,' he said quietly. He looked closely at her. 'So pretty,' he murmured. 'Your eyes be like a leaf. A new leaf in springtime.'

She felt weightless, suspended. Her own hand came up to touch his face. The skin was surprisingly soft. She traced the outline of his full lips, and touched his hair, aware of its strong texture.

'You are beautiful,' she told him.

His hands were back on her shoulders, running down over her breasts, lifting them, supporting them in the water. He held her round the waist and raised her so that her breasts were level with his face, and then he leaned his head back to look.

'Pink,' he said, as if this were something wondrous. 'Pink.'

And his mouth closed over an erect pink nipple, soft lips sucking, white teeth gently biting.

The sensation was almost unbearably pleasurable. Instinctively she wrapped her legs tight round his waist, pressing herself close to him, loving the sense of her secret parts so close to him. Carrying her while both her legs and arms embraced him, he strode from the water. She let her head fall on his shoulder.

He knelt down, still holding her, and then let her body slip downwards until she could feel between her opened thighs that he was hard and erect. She knew that this was what happened to the male, but had not imagined that the reality of it could be so demanding. She felt like a vessel waiting to be filled or emptied, she was not sure which, and she wanted him to be the one to do it.

She looked into his face. His expression was tender, questioning, asking.

'Do you know what to do?' she whispered.

'I seen others.' He said it apologetically, like a confession.

'Then do it,' she said urgently.

He laid her on the soft grass beside the pool, and for a moment all that masculine hardness was before her. She needed to touch it. She ran her hands along its length, liking the feel of the velvety softness of the skin against the strength of the flesh. He stopped moving to let her hold him, his eyes closed, groaning a little. Then she let go, and he slid his body over hers. Her legs were already opened, and he lay quietly between them for perhaps a minute while he caressed her eyelids, her hair, dropping gentle kisses on her face. She could feel the object of her need pressing against her and found herself moving beneath him. Her hips seemed to have a momentum of their own as they rose and fell. She wanted more than kisses.

And, unable to wait any longer himself, he opened her gently with his fingers and found the way in. There was a brief moment of pain and then only great, uncontainable joy.

They slept afterwards. And it seemed to Amelia it was the first true, contented sleep she had had since Colonel Lamb's soldiers came to arrest her at the school. Joshua had wiped out the misery of the weeks in Taunton Prison, the memories of terror on the ship, terror of the arrival on the island, terror of the future. She had lost all shame, and the bad dreams receded. Sleepily she wrapped her arms round him, nuzzled her head into his shoulder, and slept.

She was surprised to find that she felt no shame. Coupling before marriage was not permitted to a girl of her class and breeding. It was for milkmaids and kitchenmaids to lie in the long grass with their loves and be dammed to the consequences. The babies came, sometimes the girl was wed, sometimes not and then all that was to be done was live with the shame. She was no more than a kitchenmaid now and marriage and family life were not permitted to slaves. She loved him and what was she supposed to do with the overwhelming urges that afflicted her body whenever he was near?

35

She loved him and he loved her. The passage from Job that he had learned off by heart they quoted to each other. They would have the same people and the same gods and they would always be together. Joshua was kind, without the bitterness and fierceness of his sister. He understood Jesus Christ and his works without difficulty. Truly better appreciated the eye for an eye doctrine of the Old Testament. Neither she nor Amelia believed in turning the other cheek. But Joshua was gentle. He loved to make things grow and, for a slave, he was happy in his work in the gardens. He dreamed of having gardens of his own and she fantasised that he and she would return one day to Quick Manor where together they would restore the house and gardens for themselves.

She could not bear to be apart from him, nor he from her. They still slept on different sides of the cabin, but there were times at night, when everyone slept, when they slipped down the frail ladder and into the soft, scented, warm night to make love under the stars and in the moaning of the ever-present wind.

One night as they came back in they found their way blocked by the huge shape of Bella.

'What you two think you up to?' She managed to get truculence into a whisper. 'What you think go'n happen when the master he finds what you doin'? You his now, gal. You think I want my son kilt over you?'

'It's all right, Mama,' Joshua whispered back. 'Master never touched her that time.'

'So what he do?'

'He just wanted to talk,' Amelia said.

Bella snorted. 'Talk! That maybe what he did, but it not what he wanted to do.'

'It's true.'

The older woman considered, elbows akimbo. 'Maybe 'tis at that. You in mighty good shape when you come back that night for someone who been with the master. I tol' myself it 'cause you white you don' get hurt. Black gals he hurt real bad.'

'Joshua and I love each other, Bella.'

She snorted again. 'Ain't no room for love for the likes of you in this world here, gal. You white, my Joshua black. What you' folks go'n say? White gals don' love black boys. Ain't right.'

'Joshua's half-white,' Amelia said defiantly.

'That don' do him much good, 'cept perhaps keep him from the fields. They say he be black even if he do be half as white as they are. And what you gonna do if you gets pregnant?'

There was a long silence. Somewhere a night bird screeched, making Amelia jump.

'You ain't thought about that, have you? Well, I tell you, master's go'n be real mad if you gets pregnant, gal. He want you. No doubt 'bout it. Why you think he's always hangin' round. Maybe he don' do nuffin' 'bout it, but he ain't go'n like it one bit if he thinks someone there afore him. You just don' get pregnant, gal.'

36

'But how?' Amelia asked.

Bella chuckled, a deep black chuckle. 'Stoppin' doing it's 'bout the only way I knows, gal.'

There was a silence and then Amelia said, defiant, her hands folded over her stomach, 'The trouble is I think it's already too late for that.'

There were times when Matthew had the impression that he was going mad. His obsession for his wife's maid was a worm in his soul, burrowing deeper into his senses, eating away at all his better instincts. He thought of her constantly. Her hidden flesh flavoured his lusts, her green eyes lit his dreams on the occasions when he was able to sleep. He could not get her out of his mind. He wanted her. Somewhere along the way in the past seven months all the purity of his feelings for her had disappeared. Now he just wanted to take her physically, roughly or gently, whether she would have him or not. He was angry with himself for putting himself into this position by having succumbed to the temptation to buy her. But then the fact he had bought her helped persuade him that she was his and that it was his right to do with her what he would.

Matthew was a weak rather than a bad man and the good fought the evil in him. He longed to unburden himself of this dreadful urge that tormented him. But to whom? For the first time in his life he began to appreciate the power of the confessional. He prayed for peace from this shameful, unwanted need, but peace was not to be found, and the need grew.

Night after night he lay in his quiet chamber, imagining how it would be to lie with her. His fantasies made him rampant with desire. Then all that he could do was to relieve himself. This he considered a sin, perhaps more of a sin than taking a woman he had bought. Those breathless, taunted, nightly-induced emissions which were followed by a temporary, quivering relief only added to his anguish.

He made sure that he saw her at least every other day, though he had to plot to make certain that neither she nor his family realised that these meetings were by design. He took to calling on his wife when he knew that Amelia would be dressing her sparse blonde hair. He made his manner hearty. 'Are you looking after my mistress wife properly?' he would demand jovially of the girl who would look at him demurely with those aware green eyes, drop her curtsy and murmur that indeed she hoped so.

Amelia had taken his advice. He heard the grossly exaggerated compliments that she gave his wife and was dismayed by Elizabeth's complacent acceptance of them. These days Amelia kept her eyes carefully down, her attitude humble so that none should see her true thoughts. But when she turned that blaze of green direct on him, all the contempt, the anger, the mockery were there clear to see.

It was August, a sultry, swollen month. The trade winds blew slower and hotter; the air was damp and heavy to the lungs. Violent rain fell, unannounced, bending and bowing even the thickest leaves by its weight and soaking all who moved in it to the skin. Then the sun shone again with sullen fervour so that all was dry and thirsty again as if the rain had never been. The island glittered in the heat, dusty and somnolent. The slaves moved snail-like about their chores and in the fields even the overseer's whip was stilled. And at Windsong, Matthew's wife and daughter slept through the long afternoons.

He told himself that it was the torrid summer that was causing this unquenchable fever in him. That he was sick. But he knew that the only cure for his sickness would be to sink himself into the soft, yielding flesh of Amelia.

It was gone midnight and there was a storm rumbling somewhere to the south. He could not sleep. He rose, lit a candle and paced his room. He was tumescent, he knew that his own attentions would not help this time. He was beyond that. He fell on his knees and prayed to God to relieve him of his burden, but looking down, he saw that prayer had done nothing to reduce the stubborn erection that he carried before him.

Perhaps God meant him to have the girl for all the years of lonely, loveless deprivation he had suffered. Perhaps God Himself had directed him to the market that January morning so that he could save her from a worse fate. Maybe the girl even cared for him. He endeavoured to persuade himself that the blaze of green she turned upon him held somewhere within its depths a longing such as he felt and that she would open her arms to him and be his.

Groaning, he dressed, moving his erection flat against his stomach as he pulled on his breeches. Nothing it seemed, would make it go down. He took his lighted candle to the kitchen where he found a lantern and made his way through the garden and down to the slave quarters.

He could see the glow of a tiny light through the miserably small window of the first floor of the cabin. There should be no light, slaves were not permitted light, but he had other things on his mind. He flung open the cabin door and stepped inside, the lantern held high. The unhealthy smell of the place stopped him dead in his tracks. Though in his youth London had smelt badly enough, he had never come to terms with the stinks of the Caribbean.

Bella was raising herself on an arm like the branch of a mature tree. Her face in the lantern light was startled to the point of fright.

'The master's here,' she shouted. 'You want someone, Master?'

'Amelia,' he snapped.

'Amelia,' Bella called, 'you done come down, gal. Master wants you.'

He stepped back outside the cabin, away from the smell, aware of a scuffling from above. He moved several paces and waited. In a few seconds she came through the door. She was, he saw, fully dressed. She curtsied. It was ludicrous in the darkness and with what he had in mind.

38

'Don't do that!' he said, his voice anguished. She stood in the moonlight, her hands folded in front of her, her head bowed.

'What can I do for you, sir?' she asked, her voice low.

'Come with me,' he said harshly. 'And be quiet.'

Windsong was in darkness. The house slept. He strode up the lawn and back in through the kitchen, Amelia close behind him. He led the way onto the veranda. There was a long couch there where his wife sometimes slept in the afternoons. In some muddled way he felt the coupling he was determined upon would be more normal if it took place somewhere proper where he could show her the affection and longing he felt for her. And where maybe she would respond.

He had extinguished the lantern for fear of attracting attention. A pale moon lit the length of the veranda, one ray resting across the cushions of the bed. It seemed to him in his fevered state to be a good omen.

And then he did not know what to do next as she stood there quietly, waiting. Waiting for what? She must understand what it was he wanted.

'Disrobe,' he whispered hoarsely.

She hesitated.

'Do it,' he said louder.

She unwrapped the bodice from round her body and let it slide off. Then she untied the sash on her skirt so that the garment slipped to the ground. She stood absolutely still.

He was angry with himself for not having had the courage to leave the lantern burning. He wanted to see her body, to remember it in all the long lonely nights to come. She was nothing but a silhouette in the darkness. He could smell her. She smelt of sweat, but it was fresh sweat. He wondered if it was caused by fear. But he was glad he could not see her eyes. If the pleading had been there he would have stopped.

He stepped forward and she did not flinch. Perhaps, perhaps, she wanted him. He put both hands roughly over her breasts, registering how they filled the span of his fingers. It seemed to him that her nipples were hard. He tugged at them a little angrily. She remained silent and still. He ran his hands over her body, feeling the scars on her back. He remembered she had been whipped and naked and the memory excited him more. At that moment he wished he had been one of those who watched. Her stomach seemed rounded to him as he touched it before sliding his hand between her legs. There was a fluff of hair there and a pronounced mound. What colour was the hair? He needed to know. Russet like her curls? Next time he would take her in daylight.

He pushed his fingers between the folds of her and found her dry. She tightened against his finger probing the entrance to her. It was natural. She was a virgin. She would yield.

He wanted her to yield. He wanted her to want him as much as he wanted her. He crushed his mouth onto hers. She did not respond, her lips were as tight shut against him as the rest of her body. He forced

39

his tongue between her lips and felt her teeth close sharply over it and tasted his own blood.

'You vixen,' he hissed once he was able, and all attempt at finesse was gone. He tore off his own garments, one-handed, holding her hair with the other. Then he forced her back onto the couch. She fought him silently, legs locked tight, nails scratching at his back. He grew angrier. He had not meant it to be like this.

'You don't understand,' he panted. 'I love you.'

'Then leave me be,' she hissed in return.

It was now no more than a grim struggle and one that he found increasingly exciting. His knee brutally forced her legs apart while one hand twisted viciously at a nipple. He jammed himself between her legs and forced his fingers inside her to open her for his entrance. The way was clear. He wasted no more time but slammed himself into her. And then she lay absolutely still, rigid under him, hardly breathing, as if she were in a trance. There was no more resistance. He realised that now he could do what he liked. He remembered all those excesses with the black girls of years ago, the different penetrations, the bitten breasts, the taste of blood. None of these had ever been available to him with a white body. Now they were. And he punished her for her mocking looks, her rejection of him, for the anguish and torment her presence had caused him, for the lack of gratitude that she had shown. He punished her for all his weaknesses and she lay in silence as he turned her and used her as if she were on a spit, until he was spent and exhausted. Then, as he lay limp over her body, the shame began to creep up on him.

'You don't understand,' he said again pitifully. 'I love you.'

She did not move and as he started to lift himself off her she wriggled free. She stood, staring down at him in the pale light and then bent forward. He had the mad impression that she was going to kiss him. Instead she spat. She picked up her clothes and turned and walked away, leaving him to lie there, wiping her spittle from his cheek.

Amelia managed to stand straight until she was sure that Matthew could no longer see her. She would not let him know how badly he had hurt her, both physically and mentally. But once he was out of sight, she collapsed onto her knees and, clutching her arms round her, moaned and sobbed. Every part of her body was burning with pain, and the humiliation and the degradation burned as badly. She could barely move. Painfully, on her hands and knees, dragging her garments, she crawled back to the cabin. Those inside heard her strangled breath as she tried to move and three figures, one vast, one slight, one powerful, came running out towards her.

'He did it this time, eh, gal?' Bella said, bending over her.

Joshua held her in his arms. She could feel his tears on her breasts. They felt warm and somehow comforting.

'I'm go'n kill him,' he said.

'You not go'n kill nobody, or you get kilt you'self,' Bella scolded. 'Just get this gal inside where we can tend her.'

As Joshua carried her into the cabin, Truly was already getting water from the pump in the old china basin that did duty both for food and washing.

'Keep her down here,' Bella ordered. 'No cause to scare the little ones.'

Joshua insisted on washing her himself. His hands were tender, and as he stroked away the blood and the pain he murmured endearments. Truly and Bella busied themselves getting fresh water. Truly had torn an old bandana into strips to use as a swab. Knowing that she would be in trouble for its disappearance, Amelia tried to protest, but Truly's shrug was eloquent in the dim light. She didn't care.

Suddenly Joshua stopped sponging and leaned back on his heels. 'The baby, Mama! Will it be all right?'

Amelia instinctively put her hands over her stomach. It was the question she had been too frightened to ask. She was aware that the baby would create problems, but she longed for it to be born. She awaited its arrival with tranquillity, telling herself that it would fit in easily with the kind of family life she had found in the cabin; it would be something of her very own to cherish and a living symbol of her love for Joshua.

'If it ain't, that the best thing in the world can happen,' Bella said harshly.

'Mama!' he protested.

Bella gave the snort that always came before one of her pronouncements.

'You been keeping you head down between you legs, Joshua,' she scolded. 'You ain't been thinking. At first the master gonna think it his, ain't he? And if we's lucky, with she bein' white and you bein' half-white, maybe we go'n fool him into believin' it is. But I ain't never seen no baby born yet that didn't show the truth, and when that baby of yourn's born black, gal, or even just a little bit black, my, have we got troubles.'

Amelia stared at Bella aghast and wrapped her arms round herself. 'But I don't want him to think that it's his baby,' she said angrily. 'It will be Joshua's and my baby.'

Bella sighed. 'Ain't you learned nothing yet, gal? Don' you understand that it be fine for the white man to fuck a black gal and have the babies to grow up and slave for them. My, sometimes they gets so generous they even gives they babies they freedom. Not right away. Sometimes when the masters die there it be in the will. But it ain't the same when a black boy he fuck a white girl, like Joshua been doin' to you. If the master think you baby got a black daddy, he like to do something real bad to that daddy when he finds out who it be.'

'What sort of bad thing?' Amelia asked fearfully.

'Chop him up in some way so he can't fuck no white gal ever again.'

41

She paused and added, 'Then after that, they string him up till he be dead so he won' be wanting to fuck anyone ever again.'

Amelia clutched at Joshua's hand. 'But I love Joshua,' she protested. 'Why shouldn't we have a baby? Why shouldn't we be together?'

'You sounds like a child. White gals don' love black boys. Ain't the way things is done. White gals get whipped or worse for mixing with black boys. White men don' love black gals. They just fuck 'em.'

Amelia was appalled. 'But it's not right,' she cried.

'White folk think it right.' Bella was pronouncing judgement. 'Might just have been all right for you and Joshua since you be a slave, but not now the master's fucked you. If he think a black boy been there afore him, he go'n be that mad that no one round here go'n be safe.'

The truth of what Bella was saying was striking hard. Dimly Amelia began to perceive and accept the barriers that separated her and Joshua, barriers that she had not even considered. And the realisation that the world's implacable judgement that black and white should never be one was like a loss of innocence.

'What shall we do?' she asked, afraid of what the answer would be.

Bella's voice was weary. 'I tell you what you go'n do and you ain't go'n like it. You go'n try and keep this baby secret. The master ain't go'n know one word about it. He go'n think you just getting fatter. And when it born, its mama ain't go'n be you, it go'n be Truly. And that way we all be safe.'

Truly gasped. 'Mama!'

'But he'll guess. He's bound to guess.' Amelia was frantic.

'He ain't go'n want it to be his baby. He ain't go'n want you to be having a baby. He gonna believe what we want him to.'

'But if we say it's Truly's, the baby will always be a slave,' Amelia protested.

Bella got to her feet, and hands on vast hips stared down in the darkness at Amelia. 'And if we don',' she hissed, 'my Joshua go'n finish up swinging from a tree. You just take you pick, gal, of what you want to do. It be up to you.'

Chapter Three

Zach's lungs were tortured and he was terrified that the rasp of his breathing would wake someone in the big grey house that stood sinister in the darkness. He was bent double, his hands on his hips, trying to regain breath. He had run the three miles from the field slaves' quarters to the house without stopping as if the devil were at his heels, as indeed the devil might well be once they discovered back there what he had done.

The punishment for striking the overseer was mutilation or death. By hanging. He had already escaped that in England and he intended somehow to escape it again. But before he ran, he needed one word with his own kind. He needed to see Amelia and Ben – in case it was for the last time.

After nine months of terrible forced labour he was familiar with the layout of a West Indies plantation. He knew that the thatched huts that both he and Amelia had mistaken for stables were slave quarters. Somewhere in those still, moonlit cabins were his sister and his cousin. If he tried to find them, would the black slaves raise the alarm? He had to take a chance on it.

It was a bad night for a fugitive. The sky was awash with stars and a great round moon, blue-veined like a woman's breast, hung like a lantern in the sky. He picked his way barefoot through the gardens towards the cabins trying to stay out of the silver light. He came round to the front of the huts and groped for the gate in the picket fence. Then behind him he heard a rustle. A manmade rustle, he was certain of it. Convinced the noise of his heartbeat would give him away, he stood stock-still, his hand clutching the overseer's machete which he had tied round his waist.

'Who is it?' The voice from behind him was a hoarse furtive whisper, not a demanding shout. It was voice of someone who, like himself, had no right to be out.

He did not know what to say in return and stupidly echoed the question: 'Who is it?'

'Zach? Is it you, Zach?' It was his sister's voice, and she was running from the shadow of the trees towards him, a ghostly figure in the insubstantial clothes of a slave. She flung her arms round him. 'Zach, I can't believe it! You. Here! It's wonderful, but you shouldn't be here. It isn't safe.'

43

She felt thin and bony and yet somehow rounded in his arms as she hugged him. She smelt different. She smelt like a woman. He pushed her away from him to try and look at her, and whispered, 'Are you all right?'

'Surviving,' she whispered back. 'And you?'

He was aware of the figure of a man as tall and well-built as himself moving towards them from the woods. Again he stiffened.

'Who's that?' he said.

'Joshua. He's my – ' she hesitated, 'friend. Don't worry.'

He could see the man was black. There was no light patch in the darkness as there always was with a white man's face. What did she mean, her friend? What were they doing out of the cabin in the darkness of the night and in the woods? With a sudden sense of shock he suddenly knew what they were doing and why his sister smelt different. He drew away.

'Where's Ben?' he asked, his voice cold.

'In the cabin.'

'Can you get him out? I want to talk to him.'

'Talk to me first.'

'There isn't time. I'm running.'

Her hand flew to cover her mouth. 'Zach, what have you done?'

'Half killed the overseer.'

'Good!' she said fiercely. 'Better if you'd killed him.'

'It won't be better if they catch me. Find Ben.'

'I'll get him,' the tall black figure said and soft-footed padded into the cabin.

'I've been so anxious about you,' Amelia was saying. 'And about Ben. Something's wrong. He won't talk to me. He barely acknowledges me.'

'Perhaps because of your friend there,' he heard himself say, cruelly.

She was silent and he knew she had taken his meaning. It had always been like that between them. Words were rarely needed.

'Ben's troubles began before that,' she said sadly. 'That's why I was so glad of Joshua's friendship. Haven't you been lonely too, Zach?'

Thinking of how lonely he had been, the only white man among blacks who would not accept him, who jeered, who contrived to make his life more difficult in every way, he almost choked with emotion. The only white face he ever saw belonged to the overseer and the overseer was the wickedest person he had ever met, man who had laid the lash about him in the cane fields for no reason other than sadistic pleasure. He knew about loneliness, just as she must, and he hadn't risked seeing her only to hurt her. He put his arms round her again, and they stood clinging to each other.

Two figures, one tall, one small were emerging furtively from the cabin. The smaller, sobbing unashamedly, ran ahead through the gate to embrace Zach.

'I've missed you so,' Ben said hoarsely. 'It's been so long, so terrible . . .'

44

Zach, anxious that Ben's sobs would be heard above the sobbing of the wind, took his arm and led him into the trees.

'I'm running, Ben,' he told his cousin. 'I'm in trouble. They'll hang me if they catch me. I wanted to see you both before I went. I want you to look after Amelia for me.'

'Take me with you, Zach, for God's sake take me with you.' Ben's voice was almost hysterical.

'No. You're not strong enough. We'd both get caught. And besides, someone has to look after Amelia.'

'But I can't stay here. I must get away. Amelia's got Joshua. You know I love her, Zach. I've always loved her. But I wouldn't be able to touch her now. Not ever.'

'I understand.'

'You don't understand. It's not her, it's me. I'm destroyed. I'm filthy. Shamed.' He was sobbing again.

Zach did not recognise this abject, weeping creature as the Ben who had sustained them throughout the voyage, whose optimism and spirit had been unquenchable. Amelia was right. Something was seriously wrong.

He put his hand lightly on the smaller man's shoulder. 'Ben, what is it?' he asked.

'It's Justinian. My master. By God, he's my master, in every way. He makes me . . .' He stopped and took a pace backwards. 'I can't talk about it.'

'What does he make you do?'

Ben gulped. 'All right, I'll tell you. He makes me strip, and then he makes me bend over and he . . . you know. As if I were a woman. He makes me do other things, too. It's always when he's drunk. I can't bear it, Zach. At first it hurt. It doesn't hurt any more, but it makes me sick and ashamed, and he threatens to have me whipped until I'm nearly dead if I don't let him do it. They whipped Amelia. I saw her back afterwards. It's scarred now, terrible scars that will never go away. But he's put scars on my soul. What kind of a man am I that lets that happen to me?'

As he listened, a great wrath was growing in Zach. More wrath than he had ever felt for himself even at the worst of the agonising months cutting cane and then working in the dreadful heat of the factory yard. He had known the lash across his shoulders and constant humiliation but he had borne it. What he could not bear was that his sister had been whipped and his cousin buggered. All three of their lives ruined for these greedy plantation owners who thought of nothing but sugar and the money that it made them.

He stood there, his fists clenched, breathing heavily, and began walking back towards the cabin, the weeping Ben behind him.

The black man stepped forward and hurriedly began to explain how Zach could get to the mountains, pointing out a spot between some trees where he said there was a hidden path that led deep into the forest and up to where the mountains began. It was a path no one else knew about. He was urging Zach to take it quickly, to run, run, run.

Zach registered it all, but there was something he had to do first. 'Where does this Justinian sleep?' he asked.

Ben's eyes widened, the whites round and gleaming in the moonlight. 'No, Zach, no. They'll catch you.'

'Show me where he sleeps. But be quiet about it.'

Ben's white face shone in the moonlight, and Zach bent to grab a handful of mud from round the pump which he smeared over his face. Then using the machete, he slit a length of fabric from what was left of the linen shirt he wore. Ben hung back.

'Show me.' He snatched Ben's arm roughly and twisted it behind his back. 'Show me,' he said again.

Without speaking, Ben began to move. He lead Zach through the kitchen where they had waited to know their future nine months before, through a hallway and up a fine flight of stairs. The moon crept through a mullion window to illuminate their way. Both were cat-like in the darkness, determination on Zach's part and terror on Ben's making them silent as a bat's flight.

'It's the last room in this hallway,' Ben finally whispered.

'Now go back,' Zach said. Ben did not move and Zach gave him a firm push. 'Go,' he said and Ben melted into the darkness.

Zach stood listening. The house was silent, nothing stirred. Light-footed, he made his way down the long, wide hall, and carefully tried the bedroom door. It was not locked. He opened it and slid inside, standing still to acclimatise himself to the room. He could hear drunken snoring and snuffling noises and in the centre of the room he could see the tall shape of the four-poster bed, curtains drawn round it. Moving with caution he made his way to the head and with infinite care manoeuvred his trunk past the bed hangings. It was dark in there, but Justinian's snores indicated where his head lay. Zach had the length of fabric in his hand, and before Justinian could cry out the linen was round his face, thrust into his mouth and tied behind his head, effectively gagging him.

Only then did Zach pull back the curtains, letting some little light onto the terrified eyes of Ben's tormentor.

Zach put the machete to his throat.

'Rest still!' he growled. With his other hand he pulled back the bedclothes. It took only one pull of an arm made strong by cutting cane to pull away the silk night gown that Justinian wore. A long, thin, very white body was revealed. With exquisite care, Zach's thumb and forefinger lifted a long but flaccid, shrunken penis. He tugged a little to give it more length and then the machete, glinting silver in the darkness, spun, accurately separating the member from the body. Justinian's frame jerked twice, and what would have been a dreadful scream gurgled behind the gag. Zach held the severed penis disdainfully up to a ray of moonlight and then flung it on Justinian's pillows. He

46

carefully wiped the machete clean on the fine bed linen, and with a mocking salute at the moaning body in the bed left as quietly as he had come.

Ben waited in the shadows outside the kitchen door, every rustle from the night animals startling him. He had stopped sobbing, but he still trembled uncontrollably. Yet he was beginning to feel secure again. All through their boyhood Zach had protected him with his enormous strength so that others who might have bullied the diminutive Ben thought again when they saw Zach at his side. He felt certain that the dreadful sexual torment he had received at the hands of Justinian was over. He had no idea how Zach would deal with it, but he was sure that he would never have to bend over for Justinian again.

It could not have been more than five minutes before Zach reappeared, gliding silently through the moonlight. At first Ben did not see him in the darkness with his face blacked by the mud.

'What did you do?' Ben whispered.

Zach ignored the question. 'Tomorrow morning behave as you always behave,' he said, speaking directly into Ben's ear. 'And look after Amelia.'

Then he was gone, running light-footed towards the slave cabins where another tall figure moved to join him and ran with him, pointing out the path through the forest to safety.

Ben tried to control his shaking hands as he returned to the slave hut. He found Bella with Amelia downstairs, huddled round a tiny scrap of candle which they had lit with a flint. The other house slaves and the children slept on above.

'Why did Zach go to the house?' Amelia asked as Ben came in and slumped in a corner. 'He could have been caught.'

'He had business with Justinian.'

'But he doesn't know Justinian,' she said, puzzled.

'I can't explain,' Ben muttered.

Bella sighed a long, weary sigh. 'I s'pose that Justinian be doin' to you what he one time do to Joshua,' she said.

Ben was silent as he took in that he was not the only victim. He saw Bella's great head nodding backwards and forwards in the flickering light.

'Bad things.' She went on relentlessly. 'Things a man only s'posed to do to a woman.'

Anguished, Ben saw how Amelia's hand flew to cover her mouth but he hoped that perhaps now she would understand his withdrawal from her.

'That Justinian, he nothing but an animal, though that insultin' an animal,' Bella said dismissively. 'You not bothering you'self 'bout that boy, is you?' She was forcing him to reply.

'I was ashamed. I was afraid that somehow it was my fault,' he whispered.

47

'You 'fraid it your fault!' She gave one of her longer, more contemptuous snorts. 'How it be your fault? You think it Joshua's fault when it happen to him? You think it Amelia's fault when the master do bad things to her? Ain't any of us's fault. We slaves. We takes what comes and ain't nothin' we can do 'bout it. I tell you, boy, it a waste of time believing it you own fault 'cos it ain't.' She sank into silence for a moment. 'What you think happen to that Justinian now?' And she sounded as if she hoped it was something bad.

'Zach wouldn't tell me what he had done,' Ben said with more confidence. Bella's flatly delivered, unsentimental verdict on the torture of the past few months had helped calm him. 'He just told me to behave as normal.'

'You think he kilt him?'

'He might have.' Amelia's voice was quiet. 'He said he had nearly killed the overseer. He was very angry.'

'Umm.' Bella thought again. 'I tell you what, boy. If that Justinian dead when you find him tomorrow, you tell the master that youngster come home last night with a sailor from Basse-Terre. That gonna be the best thing to say. We don't want none of our own folks in trouble over it, does we?'

Ben was thinking. The burdens he had been carrying alone for so long were lifting. Bella was right. None of it had been his fault. He was a straightforward ordinary, normal man who had been misused against his will. How could he despise himself for that? By nature he was an optimist. He could feel his self-confidence tickling its way gently back.

'We don't want none of our own folks in trouble, does we?' Bella repeated.

'No, we don't,' Ben said slowly. But he was planning to deal with what happened in his own way. Black folk were not his folk. As long as Zach got clear away and neither he nor Amelia were blamed, he didn't care who swung for it.

Joshua ran with Zach in the blackness until they had passed the secret pool and had reached the spot where the stream came down from the mountains. There they stopped for breath, panting. The moonlight was bright enough see each other's faces.

'Run in the stream for as long as you can,' Joshua advised. 'They might try to track you.' He paused, sounding troubled. 'I never been further than this,' he said anxiously. 'The forest is thick . . .' His voice trailed away and Zach realised that the black man feared for him. 'I'd come with you,' he said. 'Two running for freedom are better than one, but Amelia . . .'

'Try to protect her,' Zach said. He sensed as much as saw the rueful smile of a frustrated man.

'I can try,' Joshua said and turned on his heel and began the run back to Windsong.

48

The glade seemed very empty, almost sinister when he had gone. Zach doggedly began to walk up the stream. The water was cold, here and there pebbles hurt his feet, but mostly it was small gravel and a smoother passage than he had expected. He tried to tell himself that it was no different from walking up the shallow Otter River in the valley below Quick Manor. The alien trees grew closer around him as he climbed until he was aware by the darkness ahead that the water was running through a steep-sided gully. Concerned that there might be no way out if he stayed in the stream, he struck off into the forest, trying all the time to keep his direction upwards and into the mountains.

He walked for what he judged to be two hours, his breath rasping in his throat, his feet bleeding and sore. Long, hanging creepers impeded his progress, frightening him as they swung like ghostly fingers in his face. The ground beneath his feet was moist and there was a smell of rotting vegetation. The air was suddenly damper and cooler than he had known it on the island. He felt as if he was fighting his way through a cloud. The climate seemed to have changed completely. It was cooler and he could no longer hear the wind. He wanted to be far away before daybreak, but exhaustion was beginning to beat him. He needed to sleep. But where? On the ground where there were snakes? In the strangely predatory fleshy trees? He fancied neither. He had no idea where he was or where he was going. The only thing to do was to stagger on, somehow remaining upright, until it was light enough to find somewhere safe to hide.

He moved on feebly, his feet like lead, his lungs bursting, but still relentlessly, muscle-tearingly upwards. He knew his breathing was too noisy, that he could be heard, but he had lost control of his lungs. Blood was pounding in his head obliterating sound, but even so he thought he heard a soft footfall behind him. He stopped, his hand on the machete, trying to find the strength to spin round. Then someone or something struck him a vicious blow on the back of his head. He knew a brief moment of pain, felt himself begin to fall and then, in a world gone dark, he lay unconscious, spreadeagled in the black soil of the forest.

When Ben went to wake his master the following morning he was calm again, ready for whatever he might find. The conviction that Justinian would never again touch him coupled with Bella's practical and logical comments, had restored his spirits and his self-esteem. He had slept well and did not feel apprehensive about what he would find behind the door of Justinian's bedroom; rather, he had a sense of eager anticipation.

The sight that greeted him was nevertheless a shock. The bed curtains were pulled back. One edge of a fine linen sheet was stained with blood already going rusty in colour and in the middle of the bed was his master, mother-naked, gagged, eyes closed, resting in a pool of his own still

49

flowing, bright red blood. It was not obvious whether he was dead or alive.

Ben heard himself let out a shout bordering on a scream. He turned and ran back down the wide hallway, calling for someone to come, and finally pounding on the door of Matthew Oliver's room.

The master came out, sleepy-eyed, his head hidden under a nightcap, pulling his gown round him.

'What's wrong?'

'It's Master Justinian,' Ben croaked. 'Something dreadful has happened.'

Without speaking, Matthew began to run down the corridor to his son's room. With Ben close on his heels, he burst in, stopped dead, and let out a strangled cry of sheer horror.

'Take the gag off,' he commanded Ben.

Reluctantly, almost retching, Ben went to the bed and lifted the head from the pillow to untie the striped fabric. It was then he saw the scrap of flesh beside Justinian's ear. At first he did not know what it was, and then, as reality sunk in, he found himself inflicted with the most unseemly desire to laugh and he understood why Justinian bled so heavily.

Suddenly the eyes in the head beneath him opened; clouded, life-fading, but open.

'Papa,' Justinian said in the weakest of voices. 'Where is Papa?'

'I am here, my son,' Matthew said, taking Justinian's hand in his. 'Ben, send Beauboy for the physician immediately and then get water and bandages. We must stem the bleeding. Tell the mistress to come.' He was already bundling the sheets round the inert body in an attempt to stop the flow of blood, but in Ben's opinion, and from his brief experience of death in the rebellion, it was too late. Too much blood had been shed. Justinian was going to die.

'Who is responsible, Justinian?' Ben heard Matthew saying urgently as he hurried from the bedroom. And he just caught the breath of Justinian's voice.

'Black . . . he was black . . .'

But he was not black. And then Ben remembered the mud that Zach had smeared on his face.

He was thinking hard as he sent a hysterical Mistress Oliver fleeing towards her son's room and woke a grumbling Beauboy in the stables. It occurred to him that if the Oliver family could be made to believe that one of the black slaves had killed Justinian, Joshua would be the obvious culprit. And if Joshua swung from a gibbet in Zach's place, that would be the end of the friendship between him and Amelia.

Ben did not know that Amelia was pregnant but he did know that he bitterly resented the affection that flowed between her and the black boy. He wanted all Amelia's affection for himself. He had told Zach the truth when he said he had always loved her. He had watched her friendship with Joshua grow, helpless, weighed down by his own

50

problems. Now with confidence flooding back and guilt and shame assuaged, he made his decision. He would endeavour that Joshua took the blame if it could be done without a direct accusation, and when Amelia's companion was no more, then he, Ben, would be there to comfort her.

It was just before midday when the house slaves were called to the compound at the back of the house. All morning there had been comings and goings and sounds of lamentation from the women of the house. The slave network missed little. They knew that the master's son was dead or dying but they did not much care about the fate of Justinian Oliver unless his death affected them. Now they stood uneasily in the blazing sun, Amelia and Ben, four black men and four black women with a few children who played in the patchy dried-out grass. They waited as Matthew walked down towards them from the veranda door. His wife was in the house, prostrate with grief, and his own heart weighed heavy.

With him was the constable and the overseer who wore a rough, bloodstained bandage round his head and whose shirt was bloodied as the slaves' were so often bloodied. He looked pale and shaky but the whip was still in his hand. It was Matthew's intention to talk to the house slaves first. Then he would go with Jake to address the field slaves on the question of the white runaway who had used Jake's own whip with devastating effect about his head and his body. If the overseer had not been so hard of head he would be dead – as Justinian was dead.

He stopped a few feet away from the gathered slaves. He could never bear the smells of the compound. They stared at him sullenly. One of the children began to cry, and its mother grabbed it from the ground and buried its face between her breasts.

'I have two things to say to you today,' he began. 'The first is that we have a runaway – the bondsman, Zachary Quick.' He saw that Amelia gave a little gasp and clutched at Ben's hand. Was she acting, or did she already know? he wondered. He had not been near her since that night when he had taken her so brutally. He had done his best to avoid her and the lust that had so tormented him before had changed to a terrible guilt. He simply could not face her. Now he had to question her.

'Have either you, Ben Clode, or you, Amelia Quick, seen Zachary Quick in the last few hours?'

It was Ben who spoke. 'No, sir. I have not seen my cousin since the day we were brought here, and neither has his sister.'

'You know the punishment for lies?'

'Indeed, sir, but he has not been here.'

'Amelia Quick, do you so swear you have not seen your brother?'

She turned the blaze of green on him, expressionless, but he felt convinced the emptiness of her eyes hid loathing.

'I have not seen my brother,' she said firmly.

He nodded, unwilling to pursue the subject of her brother. 'The other matter is one of great grief to my family. Our son, Justinian, has been murdered. His last words to me were that the perpetrator of this outrage was a slave. We shall find the man or woman who has done this dreadful thing. Ben Clode, you were the last to see him?'

'Yes, sir, this morning in his bed, surrounded by his own blood.' Matthew thought he detected an unattractive note of satisfaction. 'I heard him say to you that it was a black man who attacked him.'

'And you saw him last night?'

'I put him to bed at ten o'clock, sir, and he was hail and hearty then.'

'Do you have any idea who could have done this thing to him?'

Ben fidgeted. 'Perhaps one of the slaves who bore a grudge against him, sir. Someone he had injured.'

Matthew was no fool. He was aware that Bella was staring with astonished eyes at Ben, and that Amelia had let go of his hand. She had drawn herself up to her full height, her back was stiff and she appeared angry. Suddenly she began to speak. 'My cousin wishes to save your feelings, sir,' she said. 'The truth is that when your son came back to Windsong last night he had drunk too much ale in Basse-Terre. He brought with him for company for the night a French sailor from one of the men o' war in the bay. It was your son's habit to fulfil the needs which we all share in this way. My cousin is kind of heart and he had hoped that you would never know of your son's perverted tastes, but if the real culprit for this dreadful deed is to be found, the truth must be told.'

Matthew remembered the horror of finding the severed penis and with pain and anger understood why his son had died in such a bizarre way. He was aware of the expressionless face of the constable, and a smirk on the face of the overseer. Bella had relaxed, but Amelia's shoulders were still squared with anger and he could have struck her for speaking of his son in this way in front of others.

'Is this true?' He asked the question of Ben Clode.

The look Amelia gave her cousin was direct and challenging and Ben replied sullenly, 'Yes, it is true.'

The constable frowned. 'But he told his father a slave had attacked him.'

Ben nodded. 'He said, "Black . . . he was black." '

Amelia stepped forward and Matthew drew in his breath when she looked straight at him. Her eyes were no longer angry. They held pity, and confused with his anger he felt a sort of benefice that after everything that had happened she could still feel pity for him.

'Justinian must have said what he said because he did not wish you to know the truth,' she said, soft-voiced. 'With his dying breath he wished to save you pain. He believed it was better for you to think it no more than a murder by one of your own slaves than to expose you to his own shameful needs. You know your slaves are loyal to you. They would not kill your son.'

He was beginning to doubt her. Was all this talk of shameful needs a reference to his own? And all plantation owners deluded themselves that their slaves were loyal. He knew it was not the truth, and for her to have picked upon this delusion made him uneasy.

The constable cleared his throat. 'Taking into account the manner of the murder,' he began, and stopped, embarrassed. 'The problem is, sir, we have no rights in Basse-Terre. Our laws do not apply and there is trouble enough between them and us. If it was a French sailor who did the deed, there is little we can do to apprehend him. The runaway, now that's a different matter. If we could question the field slaves, we might make some progress there.'

Matthew knew his shoulders had slumped but he made no move to straighten them. He was full of despair. Whether the killer was black or white, sailor or slave, he appreciated that the punishment had fitted the crime. Worse was the thought that he himself might be to blame. Could his own perverted needs and desires have been inherited in a different form? He faced for the first time the fact that in his heart he had always known the truth about his posturing, drunken son, but how could he explain to his wife that there would be no tracking down of the man who had killed him? What lies would he be forced to tell her and their neighbours? He would have to lie and continue to lie, though he had little doubt that the truth would out. It was possible that people had always known about his son's predilections. Perhaps they knew about his, too. He had a wild urge to take one slave, any slave, and hang him as a scapegoat, but what good would that do?

'Ah, yes, the runaway,' he said dully. 'You deal with that, will you, Jake.' And leaden-footed he went back into the house to his weeping wife.

It wasn't until the grey hours of a sleepless night that he remembered the gag that had been stuffed in his son's mouth. He could not swear to it, but he seemed to recall that the fabric was course and striped, the sort used at Windsong for the slaves' clothing. If he was right, Amelia had been lying and so had Ben. But who had they been protecting? Zachary Quick? Tomorrow he would find the gag and take it to the constable and the search could begin for his son's killer.

He was in the kitchen at early light. Bella was already there, riddling the stove.

'Bella,' he asked, 'what happened to the sheets from my son's bed?'

'All washed, master. You want I bring them to you?'

'Yes. And the gag that was in his mouth, where is that?'

He was sure it would not have been thrown away. Slaves never threw anything away.

'Washed, too, master.'

'Bring it to me.'

Bella waddled across the kitchen and into a huge cupboard. She came back holding a piece of fabric. He took it eagerly. 'Is this it?'

'Yes, sir.'

It was a length of fine white linen.

'It from Master Justinian's shirt,' Bella said. 'I thought to get Truly to sew it back. Seem a shame to waste a good shirt.'

Her expression was unreadable, the glistening black face impassive. But he believed he could feel a kind of triumph exuding from her.

'Don't bother,' he said heavily. 'Just get rid of it.'

The light was strange, grey and shadowy, totally unlike the endless brilliance of the island that had beat about his eyes for the past nine months. It was cool, too, and there was no sound or feel of the constant wind. Somewhere behind him a fire burned. He could smell the wood smoke and was aware of the flicker of a red glow.

Cautiously he raised himself up on one elbow and winced. The back of his head hurt. He placed an exploratory hand above his neck and felt the stickiness of half-dried blood.

With care he sat upright and a deep voice from behind him said, 'Awake, are you? By God, you slept well.'

Zach carefully turned his body to the source of the voice and squinted to see better. Behind him sat a man by the side of a small fire, near to the mouth of what appeared to be a cave. Outside the cave the light was still grey, as if blanketed in cloud.

The man was not young, perhaps nearing fifty. He was hugely bearded with shrewd blue eyes set above the bush of greying hair. He wore a loose shirt, old-fashioned breeches and heavy boots. His head was covered with white hair as wild as that on his face. He appeared to be whittling a piece of wood. The steel of a thin knife twinkled innocently in the firelight.

Zach stared at him and then asked aggressively, 'Did you hit me?'

'I did indeed.' The man's voice was serene. 'You appeared like a ghost from the woods, your face blackened, wearing slaves' garb. I thought you were a runaway. It's lucky I realised you were white before I finished you off and threw you down the ghaut. I want no hunting packs here.'

Zach was chilled by the man's cold-blooded talk of finishing him off. He carefully felt for his machete, but it was no longer at his waist.

'Explain to me what you are doing here in the forest, garbed as you are garbed,' the man said. 'I find myself intrigued. You have all the appearance of a runaway, but you are white.'

'I am a runaway,' Zach said sullenly. He thought he might as well tell the truth since he could think of no other explanation.

'A bondsman?'

'Yes.'

'Why are you here? Are you a criminal?'

'They said I was a traitor.'

'Oh, that! I care nothing for that.' The man made a dismissive chopping movement with his left hand. 'So they're shipping their slaves out from home now, are they? What port did you sail from?'

54

'Bristol.'

'I'm a Bristol man. You're from Wessex yourself?'

'Yes. Devon.'

'It's a long way from here.'

'It is indeed,' Zach said fervently.

The man contemplated the vicious looking little knife thoughtfully. 'Why did you run?'

Zach hesitated. How much should he tell this man? But perhaps he was a runaway himself, hidden in this cave so high in the forest. Zach did not think he would send him back to Windsong. Kill him maybe, but not send him back.

'It was night. I was outside the cabin, trying to breath some air that smelt sweet. The overseer came up behind me, told me to get back inside and set about me with his whip. I snatched it from him and half killed him with it. I left him unconscious. Maybe he's dead. I don't know.'

'You'll swing if they catch you.'

'I know. But if I do, it was worth it.'

The man seemed to be thinking. 'Where were you heading?' he asked.

'I didn't know. I was just running.'

The man shook his head reproachfully. 'You should always know where you're going, except that here there is nowhere to go.'

Zach was silent. He felt he was being criticised in some way. And then the man asked abruptly, 'Are you hungry?'

Zach realised that he was. He nodded.

The man nodded back and got to his feet. He went to the back of the cave. Zach, his eyes now accustomed to the light, could see it was furnished with some rough pieces of heavy wood furniture and with rugs on the levelled floor. There was a long pallet where the man presumably slept, some good silver candlesticks and hanging tipsily on one of the walls was even a painting of a galleon at sea. It was a home within a cave.

The man returned with some fruit that Zach did not recognise and what appeared to be salted meat. They were arrayed on a good pewter plate.

'Eat,' he said briefly, and settled himself back by the fire to continue his whittling.

The fruit was fresh and delicious, the meat tough and too salty. Neither of them spoke until Zach had finished eating.

He wiped fruit juice from his chin with his hand and asked, 'You live here?'

'Most of the time.'

'Isn't it lonely?'

'It's better than the company of men. At least of the men on this island.' Again a dismissive gesture, then, 'Now, what's your name, lad?'

'Zachary Quick.'

'Zachary Quick! You weren't quick enough out there, were you?' he said, and slapped his thigh, laughing at his own joke.

'And yours?' Zach enquired, trying to sound polite since his life appeared to be in this man's hands.

'Tom Fowler, one time sailor, long time buccaneer and these days sometime recluse.'

'A buccaneer!' Zach was impressed.

'Still am when the mood takes me and I tire of the silence and the mist up here. But the good days are over. They outlawed us.' He sounded outraged. 'After all we did to secure these islands for England. After all our fights against the Spanish. Who forced the Spanish to recognise the French and British settlements in these seas? The buccaneers, of course. And then when they don't need us any more, they outlaw us. Suddenly we're nought but thieving rascals only wanting to line our own pockets.' He gave a rich laugh which reverberated in the cave. 'Which, of course, we are.' He laughed again and then said confidingly, 'There's nothing more hypocritical than governments, lad, when it suits 'em. They made a treaty with the Spanish who then recognised the British claim to the islands. Then they wanted us out of the way. The sea dogs were biting too hard. We continued to line our pockets. We were the terror of the Spanish main. There was nothing too strong for us to tackle. But a man can be a murderous privateer one week and a hero the next, depending on which way the political winds are blowing. There was no more vicious, bloodthirsty dog than Henry Morgan, but they gave him a knighthood and made him Governor of Jamaica. They call it setting a thief to catch a thief, and thieves we were.

'I should know, lad. I sailed with Morgan. I was with him at Panama. A month we were there, burning, pillaging, and paying attention to the women, whether they wanted it or not. We didn't leave much of the place, but there wasn't much there to take. The Spanish had removed their treasure before we came. We had better luck in Cuba . . .'

He stopped, perhaps realising that he was beginning to ramble.

'I talk too much, lad – if I get the opportunity. It was a cruel life, but every man was not for himself. There was a comradeship among the buccaneers that you'll never find on these island. If the lads were married, and a few of them were, we even paid their women a pension if their husbands died in service.' He spat noisily out of the cave mouth. 'Here on these sugar islands it's every man for himself and to hell with the human race. As you've no doubt found, lad. Tell me, would you care if the overseer dies?'

'No,' Zach said. 'In a way I hope he does. And the other one, too.'

'Huh! Another, eh? Who?'

'The plantation owner's son.'

'And what did you do to him.'

Zach explained in four words and Tom Fowler's face screwed into a parody of pain and distress. 'What did you want to do that for?'

Zach again briefly explained.

'Well, that one will be as well off dead,' Fowler pronounced. 'Though it seems a small enough thing to die over. When you're at sea it's what you might call any port in a storm.'

Zach didn't quite understand what Tom Fowler was saying, but it was almost a relief to have spoken of what he had done. He said slowly, 'It was the anger, you see. This terrible anger that I've had inside me ever since they shipped us here. It's like an ache in the guts; it's beating at my brain all the time. The only way the anger is relieved is by violence.'

Fowler stopped his whittling and stared into space.

'Anger is a carbuncle on the soul,' he said. 'There are few on these islands that don't suffer anger. The plantations are built on fear and the subjugation of others, but the white folk know that one day they will have to account for what they have done. They are afraid and angry with themselves for feeling fear. And the blacks know that one day they will get their revenge and are angry at the waiting time. There are no truly happy people in these sugar islands. Life is too uncertain. Fear blows into every heart, along with the trade winds.

'I know, lad. I signed on a four-rigger at fourteen; wanted to see the world. I found myself on the slave ships, coming across the middle passage from Africa to the West Indies. At first when they loaded on those captured blacks, men, women and children all stripped naked, I could smell their fear and their terror. The first few passages I went on I tried to make their lives easier, but it's easy to blunt the human soul, lad. I began to persuade myself that they were only animals, like the rest of the crew said, and I took my turn fucking their women. Sometimes they'd throw themselves overboard after, and then we'd be in trouble with the master. Slaves were money. I tell you, it took no time at all to turn me from a compassionate country lad into a beast, such as we told ourselves the blacks were.

'And then, one voyage, I was sick. Sick unto death. I had the ague, the pox, the flux. I lost more than five inches, and when we found landfall here at St Kitts, the master put me ashore with the slaves, and he made damn sure he sailed when I was not aboard.

'Captain Nathanial West left me here to die, without money and without friends. He didn't want any sick sailors on his ship making a bother of themselves. I'd seen it happen to others. I never thought it would happen to me.

' And die I would have done if it hadn't been for an Irish woman from Irishtown in Basse-Terre who found me collapsed on the road. She'd been shipped here by Cromwell and hadn't a pot to pee in but she took me in and nursed me back to health. I tell you, I was sick at heart at man's inhumanity to man, but I had to live. So I went buccaneering and forgot about humanity except for myself, and maybe Molly McGuire. I found in the seas it's the only way to survive, lad. And here in the forest I cleanse the carbuncles off my soul. But even

57

now I can join up with the lads and go buccaneering again when the mood takes me and grow a few more carbuncles to cleanse away. I keep a boat at the other end of the island that's big enough to take me to Tortuga where we meet. There's a great salt pond beyond Basse-Terre, and no one goes beyond it. The boat is hidden there in a creek.'

He lumbered to his feet, and Zach saw that he was a huge man, as big, if not bigger, than Zach himself.

'They'll be after you, lad, you know. The master's not going to like what you did to his son.' And Zach saw that the knife glinted in his hand. 'I don't want them led to me, so it's a choice. I kill you and throw you down the ghaut . . .' He paused, and Zach braced himself to fight against the knife. 'Or you come buccaneering with me.' There was a long silence, and then Fowler let out a great bellow of laughter and pointed at Zach. 'Your face!' he said.

Zach grinned feebly, still uncertain of the man's intentions.

'You'll have to get off this island or swing. I'm wanting to be on my way again. A man who has no compunction at killing should make a good buccaneer. So what's it to be?'

'Buccaneering,' said Zach.

Chapter Four

December 1686

'You are getting fat, Amelia.'

Charlotte, sitting in front of the glass while her hair was combed into the old-fashioned ringlets she affected, stared at her maid's reflection. She giggled. 'We must be feeding you too well. Mama will have a fit of the vapours if she notices.'

There was little chance of Elizabeth Oliver noticing, Amelia thought. The woman never looked at her. She just gave her orders and expected them to be carried out. Under the circumstances that was just as well. She was concerned that Matthew would notice her changing shape, but she rarely saw him. He continued to avoid her and the loss of his son seemed to have made him thinner, greyer and more ghostlike than ever. He moved as if he had no idea where he was. But Charlotte, now the only heir to Windsong and not dismayed by the prospect, was more perceptive.

'Not fatter,' Amelia, who had been preparing for this moment, said easily. 'It's just that I'm wearing one of Bella's old kirtles. It's too big for me.'

'It would be,' said Charlotte, and giggled again before beginning to prattle about her latest beau, a young lieutenant from one of the naval ships that was anchored outside Old Town Road. The island had been clumsily split between French and English back in 1624 when Sir Thomas Warner settled St Kitts. The island was shaped like a club and the French owned the two extreme ends of the body of the club; both countries shared the infertile handle and the huge salt ponds that lay beyond the French capital, and the English held the more fertile centre of the island and most of the mountains. They cast covetous eyes on the natural harbour where Basse-Terre had been built. There were constant small but bloody skirmishes between the two nations. Elizabeth Oliver, who despite having been born in the Caribbean never for one moment felt safe and comfortable, complained that it was bad enough being surrounded by blacks and Irish and the heat and hurricanes and infernal wind, but to have to put up with the marauding French as well was really too much.

'Mama has invited Edward to spend Christmas with us, if his captain permits it,' Charlotte told Amelia. 'I must have a new gown, and Mama, too.' Her voice changed to a coaxing note. 'Would you go into Basse-Terre and bring us back some samples of the new fabrics?'

Amelia had carefully cultivated the impression that she disliked her visits to Basse-Terre. If Elizabeth Oliver had thought they were any kind of pleasure, she would have put a stop to them.

'They say there is trouble with the sailors from the French navy,' she said, making her voice reluctant and drawing her eyebrows into a frown.

'Oh, pooh! What notice will they take of you?' Charlotte said. 'And in any case, Mama commands it.'

Amelia had not been into Basse-Terre since November, a few days before Justinian's death and the following morning she set off as early as she could, wanting to reach the Columbus Tavern before Molly's rumbustious customers arrived. Apart from Bella and Joshua, Molly was the only person who knew that Amelia was pregnant. Amelia had confided in her, and had been dismayed by the fact that even Molly was shocked when she learned Joshua was the father.

'You must be rid of it,' had been her first reaction. When Amelia told her the pregnancy was four months along, she was exasperated.

'You should have told me before,' she scolded. 'You'll have to bear it now. Your friend Bella is right. You must pretend that it's Truly's baby. Holy Mother of God! What did you think you were doing, lying with a black man? If your blood was hot, why not your cousin Ben?'

'I don't love Ben,' Amelia said firmly.

Molly looked baffled. 'You're telling me you love this black lad?' She looked to heaven. 'Well, I suppose all things are possible.'

It had taken Amelia a while to come to terms with Molly's reaction, but she eventually had to accept that it was common among both blacks and whites. She was aware that Bella did not approve of her son loving a white girl. Not that Bella said so, but she was adept at making her feelings known without words.

But neither black woman nor white woman had ostracised her. It was simply that they did not understand and now as she hurried through Basse-Terre she feared that perhaps Molly would think that she had not visited her because of that lack of understanding.

She found Molly behind the long wooden counter in an empty tavern, polishing the pewter pots in which she served the ale. She looked up as Amelia came through the door.

'Ah, there you are,' she said, nodding her head and it seemed to Amelia that she was relieved to see her. 'And where have been you all this long time?'

Without preamble and while settling herself on a three legged stool, Amelia said, 'Justinian was killed. They've all been in mourning. No one has been anywhere.'

'I know about that,' Molly said. Her eyes were twinkling and she looked pleased with herself. 'Your brother told me.'

Amelia sprang to her feet. 'Where is he? Is he safe?'

'As safe as anyone on these islands,' Molly said. 'He's gone buccaneering.'

'Buccaneering! But how?'

Molly leaned on the long counter, looked round the empty room and lowered her voice as if afraid someone might be eavesdropping.

'While he was running he met a friend of mine in the mountains. The man who gave me the money to start this tavern.'

'To start this tavern?' Amelia was bewildered.

'Tom Fowler is his name. It was long years ago. He was a sailor, and so sick that his captain, the same captain that brought you here, left him on the island to die. I happened upon him and nursed him back to health.' She hesitated, pursed her lips, frowned, and then as if having made a decision, said, 'In those days I was whoring. There was nothing else to do to live. Tom went off with the buccaneers when his health was restored and he came back six months later a rich man. It was his piracy that paid for the tavern. He gave me his first profits. It was in return for his life, he said.'

'And Zach is with him?'

'He is indeed.'

'But buccaneering is illegal now, and dangerous.'

'Most things here are illegal for much of the time and life is always dangerous,' Molly said flatly. 'What they are doing is no more dangerous than the kettle of fish you're in. Don't persuade yourself, my green-eyed little darling, that that sanctimonious old master of yours won't take his revenge in the cruellest way if he finds you are pregnant by a black lad.'

Their respective dangers seemed hardly comparable to Amelia. She brushed aside Molly's warning and asked, 'Is Tom Fowler a good man?'

Molly hesitated. She put her elbows on the counter and used her hands to support her chin. Quietly, eyes unfocused, she said, 'He's a good man attempting to be bad. He sees his goodness as a weakness but, praise be to God, it's a goodness that he cannot quell. When your brother stumbled across Tom's hideaway, a sensible man would surely have killed him. Instead, Tom has rescued your Zach by taking him away from the island.' Her voice harshened. 'But Tom's too old by far for buccaneering. He should have stayed up there on the mountain safe in his hideout, coming here under cover of night when he needed provisions, just as he always has over the years.'

Her anxious, protective tone was one that Amelia recognised. 'You love him,' she said and then realised the words sounded like an accusation.

Molly's mouth widened into a shy smile and for an instant there was a glimpse of the pretty young girl she once had been.

' 'Tis true,' she said with a sigh. 'He is indeed the love of me life. And I of his, though he would never admit to such weakness. He brought your brother here for shelter and also to give me more funds before they went away. He's ever generous with his ill-gotten gains. I save what he gives me, for it is the dream of my life that when I am old, or when he has gone to what other world it is that awaits him, I shall go to Montserrat.'

'Montserrat?'

' 'Tis an island none too far from here, the home of the Irish in these waters. Those who lived through the years of Cromwell's persecution that brought us here to these islands went there long ago. Today the Irish flee there from Virginia in the American colonies when their bondsmanship is over. It is no disgrace to be a good, believing Catholic in Montserrat. I would have gone there long ago myself if it had not been for Tom Fowler, but while this is his homing ground it shall be mine also.'

Amelia looked at Molly, baffled by her fervent tone. It seemed odd that a woman of her years should sound like a young girl in love. Did old people still know the pangs and pleasures of love? She longed to ask but thought better of it. Instead she said, 'And you think he will look after Zach?'

'Your brother is big enough to look after himself.'

'My brother is big in the body but small in the head. He does not think carefully.'

'Then you are lucky, for Tom does. Mayhap he will think for them both or teach your brother how.'

'You think they will come back safe?'

Molly sighed. 'For twenty or more years Tom has come back. Pray God he will again. But, Amelia, you must understand that your brother can never come back. He is a runaway. If they find him they will hang him. You say he does not think, but that he understands.' She stopped and sighed again. 'He left a message with me for you.'

'What was it?' Amelia asked apprehensively.

Molly hesitated. 'He asked me to tell you he loved you, to beg that you never forget him,' she said slowly. 'And then to say goodbye.'

A pain, not dissimilar from those she suffered as a child from eating too many scrumped apples, woke Amelia before dawn on an early April morning. She was downstairs in the slave cabin where for the past few weeks she had been sleeping with the older slaves, away from the children. Her soft groan roused Bella.

'It'll be time soon,' Bella pronounced, the full weight of her heavy hand on Amelia's belly. 'But you got to get through this day, gal, without them white folk knowing what going on. You just wait here a while. I be back.'

She slipped from the cabin light-footed despite her size without saying where she was going. The pain subsided and Amelia dozed a little, surprised to find she felt little fear. For the past few months she had been curiously content. The sense of the baby growing and kicking inside her, knowing that new life was flourishing, had become of uppermost importance to her. She felt every other aspect of her existence must be put aside until after the birth. Nothing else, not even Joshua, seemed to matter in comparison. She would think about her problems when the baby was born.

Her girth had increased but not alarmingly so. Elizabeth and Charlotte seemed to have accepted her rounder self and the shapelessness of the loose clothing that all slaves were given helped to hide the definite bulge of the coming baby. On the rare occasions she saw Matthew, he looked at her furtively from the corners of his eyes. She thought perhaps he might have guessed but he said and did nothing.

Bella had supervised what Amelia ate, refusing to permit Joshua to give her extra of the meagre amount of food they were provided with.

'We don't want you being too fat, gal,' she would warn. 'We don't want them knowing 'bout this baby.'

Occasionally the black woman would produce some evil tasting potion which she obtained from Bessie, an old, old slave who remembered how things were done in Africa. This, she insisted, was good for the baby.

'That be my gran'chil' you got there,' she would growl. 'Now you drink it down and do as you tol'.'

For most of the pregnancy Amelia had been under Bessie's care. Bessie, with the help of her daughter Minta, was doctor, witch-doctor, nurse and midwife to the house slaves. They were half afraid of her since it was whispered that she knew how to poison folk so that no one would ever know how it had been done. But Bessie also knew how to cure. She stopped the flux with a tea made from the leaves and bark of the guava tree. A lotion made from the fruit pods of the okra soothed eyes made sore from the dust in the sugar cane. Boils and manifestations of the skin she would heal with a potion of molasses and aloes. When the women slaves did not want to become pregnant she supplied them with a preparation made from yams that kept the babies away, and she scolded Amelia for not having come to her for help earlier.

The waiting was nearly over, and as Amelia lay in the pearly pre-dawn light, Joshua crept silently to hold her hand, trying not to wake the others in the cabin.

'Mama says it will be today,' he whispered.

'I know,' she said tranquilly. 'I wonder if it will be a boy or a girl.'

'Girl, I hopes. Just like you. Then she won't have to work in the fields.'

The thought that her baby must be a slave caused more pain than any contraction. 'Don't talk about that now,' she whispered. She was silent for a moment as another wave of pain came and went, and then sat bolt upright. 'But suppose it comes when I'm in the big house,' she said fearfully.

As she spoke, Bella came back into the cabin carrying a steaming cup. With her were Bessie and Minta.

'Bessie, here to help,' Bella explained. 'She know 'bout these things. Ain't one birth round here she don't be at.'

Bessie was so old that her skin seemed to be covered with a fine layer of ash, her hair was dull as unpolished pewter but her black eyes were still bright. She squatted beside Amelia's pallet on bowed, skinny legs, and a thin bony hand felt the swollen stomach. She motioned Minta to do the same. Everyone in the cabin was now awake but no one spoke for the long, long time that Bessie stayed silent. She waited until Amelia's body had arched twice and then said, 'It come tonight. You lucky. You be all right for the day.'

Amelia heard a soft murmur of relief from the slaves, and Joshua squeezed her hand tighter.

'You drink this,' Bessie said, taking the cup from Bella, 'then the pains they not be so bad.'

It was another vile-tasting concoction, but Amelia obediently drank it plus another which Bella managed to feed to her midday. Whatever was in the potion made her light-headed, almost giggly, so that Charlotte scolded her for foolish behaviour. But by the late afternoon the pains were coming more regularly and she had difficulty not to cry out.

Truly took over her clearing-up work and as dusk began to fall the men, including an anxious Joshua, were banished from the lower floor of the cabin, while Bella and Bessie, helped by Minta, prepared for the birth.

When the time neared and her sweat was pouring into her eyes and her lips were bleeding against the effort of not crying out with pain, the three black women made her squat, supporting her as she did so. They had placed a threelegged stool behind her back which they lifted her on to between contractions. Set between her legs was a large china basin they had purloined from the house. One of Amelia's stolen candle ends burned, giving the only light in the cabin. It glinted off shining, sweating black faces with encouraging eyes and voices. They sang low-voiced, gently clapping their hands; foreign songs with strange cadences. The shining faces, gleaming eyes and unfamiliar sounds had the quality of an alien but benevolent dream. She felt joined to these women in some shared, mysterious, feminine rite and their closeness was comforting. They gave her security. And just before midnight, the baby was born.

'It be a girl,' Bella said.

Amelia was slumped on the stool where they had lifted her after the last desperate push. She was panting, aching, weak but triumphant.

'I want to see her,' she gasped.

Without speaking Bella handed her the baby, still smeared and sticky from birth. Minta held the candle close to the child's face. Amelia saw a fluff of dark hair, tight shut eyes in a face like a button. The infant's breath made its full, bow-lipped mouth tremble and a tiny bubble shone in the light. She snuffled a little through a nose that seemed small as Amelia's own. But what colour was the skin? It was difficult to see in the light, but to Amelia, whose heart swelled with love as she held her baby, the skin looked white.

'She's white,' she said her voice full of wonder.

'She's yella,' Bella contradicted her flatly. 'Golden yella if you like, but she's yella.'

Whatever colour the baby was, it didn't matter.

'A golden-yellow flower,' Amelia said dreamily. 'My little golden-yellow flower. I shall call her Tansy.'

'Huh!' Bella's derisory snort made the candle flicker. 'You can call she what you likes, gal, but this baby ain't white 'nuff. It ain't safe for Joshua for this baby to be yourn, not from this minute on and you'd better know it. Bessie and me got all the 'rangements made for the feeding. There be two women with plenty of milk going spare.'

She leaned forward and took the child from Amelia's arms, turned and handed it to her daughter. Truly took the baby gingerly and in the candlelight Amelia saw the black girl's expression of dismay as she looked at the child.

Bella saw it, too.

'And you better know that this baby your brother's child, Truly, my gal. You its auntie and its mama all in one, 'cos if you ain't, you ain't got no brother no more.'

Truly was staring down at the tiny naked body in her arms. As if aware it was not welcome, the child gave the whimpering cry of a seabird.

Hastily Truly thrust the baby back at her mother.

'I don' know that I can do it, Mama,' she whispered. 'That baby's near 'nuff white to be white. You know what they all go'n say? They go'n say I fucked with a white man.'

The revulsion in her voice opened for Amelia the endless vistas of prejudice from both black and white that this child of hers might always have to face.

It was Ben who told Matthew that Truly had a new baby. Ben's circumstances had changed dramatically since Justinian's death. When Bella and Amelia between them had outmanoeuvred his attempt to blame the murder on Joshua, he realised he had little chance of either a welcome or indeed safety in the slave cabins if he had to stay in them. Amelia would not speak to him and that cut him to the quick. He had therefore requested permission to attend Justinian's funeral where he wept crocodile tears. He paid court to Elizabeth Oliver, flattering her whenever he found the opportunity, and comforted Matthew in his grief, all the time reinforcing the belief that it was he, Ben, who had tried to shield his master from the truth of Justinian's sordid death. Within days he had been moved from the slave cabins and now lived in the house. He slept in the attics on an old broken-down bed. He had been given a chest and there was even a cracked looking glass on the wall.

Ben's fears were not unfounded. The black slaves did not forget his short-lived attempt to involve them in the murder. None of them spoke to him. Bessie had made dire threats against him. He would not have been safe in the cabins.

He had no idea that Amelia was pregnant. Bella had forbidden her to tell him. 'That Ben, he can't be trusted,' and Amelia had reluctantly had to agree.

But one morning when he came into the kitchen to collect his master's breakfast, to his astonishment Bella greeted him with a broad smile. He was instantly on his guard.

'You heard the news?' she asked.

He shook his head cautiously, expecting that it would be bad news for him.

'I be a grandmammy. My Truly she done got herself a baby girl.'

He considered this piece of information. Why was Bella making such a point of telling him? He pursed his lips and considered the black woman, noting that her vast frame seemed to radiate happiness. He relaxed. She just had to share this news, even with him, he decided.

'Felicitations,' he said rather pompously. He picked up the breakfast tray and left the room.

Matthew was sitting up in the huge four-poster bed, waiting for his breakfast. As ever his eyes were dull and unfocused and he showed no interest when the food was placed before him. Ben fussed around and for something to say remarked, 'Bella has just told me that she is a grandmother.'

'Oh?' Matthew seemed uninterested.

'Truly has had a daughter.'

Matthew pushed away the food. 'By whom?'

'I don't know,' Ben said. 'I didn't think to ask.'

His master considered the matter, then said, 'A pity it's a girl. There are too many women slaves about the place. It's field hands we need. Still, I suppose I must go and take a look at the child since it is now my responsibility.'

Hah! thought Ben as he went to fetch hot water from the kitchen for Matthew's ablutions. Checking on the property, more likely. Responsibility for the child might technically be Matthew's, but the real truth of the matter was that Truly had just made the Oliver's richer by one more slave.

Ben might have changed sides, but he had no illusions about the motives of the enemy. One day . . . one day . . . he thought as, sweat pouring into his eyes, he carried the steaming pail of water through the huge house. And then he remembered that there were still nine years of this daily humiliation to bear before that day came.

Matthew visited the kitchen before he went out for his usual morning ride into Old Town Road. Bella was banging her pots about and singing to herself as he walked in, his riding whip hanging loose in his hand.

'Morning, sir,' she said when she saw him and attempted to drop an awkward curtsy.

The woman gets fatter every time I see her, Matthew thought. He accepted that there was no way to stop her stealing food without banning

66

her from the kitchen, and she was too good a cook to do that, but her size irked him.

'What is this I am told about Truly? Is it true she has borne a daughter?' he asked.

'Be true, sir. The baby be right there. I keeping my eye on she while Truly at work.'

Bella pointed towards an old barrel that had been sliced into a makeshift cradle. It stood on the floor where she could rock it with her foot.

More interested in where the barrel had been purloined from than the baby, Matthew moved to look closer. As he bent down a tiny white face confronted him. He straightened abruptly. Or was it white? He bent to look again, conscious that Bella was standing very still, watching him.

'Who is the father of this baby?' he asked sternly.

'That Truly she don' say,' Bella sighed. 'If you don' mind me saying so, she 'shamed cos it be so white, sir. I reckons and so do Bessie that it be that Ben's. Ain't no one else it could be. Unless . . .' She stared at him very hard.

He was about to protest that it was nothing to do with him when he realised that this would be undignified in the extreme. He stood pulling at his pointed beard to give himself time to think.

'Ben,' he said. 'I see.'

He looked again. The baby's eyes had that telltale hint of yellow in the white round deep blue iris, its skin appeared olive, but its features were those of a white girl and the small tuft of hair seemed straight enough. It yawned, the tiny mouth opening wide to an expanse of pink, and then it stared at him almost challengingly.

He had a sudden picture of Amelia and the challenging stare that she had so often turned on him since the night he raped her – a stare he tried to avoid by never looking directly at her. He had another mental picture of her moving heavily, her hand on her lower back, walking down the passage to his wife's room while he secretly watched her. He was suddenly certain that this baby did not belong to the coal-black Truly. It was Amelia's. He was sure of it. But was he the father? Was that why Bella had looked at him so hard. He went cold at the thought and did some rapid arithmetic. It was possible. But there was coloured blood there, he would swear to it. In that case, if it was Amelia's, who was the father? He was aware of Bella hovering behind him, almost holding her breath. She was not at ease. Maybe she was indeed a grandmother, but maybe the parent of her grandchild was not Truly. Maybe it was Joshua. Joshua coupled with Amelia. He felt sick at the thought.

He leaned again to look at the baby. It was definitely light-skinned, and sometimes babies did look a little yellow when they were born. Justinian had, and there was no doubt of his parentage. Maybe he was the father and maybe he wasn't. And maybe it was Truly's. He did not know and it was unlikely he ever would know. Not with any certainty. Nor, he realised, did he wish to know.

Without speaking, he turned abruptly and left the kitchen. An hour later he gave Jake orders that Joshua, Truly, Bessie, Minta and the baby were to be taken to the slave market and sold. He would have sent Bella with them had Elizabeth not protested that she was unwilling to lose a good cook. But she did add that she would be glad to see the back of that sullen, surly Truly, and really they should have sold her long ago.

It was Benson, the overseer from Macabees, the biggest plantation on the island, who bought the bewildered quartet plus baby from Windsong. He did not want the baby, and nor did he particularly want Bessie, but Jake had been told to make a bargain package of the group in order that they should be sold and away from Windsong as quickly as possible. The price was right, so the deal was struck.

Benson was in need of a young, strong gardener and a woman to take care of the laundering for the Ramillies family. The plantation had suffered an outbreak of fever in the cabins and the weakest and oldest of the slaves had died including the gardener and the laundress. It was simpler to buy trained slaves than teach the work to ones fresh from Africa.

Joshua was in total despair as they were driven from the marketplace to the huge house overlooking the Caribbean, sheltered by the staggeringly high cliff of Brimstone Hill, some ten miles from Windsong. Bessie had taken charge of the baby, hugging it to her thin shrunken breasts. Truly would have nothing to do with the child and her ever-present anger and resentment now had a target: Joshua.

'If you hadn't fucked that white gal none of this would have happened,' she hissed at him. 'And if you think I be goin' to look after her brat, I tell you I ain't, big brother.'

Bessie was to work with Truly in the laundry room of Macabees. Bessie was so old, so inured to a life of slavery, that it mattered little to her where she was. She had been bought and sold so many times that she quickly settled wherever she was put. As soon as they arrived at Macabees and had been led to the slave cabins, she made it her first task to find someone to feed Tansy. The baby grizzled with a high, thin cry, complaining to anyone that might hear that she was hungry. Her misery added to that of Joshua's who was frantic at his inability to help.

'We's been lucky,' Bessie was able to tell Joshua as he sat distractedly and awkwardly trying to soothe his daughter. 'There be a gal here just lost her baby from the fever. She still got milk. She say she'll feed the baby.' She scratched her woolly grey head. 'Just one trouble. I ain't tol' her how white that baby be. Don' know how she'll feel 'bout that. Better if you take the baby to her.'

He had been sitting on the ground, his back to the wall, the baby in his lap, his thoughts all of Amelia and how they had been torn apart.

He realised that Matthew Oliver might have guessed the truth and that that was the reason he and Truly had been sold. But what would they do to Amelia? Would she be safe or would the master come for her in the night again? Joshua's fists clenched and his stomach churned with the impotence of his situation. There was nothing he could do. If he ran, it would not help Amelia for she could not run with him, and besides, there was nowhere to run to.

He looked down at the angry face of his daughter and automatically began to rock and hush her. The child quietened and lay still, looking up at him. He believed he could see Amelia in the small face.

'Where be this gal?' he asked, glad of something positive to do.

'In the kitchen,' Bessie said. 'She called Ruby.'

She walked ahead of him briskly on skinny, bowed legs, leading him through the ornamental gardens which would no doubt become his concern. If he hadn't known better he would have believed that the old woman had lived here before, so assured was she as she led him. He had thought Windsong grand, but this house was a mansion, constructed of red brick, not stone, three storeys high. It was twice the length of Windsong and had tall twisting chimneys which were silhouetted against the sharply conical mountain that towered behind.

The kitchen was through double wooden doors at the side of the house. He could smell roasting meat. Inside, the room looked so like the Windsong kitchen that he almost expected to see his mother's huge bulk, ladle in hand, greeting him.

Instead, a young girl stood by the spit. Her black, springy hair was cut short to her head. She was tall with fine jutting breasts and her face was a mirror of Africa, broad lips and nose, gleaming black skin, as black as Truly and his mother. It was her expression that was different. Truly mostly scowled, his mother's face was almost always stern and the faces of most women slaves when in repose revealed only dignity and deep sadness. Though this girl was not smiling her face was somehow happy, mischievous, as if she were laughing at the world. The lips turned upwards, the black eyes snapped as if a light was lit behind them. Like his mother, she was holding a ladle. Bella's hold turned every kitchen implement into a weapon, but Ruby's grasp suggested nothing more dangerous than an accessory to the striped clothing she wore.

Tansy had begun to cry again.

The girl put down the ladle. 'That baby hungry,' she announced. She stepped forward and took the bundle from Joshua's arms. She pulled open the front of her chemise and thrust the baby's face towards her black gleaming breasts.

The baby's mouth closed over a dark nipple, the cries ceased and soft sucking sounds took their place. 'That be better for she and better for me,' the girl said contentedly.

Joshua could not take his eyes from those suddenly revealed womanly breasts, standing so upright, their nakedness framed by cheap striped fabric. Amelia's breasts had been smaller, pinker, a girl's breasts made for love and delicate handling. Ruby's breasts looked as if they might feed all the world and as if a man could thrust his face roughly and urgently in them, bite them, suck from them . . .

She was peering down at the child in her arms.

'This baby sure is white,' she said. 'It really yourn?'

'She's mine,' he said awkwardly.

'Yeah. My baby that died weren't properly black either,' she said. 'Guess that because that Benson his daddy.' She let out a peal of spontaneous laughter. 'How come yourn so white?'

'Her mammy's white.'

Ruby's black eyes rounded so that they were surrounded by a wide, white ring. 'Real white?'

He nodded.

She made a little tisking sound between her teeth. 'Now what you want go fucking a white gal for?' she asked reproachfully. 'Boy, you is lucky you ain't hanging from a tree some place. Or maybe she be hanging from a tree some place?'

'No.' He felt he could not explain. Instead he said, 'I sorry your baby died.'

Her smile faded. 'I not,' she said. 'I don' want to bring more slaves into this bad place. And beside, like I say, he weren't properly black.'

Something in her voice stung him into saying, 'I'm not properly black.'

'I sees that. Sad. It hard not being one peoples or other. Best to know who you be. But you do be handsome.'

He felt himself colour at the frankness of her appraisal of him. Silently, he thought she was right. He had never exactly known who he was. She looked down at the baby. 'This poor little thing ain't never go'n know who she be. But she sure happy with black milk. But they all are, ain't they, when they little?'

She looked back at him and smiled.

'You leave this baby with me for now, eh? Bessie and I do everything. You go get to you work or Benson have you hide for sure. He a swine.' Again the peal of laughter. 'You can't save you hide with him way I do.'

He had never seen a ruby, but Amelia had described them when they had read Proverbs together. This Ruby looked as he imagined the jewel. Dark and glowing, with secret depths of fire. Warm. But Proverbs had asked: 'Who can find a virtuous woman? For her price is far above rubies.'

Ruby was not virtuous, not if she slept with the overseer and called him a swine. But watching her with his child at her breast he thought that perhaps her price would be far above rubies anyway. And maybe virtue was not everything.

He discovered quickly that she was positively wanton. She had, it seemed, determined upon making him her lover even though most nights Benson sent for her to come to his quarters where she went cheerfully

70

enough. Joshua, still haunted by his memories of Amelia and what he knew had been pure, unsullied love, did not understand.

'Don' mean nothing,' she said tossing her head to show off the cheap hoop earrings that Benson had given her, 'but it sure make the living easier.'

Yet she was shameless in her pursuit of Joshua. When he was working in the vegetable garden, near to the kitchen, she would come up behind him, put her arms round his waist and gyrate her hips against him. The heat between her legs seemed to pass through her clothing and scorch him. His own body flamed. He was seventeen years old and unable to stop himself hardening into life. Her hand would roam downwards and stroke the rod that she found, and then she would laugh her uninhibited laugh as he shook her off, ashamed and full of guilt that a woman other than Amelia could have this effect on him.

'I get you yet, boy,' she promised.

Joshua was tempted, but both the Bible and his mother had taught him that for one man there was one woman, and for him that woman was Amelia. He still dreamed of her, he could smell her different body smell in his nostrils in the night, and he remembered her soft, eager yielding to him. She was not bold and provocative like this handsome black girl who plagued him. But it was hard for him to resist and it was mostly the thought of what would happen to him if he did yield and Benson found out that kept him faithful to Amelia. He now knew why Macabees had the reputation of being the hardest plantation on the island. Benson's rule of iron made Jake at Windsong seem almost gentle.

Joshua was slow to wrath. He was quiet and introspective by nature and having been born into slavery was able to live with his situation. His mother's tribe had been agricultural people. They were not warlike, and his racially inherited gift for gardening had saved him from the worst excesses of slavery. It was work he was happy to do. He had never felt the lash round his shoulders for no one had ever found him neglecting his work and supervision in the gardens was anyway less stringent than in the fields. With the shadow of his unknown father hanging over him, he tried to be a gentle person. It hurt him to feel that he was the result of an assault upon his mother. His father had been a bad man. He was determined on being good, and because of this the words of the Bible Amelia and he had read together struck a chord in him. Without knowing it, Joshua had become a Christian.

It was late in May when the situation changed. He and Ruby were sitting outside in the cool, away from the cabin. The girl was feeding Tansy who suckled contentedly. Tansy had grown fat and rosy in Ruby's care, and he was grateful.

'You ain't go'n see much of you sister no more,' Ruby said abruptly. There was something odd about her tone. He could not tell if she had a faint air of triumph or if she were troubled.

71

He had noticed that Truly had not appeared for the evening meal that the slaves shared. He suddenly felt apprehensive.

'Is she safe?' he asked.

' 'Pends on what you calls safe,' Ruby said. 'That Benson he wants some fresh flesh and he picked your Truly for that. She lucky. She safe 'nuff long as she do what he wants.'

Joshua was appalled. He remembered his sister's disgust at even the thought that people might think she had fucked with a white man. What would she do? Truly was not like him. She was not one of life's accepters.

'They bringin' in a woman from the fields to do the washin',' Ruby told him as she changed the baby from one breast to the other. 'And Truly, she moved into Benson's own quarters. She go'n be his personal house slave. He never did that for me, but he couldn't. I too good a cook. Mistress Ramillies she go mad if I ain't cooking.'

'What will happen to her?' Joshua asked.

'She be there for him to fuck when he wants it. She cook for him, she clean for him and wash he clothes. Like a wife until he want fresh flesh again.'

He put his head in his hands, feeling again all the despair of a man who could not protect his womenfolk.

'It not so bad,' she said gently. 'She get used to it. We all do. And there's the good thing – you don' have to be afeared of fucking me no more.'

He lifted his head sharply. She was sitting upright before him, breasts bared, the baby lazily half-asleep on her lap, milk round the corners of its mouth.

'It isn't that—'

'Listen,' she interrupted. 'You ain't go'n see this baby's mamma ever 'gain. Ruby be she mamma now.'

Her long-fingered, strong hands moved to support the heavy, milk-filled breasts from underneath. She proferred them.

'You a thirsty man,' she said, low-voiced. 'Ruby can see you thirsty.' Her hands lifted the shining breasts higher. A thumb and forefinger held one dark, pointed nipple and squeezed gently so that the ruby black was stained white. 'Drink of me,' she crooned. 'Drink of me.'

He stared at her breasts, mesmerised. He was a man, he told himself, a frustrated, thirsty man with a thirst that had never been quenched.

He hurled himself forward with none of the gentleness he had shown and shared with Amelia. First he licked away the white liquid from the nipple she had squeezed and then his mouth closed over it and he drank. It was warm, an unknown taste; the act of drinking from her made him feel powerful; potent. She placed the baby in the grass beside them and wriggled off her skirt so that all she wore was the opened bodice. She was rounded, polished below him and he let his hand caress her breasts while his mouth, tongue and teeth worked their way down over the flat stomach to the sparse, springy hair below. And he drank from there, too, bitter juices, more acrid than her milk, secret and

72

forbidden, yet warm and welcoming. As he licked and nibbled at her forbidden folds, her hands pulled at him, guiding him to where she wanted him to be. He felt her insert him and they were linked, one person, joined together in lust and need.

When he slumped on her, satiated and exhausted, she let out a long breath.

'Tol' you,' she said with a chuckle. 'Tol' you I get you.'

He should have felt guilty, but he did not. He felt triumphant. He knew in a flash of sudden insight that he would never feel for Ruby what he felt for Amelia; he knew too that he would never again be able to resist Ruby's strong thighs gripping him or the way that deep inside her she gripped and rode him to his rhythm and her own, almost savage, abandonment.

'I reckons,' she said as she pushed him off her, 'I reckon we might just have made another baby. And this one, he go'n live.'

Chapter Five

Mechanically and unthinkingly Amelia served Elizabeth Oliver and Charlotte tea in their small withdrawing room at Windsong. Years of performing the same task at the same time every day had produced a boredom that she automatically hid under the bright and ingratiating manner that had become habitual when dealing with the Oliver women.

For three years she had been privy to all their chattering, their speculations about Charlotte's future and sizing up of her beaux and understood exactly why the romances always foundered. She knew by heart Elizabeth's complaints about life in the West Indies and the difficulties of making any money and how much it cost to feed and clothe the slaves. She also knew how little Elizabeth actually spent on those who worked for her. Old Pottle the bookkeeper, whose status was not much higher than that of a slave, had become her friend. He had told her that Elizabeth was a very rich woman indeed. Windsong's sugar yield was one of the greatest on the island and sugar was fetching the highest prices ever on the European market. Elizabeth had little to complain of.

Most of the time Amelia no longer listened to her mistresses' gossip. She had built for herself an inner world where she fantasised that she was safe with her lost loves, Joshua, Tansy and Zach. Never a day went past when she did not think of them, worry about them and pray for them. Not knowing where they were and how they fared was slow torture. Sometimes she felt as if she were hollow and the biggest area of nothingness was the emptiness caused by the loss of Tansy and not knowing if her child were alive or dead. When Joshua and the baby had been taken off to the slave market with Truly, she and Bella had wept the length of one night, from dawn to dusk, attempting to console each other. But Amelia was aware that Bella blamed her for everything that had happened. If Amelia had not come to Windsong things would be as they always had been, but now Bella's family was torn apart and she, too, grieved every day of her life.

Amelia was lonely. It was true that Ben had made a graceful attempt at mending the breach between them. He had apologised for his duplicity and told her honestly that his actions had been caused by jealousy and his love for her. Amelia had been touched and wholeheartedly forgave him. But he was no companion. He had become more and more close to Matthew Oliver, always seeming to be three paces behind his master, and he never came near the slave cabins. It was only in the course of their daily duties that they met.

She rarely saw Molly McGuire for Matthew had forbidden any from his household to go near the French part of the island. King James II had fled first England and then Ireland and was in exile in France. The newly crowned Protestant William and Mary of Orange occupied the British throne and an allied Holland and Britain waged war against the French in Europe. It was a political situation that made the French and the English uncomfortable bedfellows on a West Indian island only nineteen miles long.

Over the past few weeks the roadstead at Basse-Terre had filled with the sails of French naval frigates and men o' war brought in on the fresh winds of the late spring. The sight of the great wooden ships at anchor filled the British with anxiety. The French kept no permanent force in the Caribbean but renewed their fleet afresh every spring, but this year the number of vessels had doubled. The British fleet consisted of only two frigates and two ships of the line which were replaced piecemeal as and when necessary. Wooden ships had a short life in the tropics and for anything more than routine repairs British ships had to return home.

Even the slaves were aware of the concern of their masters but they were indifferent to the outcome. Whether the French or the British ruled the island, nothing would change their status.

Amelia had just finished pouring the tea from a fine silver teapot when there was a discreet knock on the withdrawing room door.

'See who is there, Amelia,' Elizabeth said.

Amelia opened the door to find herself face to face with Matthew. As usual, his eyes slid away from confronting hers. He came into the room hurriedly, obviously agitated.

'I'm afraid the news is bad, my dears,' he began. 'It may be necessary for you to leave the island for your safety's sake. It looks like war.'

Elizabeth put down her teacup. 'There are more French ships in the harbour? she asked.

'No, but a huge force has been reported sailing from Guadeloupe and Martinique and the Irish from Montserrat are with them. We are disadvantaged. Our fleet from Barbados cannot be here in time to defend us.'

For all her faults Elizabeth was a shrewd woman, more intelligent than her husband. She appeared calm. 'You are sure?'

'I am sure. Sir Christopher says it.'

Sir Christopher Codrington had only just replaced Sir William Stapleton as Governor of the Leeward Islands and Matthew was more inclined to accept Codrington in the role he so desired for himself. He had again taken his place on the St Kitts Council, which was made up of ten of the wealthiest planters, and was once again busying himself with the government of the island. The two men respected each other and Matthew's life had become purposeful again.

'You know Sir Christopher believes that all turns on mastery of the sea,' Matthew said, pacing the length of the room. 'He says if we have mastery we are safe, however thinly peopled. If the French have it, we cannot raise enough men in all our islands in these waters to hold any single one of them.'

'Papa, shall we all be killed?' Charlotte said fearfully.

'Quiet girl,' Elizabeth silenced her. 'And we are no longer masters of the sea?' she asked.

'Not until reinforcement comes.' Matthew ceased to pace and threw himself heavily onto a wooden chair. 'These troubles are all the fault of governments who fight their wars in Europe. If they would permit the islands to trade freely, we need not be at the throats of our neighbours nor they at ours. We are no more than pawns in the greedy games of governments, making them rich – and at what cost to ourselves with the restrictions they put upon us! Our French neighbours have the same problems. We both must trade only with our home governments who make us sell cheap to them and buy dear from them. These islands are the most prosperous of their colonies and they milk us for it and put us into wars with no thought for our safety and wellbeing.'

'That has always been true,' Elizabeth said. 'I have said it a million times. But surely we shall fight? The King himself has declared war on the French.'

'The Redcoats are prepared and the militia are called to arms. Sir Christopher is to raise an army. I shall fight with him. But it is late. It is better if you flee.'

'Flee from the French!' Elizabeth's voice was full of indignation.

'It is better for the women and children to leave for fear of becoming hostage,' he said. 'I foresaw this and have made arrangements. You will stay with the Jeffreys on their Nevis plantation. There you will be safe until this matter is finished one way or the other. Beauboy will take you to a boat. You must prepare yourselves as quickly as possible and be on your way. Amelia,' he turned to face her directly, 'you must help your mistresses prepare. You will accompany them on the journey.'

'I do not wish to go,' Elizabeth said firmly. 'I will not be driven from my home by the French.'

'You will go and you will devote yourself to Charlotte's safety and welfare.' He was angry. 'I have lost a son, I will not lose my daughter over your unreasonable stubbornness. Not another word. Prepare yourself.'

He left the room, straight-backed and positive, and Amelia found herself almost impressed. She had never heard him stand up to his wife before, but then the word in St Kitts was that Sir Christopher Codrington believed that the sugar islands would benefit more from a governor who was a planter rather than a Crown appointee. Had Matthew hopes of becoming his own man again? As she hurried off to prepare for her mistresses' departure, she was wondering if perhaps

77

this outbreak of war might just, at some point, give her the chance of becoming her own woman again.

As it happened, it was the Oliver women's insistence on taking with them almost all of their belongings that gave her the opportunity. On their instructions Amelia hurriedly packed their clothing, jewellery, favourite ornaments, much of their silver and even some furniture into big wooden boxes. When it was all loaded onto their carriage and two following horses and carts, there was no room for Amelia.

'You will have to stay behind,' Elizabeth announced. 'You can see to the house in our absence. I shall expect to find everything in order when we return.'

This time Matthew did not argue, which filled Amelia with unease. But it proved unwarranted. Matthew was busy with men's work, conferring with Sir Christopher, helping raise an army. He had already conscripted Ben but there were only five hundred British against two thousand French. Amelia found herself in Windsong with only the black house slaves for company. Jake, the overseer, who had been left in overall charge, sent Rufus, one of his hated black deputies, to watch the house. Those black slaves who had accepted positions of power and were permitted to wield the whip against their fellow countrymen were loathed even more than the white men. Rufus, the same huge negro who had taken Zach to the cane fields on their arrival three years before, seemed uncertain of what to do about Amelia. He dealt with the problem by acting as if she were not there.

As she automatically began to clear up Charlotte's bedchamber and neaten her bed, it dawned on her that she need not perform this task. There was no one to complain that she had not done it well and for the time being no one would be sleeping in the huge four-poster bed. She heard herself laughing and with an exquisite sense of freedom, temporary though it might be, she flung herself onto the thick feather mattress, promising herself a sleep there that very night. She was stretched out, scuffling her toes in the linen sheets, when she heard what sounded like a dull thud. She sat up to hear more clearly, and then came another and another. The earth seemed to shake. She leapt from the bed and ran through the house back to the kitchen.

'What is it? What is the noise? Has it begun?' she asked Bella, who was standing stock-still by the spit, listening.

'It be the cannon. The ships be firing on us, but we be too far from the sea for them,' she said in the tone of one who had been through it all before. 'Them folk in Old Town Road, though, it bad for them.'

'What will happen?' Amelia asked.

'Them Frenchies will win for a bit, then the English will get it all back again. Happen all the time here.' She sniffed loudly. 'White peoples!' she said.

'Maybe the English won't get it back,' Amelia suggested.

'Maybe.' Bella shrugged. 'Won't make no difference for us.'

But, Amelia thought, for her things could be different, and she went looking for old Pottle, the only other white person left in the house. She found him in his little counting house in the grounds, working at his books, seemingly unaware of the constant thuds that were shaking the island.

'Master Pottle . . .'

The old man looked up, his bald head gleaming in the light from the candle which illuminated his work. He nodded and smiled as he saw her.

'And what can I do for you, my dear?' he asked.

'They've all gone away, Master Pottle,' she said. 'Did you know? There's only you and me and the slaves, with Rufus to watch us. The master has gone to fight and taken Ben with him. Jake's in charge, but he's out in the fields.'

Pottle put down his quill and stretched. 'Unwise of them,' he said in his high, reedy voice that still held traces of a London accent. 'But I suppose they were scared for their skins.' He cocked his head to listen. 'The cannon are busy enough,' he remarked, 'but they can't reach us here.'

'Bella says that the French usually win and then we get the island back,' Amelia said.

'True. Last time the French won – twenty years ago it was – they expelled most of the British plantation owners. But they all came back in time.'

'If they win this time, and the master says we have no hope of defending ourselves, what do you think will happen?'

'My dear, I'm just a bookkeeper, not a military man, but no doubt they will expel the plantation owners again.'

'So the Oliver women won't come back and the master will have to go.'

'Probably. If the French win.'

Amelia drew a deep breath. 'Then I'm going to run.'

Pottle looked startled. 'You'd do best to stay where you are. It's safe from the fighting here, at least for the time being.'

'No, I'm going to Basse-Terre. I have a friend there. I speak French. I can lose myself in the town.'

'More likely get yourself killed,' Pottle warned. 'The English fleet will destroy Basse-Terre.' Then he added dryly. 'They always do.'

'Death can't be worse than this life,' Amelia said, aware she was sounding over-dramatic but still meaning what she said.

'Oh yes it can.' Pottle smiled at her indulgently. 'There's little worse than death, my dear. It's very final. Run if you must, but not yet. Wait until the cannon stop. Wait until things quieten. You have plenty of time. The Olivers will not be back until it is completely safe. They may never come back at all. Leave when it is less dangerous.'

Amelia considered. What he said made sense.

'All right,' she said and added with a broad grin, 'But in the meantime, I'm going to sleep in Mistress Charlotte's bed.'

The old man chuckled. 'Why not,' he said. 'Why not.'

Freed of her duties, each day Amelia climbed the mountain behind the house to where she could look down onto the sea and watch the battles between the great white-winged ships. Some limped from their wounds like harmed birds, some were afire. Men, seeming as small as marionettes, clung to the rigging or fought hand to hand on the decks. The sound of musket fire carried on the wind. Divorced as she was from the effects of the gunpowder, the slow puffs of the cannon followed by a dull thud and the blaze of sudden fire had a curious beauty. She could see that both Basse-Terre and Old Town Road burned; the smoked drifted up into the clear blue of the sky, expelled by the trade winds out to sea where it was lost among small scudding clouds. Other parts of the island burned too, but she had insufficient knowledge of the geography to work out exactly where the fires were. She would not have cared if the entire island had been razed, but she feared for Joshua and Tansy. Could one of the plantations that burned be the one where they were?

Days passed and one heavy summer morning old Pottle found her when she returned from spending the day in the glade where she and Joshua had first made love. She went there most afternoons and dozed in the shade, remembering.

The old man was agitated. 'It's time you left if you want to be off,' he said. 'The master has been back with your cousin and they were looking for you. Mistress Elizabeth wants you to look after her. Apparently the Jeffreys's maid is not satisfactory. They are sending a boat for you tomorrow and Beauboy is to take you. The master was angry he couldn't find you today. He wanted you to leave with them. They're fleeing. The French have occupied Old Town Road and a troop of their soldiers are marching here to take over the plantation. The master is setting sail with Sir Christopher for Nevis where they are to reform the defence. It's said there is no ammunition left with which to fight.'

'The English have lost?'

'For the moment. It may all change.'

'What will you do?' she asked anxiously. 'Will you be safe?'

'I'm an old man, my dear. I'm in no danger. I shall continue with my work; the French will not harm me.'

'They might burn the house down.'

'More likely they will move in. But you will not be safe from the attentions of the soldiers. Go to your friend in Basse-Terre.'

She looked at him doubtfully, uncertain if he were telling her the truth. She had become fond of Master Pottle and wished him no harm.

'Will you come with me?'

'No. I tell you, I'm safe here.'

'If you are sure . . .'

Days ago she had packed a small bundle of clothing in readiness –

80

most of it Charlotte's cast-offs. She waited until dusk and then gathered the bag and set off on foot through the parklands in front of the house and on to the rough track that led to Basse-Terre. She had considered 'borrowing' a horse, but decided against it. Charlotte's old clothing she might just get away with if caught. Taking a horse would be judged as theft.

It was dark when she reached Molly McGuire's, scuttling through the town, avoiding the patrolling French soldiers by hiding in doorways at their approach. Her heart was beating very hard and she was breathless as she pushed open the tavern door. She could hear singing, men were banging their tankards on tables and she hesitated as a drunken roar greeted her arrival. The tavern was brightly lit, the light of many candles reflected off the sweaty faces of the soldiers and sailors who crowded into the big, bare room. One sailor in blue uniform lurched towards her and grabbed her roughly by the arm.

'*Regardez!*' he shouted to the bar at large.

'*Ne touchez pas,*' Amelia said fiercely, trying to shake him off, but Molly was already striding from behind her bar.

'*Assez! Assez!*' she bellowed at the sailor, giving him a sharp crack round the ear. '*C'est une amie du moi. Relâchez la immediatement.*'

Molly controlled her bar like a regimental sergeant major. The sailor sheepishly dropped Amelia's arm. Molly marched her through the bar and into the living quarters at the back of the tavern.

'Wait there,' she said, and vanished.

Molly's sitting room was as bare as the bar, with just a settle, table and wooden chair, and an open fireplace where no fire burned in the heat of the Caribbean summer night. Amelia dropped her bundle, sat at the table and attempted to compose herself. Now that she was away from Windsong, doubts were beginning to trouble her. Suppose the French lost? Suppose she was caught? Matthew would do nothing to save her now and the punishment for running away could be death. And now she had run, what was she going to do? She told herself these were questions she should have asked herself before. As she was already here, the only thing to do was to wait and see what happened. With the optimism of youth, Amelia persuaded herself that everything would be all right.

The room was dimly lit. In her own quarters Molly was economical with candles and at first Amelia did not see the door that led through into the kitchen quietly opening. She looked up to see the shape of a strongly built man standing in the doorway, his face hidden in the shadows. Frightened, she jumped to her feet and backed towards the door into the tavern, letting out a strangled scream.

'Quiet!' a familiar voice said. 'It's me. Zach.'

Then she recognised her brother. He had been a brawny lad when she saw him last more than three years ago. Now he had filled into a powerful man. His shoulders all but blocked the doorway, and his head was ducked against its height. He had an air of authority so strong that it was almost menacing. She did not run towards him but stayed, one hand on the table, looking at him.

'Zach? Is it really you?'

He came towards her with two giant strides and picked her up off her feet to hug her close. She hugged him back fiercely.

In the dim light she could see that he was bearded and the feel of his clothing as he held her was of good linen and fine wool; his boots were of fine leather.

'You should not be here, Zach. It's not safe for you.'

He chuckled. 'It's not safe for either of us in Basse-Terre,' he said, sitting on the edge of the table which grumbled creakily under his weight. 'The Irish have sided with the French. The French are looking for the English. They'll all have our guts for garters if they find us.'

'But Molly—'

'Molly was hiding me, and now she is hiding you as well. Come.'

He took her hand and pulled her to her feet. He led her to the door that he had come through and behind it in the dim light she saw a flight of steps.

'They go to the attic,' he said. 'I've been hiding there. We'd better go back up in case one of those drunken louts breaks through into Molly's sitting room.'

He guided her up the stairs and into the attic which was bare of both light and furniture.

'I fear there's only the floor for seating,' he said as they settled themselves side by side on the bare boards in the darkness, 'but now we can talk.'

'And you can tell me why you have come back.' It was so good to see him, so good to have human contact again that Amelia snuggled into his side as she used to when she was six years old.

'One good reason,' he said. 'I promised Tom Fowler that I would. It was the last promise I could make him. He wanted me to see that Molly had enough money to make her safe for life.'

'He's dead?' Remembering her conversation with Molly, Amelia was shocked. 'Molly will be brokenhearted.'

'She is. But she has expected it for years. For a buccaneer, Tom led a charmed life. He saved mine and died himself. He took the shot that was meant for me. It was point-blank. The man could not have missed me when he fired if Tom had not leapt to take the force. But I have not told Molly that. She might not forgive me. She might not . . .' He hesitated.

'Shelter you?' Amelia asked.

'Shelter me,' he agreed, his voice low.

'Did he mean to save your life?'

'I believe so. We were close. He said I was the son he had never had. He wanted me to promise to use the money I won from buccaneering to lead a decent life one day. And I hope that will soon come to pass.

There are rumours that those of us who were transported here might be given pardon.'

'Pardon! We could go home again?' Amelia leaned back, trying to see his face in the gloom, afraid he might be teasing her.

'Maybe. If there were anything to go home for.'

'But why might we be pardoned?'

'King William is busy unwinding all the Popish webs that James spun. And you will be content to hear that Judge Jeffreys is disgraced and in the Tower for his own safety from the mob. We are no longer considered traitors.'

Amelia looked at him doubtfully. 'We are so far away, I cannot believe they will even remember us, let alone pardon us. Besides, the planters paid for us. They will want their money back and where shall we get it?'

'I have money. If it should happen that we are freed, I have the money to take us all home. The three of us can, if we wish, return to Devon.'

'Home.' Amelia had a sudden and vivid picture of Upottery, the grey church in the gentle valley, the busy stream where the boys fished for trout, the deep green landscape of England with familiar oaks and elms, so different from the predatory trees of this tropical place. 'It would be good to go home, as long as . . .' She hesitated. She wanted to say as long as Tansy and Joshua could go with her, but three years in St Kitts had taught her to accept that that could not be.

Zach did not notice her hesitation. 'But for now I cannot stay here in this attic like a cornered rat,' he went on. 'I shall join with the English and fight for this Godforsaken place. I have no love for the French and it would amuse me to be given a free pardon for my services to England before Parliament decides to do so.'

'And if you are killed fighting?' Amelia said fearfully.

'So then I am killed.' She saw the broad shoulders rise and fall in a dismissive shrug. 'After three years with the buccaneers I have the habit of fighting. Killing and being killed becomes a way of life.'

'You have killed?'

'Many.' He shrugged again. 'The killing helped me, Amelia. You could not understand, but the anger in me was so great that the only way I could appease its burning fury was by killing.' He paused and then said, 'Molly tells me that Justinian died.'

'Yes.'

'Good. He was the first I helped to find his way to another world. There have been many since.'

Amelia considered what he was saying. She was not appalled. There had been times when she herself could have killed – when she had been whipped, when she had been raped, and when they took Tansy and Joshua away. She understood his anger. She had felt it herself.

'It was a good life, that of a buccaneer,' he was saying, almost to himself. 'No woman could understand the excitement of seeing the prey, sails full as we chased 'em or perhaps caught 'em in the doldrums, unable to escape. Ships full of booty. Often gold. Oh, Amelia, my heart was in my mouth the first time I boarded a Spanish vessel. They fight like heroes those Spaniards, but they're no match for an Englishman. Some we killed, some we bound and some we flung overboard. Then we took their cargo and left them to drift. The buccaneers are brothers. It was fair shares for all every time. The captain's portion was greater, but that's as it should be. I was happy enough with my share. We had no setback. The whole of the Spanish main feared us, but it was a ship of the English navy that did us in. They swooped upon us off Hispaniola at night, boarded us while we were all full of rum. Those of the crew who were not killed in the fight were taken prisoner. My comrades. No doubt by now they swing on some gibbet in some tropic harbour. I was lucky. Tom took the shot that was aimed at me and I jumped overboard, taking him with me. I held him in the water in the darkness until the ship went down and I was able to get into a lose longboat. We got away in the confusion, but Tom died in my arms.' He sank his head in his hands. 'It would all have been for nothing if he had not told me where his fortune was hidden in the cave where I first met him. He made me promise on your life to share it with Molly. He said he would rather Molly had it all, but that was too much of a promise to ask of any man. And then he died.'

Amelia moved to take his hand in hers and they sat in silence for a moment.

'How did you get back here?' she asked.

'Slowly,' he said. 'From island to island. I had the boat, and Tom had taught me always to keep some gold about my person for just such an eventuality. I took what he carried and, with my own, I had plenty to get me here, with some left over. Just in time for a war.' He laughed shortly. 'I shall never go buccaneering again. I'm rich enough to become respectable. But I do have a fancy for just one more fight – against the French. The anger is not all appeased. I shall kill a few Frenchman in its name.'

'Be careful,' she said, though in truth she felt no real fear for this changed brother.

He ignored the warning. 'And you?'

'I'm running away. The Olivers have gone to Nevis.'

'Then why run?'

'To be free.'

He was silent, then asked, 'Has it been bad?'

She shook her head. 'I learned to live with it.' She paused. She had made a decision to tell him what had happened to her, but she was not certain how he would react. 'But they took my baby.'

'Your baby!'

'They sold it.'

He sighed deeply but in a resigned way. 'Was it by the black man who led me into the forest that night?'

'You mean Joshua. Yes. He was the father.'

'And they sold it?' His voice was flat. She had no idea what he was thinking.

'I called her Tansy because she was like a little yellow flower. No one except the slaves knew she was mine. You see, the master had raped me' – she felt his arm tighten round her – 'and Bella hoped that perhaps he would think it was his baby. But the baby was not quite white enough for that.' He listened quietly as the story tumbled out. She told him how Bella had insisted that they pretend the baby was Truly's and the reasons why. 'But none of that mattered any more when the Olivers sold Joshua, Truly and my baby. There was nothing Bella and I could do.' Her eyes filled with tears. 'I think of her every day and wonder where she is and whether or not she is safe. What am I going to do, Zach?'

Her brother's heavy arm pulled her closer to him.

'Get her back,' he said. 'That's what we're going to do.'

Zach stayed at the tavern for a few more days, waiting for the moon to wane. Then one dark night he slipped away, promising to return when the English regained the island.

'Which we will,' he said confidently. 'The French never were and never will be a match for the British.'

Amelia was aware that Molly was relieved by his departure. Zach spoke little French and had to be kept permanently hidden. Amelia had less problem in letting herself be seen in public. She helped Molly in the tavern and played the demure, silent young girl, a role to which she had grown accustomed. But because she could not openly be herself she felt no freer than at Windsong.

The fighting ended and though the French did not occupy the entire island, Basse-Terre swarmed with French troops and sailors. Molly's tavern was open day and night and business was good even though the town had been badly damaged by cannon fire in the fourteen days of battle. Molly served the drunken troops and kept them in order in her usual efficient manner, hiding the fact that she was mourning her dead. She spent what free time she had in the church where she tried to find comfort from the Jesuit priests. The tavern was run with all her old skill and authority, but automatically, as if none of it mattered. She had aged overnight and seemed frozen and though Amelia longed to comfort her, there seemed no way to break the iron guard that the older woman had put round her emotions. She was kind as ever, but distracted, and Amelia sensed that her own presence at this time was not entirely welcome. She was another problem to add to the others with which Molly battled.

As the summer became unbearably humid and hot, the island seemed to be overcome by a curious lull as if the bitter fighting and burnings of the past few weeks had exhausted even the elements. The ever-present wind had dropped, leaving the trees still and silent. The palms looked artificial, as if moulded from thin sheets of copper. The sea resembled molten metal brushed with oil as it fell sluggishly against the black volcanic sand of the Basse-Terre shore. The heat was intense and thunder rumbled around the peaks of the mountains already hidden by a bonnet of heavy, livid cloud. People moved in a lethargic manner, grumbling about the oppressive heat, and in the tavern men's tempers flared into sudden violence. It seemed to Amelia that even the horses were restless, the street dogs surly. She herself felt an unexplained foreboding, as if something momentous were about to take place.

One fiercely damp and hot afternoon she found she could not bear to be in the tavern a moment longer. The walls seemed to be engulfing her and the noise of men celebrating release from war became insupportable. Leaving Jamie, the freed mulatto lad Molly employed, to cope alone, she borrowed a large shady hat from her hostess's wardrobe and went walking in the streets. Without the trade winds blowing, it was no cooler in the open air than indoors and she made her way to the shore hopeful of finding at least the trace of a cool breeze there.

She was walking down one of the narrow roads that led directly onto the Shore Road when she had the impression that the sky had dropped from its moorings and was resting on her head. Then suddenly there was a long, low rumble and the molten mass of sea before her sprang forward in a vast, white-etched wave that covered the shoreline and the road as far back as the houses beyond the beach. The roaring sea then retreated as violently as it had advanced. From where she stood she saw the water rolling back and back, Biblical fashion, revealing a wide expanse of sand as sticky as molasses. Then, with a terrible sucking noise, the sullen grey sea seemed to fall into a deep hole about a quarter of a mile offshore. It was gone for no more than a few seconds before abruptly leaping from the depth and surging back with a roaring violence that sent it swirling over the shore road and up the side streets away from the beach.

At the same moment the buildings around her began to grumble and tremble and the ground cracked into a crazy pattern beneath her feet. The violence of the tremors flung her to the ground where she lay helpless as seawater rushed over her, tossing her against the rough stones of the road before sweeping back to the beach, taking her with it. She could hear the crashing of masonry and long, low, angry rumbling noises, and then as sharply as it had all began she was lying in the shallows, drenched to the skin. Molly's hat floated on surly, eerily-still water and only the screams of people broke a sudden deathly silence.

Carefully she pulled herself upright, covered in filth, her feet squelching in the black sand which seemed reluctant to let her go. She was relieved to find that she was unhurt apart from a few grazes on her arms and legs. Trembling, she stared about her, thankful not to have been swept into that dark pit out to sea. And then she turned to look at the town and her mouth fell open. From where she stood it seemed as if there was barely a building left standing. The spire of the church had disappeared and the bulk of the Jesuit college was no longer there. The screaming had begun again. She began to run, jumping over the wide cracks in the pavement, anxious to get back to the shelter of the tavern and praying that Molly was safe.

The short journey was not an easy one. At de Lisle Street a gap nine feet wide ran across the road and whole buildings had disappeared into its mysterious depths. She shuddered at the fate of those who had inhabited the houses.

It seemed at first glance that most of the prosperous shops and merchants' storehouses were destroyed. The bigger and finer the buildings the more they had suffered. People were digging with their bare hands at tumbled ruins and she could hear the muffled cries of those who were buried. From other wrecked buildings there was only ominous silence. She could not believe that Molly could possibly be safe but to her immense relief the tavern still stood. The front of the wooden building, including half the bar and presumably the men who had been drinking there, had gone, fallen into a much narrower chasm than many she had passed, yet most of the building still stood, the interior wide open to the street, a smell of rum and wine pervading the air where casks and bottles had been smashed.

The place seemed deserted, though what remained of the bar itself looked surprisingly untouched. But where was Molly? Amelia picked her way gingerly into the back room through the door which hung drunkenly on broken hinges. The heavy furniture appeared to have been thrown into the air by a giant hand. But Molly was there, alive, white-faced, trembling and sitting on a closed trunk. At the sight of Amelia, she gave a little cry and stood up, devoutly crossing herself.

Amelia ran to put her arms round the Irish woman and held her tight. 'Thank God you're safe,' she said, but Molly felt rigid in her arms.

'I was in the cellar,' she said dully. 'I needed more rum. When I came back . . .' She gulped. 'All those good lads gone . . . Jamie, too. But you're safe, thanks be to God. That's something at least. You're soaking wet,' she added as if she'd only just noticed.

'The sea nearly took me,' Amelia explained, aware that still shocked from her brush with death her voice was trembling. 'Are you all right? What happened? Was it an earthquake?'

'It was indeed. A bad one. You ask how I am. I tell you I'm as fine as I'll ever be, but I've had enough.' Molly seemed to be on the edge of hysteria as she pulled the wooden chair upright and sat on it. 'Tom dead. War. Earthquakes. My tavern wrecked. I suppose it will be pestilence next on this poxy island. I'm going. I've been packed and ready to go for weeks now, since the day your Zach told me of Tom's death. There's a boatman who will take me, but I hesitated. Heaven knows why I hesitated. I should have gone there and then. Now I shall. Goodbye to St Kitts. There's nothing to hold me here.' Large silent tears were slipping from her blue eyes and Amelia found her own eyes were wet. She could not bear the thought that Molly was going away. Molly was the one prop in her life. Her only friend.

'You're going to Montserrat?' she asked sadly.

'That's where I'm going and I'll take you with me if you will come.'
Amelia sat wearily on the trunk. 'But I'm not a Catholic,' she said.
Molly shrugged. 'No matter.'

The offer was tempting. Amelia sat silent, thinking it through, and
then she said slowly, 'I can't. Zach and Ben are here. But more
important, Tansy is here somewhere. And Joshua. I must find them.'

The Irish woman was recovering her composure. She shook her head
fiercely. 'Better to forget the black and the baby.'

'Oh, Molly, I can't.'

Molly sighed. 'No, of course you can't.'

There was a long silence as they both surveyed the devastation around
them.

'What will you do about the tavern?' Amelia asked.

Molly threw her hands in the air. 'It's yours. What's left of it.'

'Mine!'

'I've written a paper saying so. I guessed you would not leave with
me. You can live on it or in it or run it or do what you like with it.
I want no more part of it. Look at it. They' – she sketched a gesture
that took in all the outside world – 'will be looting, no doubt, soon
enough. And with Tom gone . . .'

She put her head on the side of the upturned table and began to sob,
bitter, choking sobs. Amelia put her arms round her and held her tight
without speaking. There wasn't anything to say.

For the rest of the day they remained in the room. Molly would not
let Amelia go into the ruined streets where the buried and the living
still screamed and dust hung in the air like a pall. Occasional tremors
shook the town and, remembering the frightening widths of the cracks
in the ground, they decided that on balance it was safer to stay inside.

'But we must barricade ourselves in,' Molly said. 'The mobs will
be out, and the first places they'll go will be the taverns. Pray God they
believe there's nothing here left to find.'

There was some comfort in attempting to clear the mess, though there
was little guarantee that what was left of the building would remain
standing. They lugged all the bottles and casks down into the cellar
and piled furniture over the entrance. That night, as the ground still
occasionally trembled, they crawled fearfully into the one big bed.
Outside, the town did not sleep. All night the digging and wailing went
on broken by the occasional crash as another building collapsed. Each
tremor left them sitting up and clinging to each other lest the tavern
should be the next to go.

In the grey dawn Molly went out to find if her boatman and his boat
had survived. The broken town had quietened as the light strengthened
and Amelia thought that perhaps people had no more energy left to
cry or wail or scream. A strong wind had sprung up as if nature had
done her worst and was now relenting. A pale, watery sun lit the scene
of devastation.

An hour later Molly returned. Amelia found her standing in the street looking at the ruin of what had been both her home and her livelihood. The crack in front of the building had closed a little and the tavern seemed to be leaning backwards, as if attempting to get away from the chasm.

'It's a sad sight,' Molly said, 'but the whole town is a sad sight. Already the merchants' premises are being looted. It will be our turn when they've finished there.' She sighed. 'I'm off and it would be better by far if you came with me, for there's nothing left here. The boat is waiting.'

Molly was right but still Amelia shook her head. 'I can't.'

'Then better you go back to Windsong,' Molly advised. 'It will be safer than here.'

Amelia would do neither. She could not leave the island that held all her family, but Windsong was no refuge. Her welcome from Rufus and Jake would not be a pleasant one. The only advantage that came with yesterday's earthquake was that if those at Windsong had not perished in it, they might believe that she had.

'I have survived so far,' she said lightly, 'and I shall continue to do so.' She did not add that she had no idea how.

Chapter Six

Louis Rosier was also up early the morning after the worst earthquake in Caribbean living memory. His planation, Ailleurs, so called because it was certainly Elsewhere – and very far elsewhere – from his home town in France, had escaped lightly. The word from his overseer was that other plantations had been devastated, with sugar mills disappearing into the ground, slave quarters collapsed, and the plantation owners' magnificent homes severely damaged. Louis shook his head; as if things were not bad enough after the war.

His own house, which was not particularly magnificent, was built on flat ground at Capisterre, the far end of the French part of the island. There the force of the quake had been much less serious. His stables had collapsed and the slaves had spent half the night rounding up the frightened horses but at least his home and his sugar mills were intact.

Louis lived alone at Ailleurs, in a landscape dominated by the cloud-capped crown of Mount Misery. At twenty-eight he was a tall, elegant man, thin-faced and lightly built, whose disappointment with life showed in his sombre dark eyes and the sprinkling of early grey in his black hair. Yet looking around at the peaceful, untouched young sugar cane which surrounded his home he reflected that he had been lucky and that it was indeed time he had some luck. The British had left him alone in the fighting; perhaps his lands were too remote for them to make a special sortie against him. Also, to his great relief, since he was not cut out for soldiering, his countrymen had not sent for him to fight and he had made no effort to join them. He had no quarrel with his English neighbours and no wish to find himself at war with them. His only knowledge of the fighting had been the sight of distant fires lighting the skies at night and the boom and thud of cannonball and shot. For days now no fires had burned and the explosions had become rarer. His overseer, La Bac, was certain that the French had won.

Louis had not left the plantation for weeks and the violence of the earthquake had increased his restlessness. That afternoon he rode down to the small pier at Pointe des Sables where he kept a boat. He intended to sail down the Atlantic coast and round the end of the island past Nevis to Basse-Terre to see for himself what damage had been done. Most people who, like him, lived in remote spots relied on boats to get from one end of the island to the other. Away from Old Road Town and Basse-Terre roads were nonexistent and there were few settlements that did not hug the sea. The sea brought supplies and was the main

91

source of communication with their own and other islands. All the plantations, except those close to the two capital towns, were accessible from the coast.

Louis noted that life was not entirely back to normal. Rather too many large ships, mostly French, hovered watchfully around the Caribbean side of the island, but no one heeded him as he sailed the choppier Atlantic coast bordering deserted white beaches. Even if the French were the victors it would have been unwise to sail the shorter Caribbean sea route where he must pass both Brimstone Hill and the English capital, Old Town Road.

As Basse-Terre came into view, Louis saw that its sufferings were great. The skyline of the town had completely changed. The landmarks of the Jesuit college and the church were gone, the waterfront was tumbled, and in spite of a welcome stiff wind a cloud of dust still hung over the town.

He manoeuvered his boat as near to the beach as possible and two freed mulattos who scraped a living pulling boats ashore waded into the water to drag him in. He flung them a coin and jumped from the boat, aware that the sand was unusually viscous. He brushed the wet black stuff from his boots and set off to walk through the town.

The extent of the damage appalled him. He could not believe that so little of Basse-Terre was left standing. Man did frightful and cruel things to man, but who could surpass angry nature? he asked himself as he stared down the nine-foot-wide cavern in what had been de Lisle Street. Somewhere down there were houses and people who had lived only yesterday. They would never be seen again. He shuddered and walked on.

Round the corner from de Lisle Street was the Columbus Tavern. It was not a place that brought back good memories. There had been an unhappy time when he spent far too long and drank far too much under its thatched roof. But he saw that the front of the tavern was no longer there and only half the bar remained, and in that bar, sitting alone on a hard chair, was a girl he had never seen before. She wore a muddied, old-fashioned, blue and white gown which had certainly been expensive in its day. She appeared to be crying.

Avoiding the huge crack that had once been the roadway, he walked into the remains of the tavern and stopped in front of the girl, looking down at her. Her head was uncovered and her rich chestnut hair sprang in curls. She was perhaps eighteen or nineteen, he judged, and she had remarkably good features. She was, in fact, a beauty. Then, when she in turn looked at him, he saw she had the most remarkable green eyes; tear-washed and yet still as light and luminous as the skin on a white grape from his native Loire valley. 'Help me,' the eyes seemed to plead. 'Help me.' But at the sight of him her tears disappeared and only a small, childlike sniff betrayed that she had been distressed.

He bowed and said, 'Madame?' making the word a question.

She rose and curtsied. 'Monsieur,' she replied.

Her voice was light and pretty but somehow foreign. He did not think that she was French.

'You are alone here?'

'I am alone.'

'Why do you sit here, outside?'

'It feels safer to be outside.'

She was definitely not French but she volunteered no further information. He stood, his hand on his sword pommel, baffled as to what to say and do next. She was so remarkably attractive and seemed so helpless and yet he felt convinced that she was brave. She might cry but he judged she would not flinch.

'Can I be of assistance to you?'

She laughed, showing even white teeth, and he noticed how plump and tempting her lower lip was.

'Monsieur, if you could make this building safe . . .'

He frowned. 'From falling?'

'From falling, from men, from . . . so many things.'

'You are not French,' he said abruptly.

'I am English.' She volunteered the information almost with pride.

'Then you are unwise to be in Basse-Terre.'

'I have nowhere else to go.'

'You mean you live here?' He gestured at the ruined building.

'It is mine.'

'Come,' he said impatiently, 'it is owned by Molly McGuire. It has always been owned by Molly McGuire.'

'Molly has gone to Montserrat this day and left the tavern to me.'

'To you!' He laughed out loud. 'My dear, you are no tavernkeeper.'

'And why not?' She put her hands on her hips challengingly, even the tilt of her breasts below the décolletage of the dress seemed defiant. 'If Molly could do it, why not I?'

'Molly is older, stronger, not as beautiful, and a peasant. You are a lady,' he heard himself arguing forcibly, aware that it was none of his business. 'You will come to harm from the men who drink here. Men in drink are animals. It is absurd that you should even consider it. Where are your family to permit this? You should go home.'

Her head and her arms had dropped and her hands were folded before her. All defiance had gone.

'I have no home,' she said quietly.

He was confused. He could not understand what an Englishwoman could possibly be doing in Basse-Terre, let alone in Molly McGuire's tavern.

'Who are you?' he asked abruptly.

'Mademoiselle Amelia Quick of Devon, England.'

He bowed. 'And I am Louis Rosier of Orleans, France, and Elsewhere, St Kitts.'

'Elsewhere?' she asked.

93

'Elsewhere from France, you see.'

'I see.' There was an awkward moment while they both stood in silence looking at each other in an almost furtive manner. What he saw he liked very much, he decided.

'Will you be seated, Monsieur?' she asked rather shyly and he had the impression that she did not want him to leave her. 'I can bring another chair from the other room.'

'Do not disturb yourself,' he said, moving to lean against the bar. 'But tell me, if you will, how you come to be here?'

She sighed, turned those incredible eyes on him again and then looked at her clasped hands.

'I am a runaway, monsieur.'

'A runaway?' He was startled. The girl seemed as white of skin as he himself. How could she be a runaway?

'From Windsong where I was sent as a prisoner after the Monmouth uprising in England. They said I was a traitor.'

Some sense was coming through the fog.

'I have heard of the men who were sent and bought by the English planters – four years ago, was it not? But a girl . . .'

'I was the only one. I have had four years of slavery and I could endure it no longer. I took advantage of the confusion of the war to come here, to be with Molly who was my friend, but now she has gone.'

He stood stroking his chin, telling himself that what he was thinking was impossible.

'You should go back to your plantation,' he finally offered.

She half-smiled. 'To be whipped, maybe mutilated, maybe worse. No, monsieur. I will take my chances here.'

The thought of her being harmed decided him. It was unthinkable that he should leave her here. It was astonishing that she had survived for so long in this broken place and he knew that as soon as the town recovered its breath and the sailors and soldiers came looking for rum she would not survive.

'Mademoiselle Quick,' he said urgently. 'You cannot stay here. You will not last the night without some assault on your person. There is no possibility that you will be safe.'

'Where do you suggest I go?'

There was gentle sarcasm in her voice and he heard himself saying, 'To my plantation. Elsewhere. It is at a remote part of the island and there no one will molest you.'

She looked at him and the huge green eyes held a question.

'Mademoiselle, I am a gentleman,' he said quietly. 'You will be safe with me.'

'Then I thank you, but I cannot leave this place.' She had left the chair and was pacing the room, her grubby skirts moving gracefully round her ankles. 'My stocks will all be taken if they are left unguarded, and they are all that I have in the world. I could not run the tavern without them.'

He was beginning to be impatient. 'Which is more important, your stocks or your wellbeing? Do you not understand that your stocks will be taken anyway? That it is impossible for you to guard them until this building is repaired? There is no way that you could control the men who come to this tavern.'

'Molly controlled them.'

'You are not Molly. You cannot save your stock.'

'I must try,' she said stubbornly.

He could have shaken her, but he said, 'Then we will have to take your stocks to safety at my home.'

She clasped her hands. 'Is it possible, monsieur?'

'It is possible,' he said wearily.

The two mulattos from the beach carried the casks and bottles to his boat until it was dangerously low in the water. He was obliged to hire another craft. It took time to load everything and dusk was beginning to fall before they were able to set sail.

She had said little while the organisation of the move took place, and now she was sitting quietly in his boat, the vast red globe of the setting sun enhancing the shade of the wonderfully thick hair.

'Your wife will not be angry, monsieur?' she suddenly asked, her voice anxious.

'I have no wife.' It was not a subject he wished to pursue.

'Ah.' She was still, looking at her folded hands, and then she said quietly, 'I am glad to be with you. I was afraid there. I feared to spend the night alone. I feared the coming of the dark and it is not my nature to be afraid.' She looked up at where he stood by the sail and he felt the full power of her eyes. 'How will I ever thank you, monsieur?' she said. Her eyes were moist and one small white tooth held her full lower lip, as if she was trying to control tears.

He looked at her and felt a wave of almost unbearable desire. He knew exactly how she could thank him, but, he reminded himself, he was a gentleman. Keeping that thought foremost in his mind he turned his attention to the sails.

Darkness had fallen when they arrived at Elsewhere. The Frenchman carried Amelia ashore from the boat, carefully keeping the skirts of the old dress she had purloined from Charlotte's wardrobe away from the water. She let herself relax in his arms, breathing in his man's smell and feeling more secure than she ever had since she came to this island. She had no fears that he would harm her.

The black sand of the shore threw off silvery glitters in the light from a thin moon as he waded through the water and delicate diamonds of phosphorescence pierced the air as he strode towards where his horse was tethered waiting near the beach. It was warm, a night for courtship, and she found herself disappointed when he let her slip from his arms. He helped her to mount and then swung himself up in front of her. She put her arms round his waist and, tired out, let her head fall against his back. Though he was light of build she could feel that he was muscular and strong, and she found it reassuring.

They rode back in the darkness on narrow paths cut through rustling sugar cane. She was relieved that at this end of the island all was tranquil as if none of the horror that afflicted Basse-Terre had occurred. The only sounds on the night air were the sobbing of the wind in the cane and the labouring breath of the horse as it carried the two of them to Elsewhere.

When they arrived, she could just discern the dim outline of a long, low house set among trees. Lanterns burned at the large wooden double doors, and there was a welcoming glow of candles wavering from behind shuttered windows. He dismounted, lifted her down and set her gently on her feet. Before he had even attempted to knock, the door was opened by an elderly black man wearing a full-sleeved white shirt, a black *veston*, black breeches and long white stockings. A white woman in a cap and apron hovered behind him.

'We were worried,' she scolded as Louis came through into a large, panelled hallway. 'We . . .' She stopped speaking abruptly, silenced by the sight of the girl standing behind him.

Louis turned, took Amelia's hand, and led her into the hallway. 'This is my housekeeper, Madame Volnay,' he said. 'Madame, Mademoiselle Quick is to be our guest. Will you please prepare a room for her.'

Madame Volnay raised her eyebrows, pursed her lips but without comment scuttled off to do as she was bid. Was she hostile? Amelia wondered and realising how bedraggled she must look, decided that surprised would be a better description.

The room Madame Volnay showed her to a few minutes later was large, the four-poster hung with silken draperies and with portraits of stern-looking men and frivolous women filling the walls. Large windows were open to the night and she could hear the croaking and creaking of night animals and insects. When Madame Volnay left, she sat at the dressing table and looked around the comfortable room, savouring luxury she had not enjoyed for more than four years. She knew that she was not truly safe; that she was still a bondswoman and could be reclaimed at any moment, but she felt that this solemn Frenchman who had come so unexpectedly into her life would do his best to protect her. She turned to look at herself in the glass. In the yellow candlelight she could see that her face had fined since she left Devon and that her eyes looked enormous above high cheekbones. With her round cheeks diminished, her mouth seemed better defined, more prominent than she remembered. She smiled at herself and her reflection smiled back. She would smile thus at him and all would be well.

She was momentarily bewildered when a white maid brought her hot water and even more bewildered to find herself being served by the same maid at supper. This French, plain, heavily-built girl was the first white person Amelia had seen doing menial work in the West Indies. Louis called her Beatrice and Amelia found her somewhat surly.

He and she ate in a long, candle-lit dining room and as the well-cooked meal was served she told him a little of her history and how she came to be in St Kitts. For the most part he listened without comment, his deep-set dark eyes watching her intently, but it was Upottery and her life there that interested him the most.

'Do you miss it?' he asked.

She considered, seeing a sudden image of the tiny village in winter when a bitter wind blew in from the sea and the only street turned to red mud or became snowbound and impassable for the farm horses and carts. She realised that though she had suffered in many ways since she had come to this place, she had never once been cold.

'It's strange,' she said. 'I did at first, terribly, but as time has gone by I think of it less. It is only my loved ones I miss.'

'And who are they?' His attention was on the silver plate from which he ate but there was an intensity about the question.

'My father, but as I have said, he is dead. My brother, and he has gone to fight for Sir Christopher as has my cousin, Ben.'

'You feel alone?'

'Often.' She ventured no further. Her years in the Caribbean had brought her to accept, albeit reluctantly, that to speak of loving a black slave and bearing his child was more than unwise.

'I miss France all the time.' He could have been speaking to himself. 'I care not for this place. Not at all.'

'It has its own kind of beauty,' she ventured.

'Violent, untamed, dangerous beauty. They say rightly that life here is nasty, brutish and short.'

'That is true.' They ate in silence before she asked, 'What brought you here?'

He carefully wiped his lips with a white, linen napkin.

'Elsewhere belonged to my uncle,' he said. 'It is his creation. He never married. It seems that as he owned women slaves he felt there was no need. He survived long here, twenty-five years, but three years ago the climate defeated him. He died of a fever and I inherited the plantation. I had been married for a year and my wife and I were living in Orleans. We were happy. We were not rich, but we had sufficient to live in comfort. I was uncertain about leaving France. It was Yvonne, my wife, who was excited by the prospect of a new life in a new country. And it is true that if we had remained in France we would never have been as financially comfortable as here. But . . .' he hesitated and stared straight ahead, suddenly looking older. 'My wife died in childbirth a year ago now. Both were lost. I am convinced that they would have survived if we had been at home in France. Now I loathe this place.'

'Can you not go home?' Amelia asked.

He laughed shortly. 'Every day of my life I miss the gentle countryside of the Loire and the pleasures of life in a thriving town but in truth there is little for me to go back for. I am like the rest of the planters. It is the profits and the easy life that keep me here, though if your

97

countrymen take over the entire island one day, these will surely be lost. Why I stay I do not know. It is true this part of the island is healthier than the swamplands of Basse-Terre but I still fear the climate and the fevers that flourish here. I despise the slave system but use it and that causes me to despise myself.'

Amelia listened quietly, aware that here was a man who had been silent for too long and who needed to unburden himself. She had been able to talk to Bella and to Molly of her losses. Could it be he had no one? He was speaking so quickly she had to concentrate to understand his French, and all the while his eyes were fixed on her as if he could not bear to look away.

'But you have a white housekeeper and a white maid,' she said.

'And a cook, Marie, and Pierre, who is my manservant. In fact, the only black servant in this house is old Joseph who opened the door tonight. I cannot abide to have people serve me without proper recompense. Joseph stays here with me because he served my uncle for many years. He has his freedom but chooses to remain.'

'And the field slaves?'

He made an angry gesture. 'Are slaves.'

Rising abruptly to his feet he threw down his napkin. 'I go now to my chamber. I will instruct Beatrice to take you to yours. I wish you goodnight.'

Amelia watched his narrow straight back and square shoulders depart through the door, pleased by the way his hair curled down his back. He did not a wear a wig, and his own hair was as luxuriant and glossy as a girl's. She thoughtfully chewed on the last piece of mutton on her plate. She knew exactly why he had gone so unceremoniously. He wanted to make love to her, she was sure of it. And, she decided as she rose from the table, it was not the most terrible prospect. Not if he would keep her safe.

Adjusting to what had once been normal life was not simple. Finding herself being waited upon instead of waiting upon others proved a curious experience. All through her childhood Amelia had been surrounded by servants, but now she found herself aware of exactly what was being done for her and wondering if Beatrice and the other young French girls who worked in the house felt the bitter resentment she herself had suffered while working at Windsong.

At least the staff of Elsewhere were not slaves. She was certain that Louis would pay them a fair wage, but when her soiled underclothes were taken and washed and the water she bathed in and her night waste were emptied by Beatrice, she remembered her own disgust at performing these tasks for another human being. She tried to deal with her own personal toilet when opportunity allowed. It shamed her that another should have to do these things for her.

Louis she hardly saw. He seemed to spend much of his time in the fields. She watched him leave in the mornings booted and spurred, wearing a plain snuff-coloured frockcoat, his hair tied back. He often did not return until dusk, and dusk gradually became the high spot of her day for they always dined together.

On her third day at Elsewhere he had noticed that she was wearing the same blue and white dress. She had tried to clean it but its soaking in the sea had done it little good.

'Do you have no other clothes?' he suddenly asked.

'What I had was left behind in Basse-Terre.'

He seemed to be thinking. Then he said, low-voiced, and as if the words were dragged from him, 'I will instruct Beatrice to take you to my wife's closets. Take what you wish. You are much of a size. They should do.'

'You are sure?'

'I am positive,' he said gruffly.

She came to dinner the following night in a silk gown of green. The outer skirt was the colour of English grass, the underskirt striped white and green. She had found a lace fichu to cover her shoulders and the swell of her breasts where they rose from the low-cut bodice.

He stared at her as she came through the door and visibly pulled himself together.

'I am sorry,' she said gently. 'It is hard for you to see me in your wife's clothing.'

'It was a shock,' he said. 'I had not thought it would be such a shock. You wear a gown that Yvonne had made in Paris before we left for here. It was always a favourite of mine and hers. For one moment as you entered . . .'

'You thought that she had returned?'

'For one moment. But her hair was brown, dark brown, her skin was darker than yours. And her eyes were black.'

'And you loved her very much.'

'I loved her and I miss her,' he said painfully. 'I still cannot speak of her without distress.'

She would have liked to have taken his hand, but the table was too long and he was too far from her to reach for it. Instead she asked quietly, 'Would you rather I wore no more of her clothing?'

He shook his head. 'I would prefer that you did. There is no one I would rather see wear her things, and besides, you may lay ghosts for me.'

It was the first personal comment he had made about her and Amelia felt the colour rise in her cheeks. She had been unable to decide whether or not he liked her; he was always courteous and nothing more. She liked him very much and in her wide canopied bed each night she lay thinking about him, wondering if he might come to her and enjoying the hot feelings that the prospect aroused in her. Love in a bed would be good, she decided, and wondered how different it would be with him than with Joshua. Were white men different, or was it all the same? And then she was angry with herself for harbouring thoughts that were disloyal towards Joshua.

99

Unaccustomed to having nothing to do, she found the days at Elsewhere long. The staff rebuffed her overtures of friendship and she eventually realised that they were embarrassed. She was failing to keep her place. She asked Louis if she could ride around the plantation. He said abruptly that there was a small grey mare in the stables that she could regard as her own but that she must not go near the slaves' quarters or the sugar mill. She found an unfinished tapestry that his wife must have been working on before her death and spent her afternoons stitching in the cool of the long wooden veranda that ran alongside the carved blocks of lava stone that formed the base of the house. But she realised that she was always waiting for dusk and the moment when he would return.

She wanted to make him laugh, she wanted to make him happier. He was too tense, his emotions as tightly bottled as new wine, and she wished he was not so much of a gentleman.

After nearly six weeks at the plantation she was in an odd state of mind, driven by a kind of longing that she hardly understood. Joshua was not forgotten, but for the moment he had been superceded. She wanted Louis. She was not certain if what she felt for him was love – it was difficult to love someone so remote in manner – but she needed him. There was gratitude involved in her feelings. By simply finding her in the ruined tavern and bringing her back to his home he had restored her life. It was time, she decided, to take matters into her own hands.

He was more silent than usual that night. She chattered, as she always chattered, asking questions, trying to draw him out. His answers were monosyllabic, but the intense dark eyes hardly left her face. His long white hands stroked his wine glass and she found herself imagining that it was her body that he stroked. He was causing her to desire him with no more than a steady look and some suggestive hand movements. But did he desire her? She was sure he did. Why then did he make no move?

As usual he said his goodnights and left the table before her. She rose and dropped him a curtsy and then made her way to her own room. Most of his wife's possessions had been moved into her chamber. She opened the closet door and ruffled through the clothing. She found a nightgown in white lace with a matching peignoir. She undressed, splashed her body with rosewater and then put on the low-cut nightgown. Yvonne had been an inch or so taller than Amelia and she had been obliged to lift all of the gowns on the shoulder so that the décolletage was not too low.

This gown was cut very low. The rosy pink of half of her nipples peeped above the lace, but there was no time for alterations. The peignoir fortunately came high to the throat, though the pink still showed through the fine lace.

She stood looking at herself in the glass, wondering if she dare do what she planned. And then, pursing her lips, she nodded firmly at her reflection before walking from her room.

She did not knock on his chamber door. She just lifted the handle and walked in. He was sitting up in bed, reading by candlelight, and when he saw her he dropped the book heavily onto the bedcovers.

'What the . . .' he began, face white, then, 'My God! Oh my God.'

She walked towards him silently, no longer certain what to do next.

'Why are you wearing that?' he shouted harshly. 'Go away! Take it away! Take it off!'

'If you wish,' she murmured and let the peignoir fall from her shoulders. The nightgown only needed the smallest wriggle of her body before it, too, slid to the ground, making a lace puddle at her feet and leaving her naked and rosy in the candlelight.

'What are you doing?' He had buried his face in his hands and for one moment she feared that she had been mistaken. He did not want her. 'Jezebel! What are you doing?'

Stung, she moved closer towards him.

'I am no Jezebel, sire,' she said angrily, 'but a woman come to comfort you and love you in gratitude for all your kindness to me. Will you reject me?'

He let his hands drop and stared at her. 'You do not need to thank me in this fashion,' he said, his expression troubled.

'But I want to,' she said with the utmost simplicity. 'I want to lie in your arms.'

He groaned, and then slowly, slowly he opened his arms. She took a tentative step towards him. He nodded, and she knew she was invited to settle herself upon the bed and curl herself against him.

He held her very tightly and neither of them spoke, then he lowered his head and began to kiss her. They were long, deep kisses, his tongue searching her mouth, demanding that she reciprocate. She gave him her tongue to taste, exploring the caverns of his mouth, delighting in an intimacy she had never experienced. For a long time they clung together with the desperation of the shipwrecked. The tips of his fingers began to gather her nipples into tight points, silkily, gently. She strained closer to him and his touch roughened; he pulled the two points, stretching, lengthening them until the pain was exquisite. Then his mouth left hers and closed over the tiny blood-red penises that he had made of her nipples. He was licking, sucking and biting until the pleasure became almost too much to bear. His leg was pushed between the heat and damp between her legs, rubbing up and down against her, fanning the flames there. She could feel how hard he was, how ready, and she knew by the sweet smells of longing that surrounded them that she was ready too. She was moaning, her hands in his hair, her body arched backwards as he plundered her breasts. She reached down to find him and to hold the hardness that she wanted inside her. Insistently, urgently, she guided him to the open, waiting entrance where he plunged into her.

'Ah, yes!' she said joyfully. 'Ah, yes.'

He did not speak, but he panted as he lifted himself in and out of her. He had turned her slightly onto her side, so that his hands could still tug at her nipples. He moved slowly at first, as if savouring what he found in her depth, and then faster, faster, faster, until she too was panting, clinging, begging. Then with a huge thrust that seemed to spear her, she knew that he had come, and she pushed against him, biting at his shoulder as she shared in the explosion.

They lay breathless and clinging together before he slid out of her. She wrapped both her arms and her legs round him and slept.

She woke to find his head between her thighs and his tongue exploring the lips between. He had found a place that he teased so expertly with the very tip of his tongue that her legs parted wide.

He rolled onto his back, and lifted her to sit on his erect penis.

'Ride me,' he whispered.

She sat upright, her eyes closed, her own hands enclosing her breasts while he used one finger to torment the secret place his tongue had found. She rode him, his penis clutched and held in her with all the strength of her muscles.

'You're doing it to me,' he said thickly. 'It's good. Oh, it's good.'

Soon the great ripples were beginning from her depth. He felt them from the first tremor and, held in her iron grip, he thrust in rhythm with the growing power of the ripples until they both cried out together.

This time they did not sleep, but lay side by side, slightly apart, eyes on the overhead canopy as if made shy by what had occurred.

'You came to me because you truly wanted to?' he eventually asked.

She rolled over to put her head on his shoulder. 'Yes, and I feared for one moment that you would send me away and then how would I ever have faced you again at your table?'

He pulled her closer to him. 'Send you away! Every night since you came here I have lain in this bed, thinking of you, imagining the sweetness of you. It has,' he said ruefully, 'been a month of hell.'

'It was the same for me,' she said sleepily.

'Did I make you happy?'

'It was wonderful. Like nothing I have ever known.'

He was still. 'There has been another?'

Now what to say? she asked herself.

'The master at Windsong raped me,' she began cautiously, and instantly his anger and distress, his avowals that she would be revenged somehow concluded the subject. He asked no more questions and she volunteered no more information.

'As for me,' he said, 'my father introduced me to his mistress when I was fifteen. She became my mistress, too. It is the French way, you know. But once I married I swore I would be faithful unto death, and I was. I loved Yvonne, Amelia, that you must understand. My heart has been frozen since she died. I thought I would never desire another woman – until I met you. I will always love her, but you have wiped away the hurt, you have unfrozen me. The ice has gone. Shall we love

102

each other do you think, Frenchman and Englishwoman together? Shall we make the other happy?'

'Perhaps,' she said. 'Perhaps.'

Even though the fever had abated and the fires were quenched she knew that this man would always be able to arouse her. Satiated as she was, the thought of what he had just done to her still caused a shiver of excitement. She would want it again and again. He was a man who understood a woman's body and needs.

But love? To think of love caused Joshua's face to fill her mind. Louis had wiped out the memory of her lovemaking with Joshua, but he had not wiped out the memory of the man. Louis was for lust, Joshua for love. That was the way it was, and she had betrayed the man she loved. As Louis slept contentedly beside her, she lay awake, struggling with guilt but knowing that if Louis should ask her to marry him, the answer would have to be yes.

Amelia, six weeks' pregnant, was a December bride. She and Louis married quietly at the temporary Catholic church in Basse-Terre since the island's Protestant churches were out of bounds for her. Louis, both thrilled and fearful when she told him of her pregnancy, insisted that they were married immediately. He bought her a new gown and gave her a diamond ring that he said had belonged to his mother. Amelia could not help wondering if once it had been worn by Yvonne.

She was happy. She hoped that perhaps this new baby she carried would assuage the yearnings she felt for Tansy. Also, she had discovered that there was love in her feelings for Louis. She loved him for his goodness, and also because he cared for her and made no pretence about the strength of his feelings. And she had found that he could laugh and be light-hearted and that his solemn demeanour dissolved when he was with her. Joshua was not forgotten, and never would be, but she had been able to tuck him into a corner of her heart while she concentrated on making her husband happy.

Louis did not object when she said that she wanted to rebuild the tavern.

'Just so that it is whole again,' she explained. 'Not because I want to run it or live in it. I feel I owe its restoration to Molly. But I want to do it mostly because it will be somewhere for Zach to go when he comes home from the war.'

He agreed without question. And she thought that if she asked for the moon he would somehow take steps to get it for her.

Chapter Seven

In a series of blood-red sunsets, 1689 waned and 1690 dawned while Sir Christopher Codrington, with a force of three thousand men, retook St Kitts. This time Elsewhere was not immune. The Redcoats backed by the militia swept down from Brimstone Hill and along the coast to Capisterre. They fired the house. They also shot dead, point-blank, Louis Rosier for having the temerity to attempt to defend his wife, his home and his servants. They then marched away again.

La Bac the overseer came from the sugar mills bringing with him his black slaves. Together, with the white servants and Amelia, they fought the flames with water from the huge cisterns that Louis had always insisted were kept full. Wooden houses were prone to fire without any outside help but this fire had had considerable assistance. As Amelia dragged heavy buckets alongside plantation slaves and the house servants, she feared it would never be quelled and feared also that she might harm the child she carried.

By the end of the day, the stone foundations and one end of the house remained standing, though the entire roof had gone. The dining room was intact, Amelia's bedroom above it open to the sky. The kitchens and staff quarters were razed. Part of the withdrawing room remained, along with some blackened furniture. As the last ash-grey, filthy remains sizzled into silence, La Bac took his slaves back to their compound leaving Amelia standing in the smoky air, looking at the ruins of what had been so briefly her home. Her house servants stood in silence behind her.

Louis's body lay on the drive halfway to the front door where he had fallen, his pistol still clutched uselessly in his hand. He had been wearing his old snuff-coloured coat, and the wool was now stained with huge patches of rust-black blood. There had been no time to mourn him in the desperate attempt to save the house. Now Amelia walked slowly to his body, sat down on the ground beside him and lifted his head with it dark curls onto her lap. She found herself rocking him, as if it might help in some way. And then she began to cry. Silent tears that fell onto his dead face but did not wake him. Nothing would ever wake him.

She was aware that Joseph was standing beside her. He squatted to her level and looked into her face.

'Oh, Joseph, he is dead. They shot him,' she whispered.

'I know.' The old man's eyes were grey with tears. 'All our hearts be like to break. He were a good man, the master.'

Joseph meant it and there was no black man or woman at Windsong who would have said the same for Matthew Oliver at his death. Amelia could not control a choking sob. She put her arms round Joseph and cried into his shoulder.

He gently disentangled himself. 'Come 'long now, Mistress Amelia,' he said gently. 'We must take the master home.'

They carried his body into the house and placed him on a long settle. La Bac, who had never approved of his master marrying an English woman, came back from the fields and asked if there was anything he could do. Madame Volnay and the cook were standing side by side, tears trickling down their cheeks, hands clasped before them, waiting for instructions. Beatrice and the other maids cried helplessly.

All Amelia wanted to do was crawl into bed and sleep away the pain and horror of the day. But her bed was blackened and smoke-stained, her servants had no beds at all, and there was no roof to cover any of them. She looked around the once elegant room, gazed up to where clouds floated above her head and turned back to find half a dozen pairs of tearstained eyes watching her, waiting to be told what to do. They were looking to her for leadership but she had not the strength. The blows on this cruel island came too thick and fast.

'What shall we do, madame? We cannot stay here.' It was Beatrice who spoke in a frightened, breathy voice. It was the terror in her voice that made Amelia realise that, like her, they were far from home with no family and nowhere to go with their master dead. They had nothing. She at least would presumably have money and there was always the tavern.

The tavern! She felt a surge of optimism. They could go to the tavern. At least they'd have a roof over their heads even if it meant that she would have to be cautious if the British had taken over the town.

'No, we cannot stay here,' she said. 'La Bac, are your quarters safe?'

He nodded.

'Then you can stay at Elsewhere. Take the slaves away from the fields and get them working on rebuilding the house.'

'But it is time to cut the cane,' he protested. 'We are fortunate that the English did not fire it.'

'Probably because they are coming back for it,' Amelia said wearily. 'Can it wait to be cut?'

He thought.

'Perhaps a week.'

He was a tall, thin man with a strip of narrow black moustache. His eyes did not quite meet Amelia's but Louis had always said that he was an honest man and to be trusted. Now he had to be won over. She had no doubts that she could do it.

'Monsieur La Bac, we do not know each other very well, but my husband thought highly of you,' she began, deliberately lifting her green eyes to him. 'His contention was that you are an honest man who served him well. I cannot help it that I am English, any more than you can help it that you are French, but here at Elsewhere we are a family. Nationality is unimportant. I would like to feel that I can depend on you in the same way as my husband did.'

He bowed, his face impassive, but Amelia believed that he would help her. He seemed to have loosened, his face was less set.

'I think it best if I take all of us from the house to Basse-Terre. I own a property there which will shelter us. I am going to leave the management of Elsewhere to you for the time being. Deploy your people how you wish. Perhaps some could be spared from work with the cane. Perhaps the women could come to clean what is left here. Most important is that we get some kind of roof raised. And I will see if I can find workmen in Basse-Terre.'

'And if the British come back?'

'Maybe they will, maybe they won't, but I think we must carry on as if they will not. And before all, we must bury your master.'

Louis' uncle and his dead wife were buried beside a tiny chapel that stood behind the house. Amelia was at a loss to know what to do without the services of a priest, but she knew that in this climate she could not leave his body unburied. The alternative was to take him to Basse-Terre, where no doubt there were bodies aplenty waiting for burial after the English attack.

She made the decision to bury him beside Yvonne, and it was a decision that seemed to please his servants. She remembered little of the burial service and there was no Bible or prayer book in the house. Besides, Louis was a Catholic. It seemed best to have Joseph and Le Bac bury him while she spoke the Lord's prayer and the 23rd Psalm over his grave.

'And yea though I walk through the valley of the shadow of death I will fear no evil, for thou art with me, thy rod and thy staff they comfort me . . .' Her voice floated into the blaze of sky above the tiny graveyard in this alien place, the ruined house behind them. She spoke the words of the Lord's prayer in French as she had been taught a lifetime ago back in Taunton, and the staff who gathered round the grave spoke them with her. There was no red rose to throw on his body, but she plucked a red hibiscus flower from the garden, wishing it could be something less exotic and more European for a man who had missed his home every day of his short life in this faraway island.

And then they continued the preparations for leaving.

With La Bac and Joseph's help they carried provisions and linen to the two boats that Louis had kept by the shore. La Bac brought two of his more trusted slaves to sail them along the Atlantic coast to Basse-Terre. They left just before dawn, La Bac having judged this the safest time to go. Madame Volnay, Beatrice, Marie, and the little kitchenmaid, Marianne, settled themselves in the bigger boat, huddled together for comfort. Amelia decided that she would sail with Joseph and Pierre in the other boat along with the provisions, for among the provisions was the stock of rum, ale and wine that she had brought to Elsewhere when she first arrived. She was not entirely sure why she was taking them with her, except she had a feeling that to have the means to reopen the tavern might just prove useful in such troubled times.

Basse-Terre seemed little different from when she had seen it last except that now a few English Redcoats swaggered drunkenly in the streets and there was some rebuilding going on.

'Oh, madame,' whispered the little kitchenmaid as they made their way through the streets from the beach, each carrying as much as they could. 'Will they kill us as they killed the master?'

'Of course not,' Amelia said with a conviction she did not feel, remembering the casual way that Louis had been killed. 'Englishmen do not kill women.'

Madame Volnay looked doubtful.

'But leave the talking to me,' Amelia added. 'It might be wiser if they do not hear us speaking French.'

The tavern door when they reached it was open and for a brief moment Amelia's heart sank at the thought that perhaps this sanctuary had been taken away from her by the war. Then she was angry. This war had taken too much: her husband and her home and the safety and contentment that she had found. The tavern they would not take. She took a deep breath and held herself as tall as possible, telling herself that if Molly could be in control, so could she.

'Wait here,' she commanded her little band of followers and strode into the tavern. With the light behind her, she could not see too clearly into the room, but she could make out someone small and slight standing behind the long counter.

'What goes on here?' she demanded belligerently. 'This property is mine. Explain yourself.'

She heard a chuckle, a delighted sound and one that she recognised.

'Amelia, sweet cousin, where have you been?' Ben vaulted over the bar and hurried towards her. 'Oh such joy to see you safe and well. Zach and I believed you dead.'

He was hugging her, kissing her cheeks, laughing and exuberant as he had been in the old days before Windsong. 'Where have you been? he asked. 'I am the happiest man on earth to see you again. Let me light the candles to see you better.'

She found that her legs were trembling, and she closed her eyes. The relief that she felt at the sight of her cousin was almost painful in its intensity and she realised how much she had missed her own kind. But what was he doing here? Why was he not at Windsong?

He was busying himself with candles when she remembered that the Elsewhere servants waited outside.

'Ben,' she said. 'Wait. I'll be back in one minute.'

She hurried outside. Mrs Volnay had her arm round Marianne who looked terrified. Beatrice's face showed nothing and Marie was clinging to Pierre's hand. Joseph was not with them, he had stayed behind on the beach to supervise the unloading of Amelia's stocks and to help the slaves carry it to the tavern. The rest of them all looked towards her expectantly.

'All is well,' she told them reassuringly. 'Come in.'

The tavern was lighter now in the candlelight, and Ben looked up in surprise as the little group trooped through the door.

'They're French,' she said quietly to Ben. 'Should we hide them?'

He looked baffled. 'Your friends?'

'Servants who are friends,' she said.

'I doubt that they'll be harmed, but take them up to the attic while we talk,' he suggested.

Amelia left them in the room where she had sat with Zach what now seemed so long ago, promising to return soon. Then she went back to Ben.

He was sitting at one of the tables, his red hair bright round his head, grinning with pleasure.

'I'd offer you wine if this tavern had any,' he said.

She threw back her head and laughed out loud. 'You know it's my tavern?'

He looked astonished. 'Your tavern?'

'Molly McGuire left after the earthquake and gave it to me. I have a paper to prove it and in a moment you will have all the wine you desire.'

'From where? Heaven, perhaps? Your tavern?' Ben was bewildered.

'Look outside,' she said, hoping that Joseph would be arriving.

Ben went light-footed to the door, and Amelia marvelled at how he had returned to being the cousin of their childhood, a Puck, an Ariel, full of light and life.

Joseph had borrowed a cart and laden it with casks and bottles. He and the two field slaves were dragging it up the street.

'It's for here?' Ben asked wonderingly.

'Yes. It's my stock.'

He scratched his red curls. 'I don't understand.'

'It's a long story. Tell me first what are you doing here in my tavern. Why aren't you at Windsong?'

Ben jumped to his feet and made a little capering dance of triumph across the room. 'You don't know?' he said. 'You don't know that we're free?'

'Free?'

'Parliament disallowed the laws concerning us back in January and in February we were all given free pardons.' He slapped his thigh and laughed. 'Oh, you should have seen the anger of those planters. Paid good money, they did, for us, and they hadn't had their pound of flesh. Only four years of our labour instead of ten. But they had to let us all go. Basse-Terre is full of men who are free. But penniless. There's the rub. What are they to do? How can they get home?'

As Amelia sat taking in this news, Joseph came through the door and Ben leapt to his feet again to give instructions on where the barrels should go. Then he sat down and said sheepishly, 'I know it's your tavern, Amelia, but its men's work. As to my being here, when Zach and I got our freedom, the Olivers wanted me to stay on, but I had no stomach for it. After four years of bowing and scraping to them I wanted no more of it. Though Zach is a wealthy man now he is still in Sir Christopher's army and he'll have nowhere to go when this fighting ends. We have no home. Zach told me about Molly McGuire so I came here but found her gone. The place was empty so I broke in and moved in. I thought Molly was in hiding from the British and would come back. I was going to open it again as soon as I had something to sell.'

'Well, now you have something to sell,' Amelia said.

'I have something to sell,' he said shaking his head as if he could not believe any of it. 'Now tell me, Amelia, where have you been? And don't miss out a single detail.'

It was three more weeks before Zach returned from the fighting. The English had been quelling the far corners of the French parts of the island, and now were in complete control. Joseph, who went back and forth between Basse-Terre and Elsewhere, reported that the Redcoats had not returned to Elsewhere. La Bac was doing his best both to cut the cane and rebuild the house, but the priority was the cane which would bring the wherewithal for the restoration of the house. The damage to the house was even greater than it had seemed and it would be months before it would be habitable again.

Amelia settled down to life in the overcrowded tavern. Ben had opened it up again for business and was proving to have the perfect temperament for a tavernkeeper. Marie had taken over the kitchen where she prepared food for the customers, and everyone involved themselves in the running of the business. There were no questions about their being French. Basse-Terre had been French and the conquering English never thought to query that Amelia's people had not lived there before. In fact, Marianne was being courted by a young Redcoat, much to Madame Volnay's disgust. Madame Volnay's opinion of the English strongly resembled Elizabeth Oliver's view of the French.

It was only the sleeping arrangements in the tavern that were a problem with so many of them in such a small space, but Zach solved that by purchasing the house next door and moving himself, Amelia and Ben there, leaving the tavern quarters to the staff.

Gradually things began to return to normal on the island. The French, whose property had not been sequestered, drifted back to their plantations and businesses, and an uneasy peace prevailed. Amelia found herself curiously tranquil. Freedom felt strange; she was unaccustomed to walking in the streets of the town knowing she no longer needed permission and that she could come and go as she wished. She sometimes wondered how Charlotte and her mother were and who was feeling the lash of their tongues now. She dreamed all the time of Joshua and in her dreams they were making love. She woke wet, wanting and bereft and also guilty that the dreams were of Joshua and not Louis, but somehow she had come to feel that the child in her womb was Joshua's. She worried less about Tansy. In some odd way the coming baby had merged with Tansy and she felt that both were safe in her care.

The pregnancy, combined with a bone-weariness from the pain of the years in St Kitts and the extreme heat of summer, sent her into a mental and physical retreat. Ben and Zach ran the tavern, though Zach was determined on going home once he had seen her baby safely born. He wanted to take her and the baby with him. She herself had postponed all plans until the child came. She told him that he could live with her on Elsewhere and run it if he wished, but he wanted no more of the island. He wanted to return to Devon, purchase Quick Manor and settle down to the life of an English gentleman. In the meantime they were doing well with the profits from the tavern, though there were times when Zach complained that they had to pay Amelia's staff.

'We should buy slaves,' he said. 'One payment and they work for life.'

This saddened Amelia. She refused to dismiss Louis' staff and remembering her husband's repugnance for unpaid labour refused to allow slaves to be used in the tavern. She and Zach fought, but she had always been the stronger and her will prevailed. For the rest, she let him do as he wished.

As June passed in a blaze of sullen heat and sultry July followed, she spent her days sitting on the shore, skimming stones into the sea and watching the pelicans plunge. Devon receded deeper into her memory and she began to feel an affection for this often hostile, always beautiful island. With freedom, she viewed it differently and was beginning to see it as her home.

As her time drew near she began to think of Bella and Bessie and how they had supported her through her last pregnancy. She wanted them with her again and the thought came that perhaps now she was free and had money she could buy Bella from Matthew Oliver and give her her freedom.

She talked to Zach and Ben about it one evening after they had dined. Zach listened and then said, 'And when we go back to England what are we going to do with Bella?'

'I'm not going back,' she told him, surprising herself at how positive she sounded.

They were in the small sitting room of the house. He stood up from his chair and loomed over her.

'You cannot stay here,' he said flatly. 'What will you do?'

'Run Elsewhere. Look for Tansy. I intend to begin to search for her once the new baby comes.'

'Amelia, you must forget Tansy.' He sounded angry. 'She's black.'

'She's my daughter,' Amelia said quietly. 'And what does it matter what colour she is?'

He began to pace the room, dwarfing it. 'Ben's coming back with me. You'll be alone.'

111

Ben had been looking out of the tiny window onto the street.

'Well, to tell the truth, Zach, I was thinking of staying here myself,' he said apologetically. 'I wondered if Amelia would sell me the tavern. I find I like the life.'

Zach looked from one to the other, his expression baffled. 'But I want to go home.'

'What for?' Ben asked.

'Because it's home.'

'Maybe. Suppose Quick Manor is not for sale. What then? Much will have changed in five years.'

'Nonsense!'

Ben shrugged.' You must do as you wish, Zach, but Amelia and I are staying here.' He threw her a conspiratorial look and she remembered how once he had said he loved her. She made no response.

'You're both mad,' Zach declared, making for the door.

'Zach,' Amelia called after him. 'You will come to the Olivers with me, won't you? Please.'

He turned, sighing. 'If you wish,' he said.

The three of them went the following morning. Amelia wore one of her best gowns and a black beauty spot high on her cheek to emphasise her eyes. They arrived in the smart horse and carriage that Zach had purchased some weeks before with Joseph acting as coachman. They drove up the long drive through the royal palms, all three silent, remembering the first time they had seen the house that lay beyond, grateful that now their circumstances were so changed.

One of the house slaves was at the door, and his mouth fell open.

'It be Ben and Amelia,' he said, eyes round with amazement as he saw them in their finery. 'Now where you been, Amelia? Master that mad when you disappeared, we all thought he'd 'plode.'

'We're free, Daniel,' Amelia said. 'Master can 'plode all he likes. We're free.'

'You lucky,' Daniel sighed.

They made their way to the veranda at the back of the house where all three Olivers sat. Charlotte and Elizabeth stared at them, as open-mouthed as their doorman had been. Matthew Oliver turned deep crimson and leapt to his feet.

'Forgive us for calling unannounced,' Amelia said sweetly, offering a gloved hand, 'but we were anxious to see you. You remember Ben, of course, and my brother, Zachary. Zachary did not stay with you for long, but I sure you won't have forgotten him.'

She was enjoying the outraged expression on Elizabeth's face and Matthew's embarrassment. Charlotte was trying not to smile too broadly.

'Oh, it is nice to see you, Amelia,' the girl said, throwing an anxious glance at her mother. 'I haven't found anyone else who can do my hair as well as you did.'

Zachary stepped forward. He wore a dark burgundy fitted wool coat with a sleeved waistcoat in rich brocade beneath. His narrow breeches

112

matched the coat and below were red silk stockings. His shoes were high-heeled, making him appear even taller than he already was. The ensemble was topped by a lace cravat and a heavy golden-haired wig. His tricorn was under his arm since the weight and height of the wig made it unwearable.

Charlotte stared as he moved towards her, her pink mouth a small round O of astonishment. Then, Amelia noticed, her cheeks became very pink as Zachary took her hand and kissed it.

'My sister has often spoken of you,' he murmured, and then turned to Elizabeth's hand. 'A mother and daughter, one as beautiful as the other,' he declared.

Amelia found herself as astonished as Charlotte. Where had her clumsy brother acquired these society manners? Charlotte was visibly melting and unable to take her eyes off Zachary, and Amelia had to admit to herself that he did look remarkably fine and commanding.

'Ben, it is good to see you.' Matthew was taking in the fact that his erstwhile manservant was dressed almost as splendidly as Zachary. 'We have all missed you.'

'And I you,' said Ben, bowing gravely.

There was something absurd about the gathering, Amelia thought. She and her companions seemed so much more at ease, so much more sophisticated than these people for whom they had slaved.

'Please be seated.' Matthew waved a vague hand towards the long settle on which he had once raped Amelia. 'What can we do for you?' he asked awkwardly.

'I remember this settle,' Amelia said gently as she sat down, looking straight at Matthew who flushed scarlet. She gave all of the Olivers the benefit of her smile. 'What you can do for us is very simple. We have come to buy Bella.'

Elizabeth stiffened. 'Bella is not for sale,' she said firmly.

Amelia turned limpid eyes on Matthew, and her hand gently stroked the tapestry cushion of the settle. He seemed mesmerised by the movement.

'I am sure you can find it in your hearts to let her go,' she said, and gave a little tinkling laugh. 'We have shared so much, Bella and I, secrets, so many things, you know how the house slaves miss nothing. And now that I have my own household, I feel the need for her near me.'

'Your own household?' Elizabeth sniffed. 'Where might that be?'

'The plantation Elsewhere at Capisterre. I am not living there at this moment since the English soldiers burned it to the ground. And, alas, they killed my husband as he tried to defend us. You see before you a widow, who expects her . . .' she paused briefly, '. . . first baby.'

'You married a Frenchman?' Elizabeth sounded outraged.

'I am Madame Rosier,' Amelia informed her.

'Then Bella is definitely not for sale.'

Matthew cleared his throat. 'Perhaps we should ask what Madame

113

Rosier is offering, my dearest,' he said to his wife. 'Bella is getting older, one day . . .' He stopped.

'You will have to support her, should her health fail,' Amelia finished for him. 'And that can be an unwelcome expense. I had in mind perhaps fifty guineas, which is, I am sure you will agree, a generous offer considering . . .' It was her turn to stop and stare challengingly at Matthew.

'Fifty guineas.' Elizabeth's voice was thoughtful, but her eyes had brightened.

'You can buy yourself at least three strong, young slaves for that. Slaves new to you and your household.' She put the faintest emphasis on the word 'new'. Matthew now had beads of sweat on his forehead. She knew he feared that she would say more.

'Oh, Mama, why don't you let her go,' Charlotte said timidly, her eyes still fixed on Zachary. 'You know how she steals the food. You're always complaining about it. And I'm sure that Amelia and her brother would let us know how she was getting on if we wished to know.'

'We would indeed,' said Zachary, bowing from the waist. 'It would be a great pleasure and a fine opportunity to have the pleasure of your company once more.'

Charlotte once again turned pink, looked at her mother nervously and then dropped her eyes modestly while her mother flirted her fan with great energy.

'Fifty guineas, you say?' She put down the fan with a slap. 'Oh, very well.'

'You are too kind, Mistress Oliver.' Amelia's voice was shot silk. 'May we take her with us now?'

Elizabeth sighed heavily. 'It is a great sacrifice. She has been part of this family for many years. But if you have the money with you . . . yes, you may take her now.'

'We have the money,' Amelia said, signalling to Ben who stepped forward and handed Mistress Oliver a chamois leather bag that chinked.

She opened it greedily, dropped the coins into her lap and counted them. It took quite a while.

'It seems to be correct.'

'Good.' Amelia swished her skirts and smiled round the room again. 'Now we will find Bella.' She raised her hand. 'No, please don't disturbed yourselves. We will find her easily. As you know, we are familiar with the way.'

Bella was in the kitchen, raking out the embers of the fire. As she turned to see who had come into the room the shining ebony of her face was red-tinged, reflecting the glow from the heat of the fire. She stood upright, meat-like hands on vast hips, and stared at the three of them.

'Oh, my,' she said. 'It be you. I knew for sure they catch you one day.' Her voice was belligerent, her expression unfriendly. Amelia remembered guiltily that she had left Windsong without saying goodbye. Had Bella felt deserted? She resisted the urge to make excuses.

'No, Bella,' she said. 'It's all changed. We're free.'

'Huh!' Bella turned back to her fire. 'Nice for you.'

'And we've come to take you away from here.'

Bella turned again, her face so pinched and suspicious that it looked almost small. 'Where to?'

'My plantation.'

'You plantation?' Bella made no attempt to hide her disbelief.

'It's called Elsewhere. It's at Capisterre. We're going there.'

'Is you telling me that now I go'n slave for you?'

Amelia was becoming irritated. 'You're not going to slave for anyone. I shall give you your freedom.'

'Ho. You give me freedom, eh? And what I s'posed to do with this freedom? How I go'n eat? What I go'n do?'

'Get paid and look after me and my baby,' Amelia said crossly. 'I do declare, Bella, you are impossible. Do you want to stay here at Windsong? If you do I shall go this minute and ask Mistress Oliver to return my fifty guineas.'

Bella's eyes rolled in her head. 'You telling me you paid the mistress fifty guineas for me?'

'That's what she's telling you, Bella,' Zach said.

The black woman ignored him. Her manner had changed. Her voice was softer. 'What baby you talkin' 'bout? Be Tansy?'

'No, another baby.' Amelia put her hands over her stomach. 'One by my husband. The Redcoats killed him. Oh, it's a long story, Bella. But I'm going to find Tansy, and Joshua and Truly.'

'And what you go'n do when you found 'em?'

'Take them to Elsewhere so we can all be together.'

Bella sighed deeply. 'You still ain't growed up, gal. You still don' understand nutting.'

'Bella,' Amelia said through gritted teeth. 'Do you or don't you want to come with us?'

The woman stood thinking, then nodded her massive head. 'P'haps I get my things,' she said.

She stumped off through the outside door in the direction of the slave cabins. Amelia, still exasperated, turned to Zach and Ben.

'She is impossible!' she said.

Ben burst out laughing. 'That's what you get for acting the lady bountiful,' he said.

Amelia opened her mouth to retort and saw that Zach was grinning too. She capitulated.

'I don't suppose she's going to change now,' she said weakly.

As they waited, they heard a flutter of footsteps running towards the kitchen and Charlotte came in the door, pink and flushed.

'Amelia,' she said, though her eyes were fixed on Zach. 'I'm so glad you're still here. Mama wants to know if you will all take tea with us one day next week. Please say yes. It so boring here and' – she hesitated – 'I missed you when you were gone.'

Amelia blinked. She was framing her refusal when Zach said, 'We should be delighted. Would Tuesday suit?'

Charlotte clasped her hands together. 'Tuesday would be perfect,' she breathed. 'At about three. Such a pleasure . . .' And then she scuttled from the kitchen as if anxious that Zach might change his mind.

'Zach!' Amelia exploded.

He stretched and put one hand up to touch the ceiling. 'Is she the heiress?' he asked.

'Who should know better than you?' Amelia said crossly.

'No other brothers?'

'No other brothers,' Ben said dryly.

It was at that moment that Bella came back through the door, shaking the wood floor under her tread, a small bundle in her hand.

'I's ready,' she said.

Chapter Eight

By the late summer of 1690, Elsewhere was partially habitable and though there was still much to be done, Amelia had decided to go back. She took Zach with her leaving Ben to look after the tavern. Marie and the kitchenmaid had opted to stay in Basse-Terre. Marianne was in love with her Redcoat and did not wish to be too far from him, while Marie had found that she enjoyed cooking for the men who frequented the tavern. Amelia wondered if she had designs on Ben; if she had, Ben could do worse.

In Marie's absence, Bella took over the kitchen at Elsewhere and to everyone's surprise she seemed to be visibly shrinking. When Amelia expressed concern and asked if she was well, Bella gave a huge, round chuckle.

'I's fine,' she said, 'but I just don' feel obligated to steal the vittels all the time no more.'

Zach took over the running of the plantation. In the last months of her pregnancy Amelia grew very big, more so than with Tansy. She slept throughout the heat of the day and had taken to wandering about the house at night. She showed little interest in anything. Zach was not displeased. It was an opportunity for him to learn plantation management. He knew well enough, first hand, how the sugar was grown and processed, but he was without knowledge of the business side. La Bac was surprisingly helpful. He did not seem to resent Zach's arrival and confessed that he found it simpler to take orders from a man than from a woman. Zach talked to the bookkeeper, immersed himself in the records of the plantation and made frequent trips to Basse-Terre to talk to the merchants and the ship's captains who both sold and transported the island's crop of sugar. The spring crop at Elsewhere had been good and Amelia declared herself happy with the profits but Zach was certain he could have sold more profitably than La Bac had. He kept a careful eye on the Elsewhere storehouse in Basse-Terre where the hogsheads of sugar they had produced were kept. He was convinced that in time the storehouse would not be large enough to hold all that Elsewhere could produce.

Whenever Zach went to Basse-Terre he made a point of calling upon the Olivers where he let his wealth show. He always arrived at Windsong with small gifts for the two women, spent lavishly on fine clothes, and his height and bearing commanded attention. Though only good at the social graces in fits and starts, he was learning how to behave in society.

He never mentioned his days as a buccaneer, and Matthew Oliver did not ask where he had been in the missing years after he ran from Windsong.

Amelia never interfered. She did not even enquire why he was taking such an interest in the plantation considering that he had made clear his intention of returning to England. But Zach was no longer so certain that he was returning to England. Zach had a plan.

William Louis Rosier was born on a stifling day in August 1690, with Bella and another black slave taken from the field work at Elsewhere attending the birth. Madame Volnay did not approve. Madame Volnay made it clear that she believed babies should be born in a bed, not on a three-legged stool with a kitchen pan held at the ready.

The arrival of the baby awoke Amelia from her lethargy, but she still took no interest in the plantation, her involvement was entirely with young Will. She continued to leave Zach to deal with the management of the estate. Knowing his forceful sister, he was fairly sure this was a state of affairs that would not continue indefinitely, so he used the time while she was preoccupied to get all the experience he could. Zach had designs on a much larger plantation than Elsewhere and he wanted to be prepared if his opportunity came.

He was certain that Charlotte Oliver was in love with him. She still flushed when she saw him and either chattered too much or became too silent in his company. The mother welcomed him warmly whenever he called, and did her best to see that he and Charlotte were left alone for just a few stolen moments. Matthew Oliver showed less enthusiasm for Zach's visits and Zach guessed that he wondered where his wealth had come from. Maybe he even guessed. But so many buccaneers had turned respectable and become rich and useful members of the community that it was not considered polite to ask too many questions. And besides, Zach was certain that Matthew was ill. He had a parchment look to him; his skin was yellow and he was painfully thin and frail under the fashionable large blond wig that he occasionally wore. Most of the time he sat with a bonnet hiding his shaved head as if he could not cope with the weight of the lavish curls.

There were few on the island who were as rich as the Olivers and yet Charlotte was in need of a husband. She would soon be twenty-one years old, and was without a suitor. Zach did not dislike the girl. In fact he had become quite fond of her. Her hero-worship of him was flattering, she was quite pretty and certainly silly enough to control. He had no doubts that it was her formidable mother who had spoilt her chances over the years. The soldiers, parsons and tutors who had flitted through the girl's life had undoubtedly been deemed unsuitable by Mama. Though Mama did not know it, he, too, was nowhere near as rich as the Olivers, but his sister owned a plantation. The joining of the two plantations could be a carrot to dangle.

He had decided to marry Charlotte. He was sure she would have him but uncertain how a courtship should be conducted. His life as a buccaneer had been no training for dealing with respectably brought up young women.

One evening in the dining room at Elsewhere, when he and Amelia were alone, Zach raised the subject.

'What would you think if I married Charlotte?' he asked without preamble.

Amelia put down her knife and fork and stared at him, aghast. 'Surely you could not!'

'Why not?'

'She's so . . .' Amelia was lost for words. 'Do you love her?'

'She's agreeable enough.'

'With you maybe.'

'That's what matters. As long as she is agreeable to me and with me . . .'

'But why? For the plantation?' A look of dawning understanding replaced Amelia's amazed expression. 'Of course, that's why you asked if she had brothers that day.'

'Why else?'

'But you were going home.'

'I've changed my mind − if I can make her marry me.'

Amelia suddenly laughed. 'I suppose it has a certain irony. Their ex-slave who killed their son marries their daughter.'

'We'll not mention that,' Zach said uneasily. 'But tell me how do I go about it?'

'What?'

He was embarrassed. 'You know. The courting. The kissing . . . How do you kiss? How far can I go?'

Amelia's expression was amazed again. 'You don't know?'

'It was different buccaneering. Tom had an expression for it. He said it wasn't asking their permission. There was no time for kissing.'

'Are you telling me that you raped women?' Amelia's voice was horrified.

He stared at her baffled. 'Well, yes.'

'Zach, you are disgusting!'

'Why?' He was hurt by the contempt in her voice. 'That's the way it was. There was no time for courtship.'

'You leave me speechless. What our father would have said . . .'

'And what would our father have said about you and what you did,' he challenged. That shut her up, he thought as she coloured bright scarlet. 'Now tell me, can I kiss her?'

'If she will let you,' Amelia said, her voice cold.

'How much further can I go?'

'As far as she will let you.'

'You mean I have to stop when she says stop?'

'Exactly.' Amelia rose to her feet. 'I'm going to my bed now, Zach. I wish you joy of all your plotting. But my fears are for Charlotte. I care little for her, but she deserves better.'

He was wounded again by her words. She had always been able to wound him. She was quicker, cleverer. Her good opinion of him was important and he needed to explain himself.

'Amelia, wait,' he said, getting to his feet. 'You don't understand. When men are together as we were in the buccaneers, there's no place for weakness. They tried to knock weakness out of me in the cane fields, but it's different with the buccaneers. There each man had to be as strong as the next. I could not be different. If they raped, I raped. If they killed, I killed. There are things that haunt me still, Amelia. Once we roasted a woman on her own hearth stones because she would not tell where her treasure was hidden. I hear her screams to this day. What you call rape seemed small by comparison. But these were things we all did – together. Alone, we would never have had the stomach. It's difficult for me to explain but at the time all the cruelties seemed to be a test, a trial to see if I was worthy of being part of their brotherhood. Maybe I have some shame now for the worst of it, but no regret. I did what was expected of me by my comrades and I found it was better to be the aggressor than the victim. In the brotherhood we were never the victims. On the *Indeavour* and at Windsong, we were the victims. I shall never be a victim again and nor shall you or Ben while I can protect you both. As for Charlotte, I intend to be a good husband to her and I asked for your advice merely because I did not wish to frighten her as I have frightened others before.'

She was standing, watching him and listening, her face giving away nothing. Then she began to speak in a voice that he thought sounded sad. 'What women want most of all is to be loved and to feel that they are loved,' she said. 'But will you be able to give her that, Zach?'

She turned from the table and left the room, closing the door quietly behind her, leaving him puzzled and alone.

He decided to call on the Olivers the very next day. Having given Amelia notice of his intentions he felt that he should now carry them out. He had a new waistcoat in brilliant blue brocade that went well with a darker blue frockcoat. He pulled on white stockings under his dark blue breeches. Topped by the golden wig, the glass in his bedchamber told him that he looked a handsome and wealthy young man.

It was Charlotte who greeted him at Windsong. She looked flustered.

'Oh, sire,' she began, 'Mama is indisposed and unable to chaperone us. I fear that your visit must be short. But will you take some tea?'

Mama indisposed. That was good news.

'Your poor mama!' he said solicitously. 'Nothing severe, I trust.'

'No more than a rhume but she feels wretched and low.'

'And you have been nursing her?'

'I have done my poor best.'

'You must be fatigued. In need of air. Do you think perhaps your mama would object if we took a turn round the garden together?'

She clasped her hands together, tipped her head to one side and thought for a moment. The bundles of ringlets each side of her cheeks swayed as she moved her head.

'I am sure a walk in the garden could not be improper,' she said. 'Though I should ask Mama.' She stood undecided for a moment and then said, 'Indeed, some air would be pleasant.'

'Then come,' he said, offering her his arm.

At first she chattered, pointing out flowers and shrubs as they walked the length of the garden and past the slave cabins. He was steering her towards the wooded area where he had run the night when he escaped Windsong.

She made no protest as they moved further and further from the house, but it seemed to him that she leaned on his arm a little more heavily as the woods drew near. The opening in the brush that led through to the pool where Joshua had taken him that night was still there.

'Shall we see where this will take us?' he asked, taking her hand in his.

She still did not demur, but she was silent. He could hear her breathing and her hand felt damp in his. Was she afraid or was she excited? he wondered.

Soon they heard the faint sound of tinkling water and then the pool lay clear and sparkling before them. He had a flash of memory of the night he had run through that selfsame stream in the unfriendly dark to safety. That night the cool water had brought back memories of the Otter River, where he had fished for trout as a child.

'Ah,' he said, 'this reminds me of Devon.'

'It is so pretty, but sadly I have never seen Devon,' she breathed. 'I had no idea that this place existed. But we are far from the house. We should turn back. Papa . . .'

She looked up at him. The top of her head just reached his chin, and her girlish, doll-like mouth was trembling; her eyes did not quite meet his. As he stared down at her, noting the way her breasts rose from the low neck of her gown, he felt a surprising stirring.

He touched her cheek gently and found the skin very soft.

'I think perhaps . . .' she began.

He took no notice. Trying to be gentle, he lifted her off her feet so that her face was level with his own. And then he kissed her, full on the lips. It was pleasant holding her, but the kiss was not quite right somehow. He put her down so that he could bend his head to find her mouth. That way he could get closer to her, and hold her tighter to him.

He had no idea how she would react. He was reasonably certain that she would not kick and fight like the other women had done, but he certainly had not suspected that she would faint dead away in his arms. He had thought for a moment that she was kissing him back, and then suddenly she became a dead weight and his own stirring disappeared. Baffled, he looked down at her for a moment, and then lifted her into his arms. He stood in the glade uncertain what to do next. Her eyes fluttered open and he peered down at her anxiously.

121

'Oh! Oh! What have you done?' she whispered.

He was too confused for the social niceties and, indeed, had no idea what the social niceties were in a situation of this kind.

'I only kissed you.' He sounded indignant.

'Oh!' She covered her face with her hands. 'What would Mama say?'

He stood there, still holding her, totally at a loss. But she had taken her hands from her face and was looking up at him. Tentatively he bent his head and kissed her again, and this time he was certain that she was joining in.

'Oh, please. Oh, please, no more,' she sighed when he lifted his head from her mouth. 'If we should be seen, why, I declare you would have to marry me.'

'But that is what I want to do,' he said crossly.

'You want to marry me?' Her blue eyes were suddenly huge in her face. She lifted her head from his arm to stare almost suspiciously at him.

Zach had lost all control over the situation. He was beginning to be angry.

'Why else do you think I have kept calling all these weeks? Why do you think I would kiss you if my intentions were not serious? But will you have me?' he asked roughly. 'That's what I want to know.'

'You really mean it?'

'Of course I mean it!' he bellowed, irritated, and without ceremony dropped her legs and feet so she could slide to the ground. She landed heavily and had to grab at his arm to stop herself falling.

'Oh, such passion!' she cried, and flung herself against him, standing on tiptoe to kiss him again. He pulled her closer, wondering if he should go further or stop. Then he remembered what Amelia had said.

'I love you,' he told her. It did not sound convincing even to him, but the effect of the three words on Amelia were remarkable. First she flushed red and then she turned quite white, swaying as if she were about to faint again.

'And I love you,' she said, her voice so low he could barely hear the words. 'I have loved you, and dreamed of you, from the day when you came with Amelia to buy Bella.' She hesitated. 'You will speak to Papa?' she asked, almost timidly.

For a moment he could not think why she should want him to speak to her father, but then he remembered.

'I shall ask him for your hand,' he assured her, 'this very day.'

'Oh, Zach.' She was swaying again and he hastily took her arm. 'I declare, I have lost my senses as well as my heart.'

And he, he realised with a sudden sense of panic, was about to lose his freedom.

It seemed to Amelia that Zach was looking rather too pleased with himself when he returned to Elsewhere in time for supper that day.

'I suppose she accepted you,' she said as they settled themselves at the table.

He looked astonished. 'How did you know?'

'You look triumphant.'

He leaned back in his chair and laughed out loud. 'It was the easiest thing,' he said. 'Except that when I kissed her, she fainted.'

'As respectable girls are meant to do.' Amelia knew her voice was sour but she couldn't help it.

He looked astonished again. It was easy to astonish Zach.

'You mean she did not really faint?'

'I mean she did not really faint.'

'But she said she loved me,' he said, his voice eager.

'I'm sure that's true.'

'Her parents were delighted.'

'I'm not surprised. They must have thought they would never get her off their hands.'

'It was fortunate her mother was sick. We were left alone.'

'Conveniently sick?' Amelia asked.

He was silent. Then said, 'I am quite fond of her, you know, Amelia. She is . . .' he hesitated and then said lamely, 'not bad.'

Immediately she was contrite. 'I'm sorry, Zach. I'm really very pleased for you. When is the wedding to be?'

'Soon. When things are arranged.' He picked up his fork and began to tackle the food in front of him.

'What sort of things?' Amelia asked.

He moved uneasily in his seat. 'Financial things.'

'Mistress Oliver was always very anxious that Charlotte should marry well. Are you really that rich, Zach?'

He put down his knife and fork. 'Rich enough,' he said defensively, 'but you know what these planters are like. They're only interested in property.'

'You don't have any property.' She did not understand why he was so uneasy.

'But you do,' he muttered.

'You mean Elsewhere?'

'Yes.'

He would not look her in the eyes. He was a blushing, awkward country boy again and it was dawning on her what he had done.

'You have not told them that Elsewhere is yours?' she asked sharply.

'Oh, no,' he said quickly. 'They know it's yours, but they think it's,' he hesitated and then said quickly, 'family.'

Amelia put down her own knife and fork. 'Zach, what exactly have you told them?'

He was doing his best to look in control. 'That there could be a possibility of Elsewhere and Windsong becoming one plantation. Well, there could, couldn't there?' he asked eagerly. 'You're not interested in running it and I am. It would be good to run them as one. It would cut expenses. It would be the finest plantation on the island, bigger even than Macabees.'

123

She was beginning to become angry. 'Are you suggesting that my plantation becomes part of the Olivers'?'

'Not exactly,' he said defensively.

'Well, over my dead body, Zach.'

'It wouldn't be until Matthew Oliver died.'

'It would be never,' she said banging her fist down on the table. She made him jump and she could see little beads of sweat gleaming on his forehead in the candlelight.

'Please, sweet sister,' he said. 'What it would really mean in the end is that Windsong becomes part of Elsewhere.'

'Impossible!' she said crisply. 'The two plantations are too far apart, and besides, this belongs to my son. We'll have no more talk of it.'

She tackled her food angrily and he sat crestfallen. She could see the wheels of his mind working, but in the end he said nothing. She was not about to help him. She was furious with him.

Nevertheless, plans for the wedding went on. It was to take place in May, in four months' time and before the weather became too hot and sultry. She guessed that Zach had simply done nothing to dispel the impression that he had given the Olivers. She decided it was his problem to tell them that Elsewhere would never become part of Windsong, but this vague threat to her son's inheritance temporarily roused her from her long sleep. It was time to take some interest in her property, she decided, but somehow the plantation held little appeal. It was so much more pleasurable to take care of the baby and watch him grow. He was a happy baby who smiled when he saw her and could wave a chubby fist to say goodbye. He was, Amelia thought, probably one of the brightest and more forward babies ever born.

About a month before the wedding day she went down to the kitchen to chat with Bella. She did this at least once a week, taking William with her, in the hopes that Bella would become attached to the baby. But Bella stubbornly acted as if William were not present.

She was kneading dough for the evening's bread. She looked up, her face belligerent as Amelia, holding young William in her arms, came through the door.

'He has another tooth, Bella,' she said brightly. 'That makes seven.'

'Most babies get 'em,' Bella said sourly, bashing the dough in front of her as if she were inflicting punishment on it.

'What is it, Bella?' Amelia asked. 'Why are you so unkind about William?'

Bella put her hands on her hips in the familiar into-battle stance. 'I ain't unkind about William,' she declared. 'Don' be William's fault. I just wonder when you goin' do something 'bout you daughter, Tansy. You 'member Tansy? She be you firstborn. She be four years old come this April, and we ain't seen her since she nothing but a scrap. But now you got William you don' care about her, and you don' care about Joshua and Truly and all my family that you got sold. You brung me here in this place by tellin' me lies. Big lies. You said you find Tansy and Truly and Joshua and bring us all 'gether again. I been here near 'nuff nine month now and what you done? You ain't done nothin'. Where my family? All my family. That's what I wants to know.'

Amelia stood looking at her, appalled. 'But Bella—'

'I s'pose now you got a white baby, you don' want the little yella flower any more. That it, ain't it? She be in the way in you new life as mistress of this big plantation. P'haps she too black.'

Amelia looked at the fat, rosy, white-skinned baby in her arms and tried to visualise Tansy as she had been when she last saw her. The picture was blurred. William had blotted out the other child. But the attempt to remember stirred all the old feelings, the old sense of loss. She was ashamed. How could she have forgotten Joshua's child with such ease now there was another to take her place? And Joshua and Truly. She had been in a trance. She had not been thinking. She had neglected her responsibilities.

'Bella,' she said, 'you're right.'

She turned on her heel and went out of the kitchen door. There didn't seem to be anything else to say to Bella. What was needed was to do something. And quickly.

With William in the care of Madame Volnay, Amelia was dressed in her riding clothes, sitting bolt upright on the settle in the hallway of her home the following morning, waiting for Zach and trying to contain her impatience. Zach disliked getting out of bed and it was late before he appeared, peering at her sleepily as he came down the stairs.

'Where are you off to?' he asked.

She did not answer directly. 'Are you going to Windsong this morning?'

'I wasn't planning to.'

'I want to go there.'

He looked at her, surprised. 'Whatever for? I thought you loathed the place and all in it.'

'I do, but I want to talk to old Pottle. I can't think why I didn't think of it before.'

'Think of what before?'

'Old Pottle will know from his books where Matthew Oliver sold Tansy and Joshua.'

Zach was beginning to look alarmed. 'Why do you want to know that?'

'Because,' she said crisply, 'my daughter will be four years old in a few days' time and I want her back. You promised we'd get her back, and I promised Bella we'd get them all back. It's time to start keeping our promises.'

'Wait a minute,' he said, agitated. 'You're not thinking of getting Joshua back?'

'I am.'

'You can't. Far better to forget it all. Leave them where they are.

125

That's all in the past. All behind us.' He was almost pleading, and she looked at him, her lips pursed.

'You're afraid people will guess.'

'Amelia, we have money, we can have position if we want it, and I want it. Why put everything in jeopardy because of something that happened so long ago? If people knew about you and Joshua . . .'

'There's no reason why anyone should know. But I want to keep my promises,' she said stubbornly.

'You're mad,' he retorted flatly.

'Nevertheless, I want to go to Windsong.'

He looked at her with the expression of a man who knew it was a waste of time arguing.

'Very well,' he said, then hesitated as if he wanted to say more. 'If Matthew Oliver should mention Elsewhere,' he began, but her expression stilled whatever he had intended to say.

They rode along the shore in silence, he ahead on the black stallion he had chosen as his own from the Elsewhere stables while she followed on the mare that Louis had given her. She was thinking about what Zach had said. Nearly six years on this Caribbean island had taught her compromise. She knew that Zach was right. It would be disastrous if the white community came to know that she and Joshua had been lovers, but there must be some way in which she could bring Bella's family home without causing harm to them all. Nothing was impossible, she told herself as her horse trotted in the black volcanic sand of the shallows throwing up cooling salt spray. She'd think of something.

Charlotte greeted her effusively when they arrived at Windsong.

'My future sister,' she cried. 'Why do you never come to see us? And sadly you have chosen a day when Papa is indisposed. He has a fever and will be so disappointed not to have seen you.'

'Not a bad fever?' Amelia said, endeavouring to sound sympathetic.

Charlotte's face clouded. 'He is not well at all. Mama has called for the physician from Old Town Road. These last months poor Papa has been subject to fevers. The physicians blame the climate and there is nothing that one can do about that.' She sighed. 'But come and greet Mama.'

Mama was sitting in her usual chair on the veranda and her expression when she saw Amelia was a mixture of distaste and then suddenly sharp interest.

She waved a hand, indicating where Amelia should sit. 'And what brings you here?' she asked. 'It is an unaccustomed honour.'

'I had a fancy to see Windsong again and to visit old friends,' Amelia murmured.

'Since our estates are to be joined?' Elizabeth asked. It was a direct question delivered with Elizabeth's usual lack of finesse. Zach, who was lounging behind Charlotte's chair, his hand on her shoulder, stiffened.

126

'No, no.' Amelia gave a tinkling little laugh. 'It was sentiment that brought me.'

'But our estates *are* to be joined?' Elizabeth persisted, her thin nose twitching.

'Madam,' Zach stepped forward, his hand upraised, 'these matters of business—'

'Must be settled,' snapped Elizabeth.

'Ah, but not now,' trilled Amelia. 'It is such joy to see you again, Mistress Oliver. I did not realise until I was no longer in your tender care how much I owed you and your charming daughter. You were the mother and sister I never had. So good, so kind and so generous to one who found herself in such sad straits. Dear me, you need never doubt that somehow I shall repay all that I owe you. Every last thing.' She paused and smiled, noting how Elizabeth was beginning to preen, and wondered if it were possible to reach a point where the woman would realise she was being mocked. 'And tell me, is dear Mr Pottle still in your generous employ? How well he always regarded you. I declare you were his inspiration. And is Jake still your ever conscientious overseer?'

'Little has changed,' Elizabeth said complacently. 'Indeed, it is true that we are loved by those who serve us.'

'And rightly,' Amelia said stoutly, then lowered her voice to confide, 'It would give me great pleasure to speak again to Mr Pottle. Do you permit that I visit him? I remember so well how kind he was to me when the French were coming. Calming my fears and urging me to stay under the protection of Windsong, though as you know I fled in fear of my life. Do you permit that I pay him my respects?'

'If you must,' said Elizabeth, looking as if she would prefer to return to the subject of the joining of the plantations.

'Always so kind,' Amelia murmured. 'I shall go this very minute to him.'

Before Elizabeth could speak, Amelia was on her feet and out through the veranda door. It was all too obvious to her that Zach had been prevaricating. Elizabeth Oliver clearly had her suspicions that there was some doubt regarding the merger of Elsewhere and Windsong. But that was Zach's problem.

Pottle was delighted to see her and asked no awkward questions when she inquired of the whereabouts of Bella's family. He just said, 'You want to unite the family?'

Amelia nodded.

'And how is Bella?' he asked.

'Thinner since she doesn't feel obliged to steal food any more.'

Pottle threw back his head and laughed. Then he set about looking through his records.

Bella's family had been sold to the Ramillies' estate, Macabees, he told her. 'It is not a happy plantation,' he said. 'I hope that they are safe and well.'

'Do you think they will sell them back to me?'

'If you offer sufficient money,' Pottle said dryly. 'Those at Macabees are not sentimental. But I urge you not to go yourself. Send an emissary. Vincent Ramillies is a' – he coughed gently – 'bachelor and not one to deal with a woman. His parents died long ago, and his brother and sister-in-law have been dead a year now, struck down by fever. His brother left a child, a daughter, then only a few months old. It seems likely that one day the estate will be hers since Mr Ramillies',' he hesitated, 'shall we say, predilections make it unlikely that he will produce an heir.'

She leaned to kiss his lined cheek. 'I shall take your advice, and thank you, Mr Pottle,' she said. He was bright scarlet as she left his room.

When they had said their goodbyes to the Olivers, the ride back to Elsewhere was again silent. Zach, she could see, was both simmering with anger and anxiety while she herself was occupied in thinking what to do next.

He exploded when they were back in Elsewhere. Flinging off his riding coat he shouted, 'You should never have gone there. Now she is suspicious that the estates will not be joined.'

'And you have been begging the question,' Amelia said coolly.

'What else could I do? With your refusal—'

She put up her hand to silence him. 'I might change my mind—'

He brightened visibly.

'But only if a document is drawn up making Elsewhere one third yours, one-third William's and one third mine.'

'Ah!' he said.

'And on condition that William and any other children I might have share Windsong in equal proportions to your own offspring.'

'Ah,' he said again, but this time on a falling note.

'It is fair,' she said and he nodded grudgingly.

'I'm surprised you don't want a share for Tansy.'

'I was coming to that.' Her voice was calm. 'Pottle says Tansy and all Bella's family are at Macabees. Before I agree to this arrangement you must visit Vincent Ramillies and persuade him to sell you,' she ticked them off on her fingers, 'Tansy, Joshua, Truly, Bessie and Minta. I want all five.'

'And what am I supposed to say to Vincent Ramillies?'

She shrugged. 'Pottle says if you offer enough they will sell. Say your sentimental sister wants to reunite her cook's family. Say Tansy is yours. It's no disgrace for a white man to have a child by a slave. Say anything you like, but bring them back.'

When Zach was thinking the process was as visible as the wheels of a clock working and he was thinking now. Eventually he said miserably, 'I don't have much choice, do I? I'm only afraid—'

'That someone will guess Tansy is mine and Joshua's?'

He nodded.

'I won't let that happen,' she said. 'I'm older now. I know the

128

regulations. That doesn't mean I like them or even agree with them, but I've been forced to understand them.'

He moved to look out of the window as if he could not face her. 'You loved him?'

'Joshua? Yes, I love him.'

He turned to stare at her. 'Then it is dangerous—'

'No,' she interrupted. 'I told you. I know the rules now.'

'I wish I knew what love was,' he muttered. 'You are fortunate.'

She laughed. 'Maybe it is you who is the fortunate one,' she told him. 'It's not easy to love.'

They stood looking at each other for a long moment, and then Zach walked towards her and wrapped his arms round her.

'I do know I love you,' he said, burying his face in her hair. 'Don't worry. I shall bring them back.'

It was three days before he went to Macabees. He needed time to think what he was going to do and say, and eventually decided that perhaps his best bet would be to play the situation as it occurred. Macabees was not far from Elsewhere. It was, in fact, the neighbouring plantation, sheltered by Brimstone Hill which dominated the western end of the island.

Zach became increasingly nervous as he rode up the long drive to the plantation house. Since the death of his family Vincent Ramillies had kept himself to himself. He was never seen in society and people knew little about either the man or his plantation, except that the slaves threatened their naughty children with the punishment of being sent to Macabees.

The black footman who opened the great wooden front door of the Elizabethan manor seemed surprised to see a caller. He ushered Zach into a hall the size of a small ballroom and said he would inform his master of Zach's presence. Five minutes later, after pacing the paved floor of the hallway, Zach heard the footman returning.

'The master will see you, sir,' he said.

He led the way through the hall and into a high vaulted room at the back of the house. A log the size of a tree burned in the open fireplace and the heat was overpowering. A man sat at the side of the fire in a long, burgundy coloured, quilted robe, his own red hair arranged in luxurious curls to frame a long, thin, dead-white face which seemed to Zach to be powdered. He bore, thought Zach, a remarkable resemblance to Queen Elizabeth. A cruel Elizabeth. Beside him stood a handsome black lad, finely dressed in a brocade frockcoat but with a huge turban tied round his head. Ramillies' right hand was on the boy's thigh.

The man raised his left hand in a languid manner for Zach to come closer. Then, in a high-pitched, mincing voice he said to the black boy, 'Oh my, he's a fine big one, isn't he just, Nero?'

Nero giggled. 'Oh, very big, sir,' he said.

'And what can we do for you?' Ramillies asked, fluttering his eyelashes.

Zach made a courtly bow. 'Zachary Quick, sir, of the Elsewhere Plantation,' he said. 'Do I have the pleasure of addressing the master of Macabees?'

'Indeed you do.'

'We are, of course, sir, neighbours.'

Vincent Ramillies took a lace handkerchief from inside his sleeve and sniffed into it. 'Fancy,' he said.

'I have come to ask if I may purchase particular of your slaves,' he began.

Ramillies looked at him sharply. 'Which in particular?'

'The family, brother and sister and the girl's child whom your overseer brought from Windsong some four years ago.'

'And how should I remember a family I bought four years ago?'

'I doubt you would, sir.' Zach could feel the beads of sweat gathering on his brow. 'But your overseer . . .'

'Oh, yes. He never forgets a thing. Fine fellow, Benson.' He then asked abruptly. 'Why do you want these slaves?'

'My sister, sir, is sentimental. The girl was her nurse. They grew up together.'

'And the child is yours, no doubt, sir,' said Ramillies with a whinnying giggle. 'Oh, yes. I know what you planters are like. It means nought to me whether they are sold to you or not.' He turned to the boy. 'Shall we sell him them, Nero?'

'Depends, sir.'

'On what?'

'On what he'll pay.'

Ramillies slapped the boy's thigh lightly. 'Oh,' he said, 'you're a fine lad, you are indeed, with all the right instincts. And you, sir, are a fine figure of a man.' He licked his lips. 'Will you take a glass of claret with us while we discuss this matter further?'

'Nothing would give me greater pleasure,' Zach said heartily, longing to be gone from this place, 'but time passes. I have an appointment in Basse-Terre just one hour from now. But if I could return to partake of your hospitality on some other occasion . . .'

'Oh yes, indeed.' Ramillies was eying him up and down with special attention to the crotch. 'Oh, yes, indeed. You will be most welcome. For now Nero will take you to see Benson, my overseer. Nero, tell Master Benson that I will not take less than forty sovereigns for any one of them, but that for forty sovereigns a head this fine gentleman here may have as many of my slaves as he wishes.'

It was extortionate, but Zach managed a bow and thanks. He heard Ramillies cackling with laughter as he moved out of the room. Then the laughter ceased and the high-pitched voice filled the room again. 'Make it forty-five, Nero, make it forty-five.'

Zach felt a shiver as he moved into the cool of the draughty hall.

130

Nero was capering before him like some small monkey in fancy dress. The manservant opened the front door for them both, his face expressionless. There was a sense of brooding evil about the place. A feeling, even in the sunshine outside as they walked through the fields, that the estate was stamped with cruelty and perversity. And the first sight of the ox-like, narrow-eyed Benson did nothing to dispel that sense of evil.

Benson was not pleased by Zach's request. His almost colourless eyes narrowed further.

'The master must be mad to be thinking of parting with them,' he said. 'The child is nearly white. I had my eye on her. And the rest are house slaves. All trained.'

'And so they should be,' Zach pointed out, 'at forty-five sovereigns a head.'

'It's all very well for him. He don't have to break in the new ones,' Benson grumbled. 'All right. You'd better come and see them.'

They walked back to the house in silence, Nero still dancing and posturing in front of them. As they walked, Zach was thinking, and his laborious thoughts were troubled. He must be insane, he decided as they walked round to the kitchens at the back of the house. Here he was going to pay good money for the one man who could ruin everything for Amelia and him. Joshua had not only been Amelia's lover, he knew who had killed Justinian. Joshua had led him to safety after the deed. And Zach knew from Ben that Ben had tried to implicate the slave after Justinian's body was found. Joshua would have no kind feelings for the men of the Quick family and would have a frightening hold over both Ben and him.

Zach made a rapid decision. Joshua must stay where he was. And while he was thinking about it, it was equal madness to bring Bessie and Minta back into their lives. They were the two women who had been present at Tansy's birth. Better that they stay out of sight and out of mind at Macabees as well.

Benson led him into the kitchen where two woman stood, their backs turned to him. The shorter one turned away from the table where she was slicing vegetables and looked at them. She had a sullen black face and suspicious eyes. Then the other turned from the stove. This woman was different. Her skin was black but shone like polished ebony. Her eyes were merry, shot with red flecks like a fine brocade. She looked as if she were laughing at them both. Her stance was not slave-like. She stood proud, fine breasts jutting, her wide, deep, pink mouth curving into a smile that uncovered strong white teeth. He found himself gaping as he looked at her. She had all the force and power of forked lightning, she was provocative and yet he felt he wouldn't have to ask this one's permission because she would never say No. He wanted her.

'Now what you doing in my kitchen at this time o' day, Master Benson?' she was asking, flirting dangerously with the overseer.

'Mind your manners,' Benson snapped, but Zach could tell his heart wasn't in it. 'I'm not here for you. I'm here for Truly.'

'What you want with me?' the sullen black girl asked.

'This man wants to buy you.'

'Me?' She moved to stand with the table between them. 'Why he want me?'

'It's your mother, Bella, who wants you. And Amelia. I've come to get you,' Zach said.

She stood contemplating him. 'You 'Melia's brother?'

'That's right.'

The girl looked agitated. 'But . . .' she began and Benson snarled at her to shut up.

'You want the brother as well?' he asked.

'No,' Zach said quickly. 'I only want the child, Tansy. And I want this girl here as well.'

'Ruby?' Benson scowled. 'She's not part of the family.'

'Ruby,' Zach said firmly. 'I want her.' Ruby's eyes had opened to white circles. 'What about my baby?' she said.

'She's got another brat, a boy, as well as the girl. The boy's black as sin. Cost you the same for the brats as for them.'

'I don't want the boy. Only the girl called Tansy.' Zach could not take his eyes off Ruby who was watching him, her dark eyes flashing anger. He began searching carefully in his pockets for the gold he had brought with him. 'I'll take them now if you can make me the loan of a cart to take them to my property.'

'And which is your property?' Benson asked in a tone that suggested he did not believe Zach had any property.

Zach would have liked to have said it was none of the man's business. Instead, aware of Ruby's eyes on him, he said, 'Ailleurs,' thinking Elsewhere's name sounded grander in French.

'As I understood it, that belongs to a woman.'

'I'm her brother.' Zach did not like the feeling of intimidation that Benson created. He drew himself tall so that he was looking down on the man. 'Now, can you loan me a cart?'

Complaining that he did not know who would cook supper that night, Benson sent Nero off to the stables to bring round some transport. He then carefully counted the money Zach handed him. He counted it twice, finally reluctantly nodding agreement that the sum was correct.

'I wish you joy of them,' he said and stumped out of the kitchen.

'Why you not buyin' Joshua?' Truly demanded as soon as he had gone.

'Yes, why you not buyin' Joshua? And why you not takin' my baby?' Ruby hissed. She no longer looked provocative. She looked angry, standing with her arms folded across her breast, her very white teeth bared, her eyes sparking, like an animal at bay. There were two red patches high on her full cheeks. Zach did not answer the questions.

'Go and get your things, and the child, Tansy. It's time we left here,'

132

he ordered and turned his back on them both. He heard a long groan, almost a howl of anguish, from Ruby. The uncontrolled sound brought to mind the prospect of making her groan and cry for a different reason and he found himself excited. But he pushed the thought aside. He needed to think. He had to plot what lies he could tell Amelia when he returned home with this exotic woman for himself but no Joshua for her.

Joshua was hoeing between the rows of sweet potatoes in the kitchen gardens of Macabees when he heard Ruby calling him. She was running down the stone path, holding up her skirts so that he could see her thin legs. Her usual smile was missing and she looked distraught.

He dropped the hoe and ran towards her, surprised that as soon as they were close enough she flung herself into his arms, sobbing desperately.

'What is it?' he asked hugging her tightly. 'What's wrong?'

'I bein' sold,' she managed to gulp out. 'And Tansy. That big man, Zach, you tol' me 'bout he come to get us.'

He was bewildered and pushed her away from him gently. 'I don't understand,' he said. 'Zach? Amelia's brother? Come to buy you and Tansy? Why?'

'He come for Truly and Tansy. I think he were goin' to take you as well, but he changed his mind and took me instead. Benson tol' him 'bout Samuel and he said he don' want him either. He told Truly that her mama and 'Melia want her.'

Joshua was gradually taking it in. 'But not me?' he asked. 'They don't want me?'

'I don't know .' Ruby was wringing her hands. 'Benson seemed to think he wanted you, too, at the start but then the big man, he said no. Oh, Josh, what we go'n do?'

He stood silent, his head bent, taking in the fact that Amelia must be alive and well and that she had not forgotten Tansy. But he also had to accept the miserable fact that Amelia did not want him. She wanted Tansy and she wanted Truly, but not him. Did it mean Amelia did not dare have him near her because she was married to a white man? Or did it mean no more than that she had forgotten him? Or was it that she preferred not to remember him out of shame for what had happened between them? In the years they had been separated, had she learned to think as all the other white people thought?

'Where they takin' you?' he asked, his voice heavy.

'I don' know. Sounded like some place called Allyer. Some place I ain't never heard of. The big man said it be his sister's.'

Joshua was silent, trying to work out how Amelia could possibly own a plantation. She must be married, he decided. But how could she be free? The man who married her must have bought her from the Olivers. He felt hope. She would not love this man. She would have married him for her freedom.

'I don' want to be alone, without you,' Ruby was saying tearfully. 'And what Samuel go'n do without me? And what you go'n do on you own without us? I know why that big white man buying me. I know that look in they eyes. Oh, Josh, I been happy with you. Don' want to fuck with no more white men.'

Ruby would be right, Joshua thought. Zach would want her, just as he himself had wanted her the first time he saw her. Ruby was desirable. And exciting. He had never forgotten Amelia – how could he with Tansy there to remind him of her every day of his life? But he and Ruby had been content. Since they had been together, she had been faithful to him, ever passionate, sometimes too passionate, and she had kept her promise that their baby would not die. Their son, Samuel, was just three and as healthy as any slave child born to the deprivation of Macabees could be. He and Ruby and Truly had gone without food themselves to make sure of it. Ruby's big heart had room to love both Tansy and Samuel, though he noticed that she would go hungrier for her own son than for his daughter.

The thought of being wrenched apart from his family and left behind here to suffer the grim life of Macabees was like a mortal wound to the heart. Joshua loved his children and the thought of the break-up of the little family that he had managed to preserve in this hostile world filled him with the most intense grief and confusion he had ever experienced. And mixed with the grief was the impotent anger of a man unable to protect his own family. If Truly, Ruby and Tansy had been sold, there was nothing that he could do about it. If Amelia no longer loved him, he must accept that, too. But to take his daughter from him was the cruellest cut of all.

'Look after Samuel. Keep he safe,' she was saying, tears sliding down her cheeks. Her hands were clenched and in her grief she looked ugly. He had never seen her look ugly before.

'Listen,' he said wildly, 'I'll find you. I'll come to you. We'll all be together again, I promise it.'

'Oh, Josh,' she said sadly. 'How you go'n do that?'

He took her in his arms and they clung together.

'I go'n find a way,' he said huskily. 'Somehow. Don' you worry. Somehow.'

She looked up at him and managed a smile.

'P'haps you will, too. And I know Samuel safe with you.' She reached to kiss him hard and passionately. 'I love you, Josh, and don' you never forget it. Whatever happen, no matter how many white men make me fuck with them, it be you I love for always. I swear I never, never fuck another black man 'cept you. Never.' She sighed breathily. 'I go'n go now. I have to get Tansy and get our things together. Better if you don' come with me.'

She kissed him again, turned and ran back towards the slave huts. He stood staring after her helplessly. There must be something he could do. Harsh reality told him there was nothing. Automatically he picked up the hoe and began the mechanical task of turning the soil again. It was some minutes before he realised that he was crying.

Amelia sat under the shade of a tamarind tree where she had a clear view of the entrance to the drive to her home. Old Joseph had carried William's cradle down and placed it beside her, and while she waited she rocked him gently with her foot. At noon Bella came to join her and the two women, both apprehensive, sat waiting for something to happen, someone to arrive.

It was well gone noon when they saw the dust of a horse and cart rise in the clear air and then the cart itself rumbled into view. Zach was striding beside it, and in the back she could see only two figures. Both women. 'Where's Tansy?' she muttered to herself.

'Shush!' said Bella. 'It just that she be too little to be seen.'

But Joshua was not too small to be seen. Where was he? Dead? Her heart turned over and she found herself praying that he was not dead. She stood up, her hands clasped across her breasts, waiting, anxious, almost unable to breath with trepidation.

As the cart drew nearer a small child who appeared to be white leapt from the back.

'Just you come back here,' she heard a woman call, and it was a voice she had never heard before.

Bella was already lumbering as fast as she could towards the cart and Amelia saw Truly, a thinner, older Truly, jump down to run towards her mother. Zach, throwing down the reins, moved to where the child stood, looking about her. He picked her up and walked to where Amelia waited frozen to the spot.

'This is Tansy,' he said.

Slowly Amelia held out her arms. The child was staring at her with huge, dark, long-lashed eyes. She had a small pointed face with a full mouth, dark as a bruise, a narrow nose and rounded cheeks emerging from a cloud of dark brown curly hair that hung past her shoulders. Her skin? Not black, not brown, but not white. Perhaps yellow, as Bella had said so long ago. Golden.

Amelia smiled at the same moment as she felt tears begin to slide down her face. This was her daughter, her quite extraordinarily beautiful daughter, once lost and now found again. To her delight Tansy smiled too, a little tentatively, but it was definitely a smile.

'Oh, you beautiful little thing,' Amelia crooned, reaching to take her child in her arms. 'Oh, you wonderful child.'

Her daughter was all skin and bones in her arms. The child smelt bad, of unwashed clothes, and the garments she was wearing were near enough to being rags. At a closer look, they were not clothes at all, just strips of old linen tied round the girl to cover her.

She was aware that Truly and Bella were watching her. Both women had folded their arms as they stood shoulder to shoulder as if they were judging her in some private test they had concocted. They watched in

135

silence as the second woman jumped down from the cart and advanced towards where Amelia stood.

'She be my baby,' the woman said belligerently. 'And that man he done left my baby boy behind.'

Amelia stepped back for a moment against the fierce energy that emanated from the black woman. She was a good four inches taller and heavier and her hostility was almost tangible. Recovering composure, Amelia pulled herself to her full height and asked coldly: 'Zach, who is this slave?'

He was ill at ease.

'She's Ruby,' he said defensively. 'She says she's Tansy's mother.'

'If I ain't her mama, I don't know who is,' the woman hissed at Amelia. 'It be my milk that kept that gal alive. Where her mama what bore her when she need food, eh? Hidin' behind her white skin, I guess. Scared maybe her baby be black. Scared to say she fuck a black man.'

The scorn in her voice filled Amelia with rage at the injustice of it all. She hugged Tansy to her until the child wriggled and protested.

'What do you know about it?' She was finding it difficult not to shout. 'How can you possibly understand? How do you think I felt losing—'

'For God's sake be quiet, the pair of you,' Zach bellowed. He placed his heavy hand on Ruby's slender shoulder and spun her round. 'If you don't show respect I'll take you straight back to Macabees. And I never want to hear another word about whose baby is whose or I'll have you whipped until you can't stand.' He turned to Amelia and took Tansy from her arms.

'This child is just another slave. Truly, come here.'

Truly walked slowly towards the now silent group, her face expressionless. She looked older, her once glossy skin seemed to have a dusting of grey across it. She was stringier than before, but the sight of her calmed Amelia. She walked forward to meet the black girl and put her arms impulsively round her. Like Tansy, she was all skin and bones under the rough linen of her skirt and bodice.

'Truly, it's good to see you,' Amelia said. 'But where is Joshua?'

'Macabees.'

Amelia turned to look helplessly at Zach. 'Why?'

'Because that filthy old fop wouldn't part with him, that's why.' Zach was shouting and Amelia knew he always shouted when he was in the wrong.

Ruby pointed an accusing finger. 'When Benson asked if he wanted Joshua, that man there, he said no,' she said fiercely. 'He gone left my man behind.'

'Your man!' Amelia said.

'My man. Papa to my two chil'en. My man.' Ruby's stare was a challenge. She swung her hands on to her hips, pushed out her breasts, daring Amelia to disagree with her.

'God in heaven!' Zach groaned.

Bella joined the group. She pushed her way in until she was standing in the centre of them all.

'Now you just listen here,' she said threateningly. 'Time you all stopped to think what you doin' and sayin'. You,' she stabbed a stubby finger at Ruby, 'that gal-child ain't yor'n. Not in truth. That gal-child ain't truly ever go'n belong to no one. That child on its own, and all us can do is our best for she. And as for you, I tell you, you forgettin' your place. I don' know why you be here. This man,' she turned her thumb to Zach, 'perhaps he got ideas about you so he brung you here. But you got no call to give Mistress 'Melia here any of you sauce. She mistress of this house, and you be nothin' but a slave so don' you forget it and mind you tongue and keep you place.'

Ruby turned on her fiercely. 'And what you be but a slave? You don' have the right to speak to me—'

'I be no slave,' Bella retorted. 'I be the cook. I gets paid. I be free. And I tell you, you lucky to be here. You young folks, don' matter whether you black or white, you don' understand nothin'. You don' understand the way things is. I loves my son better than anything in the world, except perhaps my daughter Truly here, but I tell you, I glad he not here. This place be wrong for him for reasons that don' concern you, and you be wrong for him, too, with you sauce and you cheek. I knows you, gal. I knows your sort. Anyone keeps you out of trouble will do, that be the truth of it. Well, my son don' be like that. He don' be no one's man. My son his own man and I tell you, it better if you leave the brunging-up of his chil' to her grandma here.'

She turned to Amelia.

'That the way it go'n be, 'Melia,' she said in a voice gentler than Amelia had ever heard her use before. 'That baby gal gotta be brung up by her grandma. Me.'

'I want her working in the fields. I won't have her near the house.' Amelia was striding her drawing room in a fury that was making her cheeks scarlet, her eyes dark emerald and her hair rampant. 'How dare you. How dare you bring her here and leave Joshua and the others behind. Never, never will I let you have a share of Elsewhere. How could you do such a thing? How could you humiliate me so. In front of Bella, in front of Truly, in front of—'

'They were only people who knew already,' Zach ventured, so crushed by her anger that he seemed to have shrunk. Amelia turned on him again.

'Don't make stupid excuses, Zach. To have that – ' Amelia was lost for words, 'here on my own estate, claiming she is Tansy's mother, declaring that Joshua is her man. It's insupportable.'

It was obvious that Zach longed to lose his own temper, but he was in no position to do so.

'How was I to know?' he asked. 'I told you how confusing it all was. What with that grotesque man looking only at my crotch, how could I possibly think straight?'

'You rarely do,' Amelia said angrily.

'How was I to know that she had a boy by Joshua and that she had brought up Tansy? Is not my fault, Amelia, and you must stop blaming me.'

'Why did you bring the woman, Zachary?' She was standing still, arms folded, lips pursed. 'Tell me, why did you bring her here?'

The question was too direct for Zach to think up a lying answer.

'I wanted her,' he said simply.

'But you are just about to wed.'

'That means nothing. It's not the same thing. I want her.'

Amelia regarded him with undisguised disgust. 'Men!' she said.

'It's different for men,' he said stubbornly.

'God only knows why.' She sank into the large chair that stood by the empty hearth and sighed. 'They would not let you bring Bessie, Minta and Joshua?'

Now that he could fall into his prepared speech, Zach was more at ease. He visibly brightened.

'No. Vincent Ramillies said Joshua was too valuable to lose.'

'What about Bessie and Minta?'

'I don't know. He gave no reason.'

She gave him the sort of steady look that meant she did not believe him. 'You must go back and get them. Persuade him. Offer more money.'

Zach felt the sweat come out on his forehead. 'No. No. You don't understand. That place is evil, horrible. The man is evil. Nothing in the world would induce me to return there.'

This time he was telling the unvarnished truth and she was convinced. She sighed. 'What does Joshua do there?'

'Gardening, I imagine. But I don't think that was what the man meant.'

'What did you think he meant, Zach?' Her voice was weary.

'I don't know. Perhaps something . . . well, Vincent Ramillies is not married. Perhaps something like Justinian.'

'Nonsense!' She rose to her feet again, imperious with anger. 'You're lying. I always know when you're lying. You didn't bring them back for reasons of your own. Bessie and Minta because they know the truth about Tansy, Joshua because he knows the truth about Justinian. Were you afraid Joshua would betray you? How could he? A slave. And now you've created the most terrible of situations, bringing that woman here.' She made a dismissive gesture that had him moving backwards towards the door. 'Get yourself married and take the woman to Windsong and do what you like with her. Fuck her until you are blue in the face for all I care. But keep her out of my sight.'

He was hovering before the door. He drew a long breath for courage. 'I can have the paper drawn for the Olivers?' he asked tentatively.

'Just get out of here,' Amelia shouted, reaching for something to throw, as her oversized, underbrained brother vanished at speed.

She sat down again as the heavy door banged behind him, stared into her lap and attempted to recover her composure. As she calmed she told herself that though it had not worked out the way she had hoped, at least she had Tansy and Bella had Truly. Some progress had been made. But Joshua? Oh, if only Joshua were here. But how could he have betrayed her with that black harlot? She had betrayed him with Louis, she reminded herself. The sins of the flesh were hard to resist, but she had never sinned against him in her heart. Had it been the same for him?

The light was fading when she stood up, stretched and purposefully made her way to William's nursery to check that he was sleeping and well. She smiled as she leaned over the cradle where he snuffled in his sleep. The sight of him soothed her. Her temper gone, she made her way to the kitchen. She could hear Bella's voice from some way off and she could tell by the cadences that the cook was happy. She pushed open the door to see Bella sitting in a big wooden chair with Tansy on her lap. Truly was perched on the refectory table and there was no sign of Ruby. The scene was so close, so warm, that Amelia felt an intruder and heard herself say, 'Can I come in?'

'It be your kitchen,' Bella said with a squeal of laughter. 'We all just gettin' 'quainted again. Me and my grandchil' and that daughter o' mine.'

Amelia sighed and sat near the stove, holding her hands towards the warmth. She felt surprisingly cold.

'What you needs is a glass of claret,' Bella told her.

'Why don't we all have a glass of claret?' Amelia suggested wearily. 'We should celebrate.'

Bella heaved herself to her feet and dumped Tansy into Amelia's lap.

'You hold her for a whiles,' she said as she moved towards the barrel and took down some glasses from the dresser, 'but not for long. You go'n have to give her up again. You go'n have to forget she yourn. All that this afternoon weren't no good. Now that Ruby she go'n start thinkin' maybe Tansy yourn and that bad.'

'Ruby knows,' Truly said suddenly. 'Joshua never stopped telling her how he loved Amelia best. It hurt her. That's why she was so fierce today. She was hurt. Ruby's good. She's kind and good and she saved Tansy's life. That chil' was near to death when Ruby took her.'

'That's as may be,' said Bella, 'but that black gal ain't no right to sauce Miss 'Melia. But you go'n have to keep you peace, Miss 'Melia. We go'n have to decide what we go'n do with that little one there you holdin'.'

Amelia's spirits had lifted at Truly's words. Joshua loved her best. She looked down at the daughter they had created between them. The child's eyes were half-closed, and a small light-brown thumb was between the dark lips, turning them into a soft circle. She felt love so strong that it was almost physical.

'Will you have her with you, Bella? In your room?' she asked. 'I won't ask Truly. I remember how she felt when she saw how white she is.'

'Huh!' Truly said, her voice violent. 'I got one of my own like that now.'

'What you saying?' Bella demanded.

'I got one, too. Near to white. A boy.'

'But where is he?' Amelia asked. 'Why didn't you bring him with you?'

'Cause I don' want him.' Truly looked close to tears. 'I hate that baby and I hate his father. I don' ever want to see neither of them again.'

Bella's great bulk was rising in wrath. 'Do I hear my own daughter saying she hate her own chil'?' she demanded.

'Yes, Mama, you do.' Truly was standing to face her mother. 'I hates everything about him. He be here because his father raped me.'

'Joshua's father raped me, but I don' hate that boy. Don' be his fault.'

'The sins of the fathers . . .' Truly said grimly.

'I don' understand.'

'Amelia does. It was she taught me. The sins of the fathers, they get visited on the children.'

'I don' understand,' Bella repeated stubbornly.

Amelia was stroking Tansy's wild curls. 'I don't want anything like that ever to happen to my daughter here,' she said. 'We've got to keep her safe.'

Bella looked doubtful. 'We can try,' she said.

'Trying don' be no good,' Truly said passionately. 'Not if you be a woman. Look at me, I be plain. I be no beauty, and yet Benson, he want me. I don' understand it, never have. He was with Ruby and she don' care about him fucking her every night. You right about her, Mama. She use men the way they used us three women here. Fucking don' mean nothing to Ruby. She fuck anyone if it do her good and keep things sweet.'

'There's a word for women like that,' Amelia said darkly. But Truly took no notice of the interruption. She had left them, gone away somewhere they could not follow. Her eyes stared ahead, her hands were clenched into fists, she just kept on talking in a flat, expressionless monotone which made the horror of what she was recounting harder to bear.

'Benson got bored with her, and Benson wanted me. Fresh flesh, Ruby called it. He wanted fresh flesh to fuck and he took me from the slave cabins and put me into his. He'd never done that with Ruby because she had to be cook. But he tol' me that all I had to do was look after him. The master didn't even know I was there on the plantation so if I didn't do right by Benson and one day I weren't there no more, weren't no one who would miss me or know what happened to me. I had to cook for him, clean for him, wash his clothes, do everythin' for him. He gave a funny sort of smile when he said do everythin'. I knew what he meant, and I was afraid.'

140

'You lived in his cabin?' Bella asked, amazed. 'My!'

'I don' want to live in his cabin. I knew what it mean. That night he come home early. I got him food, he ate it and then he grunted and told me to clear up. I made washin' the dishes last as long as I could, and I stayed out there in that kitchen. But he come after me. He ain't got a stitch of clothing on, and he white and hairy and horrible, looking like he had a truncheon sticking out of him. I shut my eyes so's not to see. Sight of him made me sick, but he ordered me to his bedroom. Mama, I was so scared, my knees they were near to knockin' and my hands, they wouldn't stay still.

'I turn my back on him and got busy with shinin' a pan. "I not go'n in you bedroom," I said to him. "Kitchen's my place." He tried to grab at me and I ran round the kitchen table so he couldn't get me. It weren't no good. He just push that table till it held me tight against the wall and I pinned like a fish on a hook. Then he got hold of my arms and drag me across the table. Hurt so bad I wanted to scream, but I weren't go'n give him the pleasure. Then he just grab my hair and he pull me, across the kitchen and down the hall into his bedroom. Ma, I 'shamed I screamed so bad. Not got much hair best of times, but most of it be in his hand by the time he throw me on his bed.

' What made it worse, he was laughin'. All the time he was laughin'. He kept calling me a hell-cat and laughin' some more. "Scream, scream," he kept sayin' as he hurt me. He knocked me clear cross the room when I wouldn't scream no more. My teeth they rattle in my head. I fought him back then. I kicked that truncheon of his and his balls and that made him yell sure 'nuff. I scratched him. I clawed his face. Just once or twice I made him grunt a little but most time he kept on laughin', while he got my clothes off, rippin' 'em until I mother-naked like him. He held my arms back against the pillow and he put his filthy, stinking body on my legs. I couldn't move. I couldn't breath and then he started bitin' at me. He bit my breasts and my mouth and my ears till I was bleedin' like to die. My blood all over his bed and I thinkin' that it me got to wash it off and me got to mend my clothes again. And all the time he just keep laughin' until he ready to push that truncheon right in me, tearin' me apart. Then I scream like he wanted me to. I screamed murder 'cause that what it felt like. But he just kept goin' up and down in me, hurtin' me everywhere and hissin' at me, "You black bitch, you black bitch, I'll tame you, black hellcat." He did that, Mama, every night of my life for round six months. Then I made myself get clever. I stopped fighting him. I let him think I liked his filthy great truncheon pumpin' me. Then it weren't no fun for him any more and he found some new fresh flesh and sent me back to the slave cabin.'

She stopped, stared defiantly at Bella and Amelia before emptying her glass of wine in one swallow. 'And you reckon I ought to love a baby I got that way? No, Ma, I can't do that. I hate that child much as I hate Benson and that the truth of it.'

There was a long silence. Both Amelia and Bella's eyes were damp.

141

'Poor little boy,' Bella whispered. 'Who got him now?'

'How 'bout poor me?' Truly's voice was sullen. 'That boy all right. That Benson keep him like a puppy dog. He be his pet. Ruby fed him when I couldn't bear to touch him. Ruby'd feed the world if she could. And Benson likes the boy 'cause he not be too black. He even tell people he be his son.'

'What's his name?' Amelia asked.

'He don' have no name. He gets called Noname. Benson think that funny.'

'Poor little boy,' Bella sighed again. She rose and filled their glasses with claret again. 'He still be my gran'chil,' she said. 'No matter who his daddy be.'

The three women were silent. Amelia wanted to say something comforting, but Truly's description of her ordeal with Benson had brought back with horrible clarity the memory of the night when Matthew Oliver had come to the slave cabins to find her for the same purpose. The silence was becoming oppressive when they were spared from speaking by a sudden clatter of booted feet outside the kitchen.

It was Zach who burst in, pulling on his frock coat, bareheaded with curls growing tight to his head. Zach was rarely seen without his wig. Something was wrong.

'There you are,' he said breathlessly. 'I have to go. Word has just come from Windsong that Matthew Oliver is dead.'

Chapter Nine

'Who would have dreamed it?' Ben shook his head and laughed out loud. 'Zach marrying the Olivers' daughter! Do you think that from wherever he has gone, Matthew Oliver now knows the truth of what happened to his son? By God, he won't rest easy if he does.'

'He doesn't deserve to rest easy,' Amelia said as she stirred sugar into her tea. 'But it's fortunate for Zach that he did die. Matthew had his suspicions about a lot of things concerning Zach.' She grimaced. 'Elizabeth was so anxious to get her hands on Elsewhere that she never asked a single question as far as I know. She might not have been so eager had she known that I wasn't letting that happen and that Zach was leading her on. Nor could she guess that Matthew would succumb to a fever and will the entire estate to Charlotte. And though I don't care for Elizabeth, it is unjust since in truth the property is hers and always was. Maybe now Charlotte will be able to wriggle out from under her mother's thumb. Since Charlotte and Zach have married, with indecent haste considering how recently her father died, to all intents and purposes Windsong belongs to Zach.'

'And so it should. All property belongs to the husband, and quite rightly,' Ben said, sanctimoniously, Amelia thought. 'Property and the management of it is man's work.'

Amelia smiled at him sweetly. 'Which is why I shall never marry again,' she informed him. 'I do not propose to lose what property is now mine.'

Ben's face fell and he was silent. The noise of laughter and tipsy singing came from the tavern outside the room where they sat. They had come straight from Windsong and both were still in their wedding finery. There was to be a ball later in the evening, but Amelia had declined to stay, excusing herself as being too recently out of mourning to enjoy their festivities. Windsong brought back too many bad memories. She found difficulty in being a guest in a house where she had been obliged to empty the hostess's chamberpot. She had been angered to find that Jake was a wedding guest but had kept her face impassive when she was aware of Elizabeth's sly glance to see her reaction to his presence. She did not wish to be in the same room with either of them and left immediately after the wedding feast. Zach had escorted her to where Pierre waited with her carriage.

'Must you go?' he asked as he helped her up into her seat.

143

'I would not choose Jake for company,' she said.

He had the grace to look ashamed. 'He's a good overseer,' he said, an apologetic note in his voice. 'And he's frightened of me. He remembers what I did to him once before. I can keep him in order.'

But you won't do that, Amelia thought, knowing that the less the estate owner knew what their overseers did, the happier everyone was.

Ben had stood up for Zach in church that morning and Amelia knew that he had been moved by the brief ceremony. Ever since, he had been regarding her with cow eyes and had insisted that she return to the tavern to take tea with him. It was quite obvious on which route his thoughts were directed.

'I had hoped that one day you and I . . .' he began.

'Ben,' she said lightly and leaned to put her finger over his lips. She laughed as she drew away from him again. 'Is the attraction that if we were wed you would own the tavern?'

'That is unjust indeed,' he bristled, full of indignation. 'It's not the tavern I want. You know I have always loved you.'

'And I love you,' she said gently, 'but not as a husband.'

'You have become hard, Amelia.' He stood, arms crossed, his back to the open fireplace, his red hair curling down over his shoulders. In height he barely reached the mantel, but his lively face was handsome enough. She looked at him and sighed.

'We have all been forced to become hard,' she said.

'Women should not be hard.'

'Women should not be slaves, or whipped, or raped, or have their children snatched from them.'

'But you refused to join Elsewhere with Windsong as you had promised. You could have spoilt Zach's chances of a good marriage.'

'Zach and I had an agreement and he broke it. I was no longer obliged to share my property with him.'

He made an impatient gesture. 'That is not Zach's view of it. And why do you refuse to sell me the tavern? A tavern should not belong to a woman.'

'This one always has, remember?' she said. 'But in time it will be William's, along with everything else I own. I will not decimate his inheritance. Why do you complain? You have the tavern, you pay no rent, you have the profits and are becoming a rich man. What more can you ask?'

'For you to marry me,' he said. 'Amelia, please think about it. We are two of a kind. We have shared the same terrible experiences. We know each other, indeed we are cousins. We have much in common and I love you. I have always loved you, since the days when we played together as children at Quick Manor. You say you do not love me in that way, but I do not believe that you loved Louis in that way and yet you married him. You married him for security, of that I am sure. Together we could make our own security. We would be a fine partnership, you and I. And what you lack in love for me, I will make up with my love for you.'

She shook her head. 'Ben, I cannot. I am sorry. But no.'

'You're still in love with that black,' he said angrily. 'Why don't you forget him? You will bring disgrace on us all.'

'There is no disgrace in loving.' Her voice was cold and she was gathering up her shawl. 'Ben, I must go. I have much to do at the plantation.' Then she suddenly stopped as if she had remembered something and said with a mischievous note in her voice, 'But tell me. How is Marie?'

He turned bright scarlet and shuffled his small feet uneasily. 'She is a very good cook,' he said.

'And that makes you,' she paused, 'happy?'

'Her food is popular with the customers.'

'And she is popular with you?'

He shook his head, threw up his hands and reluctantly laughed. 'Amelia!' he said. 'You miss nothing.'

'And you could do worse.'

'No. For me it is you or no one. But as you say, she keeps me happy.'

The anger between them had evaporated. They hugged and Amelia found herself wishing she could love him. It would all be so wonderfully tidy. But he was just her dear cousin, nothing more, nothing less. She held his hand as he led her out through the busy tavern to where Pierre waited.

'Will you come to Elsewhere soon?' she asked.

'Perhaps,' he said, 'but I am kept busy here.'

She nodded. 'Then I must come to see you. God be with you, Ben.' She made a little salute and turned towards home.

It had been a strange wedding, she thought, Zach and Charlotte barely able to hide their triumph at what they had achieved, the newly-widowed Elizabeth unable to disguise her fury, her face set, a lodger in her own home and yet still making her displeasure felt that Elsewhere and Windsong were not one. Amelia felt out of sorts with them all. Zach sulked because she had retained complete control of Elsewhere, Ben did love her but wanted to own the tavern and accused her of being hard because she would not part with it. Men did not wish women to have any independence, she thought, and felt another positive twinge of sympathy for the odious Elizabeth. It was better to live alone and be free. And she had no need of a man except for those importunate desires of the body. She had her memories of Joshua and Louis, both cruelly taken from her, and she had William and now Tansy as a legacy from each of them. She believed those who ran her home did care about her. Then she laughed at herself. She sounded like Elizabeth and every other despotic planter, convinced they were loved by their slaves. At least within her home only Truly and Tansy did not have freedom, so those who worked for her were free to love her or leave her.

Elsewhere was quiet. Most of her staff had gone to Windsong to help prepare and serve the wedding feast and would stay the night there, returning in the morning. She went first to the nursery where William was sound asleep in his cradle. She dropped a light kiss on his forehead and made her way to the kitchen to describe to Bella the day's events.

'So you be home,' Bella greeted her. 'S'pose you want somethin' to eat?'

'No. The tables were groaning at the wedding feast and I took tea at the tavern with Ben. But a glass of claret would be welcome.'

She settled herself at the kitchen table as Bella stumped to the barrel, holding two glasses.

'Charlotte did look exceedingly pretty,' Amelia said. 'And Zach was so pleased with himself.'

'For a slave he sure done well.' Bella's face was one large grin. 'And when you comes to think about it, it just as well he murdered Master Justinian.'

'Shhh!' Amelia was alarmed. 'We must forget that.'

'I not go'n forget.' The grin had vanished. Bella's expression had become obstinate. 'That be something it p'haps useful to know one day.'

Amelia looked sharply at the black woman, even more alarmed. Now Bella's face was bland and guileless but her eyes were black pinpoints of mischief.

'Ruby, she not be coming back from Windsong, eh?' Bella was asking.

'No, she's not coming back,' Amelia said forcefully, concerned at the direction this conversation was taking. Bella had some axe to grind. She was a servant, but never acted like one. She had been too close to Amelia for too long and knew far too much about the Quicks. She had, in fact, become one of the family if only by proxy. It was the custom for slaves to call themselves by their master's name, but Bella had refused to answer to Bella Oliver. Now she was free she needed a surname. She had elected to call herself Quick. She announced that she and all her family would be known as Quick. Amelia had been pleased. It meant that Tansy would bear her name. She herself had decided to add Quick to her married name. She'd never felt quite comfortable as Madame Rosier; it seemed to her that the title rightfully belonged to Louis' first wife. She and William were Rosier-Quick.

Bella was taking a hearty swig from her glass of claret.

'Tansy cry hersel' to sleep 'cause Ruby not comin' back,' she said thoughtfully. 'By all 'counts that Ruby be a good slave. If Master Zachary go'n keep her, I reckons we ought to have one of his slaves in exchange.'

Amelia's heart had lurched at the thought of Tansy crying herself to sleep but she was not going to show how wounded she was. Instead she said crossly, 'Bella, what is it you want? What are you after? Stop playing games with me.'

Bella chuckled. 'What make you think I wants som'thin'?'

Amelia said nothing but gave her a steely look.

'You be right,' Bella sighed. 'But it not me that wants som'thin'. It Truly.'

'What does Truly want?'

Bella pursed her lips and then announced, 'Truly in love.'

'Oh!' Amelia was delighted. 'With whom?'

'That big black houseman at Windsong. Daniel. I swear he the blackest man I ever see. My Truly always like him when she be little. These few weeks while she be goin' to Windsong to help for the weddin', he find he like her, too. What she say was that she like to stay there, like Ruby go'n do, so she and her Daniel be together.'

'But Mistress Oliver wouldn't have her,' Amelia said. 'She never liked Truly. She was always a little afraid of her. And Truly's better off here.'

'That exactly what I tol' my Truly. "Ain't no good go'n back," I said to her. " 'Sides that Mistress Oliver, she won' have you. And maybe one day you get you freedom if you stay at Elsewhere." That what I said to her.'

Amelia was beginning to catch Bella's drift. Ignoring the hint about freedom she said, 'So you want me to exchange Ruby for Daniel?'

'Seem like a good idea to me. I reckons that Master Zach he be able to fix it. And if Daniel be here with you, like Truly be here with you, they go'n live like a real two people. What you think, 'Melia?' Having spoken, the black woman turned so that Amelia could not see her face.

Bella only ever used Amelia's name at important moments. Before Amelia herself was freed Bella always called her 'gal'. These days she tried to avoid calling her mistress anything. If Bella had forced herself to say Amelia, this was obviously the most serious of requests and something that really mattered.

'You want them to be a family.'

Bella turned square to face her, and her eyes were full of unshed tears. 'Yes, that's what I wants for my child'n,' she said. 'Family like it be in Africa, and like it be for white people here. Proper life. Don' matter they not got much if they be free and they be together. Can't get it for Joshua, but now there some chance for Truly.'

She stopped and waited for some response, impatiently wiping her eyes. Amelia knew that she would do exactly what Bella wanted. She would exchange Ruby (and glad to see the back of her) for Daniel (and glad to have him). But she baulked a giving them both freedom. Why, she did not quite understand herself. She was able to tell herself that there was little point in giving them freedom, except that Truly would be paid a small sum for her labours. But the problem was that if Truly and her Daniel were free, they could go where they chose. They might leave Elsewhere. Truly, Bella and Tansy had become a substitute family and Amelia did not wish to lose any of them. Free or not, Bella would never leave Elsewhere, of that she was sure, but Truly with her independent spirit might just prefer to go hungry in the town than live in the safety of the plantation where she had once been a slave. Better if things remained as they were for her and Daniel. And besides, it was important that Bella did not win too easily. Bella could be altogether

147

too domineering, though she had never before threatened to use her knowledge of Zach's past.

'It wasn't necessary for you to bring up the subject of Justinian,' Amelia as said sternly as she could. 'I would have bought Daniel for you and for Truly. You only had to ask. But since you did mention Justinian, there is a condition to my bringing Daniel here. You must swear to me on your children's lives that never, never again will you mention the manner of Justinian's death, nor will you try to use that knowledge for your own gain as you did just now.'

'Weren't for my gain,' Bella muttered. 'I ask it for Truly.'

It seemed as if Bella had not spotted the flaw in Amelia's argument.

'But do you swear to me you won't do it again?'

Suddenly Bella grinned. 'S'pose I say no?'

Or had she?

'Daniel stays where he is,' Amelia said firmly.

'And s'pose I say I go'n tell Mistress Charlotte 'bout what happen to Master Justinian unless you brings Daniel here?' She threw back her head and chortled. 'You and me, we be as locked together as the lid and the bottom of Mistress Charlotte's jewel box. But no mind. I go'n swear for you on my child'n's lives, if that's what you wants. Don' matter no way if I do swear. Truly still know the truth and she can tell what happened – unless you be making her swear, too, but you knows how stubborn that Truly be.'

Bella had not been fooled. She was never fooled and Amelia found herself laughing, if ruefully, with her opponent.

'Forget it, Bella,' she said, throwing up her hands lightly, as if throwing away something insignificant. 'No promises. It would be better if we just started trusting each other.'

'Guess trust be the best way, 'Melia,' Bella said solemnly. 'And I sure trusts that you bring that Daniel to Elsewhere.'

'I'll bring him,' she said, determined that she would do so. It wasn't until some hours later that she realised she was the one making all the promises.

After the last guests had left the wedding feast and the ball was over, Zach sat alone in the library at Windsong, a glass of fine brandy in his hand, mentally surveying the property that had, by hazard, so suddenly become his. His bride had gone to prepare herself, his indignant mother-in-law had retired to her chamber, leaving Zach to reflect on the twists and turns of uncertain fate that had led him to becoming the husband of one of the wealthiest women on the island of St Kitts.

He found himself confronted by one difficulty. He was beginning to realise that it was the estate that had made Charlotte seem attractive. Now the estate was his, her attractions had paled. Even so, in about half an hour's time he would be expected to make love to her. Indeed, if he wanted an heir to all that he had achieved he would have to make love to her.

The slaves were clearing up after the ball and he wandered out into the big open hallway where he saw Ruby walking away from him, carrying a tray laden with glasses on her head. It seemed like a dangerous thing to do, but she walked with straight-backed confidence towards the kitchen, both hands free, her behind swaying lasciviously. The two round high cheeks outlined under her skimpy skirt seemed to be beckoning to him. She was like a force of nature. Her effect on him every time he saw her was as startling as an unexpected clap of thunder. The blood rose in him as she disappeared out of sight and he found himself comparing her with his languid, silly, spoilt wife, and knew which of the two he would rather be bedding that night.

He went back into the library and poured himself another brandy. He had found that he could now recognise Ruby's footsteps from those of the other slaves. Hers were crisper, lighter, as if she bounced rather than walked. The very sound put him in a fever. The girls that Ben employed in the house next door to the tavern which he, Zach, had bought after the earthquake were skilled enough and took care of his needs whenever they became pressing, but he was sure that Ruby would provide unthought-of erotic delights, extremes of sensuous pleasure that he had never experienced. And upstairs waited Charlotte.

He drank brandy and then took himself, heavy-footed, up the wide staircase to where his bride waited in the same bedchamber and same four-poster bed where nearly five years ago he had had his one and only encounter with her brother.

Charlotte was also in a fever, but of anticipation. She was twenty-one years old, and all she knew of love was what she had overheard of the women slaves' talk of fucking. As small as she had been when they whispered and giggled, disregarding her presence in the belief that she was too young to understand, she knew that this was a bad word and not to be used but that it meant the ultimate act between a man and a woman.

'Fucking, fucking, fucking,' she whispered to herself once her maid had gone from the room, wondering what it would be like. Would it hurt? Would she really faint as she had pretended to do when Zach kissed her? She had wanted to cling to him, rub herself against him, let him touch her where he would. She had wanted him to fuck her, and that was shameful and wrong.

Yet the slaves seemed to enjoyed it. They laughed when they spoke of it, rolling their dark eyes, making bawdy remarks which her mother would have had them whipped for had she overheard. Black girls sighed and moaned when they remembered and recounted the pleasures of lying with the man they loved, but of course, Charlotte told herself, slaves were not far removed from animals. White women were more spiritual, more reserved and modest. Black people had little else to please

149

them. Fucking, they said, was free and they were free when they fucked. What was surprising was that, considering how primitive they were, they were faithful to each other, just as she would always be faithful to Zach.

Her mother, of course, would never speak of anything so coarse. The few mentions she had ever made of love between a man and a woman had subtly given Charlotte the impression that a true lady did not enjoy lovemaking. Her mother's opinion was that in polite white society love was no more than a wifely duty that a woman must endure. And yet it was a duty that Charlotte found herself eager to embrace. The very thought of Zach made her burn at the pit of her stomach and gave her strange longings that she did not entirely understand, though her own exploring fingers in the privacy of her bedroom discovered the body changes that desire could bring about.

It troubled her that those feelings lacked the spirituality of the romantic love she had learned from Shakespeare and a little book of Herrick's poetry. It troubled her also that her fantasies were so much earthier than the sonnets and verses she knew by heart. Her fantasies were not so much of a sweet disorder in the dress, but of Zach stripping her slowly of her silks, of seeing him naked, of feeling him close, and it needed no more than her imagination to bring about those wonderful hot feelings which, once they rolled in her, she tried to sustain. She did not want them to slip away and wondered if the real thing would hold the feelings longer and stronger.

But would her body please him? She inspected herself in the long glass that stood near the window. Her ball gown was flung across the small velvet-covered day bed which stood under the window and her maid had laid out her white damask nightgown but for the moment she wore only her petticoat. She stroked her white shoulders with a lingering hand, lifted her breasts lightly from beneath and then slowly undressed, watching herself in the mirror as silk slid rustling over her hips to make a pale patch on the carpet of her room.

She stood naked, smoothing her hands over the flat belly above the fluff of blonde hair that hid the rise of the mount of Venus. Her breasts were small, pink-tipped but darkened with anticipation. Should she put on the nightgown, or wait for him naked? No, that would be too bold. He might think her wanton, and yet that was what she longed to be. She wanted to spread herself on the four-poster, naked as the day she had been born, pull the curtains round her so that when he came to their bridal chamber he would pull back the draperies and find her ready for his love, white legs parted, ready to enjoy his manhood, breasts proud for him to caress, blonde hair loose on the pillow, arms outstretched to pull him to lie along the length of her. Perhaps it would be better with just a wisp of silk, as Venus wore, to cover that pale fluff of hair and the entrance it concealed so that he could strip it away from her waiting body and see and feel how wet and wanting she was.

But that would be behaving like the slave girls. He would not expect

150

that of her. He might even think that he was not the first to enter her while the truth was that all these years she had been saving herself for him. She had known it the minute she first saw him. It would not be right to behave like a harlot. She must control herself until they knew each other better, and then they would share musky kisses and she would explore his body until she knew it as well as her own.

But tonight she must be shy, shrinking, reluctant to lose her virginity for fear that he would receive the wrong impression of her virtue. But she sighed as she braided her hair before taking the nightgown from where it lay and slipping it over her head. She folded back the bed covers, slid between the sheets and pulled them back up to her chin. Then she lay, waiting for her husband to come to her.

Zach lay staring into the stuffy darkness. The curtains were drawn round the bed and beside him his bride sobbed quietly. He could not think what in the name of God she was crying about. If anyone should be shedding tears it was him tied to this frosty, unyielding lump of soft flesh. He thought of the girls at Ben's and their eager responses. They were being paid for their responses, true, but surely a wife should be able to bring the same ardour to her marriage bed as a whore who felt nothing for the man she caressed? What was the matter with the woman?

He had done his best to please her, but at every touch, every kiss, she had half-swooned and withdrawn from him with soft cries of fear. Eventually he had lost patience. It was better with whores or with women whose permission was unasked. In a lather of frustration, he had slammed into her, ignoring her cries of pain, and emptied himself into this vessel that was legally his.

It was then she began to cry, and making no attempt to console her, he lay sulking at her side, full of indignation that this first coupling with his wife had been such a disappointment. Eventually her sobs became hiccuping sniffles, and then they too went away and he could tell by her breathing that she slept.

Carefully so as not to wake her he slid from the bed. Beyond the bed curtains, moonlight was flooding the room. He crept to find his clothes, but she did not stir, just sighed and mumbled in her sleep.

He dressed swiftly and not bothering with his wig walked lightly across the room and through the door, closing it gently beside him. He was going to look for Ruby.

PART II

Chapter Ten

February 1705

It had been three weeks now since Tansy had been given her own room at Elsewhere. Mistress Amelia had suddenly and brusquely said that at seventeen she was too old to share with her grandmother any more and that it was time that Bella had some peace and quiet.

It was only a small room in the attic. Nevertheless, it was a private room, with a proper if broken-down bed and some old furniture and a looking glass. Her acquisition of this not very desirable room caused great resentment among the other slaves. But Tansy was used to others' jealousy. She had suffered from people's envy from the time she was a small girl.

She was convinced that her fellow slaves would have liked her better and her life would have been pleasanter had she not been so white. As a child, though her skin had been pale, it was obvious that she had black blood. As she grew older she seemed to become whiter. True her mouth was too full by white standards and her hair very black and curly. But it was not fuzzy. Only when she pulled it back tight against her head did the African heritage show in little springing single hairs like wires that stood out round her head, catching the light. But when her wild mass of hair was let loose, these fierce little hairs disappeared into its depth. Her eyes and her skin were light olive, and her nose, though perhaps a centimetre too broad, was straight and small. Mistress Amelia said she could have been born Portuguese.

Being so white had brought her privileges. She became Mistress Amelia's personal maid when she was ten years old, but before that the mistress had spent at least two hours a day with her, teaching her to read and write and to speak properly. It seemed that this was much frowned on by other whites and it had caused problems with the house and garden slaves. Tansy had been obliged to switch between two idioms of speech: the patois of her fellow slaves and the speech of an educated white. The only other slave who could do the same thing was her aunt, Truly, though Truly's white talk was not so practised.

Mistress Amelia also taught her to sew and embroider. She had been allowed to use the harpsichord in the drawing room and found she had a talent for music. She was also given free access to the library where she devoured any book that gave her a picture of Europe and life in that very different continent so far away.

She was about nine when she began to question her colour. Grandma

Bella was black as could be. So was Aunt Truly. The woman whom she dimly remembered as her mother was boldly black and her fading memories of her father were of a brown-skinned man.

She asked her grandmother the reason.

'It because you father be half-white,' Bella told her. 'His pappy be white.'

But she would explain no further even when Tansy pressed with questions about who her white grandfather was.

Yet her pale skin did not trouble her greatly, except for the confusion it sometimes wrought in her. Her trips to Basse-Terre and Old Road Town with her mistress had given her the opportunity to see that there were many pale-skinned blacks on the island. And she noted that they were more likely to be free than their darker brethren. She felt dimly that she would like to be free herself, and yet for what? She had her own room, she was well-fed, well-clothed in comparison to the others. It would be pleasant to have money to spend, but she was not sure on what she would spend it. She accepted that she had been separated from her parents though a vivid memory remained of the night when her mother was taken from her. She had got over it quickly enough. Everyone knew that slaves were not permitted real family.

Secretly she felt she had real family. Not her Aunt Truly and Uncle Daniel who barely spoke to her, but her wonderful, big fat grandmother who gave the same comfort as an oversized cushion. And she felt, though she would never have voiced the feeling, that 'Melia, as the slaves called her, had been both mother and father to her. She was certain that 'Melia loved her. No words on the subject had ever been spoken, but Tansy felt the love as something she could reach out and stroke. It seemed to Tansy that her mistress had never made any difference in her personal treatment of her and her son, William. As she grew older she put it down to the fact that since she was so nearly white perhaps Amelia regarded her as the daughter she had never had.

She and William had played together as children; as a baby he had often been left in her care and they had always been the best of friends. He was a quiet, gentle boy with smooth, dark hair and a sallow skin. Amelia said he was the image of his father who had been killed in one of the island's many skirmishes between the French and the English. William was inclined to be too perfect, too well-behaved. What little mischief he did get into was instigated by Tansy, and she always had the impression that Amelia was secretly pleased when her son did do something naughty or defiant that showed he had some spirit.

William enjoyed his lessons too much to get into any real trouble. He could always be found with his nose in a book. He would much rather read than play games and sometimes Tansy grumbled that best friend or not, he could be a dull companion. He never rebelled against the strictness of his tutors who had been brought out from England since he was five years old. Not that any of them stayed very long. They had an unfortunate habit of dying of a fever or finding the climate insupportable and rushing back to Europe as fast as they could.

The last one, a Mr Jott, had stayed less than a year before suddenly making up his mind to return home. He had been convinced that the climate 'would do for him' if he did not escape immediately and he had gone in a lather of impatience, refusing to give Amelia any chance of replacing him before he departed. There had been a four-month gap when the fourteen-year-old William had been without lessons. But yesterday Joseph had been dispatched to Basse-Terre to meet the new tutor, a Mr Henleigh, who had arrived as a passenger on one of the trading schooners.

Tansy had seen his arrival and thought that he looked as she imagined Hamlet might. Mark Henleigh was tall but with slightly stooped shoulders as if he had spent too long over his books. He did not wear a wig, and his own hair was as yellow as a lemon and yet his eyes were dark grey. She could make out the skeleton beneath his thin features, sharp chin, broad cheekbones and a high, sloping forehead. His clothes were elegant but shabby, his expression melancholy and he did not look very healthy. She had her doubts that he would stay long, indeed live long, but he was a great improvement on Mr Jott who was old, grey and a fusspot.

'Have you seen the new tutor?' Amelia asked Tansy as she laid out riding clothes the following morning.

Tansy nodded. 'He doesn't look very strong,' she said. 'He's very thin. And he looks sad.'

Amelia sighed. 'I hope he will stay. All these changes are so bad for William's education. But this man comes much recommended by Mr Lockett.' Lockett was Elsewhere's agent in London. 'But as Mr Lockett points out, the choice is not great. Few want to risk their health in the islands. When even the plantation owners refuse to live here for fear of their lives, it is understandable that others will not come. There's talk that even those at Macabees are considering leaving the estate in the hands of an agent. More and more return to Europe and it is not good for the islands. There's no substitute for proper management by an owner.' She sighed again. 'However, it's good that Mr Henleigh is arriving at the best time of the year. Perhaps the sunshine and the soft breezes will do him good and build up his strength before the heat arrives.'

Tansy looked out of the window to where a blue sky reigned over a few puffballs of clouds and wondered why anyone would want to live anywhere other than St Kitts. From the window she could see the turquoise sea in the distance and, nearer, the woodlands that abutted onto the side of the house, woodlands that were constantly cut for fuel for the sugar-refining boilers as well as for fencing and buildings. Elsewhere had its own orchard of citrus and tropical fruits on the other side of the house. The trees grew by the banks of a fast-running stream which tumbled from the mountains and provided the estate's water

157

supply. Amelia was planning to harness the water to create a watermill.

Tansy, who had never had to do any of the manual labour which kept the estate running and profitable, loved Elsewhere though she had never been further than the house and garden. The slave quarters and the factory yard were forbidden to her, though she and William were permitted to play on the beach. As curious as she was about Europe, she did not think that anywhere could be as beautiful as Elsewhere, and sometimes, when she said so, Amelia would laugh and say that she might be right.

It was a perfectly kept plantation. The gardens and the house were walled by a thick hedge of exotic bushes, all chosen for their brilliantly coloured leaves or flowers. Well beyond this hedge were the red-brick buildings where the bookkeeper and overseers lived and had their offices. Even further from the house was the factory yard where the sugar was brought from the fields to the mills to be refined. There, too, were the neatly-built workshops where the skilled slaves made the hogsheads that held the refined sugar. They also made furniture and dealt with repairs to the house and factory equipment. The estate had its own blacksmiths and coopers, all black. There was a small distillery where the sugar residue of thick, sticky molasses that ran from the perforated bottoms of the hogsheads was gathered and made into rum. Furthest away from the main house were the thatched quarters for more than a hundred slaves and the provision grounds where their food was grown and where Tansy was forbidden to go. Completely surrounding the big house were three hundred acres of the purply-yellow sugar cane. There was also pasture for mules and cattle. With a subsidiary crop of cotton and another of corn, both grown near the house, the estate was self-sufficient but, as Bella pointed out, it all rested on the back-breaking labour of the slaves.

'If they had to pay all them black folks for the work they does, won' be much profit in it,' she would declare. 'Takes 'bout eighteen months for a slave to earn the price his mast'r pay for him, but then he go'n work for nothin' for the rest of his days.' Remembering the conversation, the idle thought occurred to Tansy that no one had had to pay anything for her. She had been born into slavery.

'What are you looking at?' Amelia asked.

Tansy turned back from the window. 'Nothing,' she said. Amelia disliked all mention of slavery. 'I was just thinking what a lovely day it is.'

'Perfect for crop time,' Amelia said. 'They're cutting cane on the west field today.' She was buttoning up her riding jacket. 'I'm showing the new tutor the estate. Would you like to ride with us?'

Tansy was surprised. At crop times even the twelve garden and house slaves were sent to the fields and the factory to help. She had never been allowed to go but stayed working with Bella in the kitchen. Bella told her she was lucky, but her absence at this time of hard labour increased the resentment of her fellow slaves. It also had the effect of

158

giving her an intense curiosity about the areas of the estate that she had never seen.

'May I?' she asked eagerly. 'May I see the slave huts as well?'

Amelia's expression was unfathomable. 'You can see whatever I show Mr Henleigh,' she said. 'Perhaps it's time you understood a little more. Go and see if William is ready. He's coming too. And then get ready yourself.'

Half an hour later Tansy was formally introduced to the tutor who looked at her as if he could not believe his eyes. A horse had been supplied for him, Amelia and William rode their usual mounts and Tansy was perched on a mule. This seemed to puzzle Mr Henleigh.

'Would you prefer my horse?' he asked politely.

'Slaves don't ride horses,' Tansy said cheerfully and he looked at her in horror.

'You are a slave?'

Tansy opened her mouth to say that of course she was a slave, but Amelia interrupted briskly.

'We must be on our way, Mr Henleigh,' she said.

As they rode the three-quarters of a mile to the factory yard, William was eager to point out to his new tutor the river, the orchard and the field of maize which they used for bread. Tansy could see that William was delighted to have someone so much younger than Mr Jott to teach him, and looking at the young man from under her long lashes she decided she was not displeased herself. Mr Henleigh looked kind and as if he might be friendly in spite of his air of melancholy. And he had admired her. She had been flattered by his surprise at finding she was a slave, but then, though her clothes were only hand-me-downs from Amelia, they did not look in the least like a slave's clothing. Perhaps that was what confused him.

The pungent smell of boiling sugar hung in the air as they neared the factory yard. The tall lattice and canvas sails of a mill came into view, and then Amelia led them towards a group of low-fenced buildings made like a simple box with an angled roof.

'We will pay our respects to Mr Durrand,' she said. 'He is our bookkeeper, and an invaluable man.'

Tansy had met Mr Durrand at the great house when he came to report to Mistress Amelia. He and Mr La Bac were important to the estate and yet it seemed to Tansy as they went into Mr Durrand's quarters that he did not live very well. His room was small and shabby, not much better than her own, and dominated by a desk piled with ledgers. The clothes he wore seemed greasy and threadbare, but he greeted Amelia with deference and insisted on escorting the little group into the factory yard where he said La Bac was to be found.

The factory yard was seething with the shining bodies of black men and sweating mules and oxen dragging cartloads of cut cane. Yet there was a kind of method to what each man and each animal was doing. Method, but little enthusiasm. Both men and beasts wore a sullen air.

La Bac held court, whip in hand, shouting at the men to move faster, and Amelia motioned for William and Mr Henleigh to rein in their horses and watch.

It was an extraordinary scene. Carts pulled up in the big, open area laden with a cargo of what looked like oversized kindling. The carts were drawn sometimes by mules and sometimes by men. Women ran alongside picking up any lengths of cane that fell as the carts rumbled their way towards the grinding mills. As well as the windmill, there were two cattle mills, driven by oxen. They consisted of four upright rollers standing in the centre of a paved circle. Two large beams radiated from the central shaft of the rollers and at the end of these, oxen were hitched and driven round and round the mill. Fresh teams of oxen waited to take over when they tired. Men, bare to the waist and sweating in the heat of the day, unloaded the carts and fed the canes to the hungry rollers. It was surprisingly silent. The only sounds were of the oxen's tread, the shuffle of bare feet on dusty ground and the crack of whips on the backs of both men and beasts if their pace slowed. The constrained energy and the Caribbean heat combined to create an illusion of rising steam.

'You see how the bundles of cane are forced between the rollers,' said Amelia, pointing with her whip. 'Watch how the juice runs along the gutters and pipes from the mills to the boiling houses.'

She indicated the two boiling houses; long low white buildings with red floors. Each had a tall, white chimney that belched lazy smoke.

'Can we look at what they are doing, Mama?' William asked. 'I'm sure Mr Henleigh would be interested.'

'If you wish,' Amelia said. 'But you'll find it very hot and very smelly.'

All four dismounted and La Bac called to a slave to watch the horses before they moved towards the nearest boiling house. Inside was an inferno. Copper cauldrons steamed with bubbling juice as men, stripped to the waist, heaved giant ladles of hot syrup from one container to the next until the viscous liquid was poured into the hottest and smallest of the boilers.

Tansy wrinkled her nose against the smell, noting that Mr Henleigh looked as if he were not enjoying himself; he was white going on green. She was not enjoying herself either. The heat, the bare sweating flesh and unsmiling faces of the slaves and, strongest of all, an atmosphere of brooding hostility were making her uneasy.

Mark Henleigh put his handkerchief to his nose. 'What are they doing?' he asked.

'Boiling purifies and evaporates the cane juice and turns it into sugar crystals,' Amelia explained. 'From here the crystals go to a curing house to dry out and be drained of all molasses. We make rum with the molasses and send the crystals back to England to be refined into white sugar. We produce around eighty tons of sugar and forty puncheons of rum each year.'

'I see,' said Henleigh. 'And these men and women working here are all slaves? Working without pay?'

All three of them looked at him, surprised.

'But of course,' William told him patiently.

Tansy noticed that Amelia was looking uneasy. Once again she changed the subject.

'This is the skilful part,' she said, addressing herself to Tansy. 'Keep your eye on the slave who is standing just watching the cauldron. He's the most important element in the whole operation.'

Both fascinated and repelled, Tansy watched. Suddenly the man, small, black and muscular, lunged forward and thrust his thumb and forefinger into the boiling mass of liquid. She felt herself wince at the thought of how hot it must be. He quickly pulled his hand away, opened thumb and finger and stretched the gobbet of sugar between them into a long, thin brown strand, fine as a violin string. So fine it looked as if it might snap.

'Strike!' he shouted, and other men leapt to tip the contents of the cauldron into a waiting hogshead.

'The syrup was ready to crystallise. Any longer and it would have been spoilt,' Amelia explained. 'It is a moment of great skill.'

'But the man gets nothing for his skills?' said Henleigh.

Amelia did not answer. She lifted her head and turned to walk quickly back to where their horses waited.

She hurried them through the rest of the tour. They saw only one of the fields where men, women and children hacked away at the tall tough sugar cane with machetes, coughing in the dust that rose from the plants. The drivers, fellow slaves armed with whips, drove them on to work faster in a haze of sun, dust and sweat.

'Speed is necessary,' Amelia murmured, sounding apologetic. 'The cane spoils if it is not processed quickly.'

She took them to one field which had already been cut and where slaves were hoeing the land back into squares round the roots from the cut plants.

'In fifteen months it will be ready to cut again,' she said, 'and we will repeat all the processes that you have seen today.'

She spoke briefly, as if the subject were exhausted, and it seemed to Tansy that she had lost all interest in the tour. She abruptly wheeled her horse back in the direction of the great house and William and Henleigh meekly followed. Her mood affected the others. None spoke. William said little at the best of times. His silence was not unusual but his new tutor looked preoccupied, almost grim. Tansy, normally the chatter-box, was equally silent as she brought up the rear on her reluctant mule. Her head was full of pictures of the horrors of the factory yard and the cane fields; men and women used liked animals. She felt this first impression of the life of a slave would stay in her mind for ever, just as the old but faded tapestry of dying, bleeding soldiers in some long-forgotten war that hung in Elsewhere's dining room still dominated, though familiarity had blurred the horror.

She realised that she had still not seen the slave quarters. Had Amelia intended to visit them but changed her mind, faced with what was obvious disapproval from the new tutor? Tansy was dimly beginning to understand why she had been forbidden to go near the factory. The sight of the slaves working, watched over by men with whips, had been bestial. Suddenly she understood the resentment that she bred among other slaves because she had been saved from all that. She should have been one of those breathless women painfully wielding a knife against the tough cane or helping to push it between the greedy jaws of the mills. She should have known the lash across her shoulders if her work pace slackened. She should have been dressed, not in wool and cotton hand-me-downs but rough, unyielding linen. She shut her eyes and saw again that small black man waiting by the cauldron, remembered the plunge of his fingers into the boiling sugar. He had not flinched. She shuddered at the thought of what kind of life had so hardened his hands that he could use them to test the boiling-point of sugar. Whatever life it was, she had been protected from it.

But why? she asked herself. Why?

Back at the house Amelia excused herself, suggesting that William show Henleigh the gardens. But the tutor pleaded a headache and said that perhaps he would go to his room and lie down for a while.

William was instantly solicitous. 'You are not used to the sun,' he said. 'Mama tells me that in England it is cold and grey. I shall ask Bella to make you a physic that will cool you.'

He went with Tansy to the kitchen and explained to Bella what was required, then asked, 'May Tansy and I go to the beach?'

William loved collecting shells on the beach. It was his second favourite occupation after reading a book.

Bella, hands on hips, looked at them. She carefully inspected Tansy's face.

'You not be likin' the factory yard, eh?'

Tansy shook her head.

'Slaves don' like it much, either. But ain't a thing anyone can do 'bout it.' She sighed deeply and, surprisingly, leaned to kiss Tansy's cheek. 'Go an' play. Go on. Be off with the pair of you.'

William grabbed Tansy's hand. 'Come on,' he said dragging her through the kitchen door.

Outside, Tansy wrenched herself free and gave him a push. He pushed her back, and in seconds they were wrestling like two puppies. They separated, laughing, still giving each other small pushes and then, with a whoop of freedom, they ran hand in hand down to the beach.

Amelia took her mare back to the stable herself. She needed the walk back to the house to regain her composure. She had not enjoyed the morning. Mark Henleigh's unconcealed disgust at the reality of slave labour and the dismay on Tansy's face as they watched the work in the factory yard was forcing her to re-examine her own attitude towards slavery. Over the years she had suspected that she was becoming callous

162

but pushed the thought aside. Today had made her accept that she had indeed changed and hardened in the nineteen years she had spent in the West Indies. She had felt nothing watching the scenes of exploitation that morning. Nothing. She simply accepted that pain, sweat, hostility, and relentless labour were the norm for those who were black. She had not even adhered to Louis' dictum of no slaves in the house. Madame Volnay still ruled the roost as housekeeper and those French servants who had been at Elsewhere when Louis died were still employed, but they did less and less work as they trained slaves – young girls and boys from the fields who had been born into slavery – to take over for them. Truly and Daniel were still slaves, albeit privileged ones. Their ten-year-old son, Juba, worked about the house, mostly running after William, and he, too, was a slave. As was Tansy.

The hard facts of life had caught up with Amelia. It was impossible to run a plantation profitably without slave labour. Plantation owners, if they were lucky, made ten per cent a year on their investment. Five per cent was more normal, and even this could be wiped out if a hurricane or bad weather struck or a discontented slave fired a field of cane. She had discovered about a year after Louis' death that the estate was near to bankruptcy. Louis had been too generous, too easy. Her intervention, with help from Zach, had saved the plantation. Some years she made no profit at all, but she lived well and wanted for nothing, and neither did those of her household. She was thirty-five years old and had spent the last fourteen years securing her son's inheritance.

The situation on St Kitts was worsened by the constant wars with the French. Three years previously Christopher Codrington the younger had once again driven the French from St Kitts and destroyed Basse-Terre. Two years before that, the town had been burned down; it had only just been rebuilt when it was razed yet again. For the moment there was an uneasy peace, but Amelia had no doubt that the French would be back, and then burning and destruction would begin all over again. There was no guarantee that any plantation on the island would survive war. So far, since the rebuilding of Elsewhere after Louis' death, she had been lucky. The occasional field of sugar burned, causing financial loss, but the house had remained untouched, perhaps because of its remote situation at the end of the island.

Windsong was always safe in times of war. Zach had become a leading light on the island's Council, and his plantation was always well-guarded by both Redcoats and the island's militia.

Elsewhere was now at least financially secure and she had been proud of achieving that. Now, what she saw as Mark Henleigh's judgement on the running of the plantation had disturbed her. She felt an unusual self-pity that circumstances had toughened her. She had not meant to become so hard. There were times when she caught Bella's cynical eye fixed on her and she knew exactly what she was thinking. Bella was wondering where the little white slave who fell in love with a young

163

black slave had gone. And where, she asked herself, where, oh where, was Joshua?

'To hell with it,' she whispered to herself, swishing her whip, beating empty air to relieve her feelings. 'If Mark Henleigh doesn't like it he'll just have to go home again.'

She decided that she would sail to Basse-Terre to see Ben as soon as she could. A talk with Ben always relieved her feelings. He was a good listener and always sympathetic.

As she walked up the steps to her front door, Joseph came hurrying out.

'Mistress Quick come this mornin',' he said as he took her whip and riding cloak. 'She waitin' to see you.'

Amelia sighed. She had not seen Charlotte since Elizabeth Oliver's funeral five months previously, and she was not anxious to see her now. As hard as she tried Amelia could never banish the memory of emptying Charlotte and Elizabeth's chamberpots. But Elizabeth had not been the same since she had lost her fortune to her son-in-law. Amelia believed that the loss of Matthew, her husband, had been of much smaller importance. No longer mistress of her own home, the woman had slowly sickened, turning into a bag of bones, exchanging her acid tongue for brooding silence. Even though she was a comparatively young woman, her memory had begun to fail. Sometimes Amelia had thought that Elizabeth was afraid of her huge, slow-thinking son-in-law and could understand it. Zach would never be intellectual but he had become ruthlessly money-wise and overbearing. Elizabeth found herself without any say in the running of what had been her own plantation. Zach had been unkind to her, but then perhaps he had not forgotten the long hours he had spent cutting cane for the Olivers. There was no reason for him to have any love for Elizabeth. Amelia was pretty sure that he had no love for Charlotte, either.

'Where is she, Joseph?' she asked.

'In the drawin' room. Bella brought her some coffee.'

Amelia nodded. 'Tell her I must just change my riding clothes and then I'll be down.'

'Yes, mistress,' Joseph said moving towards the drawing room.

'And give her some more coffee,' Amelia shouted after him.

She was back downstairs in five minutes to find Charlotte in what looked like a brand new gown sitting with her feet on a footstool. She looked fatter, rounder in the face, and surprisingly happy. Since Charlotte had married Zach five years ago there had been a down-turn to her mouth, her air of confident superiority had vanished and she had never seemed happy. But now something must have happened to lighten her life, Amelia thought. Perhaps it was simply the death of her frightful mother.

They kissed, and Charlotte's hug and peck were full of warmth Amelia could not match. She told herself Charlotte liked her, and Charlotte was not a bad woman. She must be kinder.

164

'You are looking very well,' Amelia told her.

'I am feeling very well,' Charlotte said, all smiles, running her pale fingers through her long blonde hair. 'I am feeling wonderfully well, and I have such good news to tell.'

She's pregnant, Amelia thought.

'I am expecting, Amelia. I'm so thrilled. It's nearly five months, and this time I have hopes that all will be well. The midwife says my health is good and there is no reason why my baby should not be born without difficulty.'

Charlotte had been pregnant once before, much earlier on in the marriage, but had miscarried. Since then Amelia wondered if her brother would ever have a family but had refrained from questions.

Her sister-in-law's face was glowing with pleasure, and moved by her happiness, Amelia went to hug her.

'So I'm to be an aunt,' she said. 'That *is* good news.'

'How good you don't know,' Charlotte said. 'I have lost so many. I ceased to speak of it, afraid to temp fate, but I have miscarried six times, Amelia. I thought I would never be a mother and Zach used to be . . .' She hesitated. 'I know he is your brother, Amelia, but he was so unkind.' Her eyes were filling with tears. 'He said I was useless. I was useless as a wife, and I could not even produce an heir for him. Sometimes I think his unkindness caused me to miscarry. He was rough with me when . . .' She gulped. 'And then, after my mother's death, everything changed. He became more gentle, more tender. I began to feel that he could truly love me, and this time – well, I am pregnant. He's so thrilled that he is to become a father at last that he's tender to me all the time and in every way. I cannot tell you how different our marriage has become and how happy we both are.' The tears had vanished and her eyes were shining as if she had seen a vision, her hands clasped as if she were in church. 'You do not mind me telling you all this?' she asked, almost timidly.

'Of course not,' Amelia said. 'Remember, I know how difficult my brother can be.'

'Forgive me, but I need to talk to someone and there is no one since Mama and Papa have both gone. Not that I could have spoken of such things to them.'

'You have not been happy with Zach? I sensed it. Marriage changed you.'

'I could not please him. I did not know how to please him. And then there was the slave girl.'

'Ruby?'

'Yes, Ruby. I know he went most nights to lie with her and it broke my heart. He hardly seemed to attempt to hide it and I wanted to die of shame and humiliation. Everyone knew. Thank God she never had a child. I could not have borne that. But I did not please him in the bedchamber. Mama had given me the impression that I must be reserved and modest or he would think me not a lady, and though I longed to

165

be different I did not know how. He thought me cold and unloving. He did not realise how I burned for him, how I loved him. I believed it would be wrong to tell him, to show him. And the worst was living at Windsong. I was so conscious of my mother in the house – her bedchamber just along the hallway – and I was afraid that if I indulged in all that I wanted to do and say, she would hear me and declare me wanton. I imagined her lying there, listening to us, though I knew perfectly well she could have heard nothing. I know it was irrational, but it was the way I felt. Amelia, you have been married, tell me please, do you think it wrong for a woman to show a man how she feels and ask for what she wants from her lover?'

'No,' Amelia said firmly. 'I believe that men want a lady in the drawing room but not in the bedchamber.'

Charlotte sighed. 'I'm sure you're right. So much wasted time,' she murmured, staring at her hands in silence. She lifted her head and began to speak again. 'And then mother died. Suddenly she was not in the house any more. Her bedchamber was empty. I felt free. It was as if all restraints had been taken from me. I did' – she hesitated – 'all the things I had dreamed of doing with my love. And far from thinking me wanton, he was happy. He was tender. Our marriage is transformed. Oh Amelia, he does not even visit Ruby any more – well, not so often. And I am the happiest woman on earth. But I have such guilt because I am almost glad that my mother has gone because her death has brought me so much happiness.'

'You should not feel guilt.' Amelia leaned to take Charlotte's hand. 'You were a good and dutiful daughter to a mother who . . .' She stopped.

'You did not like my mother.' It was not a question, nor a reproach, merely a statement of fact.

Amelia found she was smiling. 'No.'

Charlotte sighed. 'Neither did I. Oh, I loved her, but she was not easy to like. I was always afraid of her. You have no idea how much I missed you after you ran away that time . . .' Her hand flew to cover her mouth. 'But I should not mention that.'

'Why not?' Amelia's voice was brisk. 'It happened. I was your slave.'

'It does not seem possible now, but there was good in it. Imagine, if all that had not happened, I would not have had Zach.'

'Very true,' Amelia said dryly, remembering the pain and degradation of those years as a slave. She was pleased that Charlotte was happy, but disappointed that even now the girl would never be able to understand the gulf that would always divide them. Only Charlotte could mentally turn the misery of what had happened to her and Zach to her own advantage.

'Please come to visit us more at Windsong,' Charlotte was saying. 'We should be closer. We are all the family we have. I know how Zach loves to see you, and now Mama and Papa have gone you will find it different.'

Ah, but the ghosts will still be there, thought Amelia, but she said gently, 'Of course I will come. Very soon.'

She woke the next morning restless and with a slight headache. It was a perfect February West Indian day. The sun was already high and a few clouds floated in a pale, washed blue. Looking down into her garden she watched the flash of kingfishers darting down to the river. Small, bright yellow birds chattered among the red leaves of a poinsettia tree. And further out, over the sea, she could see huge frigate birds wheeling. The view, beautiful as it was, somehow did not please. She wanted to get away from Elsewhere.

Tansy came in with her breakfast. Tansy always came in with her breakfast, but this morning Amelia felt a flash of shame that her own daughter was waiting on her. Later Tansy would empty her chamberpot just as she herself had had to empty those of the Oliver women.

'Good morning, Mistress Amelia, did you sleep well?' Tansy asked as she placed the platter on a table. She seemed unusually preoccupied. Tansy was normally cheerful. She had a remarkably pleasant, open nature. The girl had no secrets; she was not capable of them. She was also bright and intelligent. She should not be a slave, Amelia thought desperately, but what else could she do without telling Tansy the truth of her parentage?

'Did you find it interesting visiting the factory yard yesterday?' she asked as she moved towards her breakfast, already knowing what the answer would be.

The girl's face clouded. 'I did not like it,' she blurted out.

Amelia sat down and took a piece of bread, trying to look unconcerned. 'Why not?'

'I don't know.' Tansy's voice was miserable.

'There must be some reason.'

The girl was standing, her hands hidden under her apron. 'I kept thinking it should have been me.'

'You?'

'Yes, me. Dressed like that, and cutting the cane like that, and all that hard, dreadful work. Men and women being whipped . . . like animals . . .'

'Ah,' was all that Amelia could think of to say.

'But you saved me from all that, didn't you?'

'Not exactly. Everyone has house slaves who do different work.'

'Yes, but they aren't taught to read and write and they aren't given their mistress's cast-off clothes, are they? Or their own room?' The girl's voice was anguished. 'I was all right until I got into bed and then I started to think. I've been thinking about it all night. I don't understand why I have been so fortunate. Why me? Why did you choose me?'

Because, my darling, you are my daughter, is what Amelia longed to say. Instead, taking a deep breath, she said, 'I suppose maybe because

167

you are so white. And I liked you. You were a very lovable little girl and very unhappy without your mama. And then you were Bella's granddaughter, and Bella is free.'

'But you freed her. She told me.'

'Well, yes. She was very kind to me when I first came to St Kitts.'

'But you didn't free Truly and Daniel.'

'Well, maybe they weren't so kind to me.' Amelia was desperate to lighten the atmosphere, while Tansy was determined on saying what she wanted to say.

'If it's just because I'm nearly white, it's not fair,' she said fiercely. 'I'm a slave like the rest of them. It's wrong I should be treated better just because I look white. I don't understand why I am so white. My mama was black. I can just remember her and she was wonderfully black, all shiny and warm. Bella's black. I know my papa was half-white, but Bella won't tell me anything about it.'

'I don't know anything about his father. I can't tell you.'

Tansy looked at her doubtfully. Then she said, 'I ought to be with my own mother and papa.'

The pain of that was excruciating, but Amelia managed to say firmly, 'You know very well it's difficult for slaves to be a family. Perhaps you understand now why I didn't want you to see the cane fields and the factory yard before.'

'But why not?' Tansy asked passionately. 'Now I wish I never had. Until I saw what their lives are like I never questioned my own good fortune. What will become of me? You have not prepared me for the life of a slave. Why do you let me talk to you like this? You wouldn't permit it from another slave. It's not fair. I'm not white and I'm not black. It would be better just to be a slave like everyone else. I don't really belong anywhere.'

'But you belong here,' Amelia cried. 'At Elsewhere. It's your home and always will be.'

'It will have to be, won't it? I can't go anywhere else.' The girl's voice was bitter.

'If you had your freedom, would you go away?' Amelia put the question tentatively and held her breath, waiting for the all-important answer. Tansy considered.

'I might,' she said cautiously.

'Where would you go?'

'I don't know.'

'Well, when you've made up your mind, let me know.' Relief helped Amelia to make her tone light. 'And stop worrying about it all so much. All house slaves have an easier time than those in the field and factory.'

'Not as easy as I do.'

'Oh, don't go on so. You've made me let my tea get cold,' Amelia said, feigning irritation. 'Run to the kitchen and get me a fresh pot, there's a good girl.'

Tansy instantly did as she was told, and once she was out of the

168

room Amelia took a deep breath. She realised with dismay that she should not have let her daughter grow up without seeing the life of the other slaves. If the girl had been more familiar with the pattern of plantation life, there would have been no shock as she had suffered yesterday. In her determination to protect her child as best she could she had made a serious mistake, but it was too late to turn back the clock now.

Coming back into the kitchen carrying Amelia's breakfast platter, Tansy was neither looking where she was going nor thinking what she was doing. Her mind was on the conversation with Amelia. She stumbled and the platter crashed to the stone floor of the kitchen.

As she looked down in dismay at the broken mass of fine china, her grandmother, moving with surprising speed for one so large, landed a sizeable blow on her ear.

'What you think you doin' gal?' she hissed. 'I tell you, if you work at Windsong, them Olivers have you whipped till you hide run blood for doin' that.'

'I didn't do it on purpose,' Tansy protested.

'I don' say you did. Don' make no difference. I knew a gal once got whipped for breakin' no more than a powder bowl. You think you'self lucky you works here.'

Tansy needed clarification of that statement.

'If someone else here had broken it, not me, someone blacker than me, would they get whipped?' she asked belligerently.

'Mistress 'Melia don' like whippin' nobody, not in the house. She got whipped hersel' once and she not go'n forget it.'

'Mistress Amelia whipped?' Tansy could not believe her ears. Her elegant, even-tempered mistress who was always in control of every situation, being whipped like a field slave? 'It can't be true,' she said, 'I don't believe it. And she doesn't seem to mind people being whipped in the fields and the factory yard.'

'Hold you tongue! There's plenty you don' know 'bout Mistress 'Melia,' Bella said crossly, 'and it don' be up to me to tell you. Now you just clear up that mess there and get out of here fore you does any more damage.'

'What about the washing?' It was Tansy's job to do Amelia's personal washing each day.

'You ain't in no mood to get it clean. Just get out of here.'

Bella looked so fierce and furious that Tansy took her at her word and went out through the kitchen door into the garden. Suddenly bereft of her normal morning chores, she wasn't sure what to do with herself. She wondered if William were about to play with or would he be having lessons with the new tutor? Failing that, she could go and play with Juba, though Truly and Daniel didn't like to see Juba in her company. The trouble was that both boys seemed too young, too childish to be really good companions. She was suddenly beginning to realise how much older she was than both of them. She wished she had a friend of her own age.

She was standing, undecided, looking about her when she heard someone call her name. It was Mr Henleigh. He was loping, thin and bowed, along the path and waving an eager hand. He was quite breathless when he joined her.

'Mistress Tansy,' he said, his hand to his chest, 'such a pleasure.'

Tansy burst out laughing. 'You mustn't call me mistress,' she said. 'I'm just Tansy. You don't call slaves mistress.'

'I cannot think of you as a slave,' he said hurriedly. 'I cannot bear to think of you as a slave. It is absurd, cruel. A disgrace.'

She looked at him consideringly. 'Because I'm so white?'

'Yes.'

'You wouldn't care if I was black?'

'After what I witnessed yesterday, it is my contention that no man or woman, no matter what colour, should be a slave. But for someone like yourself, it is the ultimate wickedness.'

His voice was full of passion and he obviously meant what he said. Tansy considered his view of the matter and then nodded.

'In that case you won't like it here,' she informed him.

'I can already see that,' he said as he took a handkerchief from his pocket and began to cough into it. 'Forgive me . . . This cough . . . I had hopes that the warm climate might improve it.'

'It might,' Tansy said cautiously, thinking that the climate was more likely to finish off one as frail as he appeared to be. Then, wondering what to do with him, asked politely, 'Would you like me to show you the gardens?'

'If you would.' His voice was eager. 'I left young Master William to write an essay for me and came out for some fresh air. It will take me some while to become accustomed to the heat.'

'It is colder where you come from?'

He smiled. 'Much colder. I come from Yorkshire in the north of England. It can be bleak and bitter but it is the most beautiful place in the world.'

Tansy looked at him doubtfully. 'More beautiful than here?'

'In a different way,' he said. 'Maybe one day I will show it to you.'

There was a note in his voice that made her look full into his face. His eyes seemed to be feverish, they shone so, and his expression was intense. Then he smiled a smile of surprising sweetness, a smile with such warmth that it could have been a caress from the sun.

'I would like to see England,' she said, transfixed by the smile.

'Then you shall.' He spoke as if it were a certainty, leaving her wondering if what she had said were true. Did she want to see England? She wasn't sure.

They walked in silence for a while, but it was not an uncomfortable silence. Then he said abruptly, 'You did not care for the factory yard any more than I did yesterday?'

170

She realised he was asking her a question. 'I loathed it.'

'You had seen it before?'

'Mistress Amelia would never let me go there.'

'Why?' He was intent on her face, watching her mouth move as if what she said was of the utmost importance. It made him very easy to talk to.

'I don't know,' she said. 'I keep asking myself. I asked her this morning and she said that she had protected me because I am so white. But that is wrong.'

'I don't understand.'

'Well, I'm not really white, but I'm not black either. But to be a slave and better treated because my skin is paler is not just. It makes me ashamed. Oh, it is so hard to explain.' She looked at him appealingly. 'Do you understand what I mean?'

'Perfectly.'

'Mistress Amelia did not understand.'

He was silent, pursing his full rather red lips in thought. He was most handsome in a delicate, almost girlish manner. His blond hair was tousled by the breeze and he passed a negligent hand over it without effect.

'Perhaps those who live here have lost all moral sense. To use men as slaves must blunt the sensibilities.'

She did not understand exactly what he meant but she nodded sagely. He nodded back before taking her hand in his and saying urgently, 'But you have noble thoughts. You understand injustice even when it is at your own expense. How simple it would be for you to thank the Lord for your whiteness and revel in it without a thought for those less fortunate. Mistress Tansy, I cannot tell you how much I admire you, what a ray of light you are in this tropical darkness. Surely God will reward you and set you free.'

'That is not very likely,' she told him, 'since God is not permitted to black folk.'

'You do not go to church?' He clapped a hand to his face at the horror of it.

'No slave goes to church, but Mistress Amelia has taught me to read from the Bible. I do know of what you speak.'

'Oh, the deprivation!' he murmured. 'The cruelty to withhold the word of God from those who need comfort more than any other in this wicked world. Mistress Tansy, will you let me lead you to the light?'

She wasn't entirely sure which light he was talking about, but his face was rapt with joy as he waited for her reply. She could not bear to disappoint him by refusing, but on the other hand she had a strong suspicion that what he was suggesting would not find favour with either the white or the black folk of the estate.

'Very well,' she said making her tone solemn and then added conspiratorially, 'But we had better not let either Mistress Amelia or Bella know.'

171

The day felt all wrong, strange, as if perhaps a hurricane or an earthquake was threatening, but it was not the usual time of year for nature's more extreme manifestations. Whatever was threatening she had created it for herself. Thoroughly out of sorts, Amelia dressed and decided to make the visit to Ben she had planned the day before. She needed a change of scene.

She went by boat, Pierre sailing her, and the breeze on her face soothed her. She walked from the beach to the tavern, remembering how this walk had been a snatched freedom all those years ago. Basse-Terre now looked very different. It had been burned and bombarded so many times and each time it was rebuilt the inhabitants used less thatch on their roofs and widened the streets as a precaution against fire. Ben had tried to keep the original character of the tavern, but the building had suffered as much as any of the others. He was fortunate, though, that when fire attacked, there was no shortage of able-bodied men who rushed to fight the flames on his and their own behalf. He had turned the Columbus into the liveliest meeting place in the town. Here French and English mixed amicably, leaving ordinary folk to wonder why the two nations spent so much time trying to slaughter each other.

Ben instantly instructed one of his staff, an oversized Irishman, to man the bar when he saw Amelia walk through the door. He came towards her, lightfooted and smiling. He had never taken to the fashion of wearing wigs, and his red hair curled down over his shoulders. He seemed hardly to have changed since the day they arrived in St Kitts nineteen years before. He was still freckled, bouncy, slight, small and incorrigibly good-humoured. They settled down together over a bottle of claret in the back room of the tavern, now comfortably furnished with the best that the local merchants shipped from Europe. Ben had become rich running the tavern and without ever once employing a slave. Zach was for ever telling him that he was mad; his profits would be that much greater if he were not paying wages. But Ben said he knew what it felt like, thank you, and he would never wish to own another human being. Nothing could change his mind, and he made Amelia feel ashamed.

'Have you come to sell me the tavern?' he joked once they were comfortable. It was always his first question when they met.

'Not yet. That will be up to William one day.'

'I've more chance of talking him into it than you.'

'You probably have,' she agreed. 'I don't think he'll ever be very interested in business. He's like his father, thoughtful. But he causes me no anxiety.'

'Who does?' Ben asked gently.

'Tansy. She's beginning to ask questions.'

'Are you surprised? You sheltered her and spoilt her. One day she was bound to wonder why.'

'I realise that now, but when she was little it didn't seem to matter.'

172

He looked at her with a raised eyebrow. 'Why don't you free her and let her go?'

'Because she's still such a baby and she would go and I couldn't bear it.'

'You plan on keeping her with you for ever?'

Amelia evaded the question. 'She's only seventeen. I long to tell her the truth. This morning she said she should be with her real mother and father and I wanted to shout out that I am her mother. You don't really understand, Ben. No one understands. She is so beautiful and so enchanting, any mother would be proud of her. But Zach would never forgive me if I acknowledged her. He is so grand and important now and I have to admit that I enjoy what little social life there is myself. I wouldn't want to be ostracised. I realise I should have gone straight back to England when we got our freedom and taken Tansy with me. She would pass for white in England without any difficulty at all. Her life would have been completely different.'

'You could still do that.'

'And give up William's inheritance? I have him to think of as well.'

'You could sell up. Or put in an agent. Others are doing it. There is even a rumour that Macabees is to be sold.'

'So I heard. Ben, would the slaves be sold with the plantation if Ramillies did sell?'

Ben shrugged. 'Who knows,' he said. 'And if you're thinking of Joshua, forget it. That really would cause you to be ostracised.'

They were sitting facing each other across a small table. Ben leaned forward to refill her glass. Dismissing the subject of Joshua he said, 'It seems to me that you have been thinking about your children far too much for far too long. You need something of your own, Amelia. You need some love in your life.'

'But I get that from the children,' she protested.

'And is it enough?'

'Not always,' she admitted.

'Besides, I meant a different kind of love,' he told her roughly. 'Why don't you marry me? Give Tansy her freedom. Let her go. Even here on the islands she could pass. She could move away from here and live as a free woman. The first man who saw her would want her. She could marry whom she pleased. As indeed could you if you came out of that cocoon you've been hiding in.'

'You think I've been hiding?'

'Of course you have. The waste of it. The waste of a beautiful woman. It's not right, occupying yourself with men's matters.'

'But men's matters are more interesting than those of women. I'm happy.'

'Are you?' he pressed, and she found she could not evade his searching eyes.

'Most of the time,' she said with a little laugh. 'Not always. I suppose I do get lonely sometimes.'

173

'Then marry me.'

'It's not the answer for either of us.'

'It's the answer for me.'

'Not if I don't love you in that way.'

'I don't care.'

'Ah, but you would, in time,' she said gently. 'You would be bruised by my indifference.'

He flushed scarlet and she regretted causing him distress. She leaned forward to take his hand. 'But I'm not in the least indifferent to you as a cousin, Ben. I came to see you today because I needed someone to talk to. You're right. I am in a rut. I feel I don't know where I'm going. The estate is safe and working well. The problems there are over. I feel I have nothing left to do with my life. I'm discontented and bored.'

He considered the problem. 'Why don't you make a trip to Europe? Take Tansy and William with you. Marry her off there, and come back again to Elsewhere. Zach will run it for you while you're away.'

She laughed. 'He'd be delighted to. Have you noticed how he keeps buying more and more land, nearer and nearer to mine. He's never given up the idea of joining the two estates. At least it makes it easier to visit him. He's even driven a road through to Elsewhere.'

'Zach is a very determined man.'

'And about to be a father.'

'So he tells me.'

There was something in his tone that made her say, 'Would you like children, Ben?'

'Only if they are yours,' he told her.

'Oh, Ben,' she sighed, holding out her glass for him to refill it again.

She felt quite lightheaded when she left the tavern and full of nostalgia. She and Ben had drifted into talking of their first days on the island, as they often did, speculating what their lives might have been had they remained in Devon.

Ben declared himself well content with his lot. 'I have the temperament of a tavernkeeper,' he confessed, 'but at home it would never have been considered suitable. I would have been Ben Clode, gentleman.'

'And if Monmouth had won, maybe Papa would have found me another earl. Imagine, I might have been a countess,' she gave a little giggle, 'but I think my temperament is better suited to running my own estates. I would have hated life at court.'

They had drunk to that with a second bottle before Amelia set off for home.

As she walked to the beach she saw a cart driving down the street ahead of her. It lurched along, full of slaves, the old women sitting on the back the men standing, clinging to the sides. The shape of one head which stood out tall above the others rang a sudden bell. She stopped and squinted against the sun to see more clearly as the cart rumbled on further away from her. There was something familiar about the

174

shoulders, too, but something was wrong. The left sleeve of the rough shirt that covered the broad frame below the familiar head hung empty. The man had only one arm.

She began to run to catch up with the cart. She was breathless as she drew level. Her quarry, the one-armed man, turned as he heard running footsteps. She saw a light-brown, handsome face, lined with pain, but a face she had not forgotten and never would. She was staring straight into the astonished eyes of Joshua before the cart with a sudden burst of speed swept him and his companions away from her on the road out of town.

Chapter Eleven

Amelia returned to Elsewhere in a state of agitation. The glimpse of Joshua had put her in a turmoil. To see him and then have him snatched away from her was insupportable. To discover that he had been mutilated was also insupportable. But why had they taken his arm? What had they punished him for? Had he run, trying to find her? The confusion, longing and anger fighting in her head created real physical pain, and once back at the plantation she went straight to her room and lay down on her bed in an attempt to compose herself.

As she calmed, she asked herself whether it was a mirage brought about by sharing not one, but two bottles of claret with Ben. Was the sight of him no more than a cruel trick brought about by the fumes of alcohol and her own longings? Even after so many years, never a day went by when she did not think of him. To her it seemed that all the charm of Tansy which held her so enthralled came from him. He was the best and strongest man she had ever known. Nothing had changed. And it had been no mirage. That was Joshua, hurt, older, but still the man she loved. And having seen him again, she wanted him again.

Resting behind the closed curtains of her bed it occurred to Amelia that she was inconveniently single-minded. She loved Tansy and wanted her with her so much that she could not bring herself to give the child her freedom. She loved William and wanted to give him the world to the extent of sacrificing her own life for him. She loved Joshua and wanted him back. Louis? What about Louis? Louis was a interlude. She had never quite loved him enough. Her husband had been a convenience she had availed herself of at a time when she desperately needed help. But Louis had been no mistake. He had given her both William and Elsewhere. Elsewhere was the least important of the two. Sweet, solemn, earnest William was paramount. If she had not owned Elsewhere, she could have made a living with the tavern. She always refused to sell Ben the Columbus simply because she was never certain if her good fortune with the plantation would continue. She had no faith in her own prosperity. On these islands, with the constant warfare, it was possible to be homeless and ruined overnight. While she owned the tavern there was somewhere else for her and all her dependants to go – just as they had once before.

But now it looked as if the tavern would have to be sold. Something else was becoming more important. She lay there thinking for a long time until the supper bell, clanged by Joseph's heavy old hand, echoed through the house. Then quickly she tidied herself and went downstairs to eat with William and the new tutor. She would continue her plotting later.

Had Amelia not been so preoccupied with her own thoughts that night, she might have caught the first danger of what was to occur between Tansy and the tutor. She would have seen the burning gaze he directed at her daughter, and noted Tansy's fascination with the young man. But Amelia's mind was set on bringing Joshua back into her life and how best it could be done.

The following morning she was up early, attending to a more serious toilette than she had bothered with in years. She crimped her hair, found heart-shaped beauty spots she had not used since Louis died, and dusted her face with powder. She was well aware that none of this would create an effect with the man she intended to visit; the effort was for her own confidence.

She was pleased with what she saw in her looking glass. She had not lost her looks in the years that she had spent disregarding them. The emerald eyes were as bright and beguiling as ever, her skin clear and white, her hair luxurious. She flirted with her reflection and then laughed at her own vanity before setting off to look for Pierre. For the journey she planned, she wanted company. It would have been better to go with Zachary or even to send him in her place, but for the moment she did not wish to tell him what she had in mind, and besides, he had sworn long ago that nothing would induce him to enter Macabees again.

She found Pierre in the kitchen, chatting with Bella. The austere Frenchman and the outspoken black woman were much of an age and had become friends over the years. Bella stared as Amelia came into the kitchen.

'My, oh my,' she said. 'Where we all off to then, all dressed in our best?'

Amelia ignored her. 'Pierre,' she said, 'is it possible to go to Macabees by carriage?'

'Macabees, is it?' Bella scoffed, hands on hips.

Pierre said he believed it was possible to get to Macabees by carriage, though the road was not good.

'Then I want you to come with me,' Amelia told him. 'And wait for me while I am there.'

'And what you go'n do while you there?' Bella asked.

'Wait and see,' Amelia told her.

She felt absurdly nervous as her carriage, Joseph driving, Pierre at his side, passed through the large iron gates and along the line of royal palms that led into Macabees. It was an estate that was spoken of only in whispers. No one was ever invited there, and no one invited Vincent Ramillies. She was silent as they drove along a bumpy, ill-made road which ran through the cane fields and finally into gardens where the road improved as the big Elizabeth-style mansion came into view. Somewhere in the trees to the side of the road Amelia could hear water running, but otherwise there was an eerie silence.

As they drove up to the steps leading to the wooden door, a huge negro appeared. He stood as if he were guarding the entrance, stock-still, arms folded.

Determined not to be intimidated, Amelia climbed briskly from the carriage and firmly mounted the steps.

'Good morning,' she said. 'I have come to call on your master. Will you please inform him of my presence.'

'Mr Ramillies he don' see no callers.'

In eighteen years Amelia had learned a great deal about slaves.

'Do as you are told,' she snapped. 'Inform Mr Ramillies that Madame Rosier-Quick from Elsewhere is here to see him on an important matter. Show me into the house immediately and curb your insolence or I shall see that you are whipped.'

She stared up at him, her eyes wide and icy. He glowered and then his stare wavered. He turned and opened the door. Amelia swept in, her gown swishing about her feet, Pierre close behind.

Without speaking, the guardian disappeared down the length of the long, stone hallway.

'They are the worst,' she whispered to Pierre. 'The slaves who get some authority. Usually they take it out on their own kind, but he is not taking it out on me.' She jerked her head decisively. 'Don't worry, Pierre, you can wait in the carriage. I shall be safe enough.'

'If you are sure, madam,' Pierre murmured, but he did not look happy.

She laughed. 'If I'm not out by sundown, you'd better send for help.' He went reluctantly out of the door.

She sat down on a long settle. She had a suspicion that Vincent Ramillies would make her wait to see him, if he saw her at all. She had time, she told herself. She could wait. She had eighteen years of waiting. Another half-hour would not matter.

She had been sitting for perhaps quarter of an hour, outwardly perfectly relaxed in the heavy silence and chill of the hallway, when she heard a slight movement, like a small animal scurrying. She looked up quickly. The door opposite where she sat had been partly opened and she caught a glimpse of a pale face peeping at her round the jam. She smiled, and the face disappeared, its expression terrified. She waited on, watching the door out of curiosity and for something to do. After perhaps a minute, the face appeared again. Amelia by then had her head back, eyes half-closed as if dozing. Whoever was hiding in there was deceived by the pose and stayed in sight a little longer, regarding Amelia with a kind of frightened fascination. It was a young girl.

Then the pale, thin face with huge, sad, blue eyes disappeared again and the door of the room gently closed.

Amelia sat thinking for a moment, and then on an impulse got to her feet, walked across the hallway and opened the door of the room. She found herself looking into a library, where, seated at a desk, was the peeping girl. When she saw Amelia she gave a startled gasp, leapt to her feet, hand on heart, and stood looking wildly around her like a trapped animal.

'Why don't you come and talk to me?' Amelia asked gently, holding out her hand. 'It's lonely in this big hall.'

'I couldn't,' the girl said, backing towards the window. 'Please leave me alone. He'll be angry.'

'Who will be angry?' Amelia asked.

'My uncle. And him.'

'Then they'll have to be angry with me, won't they?' Amelia said wondering who 'him' could be, 'since it is I who spoke to you first. I am Amelia Rosier-Quick. I live at Elsewhere. I have a son of about your age.'

'Where is Elsewhere?' the girl asked, a sudden urgency in her voice.

'It is the next plantation to the west of here, further along the coast. Now, please tell me, what is your name?'

'Isobel,' the girl whispered.

'What a pretty name.' It seemed necessary to talk to this girl as if she were much younger and do nothing to frighten her. 'Do you live here?'

The girl nodded, clasping and unclasping her hands.

'It is a very beautiful house.'

'I hate it.'

The fear had temporarily gone, to be replaced by so much hatred that Amelia found herself stepping back from the force of it. Isobel then cocked her head and listened. She visibly whitened. 'He's coming back,' she whispered, 'please, oh please go. Don't let him catch me with you.' She looked terrified, eyes darting in her head, body rigid. Amelia could hear nothing, but reasoned that perhaps living in this sinister house had attuned the girl to danger. Without speaking she nodded and slipped out of the room, closing the door gently behind her.

Isobel had been right. After perhaps thirty seconds Amelia too heard footsteps. She was standing casually in the centre of the hall when the doorkeeper appeared, his face a mask of hostility.

'Mr Ramillies say he busy.' He moved towards the front door to open it. At the same time Amelia set off down the hall in the direction from which he had come. By the time he turned she was halfway down.

'You just git out,' he shouted.

Without stopping, Amelia turned her head to treat him to another blaze of green, then imperiously waved her hand for him to go away. He pounded after her, and she thought she also heard softer footsteps whispering further behind but she resolutely looked ahead.

With the doorman hot on her heels she found herself in the same, high-vaulted room at the back of the house where years before Zach had confronted Vincent Ramillies. She saw an elderly man sitting in a huge winged armchair. He was dressed in a fine, white, frilled shirt and brocade waistcoat over his breeches and pink silk stockings. His long, pale face, topped by a bright red wig, was expressionless. Standing behind the chair was a mulatto in his late twenties, equally finely dressed, his handsome looks enhanced by a huge turban.

'I said I would not see you,' Ramillies hissed, his voice reed-like with indignation.

'What you want of my master?' the mulatto asked aggressively. 'We don' want women here.'

It was obvious that no one was going to offer her a seat so Amelia took the chair on the other side of the fireplace to where Vincent Ramillies sat. She resisted the impulse to hold out her hand to him. She had a presentiment that he would not want to touch her.

She ignored the mulatto's question. Instead she said, 'Mr Ramillies, sir, it is indeed a pleasure to be in your company and in your beautiful home. May I congratulate you on your taste. Macabees is surely the finest house on the island. My brother, Zachary Quick, who visited you once long ago, had told me of its charm, and now that I see it for myself, I understand his enthusiasm. He told me too of your kindness in receiving him and has asked me to offer his very best regards to you and your household.'

Ramillies pursed his lips then stroked his nose with his thumb and forefinger, regarding her with what amounted to distaste, but the mention of Zach seemed to have interested him.'

'He was the big man?' he asked.

'My brother is *very* big,' Amelia said with a little conspiratorial smile.

'He bought slaves.'

'Yes. He was struck by your generosity in permitting them to be sold. If you recall, one of the girls had been my nurse.'

'I do not recall,' he said frostily.

'Of course not. Such a trivial matter. So long ago.'

'I do recall that he took two of the women. Today we have no women in this house. So will you oblige me by telling me what it is you want, madam?'

'To buy Macabees,' Amelia said calmly.

The man stiffened and the mulatto jerked upright and clasped the back of Ramillies' chair.

'It is not for sale.'

'Oh dear. You mean I have been misinformed?'

'If you have been so informed you have been misinformed.'

'And on such good authority.'

'Whose authority?'

'If I have been misinformed, perhaps I should not say. But it was a high authority who believed that you were to return to England and important office.'

He stared at her. She stared back, deciding it was time to let a little steel show.

'Why do you want Macabees?'

'It abuts on my own land. I wish to enlarge my plantation.'

'Elsewhere?'

'Elsewhere.'

Suddenly Ramillies began to giggle, a sound so unpleasant that Amelia found the hairs on the back of her neck rising. There was no mirth in his face or in the laughter.

'And how much would you be prepared to pay?'

'As much as it is worth and more.'

'That would be a great deal of money.'

'How great?'

'Since Macabees is not for sale it is academic.'

Amelia smiled. 'It would be interesting to know.'

'Umm.' He pulled his thumb and forefinger down the length of his long, thin nose again. 'Thirty thousand guineas.'

Her heart lurched at the size of the sum. 'I had imagined it would be that,' she said casually. 'It would, of course, include all the slaves?'

Ramillies leaned back to take the hand of the mulatto. 'Not my personal slaves. Not Nero here. Do you like him?' His voice was sly. 'He is very handsome, is he not? But, of course, you could not admit to finding him attractive. Ladies must be circumspect.'

It was the greatest insult on the island to suggest that a white woman might look at a black man with sexual interest. It was an insult that was wasted on Amelia. She stared coolly at Nero. 'Yes,' she said. 'It is an attractive mixture, the black and the white. Your mother was white, I presume?'

Nero flushed with anger, but Ramillies broke into giggles again. 'Oh, what a bitch!' he said delightedly. 'I am really quite sorry not to be able to sell you Macabees.'

'I also.' Amelia began to rise to her feet. 'But tell me, how could such a rumour have begun?'

'I have no idea.' The giggles ceased abruptly. 'And if I had, it is no business of yours.'

'Should you change your mind . . . ' Amelia murmured.

Ramillies flapped his hands on rubber wrists. 'Nero, see Mrs Rosier-Quick out. I wish you good day, madam.'

'Good day, sir.' Amelia was purring now. 'Such a pleasure . . . But do not be surprised if I should return to see if you have changed your mind.'

Without giving him time to reply she turned and walked steadily out of the room. She moved as slowly as she could, trailing behind the mincing Nero and glancing through every door to see if there were any sign of the frightened girl. Ramillies had said there were no women here but that was obviously not true. But why was she so frightened and who was she? Then Amelia remembered through the mists of time that old Pottle, now long dead, had mentioned that when Ramillies' brother and sister-in-law had died they had left a baby girl. That must

182

be Isobel. She was the right age. Poor child, Amelia thought, to have to live in this evil mausoleum with only the repellent Vincent for company. It did not bear thinking about it.

Nero opened the front door. The huge doorman stood at the top of the steps, staring at her carriage as if he were afraid it would storm the house. Pierre and Joseph rose and jumped down as she appeared, relief written on their faces.

'Are you all right, madam?' Pierre asked as he handed her into the carriage.

She nodded, realising she was trembling a little. 'Don't hurry, Joseph,' she said. 'Take your time. Let us leave with dignity.'

Joseph took the point. He fussed with the horses and reins, adjusted the canopy of the carriage and then in a leisurely fashion set off back down the road out of the estate.

'That be a real bad place, mistress,' he said over his shoulder as they neared the gates. 'We was scared you never go'n come out.'

'I had my doubts myself once or twice,' she said ruefully.

They were on the rough public road that ran through woods and skirted the Macabees estate. Again Amelia could hear running water and it seemed to her that now they were free of the plantation, birds once again sang. She shivered, glad to be away even if her plot had failed. She now understood why Zach had so hated the place.

As she pondered what her next move would be, the sound of water strengthened. Suddenly from out of the woods tumbled a small wet figure running frantically towards the carriage. As the figure neared, soaked skirts clinging to spindle legs, Amelia realised who it was.

'Oh, stop, please stop,' the girl Isobel was calling, desperately waving her arms. 'Take me with you. Please take me with you.'

Without being told, Joseph immediately drew up. Amelia jumped down from the carriage and ran towards the girl who had buckled at the knees and collapsed in the dust. Pierre followed. The girl looked up, blue eyes huge and frightened in her face. 'Help me,' she whispered.

Together Amelia and Pierre dragged Isobel into the carriage. It was not difficult; she weighed nothing. Once under cover, she slumped, panting and distraught, into a corner where she cowered low in the seat.

'Please, please get away from here quickly,' she begged, 'before they find I have gone.'

Without stopping to consider what she was doing, Amelia nodded. 'Home, Joseph,' she said, 'and quickly.'

Zach told himself he was just about as contented as a man could be. It was three o'clock in the afternoon and the heat beat down on the thatched roof of the slave hut where he lay sprawled on the floor of the upper storey, nothing but straw under his big, unclothed frame. Flies made angry sorties about his head, sizzling with sound, but he pushed them away with a negligent hand, too replete to bother to swot them. Beside him Ruby slept, or pretended to sleep, as naked as she had come into the world, glistening black, rounded belly rising and falling with her breathing, breasts still firm and nipples dangerously dark. A thin coating of sweat lay over her broad face, highlighting its exotic planes. He had fucked her three times and he was exhausted from the effort.

Back in the great house his wife was also sleeping; taking her afternoon nap to keep both herself and the coming baby away from the killing heat. These days Zach paid his visits to Ruby at times when Charlotte would not know what was going on. Previously he had not cared, but his attitude had changed now that his wife was producing an heir. He was careful to do nothing to upset her.

It would be cooler in the big, airy bedroom in the house, Zach thought, and wondered how it would be to fuck Ruby in his own bed. But that would be insulting to his wife. In any case, he rather liked the steamy heat and the unidentifiable smells of the slave quarters. It was amusing to fuck Ruby there while all the other inhabitants were labouring elsewhere for him under the hammer blows of the sun. Thinking about it, maybe Ruby was labouring for him, too. He had no illusions that she loved him or even liked him, but did it matter? She was a natural-born whore. In his opinion it would be impossible to rape Ruby. The moment she was touched, roughly or gently, breast, cunt, mouth, anywhere, she opened up. She became wet, the smell of musk permeated, her nipples sharpened and, most important, her legs opened.

He couldn't give up these uninhibited sessions with Ruby completely. Lust. That's all it was. He didn't have to *think* about fucking Ruby. He just did it. With Charlotte it was different. Since her mother had died she too had become uninhibited but in a different way. With Charlotte it was necessary to think about the act of love. She would drench her nipples in perfume. She would place honey between her legs for him to lick away. She liked to surprise him. He would come into the bedroom and pull back the curtains round their huge double-poster bed to find her stretched out there, legs wide apart, one finger buried where she wanted him to be. Or she would be playing with her own nipples, and then insist he knelt so that she could thrust them into his mouth. It was quite extraordinary how she had changed and the pregnancy had seemed to make her even more eager. Charlotte had imagination when it came to love and she expected him to match it with loving gestures and romantic words. Ruby was no more than an exciting fuck who made a lot of noise, put a lot of energy into it and took what was coming to her.

His favourite fantasy was having the two of them in bed at one time. One white and sensual, one black and sexual. He knew it would never happen.

But Charlotte would be waking soon, and when she woke she liked to find him there. Since she had begun to swell she had taken to insisting that they try new positions so that his weight was not on her stomach. She was particularly fond of being taken from behind, and these days when he pulled back the bed curtains he was liable to find her on all fours, two smooth, round, white buttocks offered as a gift, dumbly saying 'take me'.

He began to dress, knowing that he shouldn't have fucked Ruby that third time. But maybe the sight of Charlotte's two mounds of white and the dark slit between would revive him. He hoped so and sighed as he clambered down the ladder into the main slave cabin without bothering to speak to Ruby. Sometimes it was exhausting for a man to have two women in his life.

Charlotte was already awake when he returned to the house. She was waiting for him in the hall, so intent on giving him the message that had come for him that she never even asked where he had been.

'Pierre came to see you,' she said all of a fluster. 'Amelia asks that you visit her with Ben in the morning on a matter of great importance. I told him to tell Ben to come here at nine thirty so that you could go together. What can it be? What kind of importance?'

Her blue eyes were wide with excitement; she was, he thought, very pretty. Not dramatically foreign like Ruby, but definitely prettier. The thought occurred to him that he really ought to give Ruby up. Sell her, send her to the fields. Anything to get temptation out of his way.

'Amelia is not one either to fuss or to panic,' he said in the rather pompous way he had adopted since he had been elected to the island Council. 'Something serious must have happened.'

'What can it be?' Charlotte breathed, clasping her hands.

'No doubt we shall discover tomorrow,' he pronounced. He patted her gently on the shoulder and then let his hand slide down over the curve that held his son. She smiled up at him, all huge blue eyes and soft blonde curls.

'Pierre interrupted my nap,' she said with the most delightful pout of thin but very pink lips.

'My poor sweet,' he said, lifting his hand so that it cupped her full breast.

'Are you tired?' she asked, her expression coy. 'It is so hot today.'

'Not too tired,' he said, and squeezed her nipple.

'Oh, good,' she sighed. 'Do let us go upstairs.'

'Thank heavens you are both here.' Amelia had been close to the window that looked down the driveway, anxiously waiting for Zach and Ben to arrive at Elsewhere. They appeared together at about ten in the morning, expressions grave, demanding to know what was the matter.

Amelia insisted they settle themselves in her little sitting room and had Bella bring in some sweetmeats and coffee. Once they were seated and comfortable, she went straight to the point.

'I went to Macabees yesterday,' she announced.

'You did what?' said Zach.

'Went to Macabees and I can see why you didn't like it, Zach. It is the most horrible place.'

Leaning forward in her chair to command their attention she told the story of the frightened girl and her encounter with Vincent Ramillies, a tale that she could see was not pleasing Zachary.

'Why do you want to buy Macabees?' he asked belligerently, interrupting her.

'That's not the point. That's not what I want to talk to you about,' she said impatiently. 'Something much more important. When Pierre and I left we had just got through the plantation gates when we saw that the girl was waiting outside for us. She wanted to get away from Macabees. She had slipped out of the front door while that giant of a black was following me to the room where I found Vincent Ramillies. Once she was outside, she went to the stream and ran down it where it was shallow, then sort of swam where it was deeper until she got to the plantation boundary. She knew they would track her with dogs, she'd seen them catch too many of the slaves who tried to run. The dogs, she says, are lethal. They have been trained to tear a runaway to pieces. She was absolutely exhausted and soaked to the skin when we found her but—'

'You didn't bring her here?' Zach interrupted again, sounding horrified.

Amelia looked at him exasperated. He never understood anything.

'Of course I brought her here,' she said crossly. 'What else could I do? Hand her back to that monster? She's still sleeping. Yesterday when I got her back here and dried her off and fed her, I thought she would never stop talking. She has had a life of true horror. She's lucky to be alive. And, would you believe, I was the first women that she ever remembered seeing.'

'But you can't just keep her here,' Zach protested.

'She's not going back to Macabees. Over my dead body,' Amelia said defiantly. 'Her parents died when she was tiny and she only remembers being looked after by black male slaves. I did her no service when I sent you to buy Truly, Zach. It seems that with Truly and Ruby gone, Ramillies decided that he would never have another woman in the house. When she was about four – and incidentally, she has no idea of her birth date – Ramillies brought a male tutor from England, one of his own persuasion, who acted as nursemaid, teacher, everything. Isobel says he was kind enough to her, though she was neglected when they had what appear to have been male orgies which went on for days. Then when she was about seven, he died. The usual fever. The next man who was employed was another monster. From the time he arrived she was never allowed out of the house. Since there are never any visitors at Macabees, she knows nothing of the outside world at all. This tutor was determined she should learn, but not for the joy of knowledge. All his lessons seem to have been a means of imposing his will on her. Oh, not sexually, though his punishments when she made an error of any kind sound as if he was taking some kind of revenge on women. Her body is covered with scars where he burnt her, usually by making

186

her lean, naked, over a candle flame. Her poor little breasts are hardly developed and yet they are dreadfully marked. Sometimes he had her whipped – you can see the marks of that, too. He devised all kinds of tortures and pain and always with Ramillies' consent. Isobel believes her uncle hoped that he would kill her by mistake one day. She says he hates her.'

'Why?' asked Ben, who had gone quite white.

'God knows. Perhaps merely because she is female. Maybe some other reason.'

'And how old is she now?' Zach asked.

'We think fifteen.'

'Wicked!' Ben whispered.

'So, you see, she cannot return there.'

There was a long silence.

'Well?' Amelia threw out her hands. 'What are we going to do?'

'I know what I'm going to do,' said Zachary grimly. 'I'm going there to kill him.'

Pleased as she was by his reaction, Amelia shook her head violently. 'No! No killing,' she said. 'What we need is the help of the law. Ben, you know all the constables, and Zach, you know the Magistrate and the Attorney General and are a member of the Council. You are a friend of the Governor. Surely there is some way we can get Ramillies driven out of St Kitts without any scandal to harm Isobel? Or at least win the right not to send the poor girl back to him.'

'It's a pity that you asked to buy Macabees,' Ben said thoughtfully. 'He could make it look as if it was a plot to make him sell.'

'But if I hadn't gone to Macabees, I would never have known of Isobel's existence,' Amelia protested.

There was an awkward silence, broken by the appearance of Madame Volnay who stood, hands clasped in front of her, in the doorway and said, 'The young lady has come downstairs, madam. She wishes to see you.'

'Please bring her in,' Amelia said.

Both men fidgeted as they waited for the girl to appear. She slid in through the door like a gentle ghost, painfully thin, grey of skin and with the air of a mouse facing a snake. But for all that, it was still possible to catch a glimpse of a pretty young child.

'Please excuse me, Mistress Amelia,' she whispered. 'I disturb you?'

Ben rose and stepped forward to take her hand and draw her into the group. He handed her the plate of sweetmeats and patted her head.

'You do not disturb us,' he said. 'In fact, it is of you that we speak.'

'Of me?' The look of terror had returned.

'We are plotting how you may never have to go back to Macabees,' Ben said gently. 'But you will have to help us to help you. We shall take you to the Magistrate and the Attorney General and you must tell them all that has been done to you, and show them the proof of the cruelty you have suffered.'

187

'Suppose they do not believe me?'

'They will believe you because you will be telling the truth.'

'I am bringing trouble on you,' she said tearfully. 'You must forgive me, but when Mistress Amelia came to Macabees yesterday it was the first opportunity that I had ever had to escape. I feared just to run with no one to run to. It was your misfortune, Mistress Amelia, that your visit gave me the chance.'

Amelia made a dismissive gesture. 'It was no misfortune,' she said.

'Was there truly no one you could turn to for help?' Zach asked.

'No one,' Isobel said, 'though sometimes a man came asking for me. He was always sent away, told that I was sick.'

'But who was he?'

'I don't know. I heard one of the slaves say that he came from Nevis. Is that near here?'

'It is the neighbouring island,' Zach told her. 'Do you have no idea of his name?'

'No. But I once caught a glimpse of him when he was leaving. He was an elderly man in a black coat; very plainly dressed and with white hair tied back with a black ribbon. His manservant was old, too.'

'A priest maybe?' Amelia suggested. 'Or a lawyer?'

Isobel shrugged hopelessly. 'I do not know. But I have the thought that he was something to do with my parents.'

'We must find him.' Amelia had begun to pace the room. 'Zach, what do you think Ramillies will do when he finds that Isobel has gone?'

'Set the dogs searching for her.'

'And when the dogs don't find her, he will put two and two together and guess that she is with you,' Ben said.

'They will know she is with you,' Zach said grimly. 'The dogs will pick up the scent where she left the stream and lose it again where she got into your carriage.'

Amelia shivered. 'And then?'

'It depends.' Ben was thinking out loud. 'If she is unimportant to him he might do nothing. But if she is important, he will want her back.'

'But how could I possibly be important to him?' Isobel protested.

'Maybe it is really you who owns Macabees,' Ben suggested.

Amelia snapped her fingers. 'That's it! All this hiding you away will be something to do with inheritance. We need to find the man who was asking for you.'

'And if we've hit upon the truth of the matter,' said Ben gravely, 'I think Isobel here may be lucky to be alive.'

After some long discussion it was decided that Isobel should be taken to Windsong. If Ben took her to Basse-Terre, someone from Macabees might see her; the tavern was anyway difficult to guard with so many coming and going.

'Can William also come and stay with you for a while so that at least she will have him for company?' Amelia asked. 'Perhaps Mr Henleigh could go with them, too, and they can both take lessons from him.'

She stopped to consider and then said to the girl, 'Windsong is the second place they will look, so you must never leave Zachary's house until we have this matter settled, Isobel. And never let yourself be alone.'

'Tomorrow I will go to Nevis,' said Ben.

'And I will go with you.' Zach turned to Amelia. 'You must remain here at Elsewhere, Amelia. Just in case those at Ramillies discover that we are visiting Nevis and guess what we are doing.'

'You think there might be danger?' she asked.

Zach shrugged his broad shoulders and clenched his fists. 'There might,' he said laconically.

The following morning, after Isobel and William had departed for Windsong, Nero arrived at Elsewhere. Joseph was puzzled what to do with a black man demanding to see Mistress Rosier-Quick and sent him packing, muttering that he had never heard of such barefaced cheek. An hour later, a burly, overdressed white man describing himself as Isobel Ramillies' tutor and calling on behalf of Mr Ramillies appeared at the front door. Nero was with him. Joseph let in the tutor but firmly left Nero outside. Then he fetched Pierre.

Stiff and correct, the Frenchman greeted the Ramillies' tutor. 'And what is your name, sir?'

'My name is of no importance.' Amelia, listening from behind the door of her sitting room, heard the bluster in his voice.

'It is important to me,' said Pierre. 'I do not permit nameless strangers into the house of my mistress.'

'It is your mistress I wish to see.'

'Madame Rosier-Quick is in Basse-Terre on business,' Pierre informed him frostily. 'If you will have the courtesy to give me your name, I will tell her you called.'

There was a brief silence, and then the man said, his tone threatening, 'I am searching for a young girl, Isobel Ramillies, whom we believe to be in this house.'

'I am afraid I cannot help you, sir.' Pierre even managed to get some regret into his voice. 'The lady is unknown to me.'

'She is not unknown to your mistress.'

'Indeed? That, of course, is possible. But we have no young ladies here in the house.' He coughed gently. 'Joseph, see this gentleman out, if you please.'

Emerging from her hiding place after he had gone, Amelia said, 'They won't be that easily satisfied. We must warn them at Windsong. Pierre, go there. Take Truly and Daniel with you. And make sure that Truly sleeps in the same room as Isobel tonight.'

'Yes, madam,' he said, bowing from the waist. 'But I hesitate to leave you here.'

'Joseph will look after me, won't you, Joseph?'

'Sure will, Mistress 'Melia.' He nodded his grey head. 'No one's go'n get by Bella and me. That Bella, she better than two men. Don' you worry, Miss 'Melia. You be all right.'

Nevertheless, she slept badly, jumping at every creak in the old house and aware of the wind sighing in the tall palm trees outside her bedroom window. She lay awake wondering what was happening at Macabees. What were they plotting? How capable of violence were they? How important was Isobel to them? She tossed and turned, frustrated at not knowing, wishing she could be secretly transported to Macabees to learn what they were doing.

Early next morning Ben and Zach were back, windblown and sea-stained, but pleased with themselves. They had with them a frail old man in rusty black breeches and frockcoat, black stockings that wrinkled round his bony ankles, and spotless, gleaming-white ruffled shirt. His wig was white and short, and he peered about him through faded but still watchful blue eyes.

'This is Mr Butts,' said Ben. 'Mr Butts, Mistress Rosier-Quick.'

The old man bowed stiffly. 'I owe you thanks, mistress,' he said in a surprisingly deep voice. 'Your brother and cousin have told me how you saved my client.'

'Your client?'

He smiled, deepening the wrinkles on his face. 'Yes, my client who was lost and is found again.'

'Ah,' said Amelia, 'the pleasure was mine that I found her. And in my pleasure at seeing you, I am forgetting my manners. Please be seated. May I offer you some coffee?'

'That would be agreeable,' he said.

Mr Butts, for all his age and seeming frailty, was robust enough when it came to speech.

'You see,' he explained once his coffee was before him, 'Isobel's parents were my clients. I was in Old Road Town in those days, but I tired of the constant warfare on St Kitts. Most disturbing, all those frightful cannonballs flying over one's head, don't you think? And whoever wins, there is never an end to it. I moved to Charlestown on Nevis. More primitive but much more peaceful. It was only by chance that I heard that Alfred and Miranda Ramillies had died. After all, they were so young, one would not have expected it. But I suppose on these islands one should expect anything.' He paused to take a sip of coffee and let out his breath appreciatively.

'Young Alfred had come to see me in Nevis when his daughter was born, in order to change his will,' he continued. 'And . . . ' he paused, looking at the three of them.

'And?' prompted Amelia.

'Macabees is hers. Entirely. Alfred explained at the time that his brother had money of his own. Vincent Ramillies is also by far the older of the two brothers and I suppose young Alfred thought that Vincent, by the law of averages, would die first.' He shook his head, his expression regretful. 'Most unreliable, the law of averages, in my experience.'

There was a silence.

190

'So Macabees isn't Vincent Ramillies to sell?' Amelia asked.

'Not a pebble of it. When I finally heard through another client that young Alfred was dead, I went to see Vincent. He should have been in touch with me, of course, but you can't expect decent behaviour from a fellow of that kind. He suggested that he continue to run the estate until Isobel was older. Since by then Alfred had been dead for nearly three years and the place seemed to be running perfectly well, it appeared to be the most sensible way round the problem, though I have to say I can't abide Vincent Ramillies. I saw the child who seemed fit and well, and a young man who was said to be her tutor. My own thought was that a nurse would have been more appropriate but Vincent said he was waiting for a new nurse to arrive from England. I had no reason not to believe the odious fop and Alfred's will had been a sketchy affair, not making any provisions for eventualities. My fault, I suppose, but he was an impatient young fellow. One of those who think they'll live for ever and you believe 'em. Couldn't have been more different from his ghastly brother.'

'It sounds as if Isobel is lucky to be alive,' Amelia said thoughtfully.

'From what these young fellows tell me, you could be right. Seems Vincent didn't quite have the stomach for murder when it came to the crunch. But then one would guess he was a squeamish kind of fellow.'

'What do we do now?' Zach asked.

'Take ourselves off to see the Magistrate, that's what we do. But I'd like to see my client before we go. Should have made more fuss about them not letting me see her those last few times I went. Trouble with getting old. You don't push as hard as you used to. But even so, it would give an old man pleasure to tell the girl the good news.'

They went to Windsong in the carriage, in deference to Mr Butt's old bones, and as they drew up in front of the house, William burst out of the door dragging with him Isobel. The two young people ran down the steps, William most uncharacteristically excited and calling, 'Mama! Mama!'

'What is it, William?' Amelia asked once Joseph had helped her down.

'A man came looking for Isobel. We hid and Aunt Charlotte was so brave. She made him go away and she didn't tell him a thing.'

'It was my tutor, Mr Peckett,' Isobel put in timidly. 'I recognised his voice.'

'They haven't been back?' Zach asked.

'No. I think Aunt Charlotte frightened him, she was so fierce.'

'Well done, all of you.' Amelia gave them both a hug.

'And we've worked it all out,' William gabbled. 'Isobel can stay with us for always and share Mr Henleigh and never go back to that dreadful place again.'

'We'll talk about that later,' Amelia told him. 'For now, Isobel, do you recognise this gentleman?'

Mr Butts had creaked his way out of the carriage and was standing

191

on the drive, hands at his side, looking very serious. Isobel nodded slowly. 'It is the gentleman who came asking for me at Macabees,' she said.

He stepped forward, took her hand and bowed over it. 'Your servant, Mistress Isobel. My name is John Butts. I was your father's lawyer and I have some good news for you.'

'Impart it inside,' said Zach heartily, shooing them all towards the hallway of the house.

He led them all into the library and waved for Mr Butts to sit at the large desk. The others arranged themselves in chairs round the room and waited for the lawyer to speak.

He had a dramatic way with him. He waited until the room was still and silent before saying, 'Mistress Ramillies, I have here with me your father's last will and testament for you to read. It is very simple. It states that all his worldly goods are bequeathed to his only child, Isobel Jane Ramillies.'

The girl had gone very white. 'What does that mean?' she whispered.

'It means that Macabees is your property.'

'Not Uncle Vincent's?'

'No. Your uncle has no right to be there, except at your wish and will. It is your home and your plantation. You own everything on it.'

She clapped her hands together and then over her flushed cheeks. 'Oh, Mistress Amelia. You wanted to buy it. You went there to buy it. You shall. Oh, you shall. It shall be my means of thanking you for all you have done.'

'Hold hard!' Mr Butts raised a cautionary hand. 'Remember, it is your home as well as your plantation. Do nothing rashly. Take your time, young lady. You have a lifetime to make your decisions.'

'But I would rather stay with Mistress Amelia and William,' she protested.

'And so you shall, if Mistress Amelia is agreeable, until we have unravelled this ball of string. There is much to be done before we can – ' he coughed gently – 'persuade your uncle to leave. It may take some time. Perhaps six months.'

'And I can stay with you?' She had turned to Amelia, huge blue eyes pleading.

Amelia put her arm round the girl's shoulder. 'Of course you can, my sweetling. Of course you can.'

'Hurray! Hurray! Hurray!' William was hopping up and down with excitement. 'Oh, thank you, Mama.' He had taken Isobel's hand firmly in his and now his hazel eyes were making an appeal. 'Can we go and play now?' he begged. 'Isobel knows hardly any games. There's such a lot to teach her.'

John Butts was right in his forecast of the length of time that it would take before Vincent Ramillies could be evicted from Macabees. In fact it was late September, a full seven months after Isobel arrived at

Elsewhere, before Ramillies left St Kitts for England. He was accompanied by Tutor Peckett, a great deal of luggage and a retinue of slaves. Mr Butts said he thought it wiser to permit Ramillies to take his personal slaves with him, muttering they were so debased that no decent person would want them in their household.

Vincent Ramillies had fought tooth and nail to stay, but the Magistrate had seen for himself the evidence of the treatment that had been meted out to Isobel. As word spread of what had been happening at Macabees, every hand on the island was turned against him. His food supplies became harder to buy, his sugar harder to sell. There were endless arguments about what was his and what was Isobel's. Since there was no one to vouch for any of the contents of the house, in the end the Magistrate ruled he could take what he said to be his on condition that Isobel agreed. In fact, it was Mr Butts who made all the decisions. Some of his clients' possessions he remembered well, but there were items he was certain Alfred Ramillies would never have purchased. He permitted those to leave the estate.

It was also decided that for safety's sake Isobel would stay at the home of Mr Butts on Nevis until Ramillies had gone. Her death would leave him the nearest living relative; he might think it worthwhile to arrange a murder even at this late stage. With Isobel went William and Mr Henleigh to keep her company, Truly, Daniel and Juba, to help guard her, plus a couple of burly sailors who had jumped ship and worked at the tavern for Ben.

Zach was a happy man throughout the seven-month wait for Ramillies' departure. In July Charlotte was delivered of a lusty pair of twins whom they christened James and Julia. No longer a young woman, Charlotte had nearly died with the effort, and Zach had been astonished by his own grief and anxiety when her life was in the balance. But she was recovering and Zach had decided that he would buy Macabees as a gift for his children. What did his sister want with more property? It was not right that a woman without a man to run it for her had any property at all.

Zach might have been pleased with life, but it was a bad seven months for both Tansy and Amelia. Tansy, suddenly bereft of all playmates, was bored and lonely and, without quite understanding why, jealous of Isobel whose unexpected arrival in their lives had caused all these problems. She was also resentful that Mark Henleigh, with all his promise of being a good companion and leading her to the light, had been so abruptly snatched away. Had she known it, the tutor was suffering similar resentments.

Amelia, so close to the real possibility of being united with Joshua and yet still having to wait, was missing William. The house seemed empty without him and she needed something to do with her life.

On the day that Vincent Ramillies at last sailed for Bristol, Amelia walked in her garden, occasionally pulling at a weed, and feeling that after so long, Vincent's departure was something of an anti-climax.

Tomorrow William and Isobel would return with Mr Henleigh as well as Truly and her family, and life would return to normal. As soon as it was decently possible, Amelia would ask Isobel if she could buy Joshua and bring him here. She had no doubts that the answer would be yes. Her only problem was that suddenly she was uncertain. Was it the right thing to do? After so long apart, would it be better to leave things as they were?

She wandered along the banks of the stream and through the orchard. Oranges hung heavy on the branches of the trees. Even after so long it still pleased her to see oranges growing. In the distance she could see a figure walking towards her without haste. She strained her eyes against the brightness of the dazzling sun. It was a black figure, and slaves were not permitted in this part of the grounds unless they were working on the trees.

She debated whether to call Joseph and then decided to deal with the matter herself. She could now see it was a man, and he had increased his pace. For a moment she felt that frisson of fear that most whites felt when alone and confronted by an unknown slave. Then he began to run towards her. She hesitated, stood her ground, wondering if he might be dangerous. If he were, should she turn tail and run for the house? Before she could decide, she suddenly saw the unbalanced gait of the man. He had only one arm.

It was Joshua.

Chapter Twelve

Not caring who saw, there on the path, where the whole world could have been watching, she opened her arms and pulled him to her, half-crying, half-laughing, but overwhelmed with a delight she had not felt in years. The moment she had seen him, she knew that nothing had changed and she kissed him with all her heart.

'Amelia, take care,' he said, reluctantly disengaging himself from her. 'Folk might be watching.'

'I don't care,' she said.

'But you should.' He was smiling at her with liquid brown eyes that held a hint of tears. He was even more fine-looking than she remembered. He was no longer a boy but very much a man. A big, solid man with sweetness in his face – and only one arm.

'What happened?' she asked, touching where his left arm should have been and bursting with love and pity.

He gently pushed her another pace away from him.

'Not now. This is not the place to tell you,' he said. He glanced around nervously and she realised he was embarrassed, suddenly uncertain of himself. 'Can we talk together? Is it all right being here with me?'

'Why not?'

His look said that she knew very well why not. 'I shouldn't be here.' he muttered.

'True. Slaves aren't permitted here, Joshua,' she said laughing and trying to put him at his ease. 'But you are. You're permitted anywhere on what is mine.'

'This be yours?'

She nodded.

A shadow crossed his face. 'Then it won't be the same between us now.'

'But I don't feel different. Do you?' She stretched out her hand to let her finger wander down his cheek. He backed away from her.

'No. But it be different,' he said doggedly.

She made an impatient gesture.

'Come to the house,' she said. 'We need to be alone.'

'We'll be out of sight?'

She was not sure if he was fearful for himself or for her. 'Yes, we'll be out of sight.'

Moving swiftly, she led him through the gardens to a back door of the house that was only used for taking in provisions. Light-footed, like two conspirators, they went up the back stairs and down the silent passage to her bedchamber.

He stopped just inside the doorway.

'I shouldn't be here,' he said, again uneasy. She understood that his fear was brought about because a black slave could be hung for consorting with a white woman. She grasped his hand reassuringly.

'It is the one place in the house where no one ever interrupts me in the daytime. It is quite safe.'

'You are sure?'

'I'm positive. But lock the door if it makes you happier.'

He did, carefully taking out the key and putting it on a small table.

They stood, the length of the room between them, looking at each other intently, registering changes, restoring familiarity. His skin seemed greyer and he looked tired but otherwise little different. She felt as if she would burst with pent-up love.

'You came looking for me?' she asked.

'You and Tansy.' He dropped his head, looking at the floor. Then he looked her straight in the eyes. 'I have a son,' he said abruptly.

'By Ruby?'

'By Ruby.' His voice was steady, his eyes watching to see how she judged him.

'I know. She told me when Zach brought her here. I, too, have a son.'

His mouth tightened. 'And a husband?'

'He died fourteen years ago. Did you love Ruby?'

'No. Did you love your husband?'

'No. I have never ceased to love you.'

He let out his breath in a long sigh. Looking at him, Amelia felt the vital heat rising in her and found herself consumed by a need that had been suppressed for far too long. From the moment the door had been locked, both had imperceptibly moved closer to the other as if some force were pulling them. They were now only about three paces apart. They stood stock-still and silent, the atmosphere between them so strong that they might as well have been in each other's arms.

Her need to lie with him was so urgent, so compelling that she was incapable of containing it. She took his right hand in hers and said quietly, 'Please love me.'

His expression was anguished. Black spiky lashes closed over his eyes to hide the pain.

'Amelia, I shouldn't have come here. We're not equals any more. You're no slave now.'

'Your slave,' she said.

He groaned. 'Amelia!' It was a cry of pain.

'Don't you want to lie with me?' she asked, determined not to give in.

'More than anything.'

She dropped his hand and put her arms round him, pressing herself as close to his big body as she could.

He looked down at her. 'I washed,' he said inconsequentially. 'I washed. In the river.'

She smiled at him and lifted her face to be kissed. He hesitated, and then pulled away.

'We shouldn't . . .'

'Joshua, I love you,' she said. 'For God's sake kiss me.'

'I only got one arm to hold you with.'

'Then use it.'

Awkwardly he pulled her to him.

'That's better,' she told him. 'Much better.'

'Still so pretty,' he was murmuring. 'Still so pink and soft.' He gazed at her. 'Your eyes still be like a leaf. A beautiful leaf in the springtime. But you don't understand. It's all different now.'

The sun streaming in through her bedchamber window was emphasising their difference, bouncing off his brown skin as it had by the pool so long ago. He looked like a statue from the ancient world; his curly hair flat to his head, the carved face, the strong body, the missing arm.

'And you are still beautiful,' she said softly. 'Now love me.'

Their coupling was as she remembered it; gentle, yet passionate, intense yet innocent. Recalling their tentative, loving encounters long ago she felt a young girl again. They were shy together. He was embarrassed by the loss of his arm and she wondered if her body, now nineteen years older than when he had first made love to her, still pleased him. There was also the memory that he had been with the bold and beautiful Ruby. But when all garments were shed and his body folded over hers, his mouth on hers, his hand beneath her buttocks, lifting her, and they were one again after so long and so arid a time, all anxieties disappeared. She clung to him in deep content, wondering at the marvel of being able at last to consummate her long-cherished love for him in the depth and comfort of her own bed.

Fulfilled, they both slept, she with her hand between her thighs so she could feel the damp and warmth he had left behind. It was she who woke first, and leaned to stroke his face. He stirred, murmured and turned to her, pulling her head onto his shoulder.

'How did you find out where I was?' she asked quietly, kissing his shoulder.

He grimaced. 'After this went,' he indicated the missing arm, 'I worked in the house at Macabees, clearing the trash, doin' anything the master and Mistress Isobel's tutor wanted me to do. The other house slaves were all – ' he hesitated – 'like Master Justinian used to be, and I didn't want that again. I kept out of their way. I only ever spoke to the master and the tutor. I used to sneak books out from their library. Reading helped me. I read every chance I got. I wanted to talk right and be right if we ever met again. Then when Mistress Isobel ran away, they had all the dogs out after her, like they always do, but they couldn't find her. Master was like to murder someone he was so angry but he had no idea who to blame.

197

'Soon after, when I was clearing the master's room, I found letters on his desk. I read 'em. Letters from a lawyer called Mr Butts. Others, too, from the Magistrate at Old Road Town. They were just lying on his desk, some screwed up in anger. I guess he wouldn't have left 'em there if he'd known I could read. Those letters said the plantation belong to poor little Mistress Isobel all the time. I reckoned then that the master was going to have to leave the island for sure. Then another letter came that said how a Mistress Amelia Rosier-Quick of Elsewhere would give witness against him in the courts. Now I didn't know your name was Rosier, but I knew you were Quick and I knew you had a plantation, and I knew in my bones it were you.' He sighed, and turned to bury his face in her hair. 'If you hadn't taught me my letters all that time ago, I never would've found you. It be like a miracle.'

She sighed contentedly and asked, 'But how did you find Elsewhere?'

'Benson, the overseer, talked about the plantation next door and would sort of wave in the direction of it. It wasn't hard to find. There's no other plantation this end of the island. I waited until the day the master was leaving for England. He was taking his personal slaves with him, and Benson and all the officials went to see him off. Then I just ran.'

She snuggled closer to him. 'And here you are.'

'And here I am.'

Then she sat up abruptly. 'But your arm?'

'I ran once before. Just after Tansy went. I took my son and went looking to find her. They sent the dogs after me. My son weren't nothing but a baby then, and it was hard to move fast with him on my shoulders. They caught me. The dogs started my arm and Benson finished it off with a machete. That's what they do to slaves who run,' he said bitterly. 'But I knowed the risk and I took it.'

She wanted to ask if he had been looking for her or for Ruby when he ran, but it did not seem to be the right moment.

'They didn't hurt your son?'

'Samuel? No. They let him be.'

They lay quietly for a while.

'You know, 'Melia,' he finally said, 'we're doing wrong.'

'No!' she said passionately, turning to hold him.

'Wrong,' he said doggedly, his face set. 'You're not a slave any more. You're mistress of a plantation. What we just did is dangerous for us both.' His voice dropped and the depth of it sounded like a warning drum. 'We can't never be together.'

The pain she felt was because he was right. Her mind was racing like a squirrel in a cage, trying to plot a way that they could have some life together.

'We could keep it secret.'

'How?'

'Somehow.'

'There be no way.' She knew he was deeply sad. 'We ain't babies any more, like then. We've grow up and we've got to understand that it's not the same. You're rich and I'm a slave.'

'I'll think of something,' she muttered.

'Maybe,' he said gently, then, consoling her, pulled her closer to him. 'Maybe. It was wrong I came here, but you have been my dream all these years. I had to come. I had to see you.'

'It has been the same for me,' she whispered. 'But I won't let you go back to Macabees. I shall buy you from Isobel and keep you here.'

'And then I really will be your slave,' he said ruefully.

'No. You'll be a free man,' she said. 'I shall give you your freedom, like Bella. Bella is free.'

'And Tansy?' he asked eagerly.

She shook her head.

'Why not?'

'If I had given her freedom, she would have left me.'

'So your daughter is your slave?' He sounded so dismayed that tears sprang to her eyes. 'You love her?' he asked.

'Yes. Almost as much as I love you. She's beautiful.'

'And Truly?'

'Truly is not free,' she said steadily. 'But she lives with her man, Daniel, and her son, Juba, in their own quarters.'

He had moved slightly away from her and lay on his back, staring up at the panelled ceiling.

'Why did you only free my mama?'

'Because I knew she would never leave me. The others would have. I needed them. They're my family, Joshua.'

He gave a bitter little laugh. 'Black family.'

'That's right. Black family.' She knew she sounded defiant.

'And you reckon I'll stay if you make me free?'

'I don't know.' The thought of him leaving caused her stomach to churn. 'But I hope you will.'

He turned again and wrapped her close to him. 'Oh, 'Melia, where else is there for me to go? I have to be here. Here is where my heart is.'

Isobel was full of excitement when she saw Amelia's carriage waiting as she and William spilled off the boat from Nevis. Daniel and Truly, laden with luggage, moved more slowly; Joseph dropped the reins and jumped down to help them. Mark Henleigh brought up the rear. It was a steamy hot day; so hot that the sea looked silver and the white of the ship's sails bounced painfully off the eyes. Henleigh coughed dismally in his handkerchief. He had turned a pale shade of green on the short crossing from the neighbouring island, and he was, Isobel thought, feeling rather sorry for himself.

She, on the other hand, was full of optimism. The memory of the dreadful years she had spent at Macabees was fading a little, though there were days when she was full of despair and found herself crying for no reason. Sometimes she was racked by dreadful nightmares and Truly would run to wake her and soothe her.

She and William had become close and he was demanding of her company. He always wanted to be with her and she found it comforting. William made her feel safe. They united in teasing the serious Mr Henleigh who seemed, in his own solemn way, to enjoy their pranks. But more important, she had spent many hours with Mr Butts, learning about her parents and her background. For the first time in her life she felt like a real person, with roots and a family history behind her. He had even been able to give her a miniature of both her mother and father. She studied their fair English faces every night before she went to sleep and was grateful to find in them nothing of the thin, cruel features of Uncle Vincent.

'Your parents were good friends of mine, you know, my dear, as well as clients,' Butts had told her, 'and I am grieved that I did not do more for you. But then I had no idea of the wickedness you were suffering.'

He had convinced her that she should do nothing in a hurry. Macabees was hers. She could keep it, and have it run by a manager or an agent, or she could sell it and return to England. But he pointed out that there was little for her in England. He said nothing definite, leaving her to make up her own mind, but she felt that in his heart he believed that she should keep Macabees for a while and see how her life developed.

'You will find it very different living there as the mistress, young as you are,' he pointed out. 'And come January you will be sixteen, old enough to make your own decisions.'

'You know when my birthday is?' she asked, delighted.

'I know your birthday. You were born on January 3rd, 1690, and your parents said that you were the best New Year present that the good Lord could have given them.'

Isobel reckoned that once a person had a birth date this made them real and made them someone. She now knew exactly who she was.

Amelia was waiting for them on the steps of Elsewhere when the carriage drew up. She hugged William first, who shied away. William was already more than five inches taller than his mother, his voice had deepened, and he had a faint fluff of moustache on his upper lip.

'You have grown so!' Amelia exclaimed, holding his arms and standing back to look at him. 'Oh, how I have missed you!'

William reddened, shuffled his feet uncomfortably and seemed lost for words, while Isobel felt a pang of envy. There had never been a mother to miss her.

But she received her hug in turn, Mr Henleigh was greeted warmly and Amelia announced that tea would be ready in quarter of an hour.

She led Isobel up to the room that she was to occupy. Once the chamber door was closed, she said urgently, 'Isobel, my dear, there is something that I must speak to you about immediately.'

Surprised, Isobel flung her hat onto the bed and turned with raised eyebrows.

'I have stolen one of your slaves,' Amelia said, and laughed a little nervously. 'Of course, the penalty for stealing a slave is death, but I trust you will not put me to the gallows. He is Tansy's father, he took advantage of your uncle's departure to flee, and he came here. It was only yesterday. Whether they are seeking him or not, I do not know. I have kept him on the estate.'

'Tansy's father?' Isobel was astonished. 'Which slave is this? Do I know him?'

'Perhaps you would remember him. He is called Joshua. He has only one arm.'

'Of course I remember him. He was always gentle and kind. I liked him very much. And he is Tansy's father? But he is so . . . ' she hesitated.

'Brown?'

'Well, yes, but if he is Tansy's father he must stay here.'

'And I must pay you for him.'

'Nonsense!' Isobel said stoutly. 'He is a gift.'

'But I wish to free him.'

'If that is what you wish, then I shall free him.' The grand gesture somehow confirmed that Macabees was hers to do with as she would.

Amelia hugged and kissed her. 'You are such a good girl,' she sighed and Isobel was disconcerted to see that Amelia's eyes were wet.

Downstairs, tea was served and Amelia was surprised to see Zach there already seated. He rose to his feet as they came into the room, took Isobel's hand and bowed over it, murmuring congratulations before apologising to Amelia for his unexpected appearance.

Halfway through the meal he suddenly said to Isobel, eyes fixed on her face, 'I suppose that you will now sell Macabees?'

'Oh no.' She was spreading honey on her bread, careful not to let it drip over the sides. 'I have decided to keep it for a while.'

'You have?'

'Yes. Mr Butts has pointed out that it is my home and I have no other.'

'No, no!' Zach said heartily though he looked rather put out. 'Your home is Windsong if you wish it so. You can take your rest with us any time you choose.'

William had suddenly abandoned his slumped position over the table. He was sitting bolt upright. 'Or here, Isobel,' he said eagerly. 'I should prefer it if you were here.'

'I can come and visit you, can I not?' Isobel said gently. 'I should so much like to continue my studies with you and Mr Henleigh, but it is better that I have my own home.'

Zach fidgeted. 'But the plantation . . .'

'I shall have it run by a manager. And I am sure that both you and dear Amelia will give me your advice, for I shall need it,' she said.

There was a silence. Amelia glanced at her brother, a glint of amusement in her eyes. He looked decidedly cross.

'I'm sorry if I have disappointed you,' Isobel said gently. 'I know

201

you wished to buy the plantation, Amelia, but I am sure you will understand.'

'I understand very well, 'Amelia told her, and then added cryptically, 'I had, in any case, changed my mind. The need has gone.'

Isobel caught the look of deep suspicion that Zach gave his sister but Amelia only smiled, a smile that turned up the corners of her mouth in a pleased and secretive kind of way. 'Why don't you and William go for a walk before we light the candles?' she suggested. 'And tomorrow we will all go to Macabees.'

'Yes, come on, Isobel.' William was already on his feet. 'Let's go down to the shore.'

Relieved to be away from Zach's obvious irritation, Isobel pushed aside her plate and excused herself. Hand in hand she and William made their way out of the house, through the garden and down to the shore. There was a rock pool tucked away that was William's favourite spot on the estate. He considered it his secret place, and she had been flattered that he had shown her it before she had left for Nevis. But on this visit he seemed nervous. He had little to say and she thought perhaps he was cross, a state of mind that was not improved when they came down onto the black sand. They were not alone; a figure was stretched out on the beach. William stopped dead in indignation. The man, a large, light-skinned Negro with only one arm, sprang to his feet. At first he looked alarmed and then he muttered to himself, 'Mistress Isobel!'

William stepped forward to stand protectively in front of Isobel. 'Who are you?' he asked belligerently, ignoring that the black man was twice as powerful even with only one arm.

Isobel pushed him out of the way. 'It's only Joshua, from Macabees,' she explained. 'Amelia told me he was here. He is Tansy's father.' She turned to face the slave and said, her voice composed, 'I'm so glad I have seen you, Joshua. I wanted to tell you that you are free. I shall get Mr Butts to give you papers to prove it the moment I meet him again.'

Joshua stared at her, bewildered. 'You are giving me my freedom?'

She smiled at him. 'Yes, and then Mistress Amelia won't have to buy you,' she said cheerfully.

The man put his hand over his eyes and Isobel wondered if he was crying.

'You don't know what you have done for me. You don't know what you have given me.' His voice was muffled, and then he took his hand from his face to look at her. 'This is your decision? You thought to give me freedom?'

'Of course,' said Isobel, deciding it would spoil it all if she told him Amelia had mentioned it first.

'You're Tansy's father?' William asked.

'Yes.'

'She doesn't look like you.'

The black man grinned. 'And that be good luck for her,' he chuckled.

202

'You came yesterday, didn't you?' Isobel asked. 'Have you seen her yet? She is very pretty.'

The man shook his head.

'She's bound to be in the kitchen with Bella at this time,' William told him. 'Why don't you go and see her?' Then he added politely. 'Do you know the way?'

'I can find it,' the man said. He half-saluted, hesitated as if he wanted to say something but then merely murmured a quiet 'Thank you.' Light-footed, he left the clearing.

William frowned. 'I wonder how he knows about this place,' he said, almost to himself. 'And he doesn't speak like a slave at all. It's very odd.'

'Shouldn't he have been here?'

William shrugged. 'I don't know. But I shall tell Mama to tell him not to come here again. This is my special place.'

'If he's free, I suppose he can go where he likes,' Isobel said thoughtfully.

'Not if he's black.' William sounded certain of it. Dismissing the subject, they peered into the depth of the pool.

Though he was never exactly a chatterbox, today, Isobel thought, her friend and companion was unnaturally silent. Then abruptly he left the pool and plonked himself down on the sand.

'Isobel, are you determined to live at Macabees?' He sounded extremely serious.

'Yes.' There seemed no point in anything but a straight answer.

William was looking pink again and tugged at the little bit of fluff that decorated his chin. 'I wanted you to stay at Elsewhere,' he blurted out.

'Why?'

He traced a heart in the sand, and said, his voice gruff, 'Well, you see, I love you very much.'

She looked at him, startled. She had never considered herself to be lovable. 'You love me?' She could not contain her astonishment.

He nodded solemnly. 'I had made up my mind a long time ago that I was going to marry you.'

'Me!'

'Oh not yet, of course. Mama wouldn't allow it yet. But as soon as we are old enough.'

He was sitting cross-legged in the sand, his face red with embarrassment, dark eyes carefully fixed on the beach. He had a most tidy profile, with a neat nose, a well-shaped mouth and a chin that was neither too big nor too small. His dark hair was held back with a large bow but one curl had escaped and lay over his shoulder. He wore a loose shirt and tight breeches, red stockings, and shoes with silver buckles. Suddenly Isobel saw him as a rather introverted handsome man and not a shy boy and understood that he was seeing her as a woman. It was disturbing. Confused, she too stared at the sand. 'I do like you very much, William,' she said. 'But is that love?'

William considered. 'I *like* you, too, but it's more. Mr Herrick says,
"Thou art my love, my life, my heart,
The very eyes of me:
And hast command of every part,
To live and die for thee." That's more what I feel.'

'Oh, William.' She clasped her hands together, thrilled at the thought
he would die for her, though she would not wish him to do any such
thing. 'You would really want me to be your wife?'

'Yes.' He suddenly looked up and stared her full in the face. The
look was so intense that she shivered, and then he looked back at the
sand.

'And you love me?' she asked, wanting to hear him say it again, but
he only nodded dumbly.'

'Do you think it would be good if we married?' he asked anxiously.
'I shall have Elsewhere one day and Mama says the tavern, too. I should
be able to look after you very well.'

She was not sure exactly what it was she felt. Gratitude was part of it
but there was also a sort of swelling in the region of her heart as if her chest
could not contain such joy. And there was tenderness, too. And
excitement. Such a mixture of inexplicable feelings. And now she wanted
to touch his face. She needed to know how he felt under her fingers.

But she restrained herself and said 'It might be nice to be married.
Like in stories.'

'Oh, but it would be real, our marriage,' he said, suddenly full of
confidence.

She nodded thoughtfully. 'We would not be lonely if we were married,
would we?'

'Never.'

'And we would be happy and kind to each other.'

'Always.'

'And never do the other harm?'

'Never.' William's large eyes were blinking with the emotion of what
he was promising.

'Then I think I should like to marry you, William.' Solemnly she
held out her hand. He took it and then seemed uncertain what to do next.

'You may kiss me,' she said, serene as a dove.

He leaned forward awkwardly and their lips gently met. It was a
pleasant feeling and she felt her face flame. He, too, had turned scarlet.

Time paused as they looked at each other with a touch of amazement
in their gaze.

'I should like to tell Mama what we have decided,' he finally said.

'Oh, I think that we should.'

'Now?'

'Yes, now.'

He took her hand and helped her to her feet. They walked back to
the house in silence and returned to the tea room where Amelia and
Zach were still sitting, looking tense and as if they might have been

quarrelling. They turned in surprise as the young people came back into the room.

'That was quick,' Amelia said.

William moved to stand at her side. 'We have something to tell you, Mama.'

'Oh?' Amelia cocked her head and waited.

'We have decided that when you say we are old enough we will marry.'

Isobel almost giggled as she saw Zach's jaw drop; Amelia looked equally startled.

'Marry?'

'Yes, Mama.'He cleared his throat self-consciously and lost control of his voice which shot up several octaves. 'I love Isobel, you see.'

Both adults seemed struck speechless.

'And I love William,' Isobel informed them shyly.

Zach put down his teacup and gave Amelia a little salute.

'You win,' he said dryly, and Isobel hadn't the faintest idea what he was talking about.

Joshua had no difficulty finding the kitchen. With complete confidence he walked to the north end of the house where the kitchens were usually situated, just as the privies were always downwind. No man could challenge him. He was free. Freed by his mistress. To him it was important that the gift of freedom had come from Isobel and not Amelia. Had Amelia freed him, it would not have been the same. He would have been so indebted to her that he would have remained as much a slave as he had ever been. Though he could not quite believe that Amelia had no hand in his mistress's sudden decision, that did not matter. The fact was that it was Isobel who had let him go and that meant true freedom. Now he could go where he wished once he had the papers from Mr Butts, even work where he wished, providing someone would give him work.

For a moment he had heady thoughts of returning to Africa, but then his common sense told him that this was a poor idea. And his heart told him that he would remain exactly where he was – here at Elsewhere with his own family, and the woman he loved.

But being a free man without Amelia having first had to buy him changed things. Perhaps she and he could have some life since he was no longer a slave and never had been one in her household. It would have to be secret, of course, but perhaps there could be some future for them. He had a wild fantasy of becoming wealthy and taking her to a part of the world where their love would not cause offence to anyone. But what part of the world would that be? he wondered. He was still black and knew of no freed slave who had become wealthy. In fact those who had been fortunate in a good master were often worse off.

The smell of bread baking led him to the kitchen door. Would Ruby be there? he wondered. He was not sure what to think about Ruby. She was Samuel's mother, but he had not seen Sam for two years since they had taken him to work in the fields. He had hardly thought of Ruby after she had been snatched from Macabees. His dreams had reverted to Amelia. If Ruby were here, she could complicate things.

Cautiously he opened the door and the kitchen heat hit him. His mother was half-turned from him, standing near the open fire where a spit turned. She seemed to be a little thinner than before and a lot older. With a pang he remembered that she was no longer a young woman. Truly, her woolly hair greying but her face unlined, was sitting at the big wooden table preparing vegetables. She looked up at the sound of the door, stared, clapped her hands over her cheeks. 'Mama!' she said in a strangled voice. 'It's Joshua.'

His mother spun round so fast her weight almost toppled her.

'My son!' she cried, and then both women fell upon him, kissing his cheeks, hugging him while all three of them wept.

'Your arm. What happened to your arm?' Truly cried.

'You ran,' his mother said accusingly, 'and they done caught you. Why'd you run?'

'Looking for my family,' he said simply. 'You, Truly, Tansy . . . Mama, where is Tansy?'

Bella snorted. 'She getting 'Melia's tea, and they two, they'll be talking. 'Bout an hour she been gone. She be back soon.'

'I long to see her.'

'She real pretty and she real nice.'

'And she real white,' put in Truly acidly. Her mother gave her a reproachful look.

'But what I wants to know, my son, is how you be here? Did that 'Melia get you?'

He shook his head. 'I came on my own. It's a long story, Mama. But the best thing is – ' he drew a deep breath ' – I'm free.' The two words came out like a trumpet call.

'You be free?' Truly's voice was full of envy.

'I be free. Mistress Isobel gave me my freedom just this very day.'

'Mistress Isobel?' Bella was puzzled. 'Why she give you freedom?'

'Because Macabees is hers. She was just a baby when we went there. Now it's all different.'

Bella was amazed. 'Surely she can't be old 'nuff to give anyone freedom.'

'She's near to sixteen.'

Bella shook her head. 'The years! Where they go? And what you go'n do with this freedom, Josh?'

'Stay here and work with all of you if Mistress Amelia will give me work.'

Bella let out a huge cackle and slapped a vast thigh. 'She'll give you work, boy, all right. I reckon you go'n be worn out with the work she give you. So you better rest now and have a bit o' tea and tell us what been happenin' to you all these years.' She turned back to her stove and then, without looking at him, said so softly he had to strain to hear

206

the words, 'But I go'n be the happiest woman in the world now you be back, Josh. I be a woman with all her folk around her. And there can't be nothin' better than that.'

He was still waiting in the kitchen when Tansy came back. She burst through the door and stopped dead when she saw him. He was glad she stopped. It gave him time to look at her without appearing to stare. He thought he would have recognised her from the picture he had carried in his head of the four-year-old girl who had suddenly been snatched from him. Her eyes were as bright and black as he remembered, her hair springy but not woolly, her nose straight and neat like her mother's; her whole aspect was that of a white girl, an exotic girl with sun-touched skin and too full a mouth. She was extraordinarily beautiful.

'I know you,' she said, peering at him. 'I'm sure I know you, don't I?'

'That you pappy sittin' there awaitin' for you,' Bella said, laughing delightedly. 'He come to find you.'

The girl's wide red mouth dropped open and then a small smile began to dawn. She looked as if she had received a surprise present. A present of something special.

'My father? Are you really?'

Her expression begged for it to be true and he nodded, slowly, three times. His beautiful daughter was silent, lost for words, and then she echoed Bella's laugh of delight.

'My father!' she said, and moved towards him. She put her arms round him and buried her face in his chest. 'I do remember you. I loved you. And then they took me away.'

'And now he found you 'gain,' said Bella.

He hugged her to him with his one arm and stood looking down at her, grinning stupidly, trying to contain his happiness. He wanted to whoop and shout. If he had two arms he would have picked her up and spun her round, but one arm wouldn't do it.

Then she drew back, her face anxious. 'Did you run?'

'Yes.'

'Then it's not safe. Grandma, we must hide him.'

'No need,' Bella said. 'Mistress 'Melia, she fixin' it all.'

Tansy looked at him, head on one side. 'You're staying here at Elsewhere?'

He nodded, his throat so tight and full that he feared he might cry if he spoke.

'What you going to do here?'

Words came. 'I'm a free man, Tansy,' he told her.

Again the fallen lip, the look of astonishment. 'Free!' She was visibly impressed. Young, she was so young, Amelia must have guarded her well.

'My mistress, Mistress Isobel, she gave me freedom,' he told her.

'Mistress Isobel!' She rolled her eyes. 'And to think I didn't like her much.'

Now that the excitement of the first moment of meeting was over,

207

he felt suddenly shy, embarrassed, and he could tell that she did, too. She kept sneaking looks at him as if she could not believe his presence. Her glance slid away from his missing arm. That was nice, he thought. She was too polite to ask. Then suddenly she turned to him, her voice eager. 'Did you bring my mama with you?'

Bella stiffened and, realising what she had done, camouflaged the movement by putting her hand to her back as if it hurt. She exchanged a quick look with Joshua.

'You pappy say you mama's dead,' she said. 'Since long time now.'

Tansy's eyes misted over.

'You remember her?' he asked, anxious to know exactly what she could recall.

'I think so. She was soft and black and she laughed a lot. She gave me her food sometimes. That was my mother, wasn't it?'

He hesitated, then said, 'Yes.'

'I wish she wasn't dead,' she said sadly. 'I loved her like I loved you.' Then she brightened. 'But I've got you back.' Again she hugged him. When she had released him he held her away from him to drink in her beauty again. As he smiled down at her, her expression changed. Two lines bisected her straight, black eyebrows, and the corners of her mouth drooped.

'What is it?' he asked.

'I'm puzzled.'

'What about?' His tone was indulgent, fatherly.

'About being so white.' Then she brightened. 'But it doesn't matter any more, not now I've got you, and now I know that lady really was my mama. I am black really, aren't I?' She sighed a touch theatrically and hugging him again said, 'Oh, it's such a relief to know what I am.'

He did not reply, but his eyes and Bella's met over her head and in both there was a look of hopeless resignation.

Tansy looked sideways out of the corner of her eye at Mark Henleigh as they walked down towards the beach. He had been back from Nevis for nearly six weeks now, and every day he contrived to take a walk with her. She was sure Mistress Amelia did not know this was going on; it was her grandmother who seemed to be encouraging her to keep the young man company. When possible, Bella did her granddaughter's work so that she was always free in the early afternoon. Where once Tansy was made to wait in the kitchen until Mistress Amelia wanted her tea, now she was allowed to accompany Mr Henleigh on his little walks.

As they ambled in the fierce heat it seemed to Tansy that the tutor looked frailer and more romantic than ever. The sun had bleached his hair to a white blond and he wore it tied simply back. He explained he could not bear the weight of a wig in the heat of the islands. His skin had also taken colour from the sun, but he was bone-thin and yet somehow elegant in his high boots and breeches and a loose white cambric shirt.

A few days after he returned from Nevis he had come to the kitchen looking for her and asked if she would guide and accompany him on his afternoon walk since he was still so unfamiliar with the estate. Tansy had looked askance at Bella, but Bella shooed her off and said she would take care of the mistress's tea. That day they had walked near the house, alongside the stream.

'Did you enjoy Nevis?' Tansy asked politely.

'It is very beautiful,' he said, 'more lush than here. But I should have liked it even more if you had been my guide.'

Tansy laughed. 'But I would have been a poor guide for you,' she said. 'I have never been to Nevis.'

He turned to look at her and his blue eyes seemed feverish.

'Then we could have discovered it together.'

'I would have had my duties to perform,' she reminded him.

'Ah, of course,' he said angrily. 'I forget. You are a slave. Oh, the iniquity of it! If only I could rescue you.'

She did not know what to say. He understood nothing but his innocence and his anger made him somehow touching and she was flattered that he wanted her to be with him.

'My life is not so bad,' she told him. 'I am one of the fortunate ones. Others do not fare as well. My papa has come back and he and my grandmama are free. All my family are fortunate.'

'Slavery is wicked,' he muttered. 'A blot on this fair earth.'

'I fear you will never be happy here, Mr Henleigh,' Tansy told him, shaking her head.

He turned the burning eyes on her. 'Oh, yes, but I will,' he said fervently. 'While you are here too, I shall be happy.'

'And I am happy that you are here,' she said politely. 'It is so pleasant to have company.'

He bowed at the compliment, but he seemed disappointed, as if she had not said what he wanted to hear.

She had seen him for at least half an hour every day since and had begun to look forward to their meetings. William was always off and away with the soppy Isobel who most of the time still looked like some frightened animal. That only left Juba for company and Juba was too young. Mark Henleigh was twenty-one, which wasn't that much older than she was. And he was always so flattering, quoting little love poems to her, writing her notes saying that she was beautiful, and always telling her about his deep, religious feelings. It was his dream that she should follow what he called the shining white path of the Lord, but his religious lectures left Tansy unimpressed. She was too cheerful and outgoing by nature suddenly to embrace religion. Nor was she looking for consolation of any kind. She even had her father back in her life and there didn't seem to be much more she could ask for. The memory of the day she had spent at the factory and in the fields still troubled her but she felt somehow that Mr Henleigh's good Lord could not do much about that. And if he could, why hadn't he?

209

Today he wanted to walk down to the Atlantic shore, a much longer walk than to the Caribbean. As they strolled between the rows of fast-growing sugar cane, trying to find shade from the sun, and then into wooded country, he was silent. Not until they reached the yellow sand of the beach did he start to speak.

'Amelia, I find myself confused,' he said

He did seem rather agitated and she put her hand on his to calm him. He jumped as if she had stung him.

'Confused? By what?'

To her dismay, he sank on his knees into the sand in front of her.

'I missed you so much in those months on Nevis. Oh, I know you will say I hardly knew you and it is true, but I could not get your sweet face out of my mind; your gentle laughter rang in my ears and I swear I heard your soft voice speak to me in the dark watches of the night. And I could picture you as clearly as if you were there in the room with me.'

'Goodness!' Tansy said faintly.

'I knew then that I loved you and that I wanted you. I returned with the intention to court you, as I would court any young woman who so seriously caught my fancy.' He smote his forehead with his hand. 'But all,' he cried, 'all tell me that this is not possible because you are a slave.'

'You mean courting like before wedding?' she asked, astonished and wishing that he would get up from the ground. If he didn't he was liable to get sunstroke from the blazing sun.

'That is what I mean.'

She decided it was less embarrassing to get down on the hot sand with him and sank in a heap, pulling her skirt over her ankles.

'But white folk don't do that with slaves.'

'That is my dilemma. What am I to do?'

She considered his problem. 'No one seems to mind us being friends.'

He groaned. 'Friends! When I want so much more.'

'You mean you want to fuck me?'

His expression was one of pure horror. He looked as if he had been kicked in the stomach.

'Truly says that's all white men want from black girls,' she told him hastily by way of explanation.

'Tansy, you must not use that word. And it is not all I want from you. Nor are you black.'

'You've seen my papa.'

Henleigh faltered. 'Well,' he said feebly, 'he's not very black and he doesn't sound black at all. Any more than you do.'

She sat looking at him. He seemed so sad and romantic, his blue eyes no longer feverish but as if a shade had been pulled over them. He was extremely attractive.

'I wouldn't mind,' she said thoughtfully.

'What?'

210

'You fucking me. If that's what you want to do to me I think you are meant to do it. All white men do it when they want to. But I don't think I'd mind like Truly did before she came here and Mistress Amelia said she could live with Daniel. I like you very much. I think I might even like it if you did it to me.'

He groaned again. 'Tansy, I am not a man to do such a thing. But are you telling me that you would not protest if I or some other man took you without the benefit of clergy?'

She wasn't sure what he meant by benefit of clergy. 'If it was a white man, I *could* not protest,' she explained, patiently trying to make him understand. 'I'm a slave.'

'Oh God. My poor child. The wickedness of it.'

He bent lower to put his arms round her and pull her close to him. Then suddenly he was kissing her, his mouth on hers, his tongue pushing between her lips. She had never been kissed before and she found herself responding, excited, liking it, kissing him back. Then suddenly he pulled away.

'Forgive me, forgive me,' he gasped. 'Oh God, help me!'

He leapt to his feet and backed away from her, his expression frantic, then he turned and ran across the beach back towards the house at the speed of a slave with the dogs on him.

Pensive, Tansy remained on the beach, sitting cross-legged, letting handfuls of sand run through her fingers while the waves from the other side of the ocean where England was broke with a gentle splash. Just how cold was this place he called Yorkshire? she wondered.

'Mistress Amelia, are there slaves in England?'

The question made Amelia sit bolt upright. She had been feeling languorous and sated with love as she sat before her dressing table while Tansy arranged her hair for dinner. She had spent the early afternoon with Joshua in the quiet of her bedchamber, just as they had spent every afternoon together for the past six weeks. These meetings would not have been possible without Bella's help. Bella saw to it that Tansy and the black staff were occupied elsewhere. It had worked out very well. Joshua had a room up in the attics of the house that led off a staircase near to her bedroom. Providing he slipped away well before the day began to cool, they were safe. The white staff, Madame Volnay, Pierre and Beatrice, rested in the afternoon in their own quarters, as did most people on the island. William could have been a problem, but he asked if he could ride over to see Isobel each afternoon and she did not discourage him. After all, though she could not get used to the thought, they were engaged and badgering to know when they could marry. She smiled, remembering Zach's chagrin when Isobel announced that she was keeping Macabees and his outrage when he realised that once Isobel and William married, Macabees would, in time, become part of Elsewhere.

These short afternoons which she and Joshua spent together had

211

become a life. They did not always make love. Sometimes they would talk, sometimes simply sit and read and Amelia would help Joshua with words he did not understand. The brevity of these meetings intensified everything that they did. Joshua was hungry to learn and, as she had discovered when they were both barely grown up, he had a keen and quick intelligence. So much of European life as she had known it was completely outside his experience, and yet he seemed to understand Western philosophy and mores without difficulty. He had even begun to learn a little Latin. It saddened her that in a different world he would have been a man with much to offer. As it was, the best she could do for him without offending Joseph was to put him in charge of her gardens, with three slaves working under him. It was not enough for a man of his ability, but it was better than emptying rubbish at Macabees.

Their lovemaking was intense also, but for Amelia deeply satisfying. She realised that she had buried that aspect of her nature in the years that she and Joshua had been separated. Now she was able to unleash her passions. Every morning she awoke to know that she was happy, or at least as happy as it was possible to be in the circumstances, and she felt the hard shell that had been growing over her slowly melting away. She felt mellow, loved, and like butter melting in the sun.

Neither of them kicked against the conventions. They were not children any more. Both accepted the way life was on a Caribbean island and though they broke the rules, they broke them secretly. It was too dangerous to do anything else.

But Tansy's question startled her, reminding her of long ago when Joshua had asked the same question.

'Slaves in England? No, not really,' she said.

'If I were in England, would I have to be a slave? Or would I be free?'

Amelia realised she did not know the answer. 'I think perhaps some very rich people might have slaves,' she said doubtfully. 'Perhaps Vincent Ramillies will keep those men he took back with him as slaves. I do not believe there is a law against it.'

'But what if no one knew the person was a slave?'

'Why do you ask, Tansy?'

The girl shrugged. 'I just wondered,' she said.

Amelia regarded her, perplexed. 'Do you want to be free?' she asked. It was the first time she had ever broached the question.

Tansy shrugged again. 'What would be the difference if I were free?'

'You could leave here, go where you like, work where you like.'

'Doing what?'

'You could be a lady's maid and be paid for it.'

Tansy put her head on one side and thought. Then she said candidly, 'But I don't want to leave Bella and Papa now he is back. I'm happy here with you. I don't understand why Truly frets so about being free. I'm sure she wouldn't be half as comfortable.' Then her face clouded.

212

'Of course it's different for those poor men and women in the fields and the factory yard.'

Amelia did not wish to talk about the poor men and women in the fields and the factory yard. The mention of them had spoilt her enormous relief at hearing that Tansy was happy. But she still did not know what had caused the girl's sudden interest in England, unless that young Mark Henleigh had been putting ideas into her head.

'Have you been talking to Mr Henleigh about England?' she asked.

Tansy's face broke into a wide smile of brilliant white teeth and red lips. Her mouth was perhaps a touch too big for true beauty but, thought Amelia, a pale, bloodless man like Henleigh would find the girl's vibrant good looks irresistible. She should have realised before that he might be attracted.

'Oh yes,' Tansy said. 'He's been telling me about Yorkshire where he comes from. It sounds very cold. But he's nice. I like him very much and I think he likes me.' She put her hand over her mouth and giggled, dark eyes bright with merriment. 'But he can't seem to understand that I'm a slave.'

Amelia did not answer. She had a feeling that Tansy was keeping something from her and she wasn't sure she wanted to know what it was. If Henleigh were falling in love with Tansy, she needed to think long and hard about the implications. And again she felt the frisson of fear that always attacked her if it seemed she might lose someone she loved. Perhaps the girl's walks with him should stop; it would be so easy for them to make love on those walks. But Tansy was so young, so childish, she could not believe that a man as immersed in religion as Henleigh was would take advantage of her. Also, if the walks stopped, it could spoil the marvellous intimacy that she and Joshua now shared. It was all too complicated and Amelia mentally threw up her hands.

'I'll just leave it all to fate,' she told herself.

Chapter Thirteen

'The news is not good.' Zach, in a state of high agitation, was striding the length of Amelia's drawing room, a cup of coffee dwarfed by his big hand. 'The French are amassing ships and men. They outnumber us two to one. They have seven men o' war and twenty-three brigantines. The Government has depleted our fleet in these islands. If the French strike, I see no way that we can beat them. We shall be overrun, our property taken or burned. God! These damned wars. I shall fight of course. We will all fight. I've come here to suggest that you and your family come and stay with us at Windsong. Your plantation is so remote and being on French land it is likely that they will be determined to seize it back.'

'It was the British who burnt us down and shot Louis,' Amelia reminded him.

'Ah, but I am now in a position to see that that does not happen,' he said grandiosely. 'I can control our own troops but not those of the French.'

It was a wonderfully cool, sunny morning. Outside in her garden Amelia could see the heads of the king palms gently fanning the air, huge red hibiscus and a deep purple bougainvillea bloomed, their heads knocking gently in the breeze on the leaded windows. Somewhere she could hear Joshua whistling as he worked in the garden. War yet again? Her heart sank.

'What do you think?' Zach was pressing.

'Naturally I am most grateful, and if you think it wise, of course we will come,' Amelia said, thinking that this move would curtail her freedom and her life with Joshua. 'But why don't we wait and see how things develop.'

'Amelia, I beg of you. Next time it may be you who gets shot.'

'I could be shot at Windsong.'

'Windsong is well guarded.'

She sighed and considered the matter. 'If I may bring some of the personal servants.'

'If by that you mean Joshua, the answer is no,' he said crossly.

'I meant including Joshua,' she said. 'And if the answer is no, we will all stay here.'

He gave his silk stockings an impatient hitch. 'I should remind you that Ruby is one of my personal servants, and I am not sending her away.'

215

She looked to heaven and shook her head. 'And you have the sauce to disapprove of me!'

His laugh had a note of embarrassment in it. He flung himself into a large wing-backed chair. 'Enough of our romantic arrangements. What shall we do about Isobel? Do you think she should come as well?'

'If she wishes, but trouble usually bypasses Macabees. It's so well protected by Brimstone Hill.' Brimstone Hill was considered impregnable.

'It won't be if the French storm the garrison. The fortress is nowhere near finished and it is undermanned.'

Alarmed, Amelia said, 'You really think it is that serious?'

'I know it is that serious,' he said grimly. 'You would think that the Government back home would keep us safe. These islands sent them more than twenty-five thousand tons of sugar last year. The West Indies are the richest of Britain's overseas colonies. Yet they wreck it all by fighting with the French over who should sit upon the Spanish throne, afraid that the French and the Spanish empires will combine to steal British trade and colonies. We here in the West Indies are nothing but pawns in a game we cannot control. Queen Anne's government manufactures any excuse for war while the true reason they fight is nought but a struggle to remain supreme in trade. And by bringing their battles to these waters, they wreck the profitability of the colonies. I tell you, there will be little sugar sent to home ports from these islands if the French attack.'

Listening to him it seemed to Amelia she had heard it all before, from Matthew Oliver years earlier. Kings and queens came and went – Queen Anne had succeeded to the throne in 1702 – but nothing changed. She thought of Louis' dead body, the blazing house, the terror of her servants and of being left alone to cope. She had coped well, but that was long ago when she was more resilient. She did not wish to cope again. Suppose this time the dead body on the drive were Joshua? Or Tansy? She had no right to put those she loved in danger just because she wished to continue to spend her afternoons in bed with the man she loved.

'All right, if war comes, we'll all go to Windsong,' she said, resigned. 'Ben, too, for they will surely destroy Basse-Terre yet again.'

'It would be wise. His luck can't hold out for ever.' He sighed. 'And war will come. There is no doubt about it. At the first sign of hostilities, you should leave here.'

'Very well,' she said. 'I will prepare myself. La Bac will look after Elsewhere – and Macabees, if Isobel wishes him to do so. Like others,' she added with a mischievous grin, 'he has been longing to get his hands on the place.'

Zach glared, caught her teasing look, and they both burst out laughing.

'Amelia,' he said, 'you really are impossible.'

A few weeks later the first French cannonballs, the size of calabashes and fired from the massed French fleet, landed on Old Road Town. The British retaliated by bombarding Basse-Terre. When both capital

216

towns were reduced to smoking ruins, the combat between troops and the assaults on property began in earnest.

As the first puffs of smoke from the cannon mingled with the few whiter puffs of cloud in the Caribbean sky, Amelia and her household moved. Windsong, set high on a hill and with the mountains behind, was too far inland for the ships' cannon to be effective against it. Madame Volnay and Pierre had been packed and ready for days. Elsewhere was shuttered and barred. 'Not that that will help against fire,' remarked Pierre with a last look at the blind, covered windows as the carriage moved off down the drive.

'Better the house should burn than any of us be hurt,' Amelia said. She turned to look resolutely ahead, then muttered to herself to take her mind off the thought of Elsewhere burning, 'Heaven knows where poor Zach will put us all.'

Those who lived on St Kitts were used to battle. Every few years there was a skirmish of some kind, but this was no skirmish. The night skies were red with the flames of burning villages and plantations, and the days thundered with the sound of cannonballs. Grapeshot was the worst – clusters of small balls that scattered in mid-air and did appalling damage. The attics at Windsong were turned into a makeshift hospital and Amelia and the other white women, along with Tansy, spent their days and nights nursing the wounded.

Zach was at the front, though he made brief visits to Windsong whenever there was a lull in the fighting. He came with tales of gloom. The British were hopelessly outnumbered. 'We have always been outnumbered and won before,' he said, 'but this time the odds are too great.'

Everyone had their tasks and their place. Joshua, Tansy, Bella and her family were put into the slave quarters. There was nowhere else for them to go. If Amelia had not been so exhausted and preoccupied with life and death, the unaccustomed discomfort her people were suffering would have troubled her greatly. But at a time when men, some pathetically young, were blinded, mutilated and dying, needing constant care and attention, there was no opportunity to concern herself with the hale and hearty.

At least there was no shortage of food – not yet. Windsong had always been self-sufficient and there were large stocks of flour, salt fish and imported goods laid in and Isobel had brought food from Macabees with her. Bella and her family spent their days endlessly preparing meals. Amelia knew that Ruby was working with them, but she pushed the thought out of her mind. Her main fear was that Ruby and Tansy would meet and recognise each other. She arranged for Tansy to eat her meals in the attic with the patients and did her best to keep Tansy away from the kitchens.

Ben, with Juba as his young lieutenant, had organised the men, both black and white and including Joshua and Mark Henleigh, into a round-the-clock guard on the house. Most of the field slaves were brought in to make up the numbers. The sugar crop was neglected. Fire was the biggest fear; if the house were fired, every man would be needed close at hand. Every possible container was filled with water, and the roof and walls were constantly wetted down in hopes that the flames would be discouraged. It seemed as if the whole island was burning. The mountains were blotted out by smoke and there was no escaping the smell of it. Amelia thought she would never get the acrid, sinister stink of it from her skin, hair and clothing. There was no time for baths. The slaves were too busy to heat water for their mistresses and every time she woke from a brief, snatched sleep, she found black soot encrusting her nostrils, ears and eyes. Before dragging herself out of the bed in the room she shared with Isobel and going back to the improvised ward upstairs, she lay for a moment worrying about Elsewhere and feeling like a miserable traitor for having left her home. But she rarely went to bed. The women mostly dozed when and where they could in the ward.

It was quiet in the attic early this morning. The patients, laid out in rows on straw from the stables covered with fine sheets from the house, all seemed to be sleeping. Amelia was sitting quietly, hands folded in her lap, when she had a sudden sensation of being trapped and that her life would never extend beyond this lofty, malodorous, hideously hot room, lit only by candles and inhabited by dying men. She was gripped by a uncontrollable need for sunshine and fresh air.

'I'm just going out,' she whispered to Tansy and Isobel who were sitting either side of a boy whose stomach had been torn out by grapeshot. Miraculously he still breathed, but he would not for much longer. He whispered to himself feverishly, eyes open, staring into the flickering light.

Both girls were too engrossed in the boy to pay her much attention. Tansy nodded absently; Isobel did not respond. Charlotte was dozing at the far end of the room. Charlotte had worked as hard and been as brave as any of them, a fact that had surprised Amelia. She slipped down the ladder that led from the attic and on down the house stairs before running along the passage and into the kitchen. Bella, her black skin grey with fatigue, was seated in a chair, her arm propped on its arm, her face in her hand, sleeping where she sat. Amelia tiptoed past to the garden door so as not to wake her. Outside, the sun had just burst through in a great flower-pink dawn that splattered over the sky. It was strangely quiet; no shot howled or crackled and the lingering smoke had risen high enough to masquerade as a cloud. The air seemed clean and fresh, blown across the Atlantic, perhaps from peaceful England.

Amelia sat on the garden seat where long ago she had sat with Matthew Oliver, and gulped in the clean air gratefully. She stayed for perhaps five minutes. Refreshed but conscious-stricken by the weakness that had attacked her, she rose to return to her duties. She was standing, stretching her tired bones, when suddenly she saw Joshua walking along the rough path from the slave cabins. Her heart lifted and she started to run towards him – then stopped dead.

She felt her fists and stomach clench in ferocious anger, for walking close behind him, in the direction of the secret pool, was Ruby.

For a day or two Joshua had been resentful at finding himself back in slave quarters, ordered around as a slave and, worse, being so abruptly separated from Amelia. But his gentle nature quickly wiped out the resentment and he was able to rationalise that this was war, serious war, and there was not much to be done about personal feelings. He was placed in one of the two slave huts that had been allocated for the fire-fighters, but during the day he continued to help out in the vegetable gardens. It was important that the production of food continued since nothing edible was being shipped in to the island. He never caught sight of Amelia or Tansy, but word was that the women were working day and night, nursing the wounded brought to the house from the battlefields.

He hated this war which had suddenly separated him from those he loved, grieved when his fellow blacks were called upon to dig makeshift graves. Black or white, young blood should not be shed so wantonly. The estate carpenter was constantly busy making rough coffins for use until the day when the dead would rest decently in one of the island's graveyards.

Bella had warned him that Ruby was working in the kitchens. 'And I not go'n tell her you here unless you wants me to,' she said.

'It's better if she doesn't know I'm here,' he said. He half-wanted and half-feared to see Ruby; what would he say to her if he did see her? He had no news of Samuel and he did not want to start up their relationship again. Remembering Ruby's boldness, he felt that meeting her again could only cause complications.

'Then I'll get young Juba to bring you food down to you in the garden,' Bella said. 'You just better keep you'self out o' her kitchen.'

It was, of course, inevitable that they would meet. She saw him in the gardens one morning as she was walking through to the slave cabins with a huge pot of food balanced on her head.

She looked wonderfully strong and graceful, tall and erect, one hand on her hip and the other balancing the pot on her turbaned head. He should have turned his back, he should have moved away before she saw him, but he did neither. He stood up to face her as she moved nearer.

'Hello, Ruby,' he said quietly.

She stopped dead and had to grab at the pot to still it. She looked at him, her carved ebony face grave.

'They tol' me you was here. Truly tol' me 'bout you arm,' she said. 'So she got you back, did she?'

'Truly?' He was deliberately misunderstanding her.

'No. Whitey. Mistress 'Melia.'

219

He said nothing and she lifted down the pot and rested it on her hip. 'Where be Samuel?' she asked, her face set.

'Working in the fields at Macabees. I haven't seen him for two years.'

'But you got Tansy instead, eh?'

'Not instead.'

'You fucking that 'Melia again?'

He ducked the question. 'I'm a free man, Ruby. The mistress at Macabees gave me my freedom.'

Her expression softened. 'Oh Josh! I be glad for you. What you go'n do?'

'Don't know yet.'

She was like some fine statue standing there, her strong legs widely set, proud breasts jutting, but he felt no stirring.

'There's never been no one but you, Josh,' she said, her dark eyes fixed on him. 'I tol' you I'd never sleep with no other black man and I ha'nt. The master, he on top o' me most days, but that don' count. I guess that be my job and it better than cutting cane.'

He nodded but said nothing.

'I go'n get this food to the cabins,' she said abruptly. 'Where you sleepin'?'

'With the men.'

'Right.' She swung the pot back on her head, turned on her heel and made off in the direction of the women's cabins, her back straight but the stiffness of her shoulders showing that she was hurt.

He stood looking after her. She was still a wonderful looking woman, but in their brief exchange it seemed to him that she had changed. Some of the light had gone out of her. But some of the light had gone out of all of them.

He hoped that would be the end of it, but it wasn't. A few nights later, close to dawn, she had come to the men's cabin asking for him. Sleepily he stumbled out of bed and went out into a dawn-washed morning. She was fully dressed, her brightly coloured turban in place, impatiently waiting for him.

'Josh, I needs to talk with you,' she said. 'Is there someplace we can go?'

He remembered the pool where he and Amelia had first made love. That should be safe so early in the day. He nodded and without speaking began to lead her through the garden towards the concealed entrance. Somewhere in the distance to his left he thought he caught a glimpse of someone standing by the garden seat but he decided to take no notice and move positively as if he were busy about his master's business. Ruby was following close on his heels and he was surprised to find that the pathway had not grown over. Someone else must have discovered the pool.

'It be pretty here,' Ruby said looking around.

'Yes.' He wasn't sure what to do or say next, but Ruby smiled her huge smile and advanced determinedly towards him, wrapped her arms

220

round him, put her head on his shoulder and murmured, 'Oh, Josh! It's been so long.'

He put his arm awkwardly round her. 'I'm sorry I had no news of Sam, Ruby,' he said.

'What he look like? Be he handsome?' she asked, pulling away from him.

'He's a fine boy.'

'Black like me?'

'Black like you. More like you than me.'

She sighed. 'Josh, you go'n kiss me or not?'

He hesitated and then bent his head to kiss her gently on the lips. She laughed. 'Can't you do better than that? Come here.'

She kissed him deeply and passionately but to his dismay he felt nothing. She smelt wrong, she felt wrong. There was too much of her; too much black, smothering flesh. She wasn't Amelia. She must have felt his lack of response because she drew away from him.

'It be whitey. That 'Melia. It be her you love still.'

He could not confess to it. It was too dangerous. 'Ruby, it's nothing to do with you. It's me. I've changed. There isn't anyone. I've learned to live without anyone.'

She had backed away from him but still looked full into his face.

'Oh, Josh,' she said sadly, 'you not even tellin' me the truth. I knows you love her. Truly told me . . . ' She saw his start of alarm and raised her hand, pink palm facing him. 'Don' be afeared. I not go'n tell. But, Josh, it be wrong. You a black man and she be white. It not right. It be bad enough that black womenfolk must be whores for the white man. Not much we can do 'bout that. But we need our men for us. Not them white women. And Josh, they go'n kill you if they finds out what you and she doin'.'

'Truly shouldn't have told you.'

'Truly don' think it right either. Truly be black and proud to be. Like me. She want for you and me to be together 'gain like we was at Macabees.'

'I tell you, Ruby, it's not like that. I don't need anyone.'

'Don' be no man that don' need someone if the someone be there. And if you don' love that white gal, you prove it to me by makin' love with me.'

She was smiling again, advancing on him. Her strong arms went round him, her breasts pushed into him. She was grinding her hips over his, rubbing against him until unbidden he felt himself spring into life. Then her hand went down, finding its way through his clothing until she was grasping him, moving her hand up and down the length of him while helplessly he felt the waves of excitement beginning.

'That better, Josh. That much better,' she chuckled. 'Now what we go'n do with that beautiful big thing? What you think the best thing to do, eh? I reckon we go'n put it where it belongs. We going to ride that cock horse together that's what we go'n do.'

She seemed to be stronger than he was. She was forcing him backwards to lie on the ground, not far from where he had lain so long ago with Amelia. Once he was on his back, still clothed except for his opened breeches, she flung up her skirts and tucked them in round her waist. She was naked beneath and he saw the gleaming ebony of her belly and the coarse mass of black hair below descending until she was skewered on him, her hands on his chest, her face triumphant above him as she rode him. He groaned with the unwanted pleasure of it, trying not to respond. If he did not respond he could convince himself that he had not been unfaithful. But she was grinding into him, twisting herself from side to side and round and round. Then she lifted herself off him and bent down.

'Let's see what I tastes like,' she murmured taking him into her mouth.

He heard a terrible groan and realised it had come from him. Her body riding him he could resist, but her mouth working at him, nibbling, biting, sucking, was not to be withstood. He could not contain himself. He felt his body heaving under her mouth and then, explosively for him, it was all over. He sensed the ripple of her throat as she swallowed.

'That real good,' she said contentedly, her hand now clasping him.

He pushed her away and drew his knees up to his chin, guarding his sexuality against hers. She was sitting beside him, laughing at him.

'Don' that be better than some white thing?' she asked.

'Ruby.' He did not know what to say. 'Ruby I must get to work.'

He clambered to his feet, fastened his breeches and with guilt not unmixed with anger at her importunity left her where she sat and hurried back towards the house.

Just as Ruby and Joshua had inevitably met, so a week later did Tansy and Ruby.

That morning two young lads with only fluff on their cheeks had died, and Tansy was inconsolable. She was near to breaking point. Too many boys, barely older than the two young girls who helped nurse them, had died and the many deaths had given Tansy intimations of her own mortality. The normally happy and cheerful girl was full of gloom, convinced that they would all die in this dreadful war.

'Go and have a walk around the garden,' Amelia told both Isobel and Tansy. 'Try and relax for a little while.'

Tansy looked at her with tragic eyes. 'It wouldn't feel right,' she said.

'Try,' said Amelia firmly.

Isobel, knowing more of pain and suffering, had proved the stronger, Tansy thought as they went down to the ground floor of the house. Isobel might seem soppy, but she was undoubtedly the braver. It rankled.

Isobel wanted to find William, whom she had not seen for days. Tansy decided that she would look for Mark Henleigh, but before doing so she would drop in on her grandma and aunt in the kitchens.

The sorrow and fatigue that had been weighing her down these last few days seemed to lift as she got further and further from the attic, and she felt a little more cheerful as she went through the kitchen door. Bella, who was skinning salt fish, looked up in surprise as she came in.

'Mistress 'Melia know you here?' she asked, sounding cross.

'She sent me down.'

Bella looked doubtful, thick lips pursed and as if she were about to send her granddaughter away.

Tansy took no notice of the miserable greeting. The kitchen felt warm and welcoming. Too warm as always, but nowhere near as dreadfully hot as the attic where the sun beat unimpeded on the roof. There were several women in the kitchen, all busy. One handsome woman, cutting up a huge mango fruit at the table, had put down her knife and was looking at Tansy intently. The woman was very black with full breasts under her coarse linen bodice. She seemed to want to say something, and Tansy, staring back, felt some stirring, some tickling of the memory.

'Hello, Tansy,' the woman said, provoking a ferocious glare from Bella.

'Hello.' Tansy put her head to one side. 'Do you know me?'

The woman smiled a huge, white smile in the blackness of her face. 'I used to.'

'Where?'

'At Macabees, when you were little.'

It was the breasts that triggered the memory. Tansy had sudden total recall of those breasts thrust into her four-year-old greedy, waiting mouth, and the woman's voice crooning, 'Who want her titty-bottle then?' When they had brought her to Elsewhere, those draughts of mother's milk which the woman enjoyed giving as much as Tansy had enjoyed drinking had ceased. But it hadn't mattered because there was plenty of other food and drink. She had never been hungry since.

'Did you used to feed me?' she asked.

'Sure did,' said the woman.

'Are you my mama?' Tansy asked, holding her breath.

The woman gave out a joyous peal of laughter. 'You remembers Ruby then?'

'I think I do.' Tansy felt shy, awkward. Was the woman her mother or not?

'Then come and give me a kiss.'

Relieved at having something positive to do, Tansy went dutifully towards Ruby and found herself in a bear-like embrace. Ruby smelt musky, and felt incredibly soft like some deep, comfortable pillow. Her skin was damp with sweat, but it didn't matter.

'They told me you were dead,' Tansy said when she was free of the woman's embrace.

'Well, that's 'cause we all thought she were,' Bella said, and then shut her mouth as if it had been sewn with fine thread.

223

No one said any more and Tansy was puzzled, expecting an explanation.

'We got work to do in here, gal,' Bella growled at her. 'Get you' self off. Go find that Mr Henleigh. He sittin' in the drawin' room, readin'.'

'But—'

'Git! Shoo!' Bella said, clapping her hands. 'Out o' here.'

Reluctantly Tansy did as she was told. 'Goodbye, Mama,' she called back defiantly. 'See you later.'

Mark Henleigh looked up from his book as Tansy came into the drawing room. He jumped to his feet, his face alight.

'Mistress Tansy,' he breathed. 'What pleasure.'

'I wondered if you would like a walk,' Tansy said.

'Is it safe?'

She shrugged. 'Mistress Amelia says that nowhere is safe and just to live as near to normal as is possible.'

'But it's stupid to take risks.'

He hadn't understood what she was saying. Sometimes, she thought, he was not very quick.

'Well, I'm going for a walk,' she told him.

'Then I shall come.'

They left the drawing room in silence. Outside, Tansy hesitated. Windsong was strange to her.

'Where shall we go?' she asked.

'I've found a charming, secluded pool,' he said. 'It's cool there and quiet. I'll take you.'

As they walked side by side, it seemed to Tansy that the sound of gunfire seemed closer and more threatening out here in the open air. She looked up nervously to where puffballs of smoke hung lazily in the sky. Today there was no black smoke. Perhaps there was nowhere left to burn and only Windsong had escaped. A particularly loud crump moved the ground under their feet, making her clutch at his arm. Henleigh moved faster.

'We'll be sheltered in the woods,' he told her.

The morning had become heavy. With the weight of it hovering over her head she felt a deep unquiet. To take her mind off her anxieties she began to talk.

'A wonderful thing happened to me this morning,' she told him.

'Oh yes?' Another explosion shattered the air. Henleigh was walking very quickly.

'I found my mother again.'

'Your mother?' This news stopped him in his tracks.

'Yes, here in the kitchen. She's called Ruby. She's the cook.'

'Ruby! That – ' his hands sketched a pair of breasts ' – black woman is your mother?'

She nodded. 'She's nice,' she said simply.

He looked at her, perplexed. 'I don't understand.'

Something streaked over their heads with a shrill whistling noise. It landed with an almighty bang too close for comfort.

He muttered something and took her hand, looking back to see how far they were from the house. She could tell he was deciding which way to run. The woods were nearer and he pulled her in that direction.

'Quickly,' he said. 'Let's get under shelter.'

Another cannon ball whistled high above them as they ran for the trees. Breathless, he led her along a narrow path until they were in a gentle glade that sheltered a pool.

Another whistle and crash, much nearer.

'They're targeting the house,' he said, dismayed. 'Quick, lie down. It's safer.'

He put his arms round her and dragged her down onto the soft damp soil of the glade. The whistles and crashes were coming thicker and faster, and the ground moved as if the island were in the throes of an earthquake. The noise was deafening. There was a sharp smell of gunpowder and fire. Terrified, she clung to him, and he rolled so his body was on top of hers, protecting her. He put his hands over her ears to shut out some of the terrifying noise, and whispered over and over again, 'Don't be frightened. It will all be over soon.'

They could hear urgent voices shouting between the blasts of cannonfire.

'I think they must have hit the house.' He sounded surprisingly calm.

'Oh, God!' she said. 'We must go and help.'

'Not yet.' His weight was pressing her into the soft earth and she could hardly breathe. 'When the bombardment stops. For the moment we are safer here.'

She knew she was trembling and was ashamed of herself for her fear. She had seen what cannon and musket shot did to the frailty of a human body and she could not control her terror. She did not want her guts torn out, her eyes put out, her limbs blown off. She could not stop shaking.

He was the brave one, holding her close, comforting her, telling her that it would be all right. Time stopped while the terrible din assaulted her senses and then suddenly there came an unreal calm like a curtain. The unexpected silence was almost as terrifying as the noise of the bombardment. She clung to Henleigh, hiding her face in his shoulder.

'What is it now?' she asked, her voice muffled. 'Why is it so quiet?'

'It's over for the moment,' he soothed, stroking her hair. 'Don't be afraid. But we'll wait here for a little while to make sure. It's safer here, away from the house.'

Cautiously she lifted her head. 'You were so brave,' she whispered.

'Only because I had you to look after. Now calm yourself. We are both safe in the hands of the Lord.'

She still clung to him. 'I feel safer in yours,' she said. She hugged him hard and turned her head to give him a 'thank you' kiss on his cheek. But his face moved. It was his mouth that her mouth found, and he let out a small cry, almost a cry of despair as she kissed him. Then he was kissing her as he had on the beach and again she found pleasure in it. She wriggled closer to him and discovered the body change that signalled his desire. It was exciting, this stiff, hard rod pressed against her. Now it was over she felt that even the bombardment had been exciting; terrifying and exciting. She felt elated. She had been so sure they would die but they had survived, clinging to one another, and she made up her mind then and there that if she was going to die in this stupid war she would not die a virgin. She would not die unfucked.

'Fuck me,' she whispered in his ear.

Again he groaned. 'Don't say it, Tansy,' he wailed. 'Don't say it.'

'Do it! Do it!' She was in a fever of impatience. The bombardment might start again and the next cannonball could kill them. 'I know you want to. Do it.'

She was scrambling to make a way clear for him, pushing up her skirt until she was spreadeagled in the glade, naked from the waist down, her own hands parting the thick black hair to show him the way. He seemed to be murmuring prayers. Impatient, she checked to make sure that he had not lost all desire, and finding the rod still there, set about releasing it from its coverings. It did not look much, long and thin, but exciting to know that it was she who had had this effect on him.

'Put it in me,' she whispered.

'We mustn't.'

'But we both want it,' she protested.

He groaned and rolled over, lifting himself on his elbows, and plunged into her waiting body. Their movements were frenzied, unco-ordinated, one pushing clumsily against the other. For him it was over all too quickly. He collapsed, gasping, on her, squashing her, breathing, 'God forgive me! Oh, God forgive me.'

Tansy slid her finger into herself, wishing he had gone on longer and that it had got better. She marvelled that there was space there where she was touching for all that, but thinking nevertheless that really fucking wasn't all that people said it was. Not anywhere near as exciting as the bombardment.

The first few cannonballs aimed at Windsong fell short. One buried itself in the formal gardens at the back of the house, chipping a few of the statues and blowing off a stone nymph's head. Another blasted a great crater in the lawn which also broke most of the leaded windows in the house. Then, mercifully, there was a brief respite which gave Ben the opportunity to get his team of fire-fighters to the attic in an attempt to bring down the wounded. The women had already run downstairs to see what was happening. White and dazed, they were standing around Amelia in the hallway. The kitchen staff, including Bella and Ruby, were running down the hallway in panic like a flock of headless black chickens.

'Get down to the cellars,' Ben shouted at them. 'Get everyone down to the cellars.'

Amelia detached herself from the group. 'Ben, the wounded – if the shot hits the roof . . .' She was shouting and it occurred to Ben that he hadn't heard her shout since they were about ten years old.

'Just get down to the cellars!' He was shouting, too, and his voice seemed too big for his small frame. 'Just get out of the way.' Then realising that Amelia would refuse to do anything so sensible unless she had something positive to contribute, he bellowed, 'Amelia, you and William are in charge of the safety of these women. Get them under cover at once.'

He wanted William out of the way. The boy was not going to be much use. He was trembling uncontrollably and had turned a pale shade of green as he hovered at the back of the group of fire-fighters.

Ben gave William a hefty push. 'Move! Look after the women. In the cellars,' he ordered.

With relief, William leapt towards the cellar stairs.

'Now the wounded.' Ben waved his arm in a movement that suggested he was leading men into battle. Eleven large black men led by the single diminutive white man pounded up the stairs to the attic. Young Juba, Daniel and Joshua were close behind Ben. He felt surprisingly calm, in control, in charge. He had the impression that he had been waiting for this moment of authority and strength all his life.

Another cannonball landed with a shuddering thud, and the heavy wooden front door of the house blew in, crashing where the inhabitants of the house had stood seconds before. The house swayed and the sound of breaking glass could be heard.

'Pick up the wounded and carry them down to the cellar,' Ben ordered. He was sweating; he could taste the salty drops as they ran into his mouth. Suddenly he felt a frisson of fear, communicated to him by the terror of the wounded who struggled to get to their feet or crawl towards the attic steps. One man who had lost both legs screamed, 'Help me, help me,' in a voice so high-pitched it could have been a woman's. More explosions were shaking the house and Ben had the impression that the entire structure was sinking into the ground. Smoke was thick in the air. Did that mean fire? Maybe. But first these men must be rescued. The walking wounded were already frenziedly making their way to the ladder, fighting for space, some letting themselves drop from the attic doorway into the hall below. The dreadful heat, the stink of smoke, the noise and the screams of the seriously injured as they were lifted had created a minor purgatory.

'God, God, get us out of here safely,' Ben was repeating to himself as he tried to keep the way down clear.

By this time the house had been hit more than once, but so far nothing had come through the roof. Now only he and Joshua and one young British Redcoat were left in the attic . With his single arm Joshua was supporting the soldier who had only one leg – the blind leading the blind, thought Ben wryly. He still had his eye on them when, almost silently, a cannonball penetrated the roof. It hissed gently and then exploded in the far corner of the attic. The blast blew Ben straight down to the hallway below. He landed in a heap, his leg twisted under him. Dazed, he managed to stagger to his feet. He had sprained his leg badly but found he was able to walk. Bizarrely, the ladder up to the attic still stood, but a few feet beyond was a gaping black hole. Exactly below the hole on the hall floor lay the Redcoat, unconscious. Above, Ben could see the crumpled figure of Joshua hanging half in and half out of the cavity, pinned at the chest by a giant pincushion of the solid rock fabric of the house. Blood bubbled at the corner of his mouth.

'I can't move . . .' Joshua said hoarsely, his eyes white in his face. 'Only one arm . . . can't push . . .'

Ben's first reaction was to get back up into the attic. The stone was so balanced that it would be easy enough to push away from Joshua's body and through the hole, but it might fall on the soldier, crushing him. He would have to move the soldier first.

'Wait!' he said, and dragged himself to push the soldier's body out of the way. He looked back up at Joshua. The blood round his mouth was thicker, a dark black stain, and he could hardly breathe. A terrible harsh sound was coming from Joshua's lungs. And he was turning a curious grey colour. If something was not done, and quickly, he would die. The light was near to snuffing out already.

Die. He would die. This man whom Amelia loved, and who had fathered her child; a slave, now free, who had come back into their lives, destroying Ben's dreams once again. If he were dead, he would be gone for ever. No longer a threat, no longer an obstacle. And surely Amelia's life would be the better for it.

Ben hesitated and then made up his mind. He turned his back on the dying black man and busied himself pulling the unconscious Redcoat down the stairs towards the comparative safety of the cellars.

Ruby found herself sitting close to Amelia down in the dark, musty cellar. Someone had produced a few candles, and the flickering spears of light lifted the gloom. There was a heavy, heady smell of red wine.

The women were seated on wine barrels, discarded furniture, old packing cases – anything on which they could perch. The noise of the bombardment penetrated even the depth of the cellar and Ruby was not sure she wanted to be underground. They could all be buried alive down here if the stone pile of the house collapsed. She would prefer to be in the outside air and take her chances under a clear sky. Not, she thought ruefully, that there had been many clear skies since this war had begun.

They were a motley collection of black and white women, all listening for the next explosion and yet doing their best to appear calm, following the example of their mistress, Amelia, who sat, back straight, hands folded in the lap of the large white apron that covered her green silk gown. Her face wore an expression that damned the French to hell. The wounded, now quiet and exhausted, had been made as comfortable as possible at the far end of the cellar.

Beside Amelia, Truly had curled herself into a ball so that only the curve of her spine and the back of her head could be seen. Next to her on a wine barrel sat Bella, head down, staring at her hands. Charlotte, her arms round her children, and Isobel were seated on the other side of Amelia, looking surprisingly calm and resigned. Amelia's white servants had bunched themselves together at the other side of the circle. There was no sign of Tansy.

'Where is Tansy?' Amelia asked suddenly.

Presumably no one knew the answer since no one answered.

'Who saw her last?'

Bella grunted and straightened herself. 'She come in the kitchen and she went off with Mr Henleigh, far as I knows.'

Amelia's expression sharpened. 'She went into the kitchen?'

'Said you'd sent her down.' Ruby noted the anxious look that Amelia threw in her direction. She thought it best to say nothing.

'They could be safe.' Amelia was reassuring herself, Ruby thought, and felt a stab of pity for her. But how could one feel pity for a woman who would not acknowledge her own daughter?

'Safer outside,' contributed Bella.

Another silence, then Amelia's anxious voice. 'Is it over? If so, I shall go and search for her.'

Truly's head rose from the foetal position. 'The mistress lookin' for a slave in all this trouble. My!'

Amelia flushed, Ruby was not certain whether it was with embarrassment or anger. Without speaking Amelia rose to her feet.

'William,' she said, 'see no one else leaves here until Ben gives the word.'

In a swish of emerald green she left the cellar, her head high. She had chosen for her exit a moment when another explosion rocked the house. Ruby noted that the mistress never even flinched at the crash.

Ain't no yaller-belly, that woman, she found herself thinking with some reluctance. And there in the cellar where they waited in silence, blacks constrained by the presence of the white mistresses, Ruby came to the conclusion that she was not that jealous of poor Amelia. What had Amelia got? Joshua's love, and what good would that do her except perhaps to get her lover hung by some rope-happy gang of white men and herself despised if it ever came out. And as for the sex, Ruby knew that if she wanted sex from Josh, she could get it any time. No problems. She'd touch him, kiss him, arouse him and fuck him and he weren't never going to resist. She had his son, and sons were better than daughters. Amelia couldn't even bring herself to admit that Tansy was her own child. And the irony was that Tansy believed big, black Ruby was her mother. Ruby reckoned she was winning this particular battle. She felt confident that she would triumph in the end.

These self-satisfied thoughts were occupying her mind when she heard the clatter of Amelia's elegant little shoes coming back down the cellar stairs.

'Bella, Bella,' she was calling frantically. 'Oh, Bella, please come. It's Joshua . . .'

Bella's bulk lifted itself from the wine barrel and with surprising speed she moved towards the cellar exit.

'I's comin',' she shouted.

All self-satisfied thoughts were wiped away to be replaced by fear, and Ruby found herself following Bella. In the darkness of the stairs Amelia bore one single candle aloft, which lit her tragic, tear-stained face. When she saw the two figures coming towards her the candle wavered and she said, 'Oh, Bella. He's dead.'

Bella threw her hands high in the air and howled like a dog on a moonlit night. Then she advanced almost threateningly on Amelia.

'Where be he?' she asked.

'Still in the attic. He's pinned under some masonry. I couldn't move it.'

Brushing Amelia out of the way, Bella ran clumsily up the stairs and through the house, closely followed by the other two women. Ruby gasped when she saw Joshua's lifeless body hanging through the hole in the ceiling above the top landing, a chunk of the house pinning him in place. She felt tears begin to flow as all three of them clambered in turn up to the attic, Bella's weight rocking the ladder as she scrambled ahead.

It was Bella alone who with one mighty heave pushed the masonry from Joshua's body, leaving it to crash into the hall below. Then her great arms lifted her son and laid him gently on one of the attic's empty pallets. She took the corner of her apron, moistened it with her tongue and gently wiped the blood from his mouth.

'My son,' she whispered, 'my beloved son.'

Ruby looked at Amelia across Joshua's body and was startled by the shock and anguish on the white woman's face. This time the pity was not withheld.

'I's sorry,' she heard herself say.

Amelia was whiter than white, her eyes huge and green in her face, full of unshed tears, her fingers frantically pleating the hem of her apron.

'You loved him, too,' she cried. 'He betrayed me with you. I saw you with him that morning. You were going to the pool. Our pool. How could he have done it?' She covered her face with her hands. 'Oh, God, oh God, oh God, what am I going to do?'

Bella had risen ponderously to her feet. She put her hands on Amelia's shoulders and shook her hard.

'You go'n keep you dignity, that's what you go'n do,' she said. 'That what my Josh want of you. And don' you let you'self be taken in by this trash here.' She turned her glittering eye on Ruby. 'Now you just tell the truth 'bout you and Josh. You tell how he loved this gal here.'

Bella looked dangerously angry, but Ruby was full of boiling indignation at being called trash and surprised at the ferocity of Bella's defence of Amelia. She opened her mouth to tell how she and Josh had fucked and how he could be hers anytime she cared. And then she stopped. Fucking didn't mean loving. No one knew that better than she did. Amelia was staring at her, almost hopefully, and again that twinge of pity came hard on the heels of a sharp attack of guilt. Josh hadn't wanted to fuck her. She'd made him do it. She'd made him unhappy just to prove that she could make him do it. She loved him, sure enough, but he hadn't loved her. She had to face the truth of that. The best she could do for Josh now was to give this distraught white woman whom he had loved and who now stared at her so desperately some word of comfort.

Mistress Amelia had risked much for Joshua. She had truly loved him. Ruby knew she loved him, too, but what did any of it matter now? He was dead and neither of them would ever hold him again. All that mattered was that he should rest in peace.

'It be true I loved him,' she heard herself saying, 'but he loved you. He tol' me. He didn't want me. He didn't even want to touch me. He only wanted you.'

She realised she was telling the absolute truth though that had not been her intention. The hope in Amelia's face was growing.

'But you have his son,' she whispered.

'And you got his daughter.'

There was a long silence. Outside, the bombardment had stopped but a distant sound of musket shot could be heard. Smoke was drifting into the foetid room.

Then Amelia gave a choking cry. She took two long paces towards Ruby. Ruby backed, afraid that the white woman was going to strike her. But Amelia didn't strike her; to Ruby's amazement her long white arms, encased in green silk, wrapped themselves round her. Spontaneously Ruby put her own arms round the white woman. She felt bony and brittle, but she smelt sweet, like flowers, and Ruby was aware of her own sweat. But without embarrassment the women hugged each other tight, both crying out their grief on the other's shoulder. It was Bella's voice that drew them apart. 'Time we was out of here,' she said. 'I reckons this old house is burnin' down.'

Zach, with a detachment of Redcoats, finally routed the detachment of French artillery who had fired on Windsong, but though the British won that particular battle they were not destined to win the war. By the end, with most British property in smoking ruins, the war was lost, though the French, having heard of a big English fleet in the area, abruptly and surprisingly fled.

Windsong did not burn down. Ben's fire-fighters put out the worst of the flames, though both smoke and cannonball damage made the house uninhabitable. Isobel's plantation, Macabees, had lost most of its crop, burned by stray cannonshot. The smell of burning sugar hung over the property and drifted down to Elsewhere which, astonishingly, was untouched. Macabees had also suffered some direct hits from the cannons, and the house needed major repairs. There was a mass migration of the Quicks and their servants to Elsewhere when the war abruptly ended.

Zach's theory for Elsewhere's survival was that the French had believed the property to be theirs and the British had not been strong enough to attack it. Amelia forbore to point out that he had held the reverse view before the war began and had she stayed at home, Joshua would still be alive.

For Ben, it was business as usual at the tavern. He rapidly patched up the damage and opened his doors again.

Amelia had been back at Elsewhere for a month when Ben sought her out. He found her sitting in the garden outside her drawing room window, a deep red hibiscus bloom in her hand which she turned over and over, catching the sunlight on its blood-red flesh.

'Can we talk?' he asked.

She looked up. 'What about?'

'You.'

She shrugged. 'What about me?'

'You're not happy.'

'That's true'

'Amelia,' he seated himself on the garden seat next to her and took her hands in his. 'Can't you see it's all for the best? It would have ended in disaster. If anyone had found out . . .Now you have a chance to live normally, be happy like other people. You could have more children. We could have children . . .'

'What are you talking about?' she asked, vacant-eyed.

'You know what I'm talking about,' he said impatiently. 'Joshua's death. You must try to forget it. Get over it. Live.'

It seemed to her that he was pleading, begging her to be happy. But his forehead was sweating, and his eyes avoided hers. He looked down, staring at the hand which held hers.

'It's better he's dead,' he muttered. 'Can't you see that?'

She had a sudden memory of the two of them, long ago, standing in front of the master at Windsong with all the other house slaves. She remembered Ben's deliberate attempt to place the murder of Justinian Oliver on Joshua's shoulders.

'Could you have saved him, Ben?' she asked abruptly.

He looked as if she had struck him. Then he straightened his shoulders, his face suddenly scarlet – with indignation? Or with guilt?

'God no!' His tone was certainly indignant. 'How could I have? I was blown from the room. I was not even conscious. And my leg . . . It's still not right.'

How could he whine about his leg when a man was dead? Amelia thought dully, and then told herself she was being grossly unfair to Ben.

232

No one would leave another man to die. Not Ben. Or would he?

'I'm sorry,' she said. 'I should not have said that.'

He shuffled his feet. 'It doesn't matter.' His manner had become formal. 'But it hurts me you should think such a thing of me. You know how I love you and how I have always loved you.'

'Perhaps that's why it came into my mind,' she said dryly. 'There was a time, long ago . . .'

'Have you still not forgiven me for that?'

He sounded sad, and she reached to hold his hand. 'Of course I have,' she said.

It was a mistake to touch him. His arms went round her and he tried to kiss her.

'Ben!'

'You know how I feel. Amelia, marry me. Please. We would be happy together. He's gone, and you are alive. And I love you.'

She sighed. His freckled face had lined, but the red hair was defiant and springy as it had been when he was a lad. He looked somehow pathetic and for a moment she found herself wondering, 'Why not?' She had thought 'why not' once before with Louis and it had not been a bad decision. But that decision had been brought about by a necessity that no longer existed. Better to live alone than with a man who could never in a millennium take Joshua's place.

'Nothing has changed, Ben,' she said gently.

'It has. He's dead.'

'Nothing has changed.'

He was motionless, his eyes lowered, hands at his sides on the garden seat. 'Nothing has changed for me either,' he said, 'and it never will.' Then he shook his head and left her.

Surprisingly quickly after the end of hostilities Charlotte and her family were able to return home to a rebuilt Windsong. Charlotte asked if she might take Juba with them.

'The children are so attached to him,' she explained, 'and I feel they are safe in his care.'

Amelia hesitated, knowing that Truly and Daniel would be unhappy at the separation from their only son.

'You look doubtful,' Charlotte said, preparing to be offended at not getting her own way.

'It's just that Truly and Daniel will miss him so,' Amelia said.

'Then we will take them too, if you permit it. I always have room for a well-trained house slave or two.'

Amelia felt there was no way she could refuse even though Zach grumbled when he heard what was to happen, saying he could not abide Truly's surly manner.

In the first few days after Joshua's death she had thought to bring his son to Elsewhere. Any animosity that she had felt for Ruby had gone, and it was in her mind to reunite mother and son. Isobel readily agreed that he could be moved, but on making enquiries of Benson they discovered that Samuel had been sold with a batch of slaves whom the overseer considered either troublemakers or too old. Samuel had fallen into the troublemaker category and now Benson had no idea where the boy was. Not wishing to disappoint Ruby, Amelia never mentioned her efforts.

By the beginning of 1707, much of the island was still devastated, so much so that Parliament in London sent £103,000 to help finance the repair of the war damage. Slowly everything went back to much the way it had been before.

Amelia found herself in the same state of mind that she had been after Louis' death. Nothing seemed important. She shut herself in her room for most of the time and left the running of the estate to La Bac. She took little interest in anything; she was too busy coping with overwhelming grief. She could not banish the image of Joshua's limp body, crushed by the piece of masonry. Each night when she shut her eyes to sleep the picture of his agonised, bloodstained face, mouth open in a silent scream, was imprinted across her eyelids. She would gasp and open her eyes, but the same picture returned the instant she closed them again. He was dead, dead, dead. She had found him, only to lose him again. It was a loss from which she was convinced she would never recover. Her single-mindedness would not be set aside simply because he was no more.

She knew she neglected William but she had at least agreed that he could marry Isobel in August, on his seventeenth birthday. But that was some months off. She would think about it later. She could hardly bear to see Tansy. Not only did the girl speak constantly of 'her mother', Ruby, but she reminded Amelia so much of her father. Not for her looks, but for her gentle yet spirited, cheerful ways. Like her father, Tansy never complained. She was back at her old duties now there was no need to keep her in ignorance of her mistress's secret afternoons in her bedchamber. Through the fog of indifference in which she existed it sometimes seemed to Amelia that her daughter was unusually preoccupied but she put this down to the death of Joshua. Tansy had been inconsolable at the death of her father and Amelia believed that she, too, still grieved.

It was at the beginning of March, the time of year that Amelia liked best in the Caribbean, when the heat was not too fierce, the trade winds blew and her garden was a mass of wonderful colour, that Mark Henleigh sent word that he wished to see her. Pierre, disapproval writ all over his face, brought the message.

Amelia groaned. 'What does he want, Pierre? He's not leaving, is he?'

'I have no idea, madam,' Pierre said, wooden-faced. It occurred to her that she had not seen the tutor for weeks, if not months. Nor had she checked on how well he was teaching William and Isobel. It was just another of the many things that she had neglected.

She sighed. 'Tell him he may take tea with me this afternoon.'

It was a very nervous Mark Henleigh who sidled into her small sitting room. He had all the appearance of one who was about to be punished for something. His pale face was set in lines of anxiety and he looked as if he had not slept for some time.

'Whatever is the matter, Mr Henleigh?' Amelia asked at the sight of him.

'Oh dear, madam,' he began, and clasped his forehead dramatically. 'Oh, madam.'

'Sit down,' she said firmly. 'Have some tea.' She thrust a cup in his direction which he automatically took, slopping the liquid in the saucer. 'Now, what is it?'

'I love your slave, Tansy,' he blurted out.

Amelia found she was not overly surprised. She had left all that to fate and fate had taken its course.

'I see,' she said. 'And does Tansy love you?'

'I think she must,' he said, his voice barely audible, 'for she is pregnant by me.'

Her first thought was one of outrage. How dare he make her daughter pregnant. She rose to her feet, feeling her cheeks redden with anger, and his hand began to shake, slopping the tea even more vigorously. Then common sense prevailed. No mistress would be angry if a slave girl was pregnant. Most mistresses would welcome the coming arrival as free future labour. Certainly the man responsible would receive no word of censure. Amelia sank back into her chair, trying to control her anger and think what to do.

'I want to marry her,' he blurted out. 'I want to marry her and take her and the child back to England. I fear, madam, I cannot live here much longer.' He was overtaken by a fit of coughing. He groped for his handkerchief and covered his mouth, delicately spitting into it. 'The climate . . . my health . . . Tansy says she would like to live in England, but of course the problem is that she is your property.'

His disdainful tone revealed all his feelings about slavery.

Amelia was torn and perplexed. In England Tansy would begin a new life and it was most unlikely that any would guess her ancestry. Only here in these colour-conscious islands would anyone look at her twice. It would be a wonderful opportunity for her if she were to marry this earnest young man, but if that happened, she would be lost to Amelia for ever, and Joshua's loss was too close for her to contemplate another. But . . . but . . . she was being selfish again.

'How pregnant is she?' she asked stiffly.

'We think perhaps five months. It was all my fault, madam, and I have prayed and prayed for forgiveness for taking advantage of her. But I love her.' His face was alight with the fervour of a man able to confess. 'It began the day that Windsong was bombarded. We were walking together – oh, quite innocently – and then the explosions began. We lay down in shelter and I held her close to keep her from harm, and as you know the bombardment went on and on. We were close for so long that we both lost our heads. I know that should have

235

been the end of it, but I could not resist her, nor she me. We have been lovers ever since. It was only this week that she confided to me that she is pregnant. The poor child was afraid to tell me in case I was angry with her.'

'And are you?' Amelia asked dryly.

'Angry? I am delighted. To have a child by Tansy is my wildest dream and it has come true. If you give us permission to marry here no one at home will ever know that our child was on the way before we wed. No one but God, that is, and surely he will forgive such love as we have for each other.'

'You do know that slaves cannot marry?'

'So Tansy says, but I cannot believe that such a basic right is not permitted to any of God's creatures.'

Amelia sighed. 'Mr Henleigh,' she said patiently, 'these islands are not the right place for you. You will find yourself in trouble with your fellow whites if you voice such sentiments publicly. You would be wise to return home.'

'With Tansy?' His voice was eager.

'With Tansy.' She made the plunge. 'I will give her her freedom.'

'Oh, madam. You have made me the happiest man on earth.'

She gave a rueful little laugh. 'Hopefully Tansy will do that. But I beg you to think carefully. She has black parentage.'

'It is impossible to believe. I am certain there is a mistake. But even if she has, Africans are just as much God's creatures as the rest of us.'

'As long as you are certain *you* are not making a mistake.'

'I am not making a mistake. May we tell her? May she come in? She is waiting outside the door, as eager for your decision as I myself was.'

Amelia made herself smile, but it was with deep sadness that she said, 'Of course.'

He hurried to open the door, a tall, thin romantic figure with his blond hair tied in a broad black ribbon. Amelia could understand why her exotic daughter had fallen in love with him. Opposites attracted.

Tansy came into the room almost timidly, and Amelia gave her a closer look than she had for a long time. Yes, the girl was definitely rounder. No doubt Bella and others had noticed it, but she, her mother, had been too absorbed in her grief to spot the obvious signs.

'Come here, Tansy,' she said gently.

Hands folded over her striped skirt the girl came forward, her face grave, the brilliant black eyes shaded by creamy lids as she looked down at her feet.

'I'm going to give you your freedom, Tansy, so that you can marry Mr Henleigh and go and live in England.'

The creamy shades were raised, but it was not delight that Amelia saw in the dark eyes beneath but apprehension.

'Thank you, mistress.' Her voice was subdued.

'It is what you want to do?'

Tansy nodded.

236

'You don't seem sure.'

'Will it be very cold in England?' she asked abruptly.

'Much colder than here. But very beautiful. And you will be the mistress, not a slave,' Amelia pointed out.

They were speaking as if Mark Henleigh was not present.

'I shall miss Mama and you. And Bella and William. Oh, everyone,' she said sadly.

Mama! She would miss her mama. At least she had said 'you' also. Amelia ignored the pain.

'But you will be with your husband. You love him?'

The eyes lit up. 'Oh, yes. He is so kind. And so loving.'

'Then that is all that matters,' Amelia told her.

Tansy was quietly married to Mark Henleigh a week or two after she had been given her freedom. Her child was born in July 1707, a month before William's wedding. It was a lusty, healthy girl who arrived with a mat of black woolly hair, walnut brown skin, a broad face and large mouth. She was unmistakably part-African. She was to be called Delilah. Mark and Tansy had agreed on that before her birth.

Mark took one look at his offspring and turned white. He also turned tail. Within two weeks, his Christian principles scuppered, he had returned to England on Captain West's ship, leaving behind his wife and his baby without explanation.

He did leave a brief note for Amelia. 'You were right,' was all it said.

PART III

Chapter Fourteen

'Gentlemen,' bellowed a red-faced, beaming Ben, 'the toast is St Kitts for England and Her Majesty, Queen Anne.' He raised his rummer high. 'The drinks are on me.'

An answering bellow of a cheer rocked the Columbus Tavern, and Tansy rapidly refilled glasses as they were thrust at her. The smoky, noisy room was crowded with red-coated soldiers, sailors from the slave ships, traders and merchants, men of quality and even a few mulatto free men. The only other women were Marie, Ben's long-time mistress who also attended to empty glasses, and the four not-so-young whores who had worked for Ben for years. He kept complaining he must bring in some young blood but his problem was that, like Marie and Tansy herself, the whores who lived and worked in the house next door to the tavern had become family.

It was a time to celebrate. France and Britain were at peace, the newly-drawn Treaty of Utrecht had established once and for all that St Christopher was a British possession in entirety and after years of warfare the island was at last secure from shot and cannon. There were few sober Englishmen on the island as the health of the Queen, who had demanded that the island be ceded to Britain, was drunk and drunk again.

It was a new era and perhaps it would prove to be a new era for her also, Tansy thought as she smiled her exotic smile at the men she served. She poured the rum, the claret and the brandy automatically, no longer aware of the lascivious glances that her presence invariably invoked. She had been working and living at the tavern for nearly six years now, ever since her husband had disappeared back to England. She was twenty-six years old and looking back over the years she found it hard to believe how young and naive she had been when she married. Mark's defection had come near to breaking her heart. She could not believe that he could so callously leave her and their baby when she had been convinced of his kindness and his good heart. He had been a dull fellow, but she had loved him for those admirable qualities, so rarely encountered in the West Indies. But he had gone without a word of explanation. She understood why. The man who had protested about slavery, who had piously sworn that all men were God's creatures, could not face the fact that his child was not shining white, like the path of the Lord he wished her to follow. His reaction had been a bitter, bitter disappointment. She had told Mistress Amelia that she could not bear to stay at Elsewhere, the scene of her humiliation, where everyone knew she had been deserted. Mistress Amelia had said it was best if Delilah stayed on the plantation but that she, Tansy, should go to Basse-Terre.

'You are Mistress Henleigh,' Amelia had said. 'No one can take that from you. Begin a new life. Ben will give you shelter.'

At first Ben was reluctant, but something Amelia said to him – Tansy never knew what it was – had made him agree. Then when she began to help out behind the bar and Ben saw her effect on the takings, he became more enthusiastic. Two years later, some further intervention from Amelia had the effect of persuading Ben that Tansy should have some status in the tavern. She was made the Mistress, though Ben made it clear that all authority was his.

Her mind was not on the Treaty of Utrecht as she automatically served drinks. She had very good reason to believe that her life, as well as that of St Kitts, would change. That morning she had received news of her own from England that had sweetened the bitterness she could not shake off. The letter had taken nearly three months to reach her and the news it contained brought both shock and relief. There were two separate documents folded within the envelope. The first was from a London lawyer, informing her in grandiose language that he regretted to inform her that her husband, Mark Paul Henleigh, was deceased but that his estate of 2,750 sovereigns had been left to provide for both her and Delilah, the daughter of the marriage. He begged to receive her instructions on this matter.

The second letter was from Mark himself. She recognised his handwriting from the days when he had sent her love notes and poems; secret missives always in praise of her beauty. The sight of the neat, elegant hand made her heart lurch.

'My dear Tansy,' the letter began, 'when you receive this I shall no longer be of this earth but gone to meet my Maker. My health, as you knew well, has never been good, and now the dreaded consumption is rapidly leading me towards the end. I have no fear of death; indeed, with the guilt and pain I must carry, the final curtain will be welcome and I shall cast aside these mortal coils with joy.

'But there is one thing I must do before I depart and that is to humble myself before you. Since I left St Kitts six years ago I have had much time to reflect upon my behaviour, my cowardice and my cruelty. If there is a hell, no doubt those crimes that I committed against you will send me there, and with good reason. I shall bear the flames with fortitude.

'I have never stopped loving you. Never a day goes past that I do not think of you and blame myself for all that happened. The truth is I had not the courage to return to England with Delilah. When we wed I did not believe that it was possible that we could have a black child and I am deeply ashamed of my reaction when I first witnessed our daughter. But when I saw her African cast of features I thought of my parents and their dismay to see such a granddaughter. I thought, too, of myself and my own embarrassment, and my Christian beliefs did not sustain me as they should have. I did not think of you, or the child, only of my own selfish fears. And so I left.

'Now as death holds out his icy hand to me, I feel the need to repent of my sins towards you. I do not know how your life has progressed in these last years but I pray that you are content without your craven husband. I pray also that you will find it in your heart to forgive me and perhaps even thank me a little for procuring your freedom. I pray, too, that our child is well and happy – and free. My one consolation is that though I was always aware that you loved me (I am convinced of that), your heart was full of doubts that you would find happiness in England. And, indeed, maybe you would not have done so.

'I have left you what little I have of worldly goods in the hope that this money will lighten your and Delilah's life. She will be nearly six. I think of her often.

'I now say farewell as I beg your forgiveness once more.

'Your shamed but loving husband, Mark.'

Tansy had read the letter a second time, more slowly, and as she carefully folded it, she realised she was crying. In six years much of the pain of Mark's departure had vanished, but the sense of rejection had never gone away. She had divorced herself from the company of men, preferring to be on her own. Tansy, though she did not know it, had much of her father in her. Since leaving Elsewhere she had worked to the best of her ability and she knew that Ben valued her, whatever his initial thoughts had been. In the small amount of time that was her own she shut herself in the room that Ben had given her in his home and read whatever books she was able to find. William, when he came into town, would bring her selections from his library. Amelia was also eager to press books upon her, and had also presented her with the harpsichord on which, as a child, she had learned to play. Now she practised for at least an hour a day, playing the latest music of Antonio Vivaldi and J. S. Bach which Amelia had especially sent by Mr Lockett, her London agent.

It was a solitary life, but she was content. She was able to visit Delilah whenever she wished though the child did not know that she was her mother. Amelia had made it clear that the little girl would be brought up as if she were free. Tansy took tea at Elsewhere at least once a fortnight, arriving in her own carriage, supplied by Ben, amazed that she was received there with no mention of the days when she had been just another slave. Her only regret was that her new status appeared to have changed things between her and Ruby. Ruby was withdrawn and she could appreciate why. On her visits to Windsong she was dressed as a white woman in fine clothes, her voice and tastes were those of a white woman her life was now far removed from that of a slave. Yet Ruby's withdrawal puzzled her. Sometimes she wondered if the black woman really was her parent. When she thought about it, at no time had anyone confirmed the relationship, not even Ruby herself. But if Ruby was not her mother, who was? There was no other candidate. Sometimes she felt that people kept secrets from her. There were times when Bella's mouth would close like a trap if she asked questions, but then she told herself she was being fanciful.

Tansy grieved that Mark Henleigh was dead, but his letter had wiped away much of the bitterness she had felt, for she was not one to harbour grudges. And as she served the tavern's customers, she considered what to do with his bequest.

The tavern closed late that night. Even the constable did not stagger out through the doors until gone three in the morning and the three large Irishmen that Ben employed to remove obstreperous guests had had their hands full. It was even later by the time the tavern was cleaned and tidy for the morning and Tansy could go to bed. Nevertheless she was up early. She wanted to talk to Amelia about her news. She had it in her mind that perhaps this was the moment to take back her child and live as a mother instead of a tavernkeeper. With the money that Mark had left her she could buy a home of her own.

Amelia greeted her warmly and suggested that they walk in the cool of the garden where a gentle breeze ruffled the tops of the palm trees. Later it would become hot and sultry and would be cooler inside the house. They should enjoy the air now, she said, and took Tansy's arm as they walked down the path.

'Have you heard?' she said. 'I'm to become a grandmother. Dear Isobel is pregnant at last.'

'You look too young to be a grandmother,' Tansy said. It was true. Amelia seemed to defy time. Her russet hair had lost none of its colour, the green of her eyes seemed to deepen with the years. She had eventually overcome the depression she had suffered after the war and was as cheerful as she had ever been. Yet now that Tansy was free and on equal terms with her, she was conscious of being less at ease with the older woman than she had been as her slave.

'I'm so happy about it,' Amelia said. 'I need another diversion or I shall totally spoil your Delilah.'

'It was Delilah I wished to speak of,' Tansy said.

Amelia raised her eyebrows in question marks.

'I've heard from Mark.'

'Oh!'

'He's dead. He wrote the letter before he died. He has left me his estate — 2,750 sovereigns.'

Amelia did not speak but led Tansy towards a garden seat placed under the shade of a tamarind. Tansy produced the two letters from a pocket in her gown. Still silent, Amelia took and read them.

'It is right he has recognised you at last,' Amelia murmured, carefully folding the two papers. 'Are you distressed by the news of his death?'

'A little, but in a way more relieved that he has been honest enough to tell me his reasons. I felt such a failure, so rejected when he left.

244

And yet there was relief there, too, that I would not have to go to England. I had thought this was what I wanted, dreamed about, but in the end, as he sensed, the thought of leaving the island frightened me.'

'Did you love him?' Amelia asked.

'I did love him because I admired him so, though I must allow he never seemed manly until we became lovers. Then it was different. And I was flattered by him. He seemed to adore me and could not accept that I was merely a slave. It angered him that I was not free. I had never even considered it. And he was so intelligent and clever. The fact he thought I was wonderful was seductive in itself. And, of course, it was I who seduced him.'

Surprisingly, Amelia burst out laughing. 'But he blamed himself.'

'He did?' Tansy laughed ruefully. 'It was all my fault. I thought I was going to die in the war and didn't want to die a virgin. He kept telling me how much he loved me and I believed I loved him. I could see no point in not doing something about it.'

A broad smile covered Amelia's face. She looked as if she was going to say something significant but then stopped. 'And now?' she asked.

'And now I wonder if it is time to stop being a tavernkeeper and become a mother.'

'Ah.' Amelia had become motionless except for a few russet curls ruffled by the breeze. 'Do you think that is wise?'

'Why not?'

'Because, it may not be wise.' Amelia seemed to be measuring her words. 'Tell me, how do you think people in Basse-Terre treat you? As a white woman or as a black woman?'

It was something that Tansy had not considered. She considered it now.

'As a white woman,' she eventually said, realising with surprise that this was true.

'And how do you think they would view you if you set up home with Delilah?'

'I don't understand what you mean.'

'They would regard you as either a white woman who had slept with a negro or as a black woman masquerading as a white woman.'

'But I am a black woman,' Tansy said.

'You are not. No more than you are white. You are neither and you can choose to be exactly what you wish. And I tell you that to be white is better. As time goes on you will be able to take your place in the white world and no one will be the wiser.'

'But that would be a betrayal,' Tansy cried.

'Why? You are neither black nor white. You owe no loyalty to either side. It is up to you to make your own choice. One might just as well say that you are betraying your white blood if you insist on being black. I ask you, what do you have in common with your fellow blacks? They are good people, but they are peasants, uneducated, admittedly through

245

no fault of their own. You are a cultured, intelligent woman. You could not live in a black world and be happy.'

'But why do I have to decide?' Tansy asked passionately. 'I don't know myself what I am.'

'I just told you. You are cultured and intelligent. Your colour has nothing to do with it. You need to be in a world of cultured and intelligent people.'

'And where does that leave my child?'

'Here with me, where she is safe, learning to be cultured and intelligent also in the hope that one day her life and the lives of black people here will change. If you take her from here both your lives will be spoilt. Unless you take her as a slave or a servant.'

'I could not do that to my own child.'

Amelia turned her head and stared fixedly towards the stream. 'It would be painful but not impossible.'

'Never. Never would I do that, but you don't understand the pain of not having her.'

Amelia's eyes closed as if she were trying to hide her expression. 'Oh yes I do,' she said quietly. 'I understand very well.'

Tansy sighed. 'So what should I do with my own life?'

'Come out of the shell you have built round yourself. Continue at the tavern – it's better to have some purpose. And think about marrying again.'

Tansy shook her head violently at the mention of marriage. 'And suppose the same thing happens again? I marry and have a black child?'

'That you can only leave to fate.'

Tansy stood and moved a few paces away from where Amelia sat. 'I will think about it,' she said. 'But if I decide that I want Delilah back, I shall take her.'

'That is your right.' Amelia's voice was resigned, but she smiled and held out her hand. 'Come and see her now.'

Delilah had a round face, coffee-brown skin, narrow, almost Oriental, dark eyes and already her hair had grown long in a way that it would not have done without white blood. It was frizzy, but there was a great deal of it, and her mouth was large like her mother's but her nose broader. If these childish good looks did not disappear, she would be a remarkably beautiful young woman, Tansy though. But never in a million years could she pass as white.

The child was also clever. Playing with her daughter, reading a child's book together, watching her carefully write her own name, Tansy understood what Amelia had been trying to say to her. Along with the pride she felt for her daughter, she also felt despair. Whatever would Delilah, with her obvious African heritage, do with this cleverness on these sugar islands? Tansy forced herself to accept that her child's abilities had little hope of ever being realised. Amelia was right. It was better to be white than black. And she, Tansy, was lucky. Unlike her daughter, she could pass.

Sitting in the coach on the way back to Basse-Terre, driven by a black coachman, Tansy made her decision. She would become white. Portuguese, perhaps. More and more Portuguese were coming to the islands, many from Madeira where life, it appeared, was even harder than here. The Portuguese were dark-eyed and dark-haired. They had olive skins. They looked exactly as she did. She would become a Portuguese.

The decision did not make her happy. She still felt as if she were betraying her heritage, but then she remembered Amelia's words, 'One might just as well say that you are betraying your white blood if you insist on being black.' Of course, that was true. She giggled suddenly into her gloved hand. It would be fun fooling everyone. All those superior whites – she would be whiter than any of them. Maybe she could become rich and a member of society, have them clamouring for invitations to her soirees not knowing that their elegant and beautiful hostess (for she would be both) had a coal-black mother and a half-white father and a big black grandma who was a cook. It was a prospect that pleased her a great deal – as long as no one told the truth about her.

She arrived back at the tavern in high good humour and went to her room to prepare herself for work. Tansy was always very much the hostess to the tavern. She wore elegant gowns made by the town's most fashionable dressmakers. She had learned to be so skilful in dispensing drinks that the French silks and satins she wore were never stained by so much as a drop of claret. Her black hair was always arranged in the height of fashion. Having dressed Amelia's hair all her young life she was clever with her own. She used a little discreet powder against the heat of the tavern and, though they were somewhat dated, she liked to wear beautyspots on the smooth olive skin of her cheeks. She dressed for the male customers, but she never teased them and was never less than a lady. She had realised her beauty combined with dignity made her more desirable than the leg and breast shows of the tavern's harlots. In fact, Prissie, the youngest of the four girls, had said to her one day, 'Thank God for you, mistress. It is you they want to fuck, but they know they cannot so they settle for us.'

Tansy rarely noticed the customers. Early on she had made a point of smiling into their faces, eyes warm and interested, while never seeing them. She had learned to drop a curtain behind her smiling eyes so that no detail registered. But coming down into the tavern that morning, the habitual curtain let through some light. It was hardly surprising: there was only one customer in the room, and he was one of the biggest men she had ever seen. She had always thought Zachary Quick was remarkably large, but this man was a giant. He was by no means fashionable. His wild shock of light brown hair fell in spaniel ears beside his long face. He resembled Charles I and the mass of hair made him appear even taller. He was standing, neck bent so as not to knock his head on the ceiling, and a pair of eyes with the blue of the sea in them lit up as she came through the door. It was the sea he had come from, she thought, for he wore a uniform frockcoat and sword topped by a seaman's tricorn and there was an odour of fish about him that caused her to wrinkle her nose.

'Ah,' he said in a voice like a drumbeat. 'I have a prodigious thirst. Two tankards of ale, if you please, mistress.'

She drew his two tankards from the barrel beneath the bar and pushed them across to him. He downed the first in one gulp, took a deep breath and downed the second. Fascinated, she watched the ripples of his huge throat. Then, with a surprisingly sweet smile he said, 'And again, if you please.'

She found herself smiling back as she refilled the two pewter tankards. A beefy hand stretched and the third ale disappeared into the maw of the man. What height was he? she wondered. More than 6 feet 6 for sure.

'My thirst, you understand, is entirely your fault.'

'Mine?' She looked at him startled, trying to place his accent. He was certainly not British.

'Yours,' he said solemnly. 'You served me far too much of your fine claret last night. This morning I have a mouth like the hold of a slave ship.'

'You were here last night?' She could not believe that she had not seen him.

'Aye. But I could not get through the door. I did my drinking on the street. I sent in the smallest and nimblest of my crew to get through the crowd. But I saw you.'

'Oh?'

'Oh, yes.' He grinned and the skin round his blue eyes crinkled into a mass of lines. 'There are advantages to being my height. I could look down on you from above the heads of your customers. And what I saw was a most unlikely serving wench.'

'I'm not a serving wench,' she said sharply. 'I'm the Mistress of the Tavern.'

'Married to the Master?'

'No. The Mistress in my own right.'

'I see. An exceptional woman. I knew it.'

She did not reply. A group of men were coming in through the open door, and she turned to call up the stairs for Marianne to come and help her serve.

'Now that is a pity,' he said as he picked up his undrunk ale.

'What?' she asked as Marianne's footsteps clattered down the stairs.

'Those gentlemen come to quench their thirsts. I came early as I had hoped to spend a little time with you alone.'

'Indeed,' she said, wondering why she was engaging in conversation with this particular customer when her rule was no more than the courtesies.

'Indeed,' he repeated. 'You see, there is little time.'

With some difficulty he had leaned his elbows on the bar so that his

248

tanned, cheerful face was nearer to hers. 'You are very small,' he remarked conversationally. 'In fact,' he said reverting to his original theme, 'there is hardly any time at all.'

'Time for what?'

'To tell you that I have decided to marry you.'

She felt her mouth fall open as she stared at him. One finger all of half a foot long gently put itself under her chin and pressed upwards to close her mouth.

'No woman looks her best with her mouth open,' he remarked. 'Let me introduce myself. Captain Robin Darnley, seaman and trader of Boston, Massachusetts, at your service. Captain of the *Queen of the Seas* which alas must sail with the tide. That is in no more than twenty minutes. My ship is ready laden with molasses and my crew await me. Therefore there is no time for you and I to get to know each other better. And should I smell of fish, salt cod to be exact, I beg you to disregard this. It is the last residue of my cargo from the north of the Atlantic. Had I known of this encounter I would have taken more care before coming ashore. But I shall be back, next time bathed, to continue this courtship.' He pulled out a turnip of a watch. 'Shall we say in nine weeks, five days and twenty-three hours?'

She stood speechless as he leaned over the bar, lifted her off her feet as if she were a doll and gave her a smacking kiss directly on the lips before carefully placing her back where she had been standing. She was too astonished to react.

'*Au revoir*,' he said. He flung a few shillings on the bar, saluted her and marched from the tavern with a tread that shook the glasses on the shelves.

Tansy watched his broad back disappear through the door, her hand on her mouth where the kiss had landed. Marianne could hardly contain her giggles and the other customers were slapping their thighs with delight. Scarlet with embarrassment, Tansy busied herself washing the tankards he had used.

'Well, are you going to accept?' Marianne called out.

'Oh, really! Don't be so silly, Marianne,' she said crossly, and yet the truth was she didn't feel cross at all. Elated would have been a better word. And the feel of the kiss still burned on her lips. Nine weeks, five days and twenty-three hours. That, she thought, would be somewhere in the middle of February. Perhaps St Valentine's Day.

But nine weeks, five days and twenty-three hours was a long time. By the time Christmas came and went she realised she was much happier. Mark's letter had soothed wounds and she was beginning to shake off the past. Ben had taken her with him to the homes of some of the grand ladies of the town, introducing her as his niece. With Marie and Marianne at home, getting on with the work of the tavern, he had become quite a lady's man and she his escort. And she had been accepted without question – so far.

She had almost forgotten Captain Darnley, having put his words and actions down to those of a man still drunk from the night before. But there was something about him that had attracted her and she still smiled to herself as she thought of his vast presence dominating the tavern and how easily he had lifted her off the ground. And perhaps, who knew, he might come back and if he did, she would, she had to admit, be pleased to see him.

Bella was making dough, when Joseph, creaking on old limbs, put his head round the kitchen door to say that the mistress wanted to see Bella.

'Now what be the matter?' Bella grumbled to herself as she wiped the sticky mixture from her hands.

Bella, heavier than she had ever been, huffed and puffed her way through the house to Amelia's sitting room. Since her woolly hair had turned white she had taken to wearing brilliant silk turbans, mostly manufactured from Amelia's cast-off gowns. She was well into her fifties, a great age for an African in the West Indies, and since she was a free woman she sometimes talked about retiring, though she had no intentions of doing any such thing.

Amelia was standing, looking out of the window and into the garden. She turned as Bella came through the door.

'Now what you wanting?' Without waiting to be asked she sank into a chair.

'To talk,' Amelia said. 'I've had something on my mind for weeks.'

She looked peaky, Bella thought. Peaky and preoccupied, just like she always did when she was uncertain what to do.

'So what's troublin' you?'

'Tansy.'

'And what she gone and done?'

'Nothing. Yet. But some time ago she talked about taking Delilah from here.'

'And what's she go'n do when she got her?'

'That's the problem,' Amelia said. 'You see, Mark Henleigh is dead and has left her his estate.'

'Who? Tansy or Delilah?'

'Tansy,' Amelia said impatiently and Bella listened while her mistress recounted the conversation that she had had a few weeks before with Tansy.

'She has to decide where she's going to be,' Amelia concluded. 'What she has been left is no great fortune, but it will make her independent. She could bring up Delilah, but how does she explain her?'

'What you mean, explain her? She be her daughter, don' she?' Bella knew her tone was belligerent.

'Of course, but you know as well as I do what people will say if they know she has a mulatto daughter.'

'Ain't nothin' wrong with black blood. What you be sayin' to me is that you think Tansy go'n have to pretend to be white.'

250

'To all intents and purposes she is white. Oh, Bella, stop being hostile. I'm not saying there is anything wrong with being black and, for God's sake, it was you who all those years ago kept warning me of the problems when I was having her. You were right. But it's better she chooses one side of the fence or the other.'

'And white side's the best side. That what you sayin'?'

'Well, isn't it?'

Bella heard her own gargantuan sigh. 'Yeah. It better.'

'I've been thinking of the dangers if she does opt to be white. How many people know I'm her mother, do you think? And how many people know about Delilah? We're lucky in being so remote down here at Elsewhere, but one breath of scandal could ruin everything for her.'

'And for you.'

Amelia shrugged dismissively. 'Bella, I'm too old to care any more. What can they do to me? I'll never for one moment regret having loved Joshua. I just wish I still had him. Now I want Tansy to be happy as I never was.'

Bella snorted, but her heart wasn't in it. 'Well,' she said, 'I knows she your child, Truly knows and I guess that means Dan knows, too. Maybe not Juba. How 'bout Ben and Zach, they know?'

'Yes, they've always known, though I'm certain they won't have told anyone else. Zach because he wouldn't want it known and Ben because he doesn't want to believe it.'

'Ruby knows,' Bella said thoughtfully, 'but Ruby don' be the kind to do someone hurt. Old Bessie she go'n know, but I knows she be long dead and gone. Her daughter, Minta, know. Guess she still somewhere at Macabees if she still 'live.'

'The question is, did any of them tell anyone else? And as for Tansy and Delilah – well, everyone on the estate knows that Tansy was once a slave and that Delilah is her child. It's going to be so difficult for Tansy, but what else can she do but take a chance on it?'

'Be what she is. Learn some trade like other freed folk. Or just stay Mistress of the Tavern.'

'I want better for her than that. She's too young to live alone.'

'What you really talkin' 'bout be marriage to a white man. And you knows what happened last time.'

'It might not happen again,' Amelia said defensively. 'But you know what she's like, how clever she is. She can't marry a slave or even a freed one. What would they have in common?'

'If you don' want her married to a black man, better if you'd claim her as yourn,' Bella said decisively. 'Pretend she had a white pappy.'

'That won't explain Delilah,' Amelia pointed out.

'You could say she fucked a black man.'

'That wouldn't help at all.'

This time Bella's snort was heartfelt. 'Don' know why you don' just tell her now.'

Amelia grimaced. 'I want to with all my heart, but I feel I've left it too late. She would never forgive me for all the years of deception. At least now we're friends. And if I tell her, what do I say to William? If I don't tell him, I shall have to inform Tansy that it must still be a secret.'

'Well, seems to me she just go'n have to take her chances, like the rest of us.'

'Will you talk to Truly and Ruby and ask them to be discreet?'

'Ruby don' need no word from me. Seems to me that if I ask that Truly, she go'n do just the opposite out of sheer pig-headedness. Better be quiet. Come to think of it, that Truly got a lot of your secrets in her head. P'haps it time she got her freedom.'

'What good will that do?'

'More good than harm, I reckons.'

'But she belongs with us.'

'Then why she at Windsong? How long it been since you seen her? And I wants her home.'

Amelia was silent and Bella knew she had won. She knew Amelia like her own daughter; sometimes liked her a lot better than her own daughter. And though torture wouldn't have dragged it from her, she loved Amelia. Amelia, she often told herself privately, would have been the perfect daughter – if only she hadn't been white.

'You're right.' Amelia's voice was thoughtful. 'Her freedom is long overdue. I'll do something about it tomorrow.'

She decided to ride to Windsong in the morning. Her mare had died a few years previously and been replaced by another, a pretty little black beast that her stable hands promised her was a descendant of her much loved predecessor. The sun shone down from a clear January sky, there was no sign of much needed rain, and it looked as if it would be a scorcher of a day.

Amelia rode through the sugar cane and the forest where parrot-like birds peered at her from the trees. She was singing quietly to herself. The thought of giving Truly and Daniel their freedom had made her feel good. The more she thought about Tansy's chances of leading a white life, the better they seemed. Most of the slaves who had been at Windsong at the time of her birth were dead. There were those at Elsewhere who knew Tansy had been a slave, but she had no fear of malice from her own people.

Truly was the one serious problem, but maybe if Truly were free she would feel no reason to cause harm. In fact, the truth of the matter was that Truly, for all her awkward nature, would be unlikely to do anything to hurt her family.

Charlotte greeted her with pleasure and insisted on calling in the eight-year-old twins to greet her. They were charming children, full of life, with the Quick reddish hair and cheerful temperament.

'Don't you think they've grown?' Charlotte said fondly after they had been shooed off back to the nursery. 'Zach is already speaking of bringing out a tutor from England.'

'Ah,' said Amelia, settling her skirts about her. 'In that case perhaps I can have Juba back.'

Charlotte let out of little cry of anguish. 'But they'll be brokenhearted to lose him. They're all such friends.'

'Well,' Amelia began carefully, 'that's really why I've come this morning. You see, I have decided to give Truly and Daniel their freedom and I can hardly not do the same for Juba.'

Charlotte had gone quite white. 'Freedom? Oh dear,' she said faintly. 'I do think that perhaps you had better have a word with Zach. Please excuse me for one moment.'

She shot out of the room with a puzzling turn of speed. Amelia knew well that giving slaves freedom was akin to giving away her fortune as far as Charlotte was concerned, but she did seem to be over-reacting since Truly and Daniel were not even hers.

It was some time before she returned with Zach. He was still in his night cap and robe and looked uneasy as he came through the door.

'Good morning,' he said.

'Good morning, Zach.' It was gone ten in the morning and she looked pointedly at his attire. 'I'm sorry to have disturbed you.'

'I had a late night at the Assembly,' he muttered.

She said no more and waited. Her sense that all was not well was growing.

'You came about Truly and Daniel?'

She nodded. 'I want to give them their freedom.'

'I'm afraid that will not be possible.' Zach was not meeting her eyes. He seemed to be having difficulty keeping his hands still.

'I don't understand.'

'They've been sold.' The words were blurted out.

Amelia stared at him appalled. Charlotte, white-faced, hands flapping, seemed to be trying to intervene.

'What do you mean they've been sold?'

'Exactly what I say.' Now he was trying to bluff it out.

'But you can't have sold them. They're not yours to sell.'

Her confusion was giving him confidence. 'Nevertheless that is what I have done.'

'How dare you!' Her anger was mounting like a furnace inside her. 'What an unspeakable thing to do. How dare you! Where are they? You will get them back at once.'

'I'm afraid that will not be possible. I sold them to a visiting slave trader who sold them on. He promised they would be sold to a plantation on another island. I have no idea which.'

For the moment she was controlling herself, but the control was slipping.

Through clenched teeth she said, 'And why did you do this wicked thing?'

253

'I had reason to chastise her. She was surly and insolent. I meant to have her whipped. Then she made some threats about what she would do or say if I did any such thing. I did not whip her. I got rid of her for good.'

'I see. And what were these threats?'

'I would rather not go into that.'

Truly and Daniel had been sent away, at their ages, to another place, torn from their son, never to see their family again, and he dared stand there complacent and confident. Rage took over.

'I can understand why you would rather not say, brother,' she said, her voice shot silk. 'I would imagine that Truly suggested she might mention how it was you who murdered Charlotte's brother that night long ago, and that Tansy is not my slave but my child and that her brother, Joshua, was my lover. Is that what was frightening you? Well, now it's all in the open,' she stabbed a finger to where a horrified Charlotte stood, 'and you will never have to get rid of anyone again to hide the family secrets. Unless, of course, you decide to try and get rid of me.'

Zach's self-possession had shattered. He backed away from her, his hands over his ears.

'Oh, no!' The breathless cry came from Charlotte, her childish blonde curls trembling against her cheeks. She took two tottering paces forward, her hand held palm out as if to ward off the ruth. Then she swayed, buckled at the knees and fell to the ground.

'I think your wife has fainted,' Amelia said calmly looking down at her. 'Perhaps you'd better do something about it. I wish you good day, Zach.'

Outside the door she began to tremble at the enormity of what he had done and she had said. But she was not leaving without Juba. Trying to control her shaking hands she went looking for him in the kitchens. Ruby, who was there alone, looked up in surprise as she came through the door.

'Good morning, Ruby,' she said, the words staccato. 'I have come to take Juba home. You look startled to see me here. No need. I am familiar with these kitchens. I was a slave here myself many years ago. Only for four years but enough to know what it is like. I lived in the slave cabins at the back there.'

Ruby raised her arms high and wide as if surrendering to the flow of truth. 'I know,' she said. 'I know. Josh told me.'

The quiet acknowledgement calmed Amelia. She let out the breath she realised she had been holding and said, 'And you have never mentioned it?'

Ruby shrugged. 'Don' be my business.' The black, shrewd eyes searched Amelia's face, then she bit her lip and nodded. 'You heard about Truly and Dan, eh?'

'Yes. Why didn't someone tell me?'

' 'Cause it weren't no one's business, I guess. And I don' want to be the one to break that Bella's heart.'

254

'Then it will have to be me who does it.'

'Guess it will.'

Amelia felt her face begin to crumple. 'I can't bear to think about it. I know Truly was difficult, but I loved her. We were young together. She was my family more than my real family. Why did he do it?'

'Fear. But she'd never have told on *you*. You taught her to read. Just like she's taught Juba. And she were teaching me, too, 'fore they took her away. Might have told on *him*, though, come to think 'bout it. And serve him right if she did.'

The black woman's eyes were full of tears and Amelia could contain hers no longer. Ruby held out her hand across the kitchen table. Amelia took it tight in her own. They stood, heads bowed, grieving until Ruby pulled her hand away and dashed it across her face.

'I guess I'll just go find Juba for you,' she said.

The little black horse made light work of the journey back to Elsewhere, even with Juba riding behind her. He was a slightly built seventeen-year-old, solemn, but with a sudden, almost mischievous smile. Today there was no sign of the smile.

She did not speak until they had dismounted in front of the house.

'Come with me, Juba,' she said. Still in her riding clothes she walked through the house to the kitchen. 'I want you to greet your grandmother and then wait for me in my sitting room.'

'You not go'n sell me?' he asked, his face full of apprehension.

'Of course not.'

'Then why you let 'em sell my mammy and my pappy?'

'I did not let them. I didn't know it was happening. I'll try and get them back. And I'm going to give you your freedom.'

He looked at her goggle-eyed, but before he could say anything she strode into the kitchen and he followed. Bella hugged and kissed him, and then looked around enquiringly.

'Where be Truly?' she asked.

Amelia nodded to Juba to go and as the lad disappeared, Bella asked, her voice full of deep suspicion, 'Is somethin' wrong?'

'Badly wrong.' Amelia flung down her whip, sat on a kitchen chair and began to pull off her boots. She needed to hide her face. 'Zach sold Truly and Daniel.'

'Sold them?' Huge white-rimmed eyes stared at Amelia in bewilderment.

'He was going to have Truly whipped for insolence. She apparently threatened him with what she'd do and say about things that happened long ago if he did it. So he sold her and Daniel.'

'Where?'

'I don't know. Somewhere far away. He says he got rid of her for ever.'

'You don't think . . .?'

'I don't think he'd do that.'

255

'He did once before.'

'And that's what he believed she was threatening to tell. Well,' Amelia banged her hand on the table, 'he won't have to get rid of anyone to keep that secret any more. I told his wife everything. About him killing Justinian, about Josh and Tansy and me. She knows all the family secrets now.'

Bella was rocking backwards and forwards, her arms clasped over her breasts. 'And what she go'n do now she knows?'

'Nothing. Charlotte will not want her place in society threatened by a murderous husband and a nigger-loving sister-in-law. She'll keep all the secrets.'

Her anger was beginning to abate and suddenly she felt exhausted and also regretful that in her rage – her justified rage – she had shocked Charlotte with knowledge with which she might not be able to cope. But, she thought, Charlotte should have been told right from the beginning. Such secrets were too dangerous. But then who was she to talk when she still kept her own secrets from her own daughter?

Bella seemed to have shrunk. 'What we go'n do?' she asked in a pitifully small voice.

'Try and find them.'

'That Zach, he not go'n tell you anythin'. Not after what you said.'

'No. He's not going to tell me anything. It may take years, Bella, but we'll find them. And at least we have Juba.'

'But Truly don' have him and he don' have her.' The woman leaned her head on the table and began to cry. 'I wish they'd let me be in Africa,' she wailed. 'We was all so happy there.'

Amelia brooded about how best to find Truly and Daniel. It would not be easy without information. There were a great many islands and even more plantations in the West Indies. It was difficult to know where to begin to search.

Just recently a Sunday market for blacks and mulattoes had been permitted on the site of the Jail Yard in the New Town section of Basse-Terre. The slaves came in from the country districts and from the estates, bringing with them their produce, vegetables, poultry, fruit, anything that they had grown in their own small plots of land behind the slave cabins. The money they made for themselves was small, but they lived in the hope that in time they might save enough to buy their freedom. If a slave were skilled, perhaps a blacksmith or a cooper or carpenter, he could then hire himself out to those townsfolk or small businesses in the town who did not keep slaves. The Sunday market was where the slaves spent their only free time and it was the one place where they could gather news of each other. Bella began to go there on Sunday mornings, ostensibly to buy produce but really to ask if there was anyone with word of Truly and Daniel. So far she had learned nothing.

Amelia managed to track down and question the slave trader, but he would tell her nothing. She suspected that he had been advised to keep his mouth shut. And Zach was quite powerful enough on the island to have his word obeyed. People said that he would probably be the next Deputy Governor. Without co-operation from Zach, Amelia realised that she would never get anywhere.

Two weeks after the scene at Windsong Ben arrived unexpectedly at Elsewhere by boat. There had been a sudden tropical rainstorm and he was wet, gently steaming in the warmth of the house. Amelia greeted him with pleasure as he shook himself like a dog, making the candles splutter.

'Zach sent me,' he said briefly.

'Ah,' she said.

'He told me what happened.'

'I see.'

'You shouldn't have said all that in front of Charlotte, Amelia. It was very wrong of you.'

'It was very wrong of Zach to sell Truly and Daniel.'

'Two wrongs don't make a right.'

She let out a snort of exasperation. 'Don't be so sanctimonious, Ben. I said nothing that was not true.'

'Well, you're going to have to go and visit him and tell Charlotte that you were lying when you said Zach killed her brother. She's been suffering from the vapours ever since, and Zach can't bear it a moment longer.'

'Indeed,' she said dryly. 'And what makes you think I will do that?'

'Because he's your brother and because he did it for me. I have to be grateful to him for that, which is why I'm trying to persuade you. He didn't mean to kill Justinian. That was a mistake. He just wanted to maim him so that I would be left alone. Damn it, Zach is no surgeon. How could he know the little bastard would bleed to death?' He made an impatient movement of the hand. 'Listen, Zach doesn't really care about her knowing, it's just that all her weeping and wailing is driving him insane. Come on, Amelia, he is your brother. He doesn't understand why you're making so much fuss about what he calls a couple of black slaves.'

She looked at her cousin sadly. How self-seeking and cruel they had all become in this lush, tropical island where the living was so easy.

'He doesn't even begin to understand,' she said. 'Truly and I were slaves together. She was good to me in her own way, as much as she despises white people. And sometimes I think she is right to despise us. Zach has forgotten and you have forgotten what it was like to be a slave.'

'Maybe Zach has,' he said sharply, 'but I have not. Never have I used slave labour. You cannot say the same.'

She winced. 'Touché,' she murmured, and then said slowly, 'I might just do what he wants if he will tell me where he sold Truly and Daniel.'

'He doesn't know.'

The answer was too pat; too prompt.

'Then why has he paid the slave trader to be silent?'

257

'Has he? I don't know.' Ben shrugged. 'But my guess is that even if he did know he wouldn't say. Zach wants to be Deputy Governor of this island. Actually, he wants to be Governor, but we all have to start somewhere. He's not going to tolerate a black woman slave threatening to blackmail him. In his shoes, I wouldn't tell you where she is either.'

Amelia walked to look out of the window at her garden. Then, with her back turned to him, she said, 'Ben, do you still want the tavern? For yourself?'

There was a long silence and she turned to face him. His expression was enigmatic, but his face had lost some of its colour and the freckles stood out on his cheeks and nose.

'Why do you ask?'

'Because if you do, and if you find Truly and Daniel and bring them back here, it's yours.'

He puffed out his cheeks and blew out a yard of air.

'Sorry, Amelia,' he said. 'But no.'

'Why not?'

'I told you, Zach did it for me. I owe him that. And besides, you should be thinking of Tansy. You don't want the tale of her background going round what society there is on this island. She's coming along well as a white woman.'

'Do you think I care if people know about Josh and me?'

'No. But you'll care if they know about Tansy. And so will I. I've become fond of the girl.'

She regarded him as if he were an interesting specimen, her head to one side.

'Is that why you let her father die?' she asked softly.

Now he turned so red that the freckles blended into the scarlet of his skin.

'What did you say?'

'You heard what I said.'

He opened his mouth to protest but she lifted both arms, palms out, to silence him.

'I know you did, Ben. I'm sure of it. I've been over that day again and again in my head. You could have saved him if you had wanted to. Don't lie to me any more.'

The silence seemed interminable, and then he said, his voice so low she could hardly hear him, 'He was ruining your life. And mine. His death did not help my life – you still rejected me – but I don't care what you say, it has helped yours. And Tansy's. Zach killed for me. I didn't kill, but I didn't save – for you.'

'I ought to hate you,' she said sadly, 'but I can't. I ought to hate Zach, but I can't. But it will take time for all of us to come together again. We have hurt each other too much.'

'For God's sake!' He was angry. 'All any of us has done is to survive as best we can. And that includes you, Amelia. What you did to Zach and Charlotte was cruel and wicked. And you're going to have to live with it just as Zach and I are going to have to live with the memory of things we would rather had not happened.' He picked up his tricorn, jammed it over his wig and slammed out of the room.

He sailed back to Basse-Terre, took his horse from the tavern stables and rode straight to Windsong. Zach and Charlotte were about to sit down to supper, and they invited him to join them. It was the first time he had seen his cousin's wife since Amelia's revelations; she looked pale and as if she had lost a great deal of weight. She was a silly woman, Ben thought, but she had shown surprising strength throughout the wars which was to her credit, and she was a good mother to Zach's children. She was pretentious, it was true, and full of herself, but somewhere there was hidden a good, if ingenuous heart. He found himself feeling sorry for her.

After the slaves had served the food and left the room Zach said angrily, 'I must tell you, Ben, that my wife continues to believe that it was I who killed her brother. Were you able to persuade my sister to reconsider her lies?'

He sounded so aggrieved, his face showed such moral indignation, that Ben wondered if he had convinced himself that it was not the machete in his hand that had caused Justinian's death.

'Amelia does not lie,' murmured Charlotte.

'Everyone lies, when it suits them to do so,' Zach snapped.

'I do not believe that to be true,' Charlotte said with dignity.

'Perhaps Amelia believes, mistakenly, that Zach was responsible for Justinian's death,' Ben began tentatively.

'But what did she say?' Zach's tone was bullying and it irritated Ben.

'That she would discuss the matter further when you have told her where Truly and Daniel are.'

'I told her, I don't know. I made it my business not to know. They are better out of the way.'

'What I don't understand, Zach,' Charlotte said, her face pale in the candlelight, 'is that if you are innocent, why were you so anxious to sell them?'

Zach seemed to swell. 'You question my innocence? I am the most maligned of men. I sold them to protect Amelia and Tansy, and what happens? My well-meaning actions rebound on me. In any case, you should be glad that your brother is dead. If he were not, you would not be mistress of this plantation.'

'And you would not be master,' Charlotte said quietly. 'I declare, Zachary, there are times when I cannot believe how insensitive you are.'

'He was always insensitive, Charlotte,' Ben said cheerfully, trying to lighten the atmosphere. 'But as I was saying, maybe Amelia mistakenly believes that Zach was responsible for your brother's death. For as you say, she does not lie. Remember I was there that night. And it is true that Zach went into the room, but all he did was wake your

259

brother and threaten him with dire and dreadful retribution if I was ever hurt again. Amelia saw him leave the house and then run for safety in the woods. Later I saw this dark figure in the hallway, the moonlight gleaming off the machete he held upraised in his hand.' Ben was warming to his story. 'He was creeping towards Justinian's bedroom. To tell the truth, the sight of him made me afraid. I was easily frightened in those days, and I quickly ran downstairs not wanting to be involved. I was even afraid to admit what I'd seen. But if you remember, your brother's dying words to your father were that it was a black man who had attacked him. I myself always believed it was Joshua though I did not say so at the time,' it was safe enough to blame Joshua now, he thought; Joshua was dead, 'but the slaves never forgave me for even suggesting the possibility that it might have been one of them. If you remember I had to be brought into the house for my own safety.'

A look of relief was spreading across Charlotte's face. Already she seemed to have gained some colour.

'Why didn't you tell me this, Zach?' she asked.

'Because he didn't know,' Ben said quickly. 'He wasn't about, remember? He was hiding in the mountains. And we have never spoken of it since.'

He speared a piece of meat on his fork and looked at it with satisfaction as Charlotte rose to her feet and came the length of the table to where her husband sat. She knelt beside him, bowed her head, and said, 'Forgive me, husband.'

'There, there,' said Zach, patting her golden curls and throwing a grateful look at Ben. 'There, there.'

'But of course, one cannot blame Amelia,' Ben said thoughtfully. 'She said what she believed to be true.'

'But how could she believe such a thing of her own brother?' Charlotte cried. 'I shall never forgive her. She will never be welcome here again.'

That won't worry Amelia, Ben thought, as he finished the last chunk of meat on his plate.

260

Chapter Fifteen

Robin Darnley debated whether or not to wear his new brown frockcoat or the burgundy one as he began dressing in his cabin on the *Queen of the Sea*. He had sailed into the Basse-Terre roadstead the night before just as the sun was sinking like a huge ball of blood into a deep turquoise sea. He reckoned that he had twelve hours to keep the appointment he had made at the Columbus Tavern. He checked that the anchor was secure and everything made fast. Then, while his crew made for the shore and the few pleasures of Basse-Terre, took himself off to his bunk. A good night's sleep was what he needed. In the North Atlantic the seas had been wild, and it had been a rough voyage.

He read a little until sleep overtook him. Robert liked the poets, Marvell, Spenser, Shakespeare; he carried copies of their works on his voyages. Though he cultivated a bluff and manly exterior and was by nature boisterous and devil-may-care, a romantic heart beat under his wide and muscular chest, a heart that had turned somersaults at the sight of the black-haired girl serving at the tavern.

He thought he had never seen a more beautiful woman. Her face was perfection, small, neat features, dimpled chin, as British as British could be, yet she was no rosebud, no milk and water maiden. The skin that covered those gentle features was golden as if lit from within by the sun, her mouth was large and a natural deep pink, pinker on the inner edge that covered even white teeth. Her eyes and hair were dark as the night, and the smile she constantly smiled he knew was not her true smile. She was a secret person, he was convinced of it. He wanted to know the girl behind the smile, behind the languorous black eyes, and he wanted to pierce with love the heart beneath the small jutting breasts which peeped discreetly over the jade silk of the gown she wore.

He had not been jesting when he had told her he intended to marry her. The words, true as the ocean was deep, had leapt from his mouth. He was twenty-seven years old and had been at sea since he was barely fourteen. No woman had ever before impressed him so much. The sight of her had struck him with the intensity of a thunderclap, a lightning bolt. He did not know what had hit him.

Robin Darnley was a confident man. It never occurred to him that the girl would refuse him; nevertheless, he was nervous as he washed and dressed himself the following morning. Their cargo to the islands was always dried cod – good quality cod , for the whites, and vast quantities of the cheapest, most dubious fish, for which there was no

261

market in the north, for the slaves. The profit was good. The only snag was the overpowering smell, which was hard to shift; he was so accustomed to it that he could no longer tell whether he stank of the stuff or not.

He not only washed himself from head to foot that morning, he also swam in the limpid sea that splashed idly against the wooden sides of the *Queen of the Sea*. He unwrapped the new clothing he had bought for himself in Boston; he had folded it in layers of linen as protection against the smell. He settled on the fine brown velvet frockcoat, gold-frogged and buttoned, with deep, satin-bound cuffs. He also had a fine damask shirt and cravat and a splendid brocade waistcoat. His stockings were beige silk and his breeches of the finest wool. He would undoubtedly sweat like a stallion as the sun grew higher in the sky, but as long as he did not smell of fish . . .

Two of his crew rowed him ashore and gave him a granny-lift to keep his polished and buckled shoes out of the salt water. Then he strode along the rough wood boardwalk by the sea jetty and into the town. He decided he liked Basse-Terre. It had a prosperous feel to it. The streets were reasonably wide by order of the town council, to reduce the risk of fire spreading. For the same reason there were only a few thatched roofs left and the modern shingle roofs gave the place an up-to-date appearance. Perhaps it would be a good place to buy a warehouse and become a merchant-trader as well as a seaman. As long, of course, as the girl he was going to marry liked the idea. He did not wish to give up life at sea just yet, but one day perhaps he would want to settle his feet on terra firma. There were worse places than this sleepy tropical island.

He arrived at the Columbus Tavern. Pulling his tricorn to a jaunty angle over the mass of his own hair, he checked his watch to make sure that he was spot on time, then stepped confidently through the door, careful to duck his head. It was just nine o'clock in the morning.

Inside he stopped dead. There was no girl with black hair waiting, only the one she had called Marianne standing behind the counter drying glasses.

'Good morning, sir,' the girl said in strongly accented English. 'What will you have?'

'I have an appointment with the dark girl – the Mistress,' he said. 'Where is she?'

'I believe in her room. Do you wish me to call her?'

'At once.' His manner was imperious.

After an anxious look round the bar as if worried he might steal something, the girl scuttled out. She was gone only a minute and he heard her bellow up the stairs, 'Tansy, there's that man to see you.' On return she said breathlessly, 'She'll be with you soon, sir.'

Tansy, so that was her name. He paced the length of the tavern while he waited. His sword kept tangling with the backs of chairs and he jerked it irritably back into place. He should not have worn the wretched thing.

Then he heard a light patter of footsteps and spun round, hand on sword to prevent it doing a mischief. She was just coming into the tavern and at the sight of him she stopped and seemed to take a pace backward. This morning she was wearing grey.

'It is you!'

He did not know if she was surprised, pleased or dismayed. 'We had an appointment, madam.' Both his expression and his demeanour were reproachful. 'And you were not here.'

'But I never thought . . .' she was flustered and that put him at an advantage.

'I am a man of my word, madam, as you will discover. We agreed to meet in nine weeks, five days and twenty-three hours. I was here to the minute.'

'I never agreed to such a meeting.'

'But my dear madam,' he said, his face breaking into a wide grin, 'you sealed it with a kiss.'

She flushed scarlet. 'I did no such thing,' she said indignantly.

'I felt your lips respond to mine,' he told her solemnly. 'There was no doubt of it.'

'I beg your pardon, sir, but it was you who stole a kiss.'

'And I hope to steal many more.'

She was definitely flustered, but it seemed to him that she was not in any way angry with him. He smiled down at her, marvelling at how neat and lovely she was.

'You are so small,' he murmured and put all the admiration that he could into his voice. 'A miniature Venus.'

As the colour rose in her cheeks once again, it was as if her face held the setting sun.

'What do you want of me, sir?' she asked, trying to regain composure.

'I told you. To marry you. I am here to court you, but it seems to me that this is not an appropriate place. Where are your father and mother so I can ask for permission to walk with you in the town?'

'I am my own mistress. I make my own decisions.'

'Then I will make my request of you. May I walk with you in the town?'

Marianne had been watching and listening, her brown eyes twinkling with amusement. 'Walk with him,' she said. 'Go on. Prissie will help me here.'

She looked undecided, and then said, 'I must find my bonnet and shawl. Will you wait a moment, Captain Darnley?'

She had remembered his name. That was a good sign.

She returned with bonnet, shawl and also a parasol, for the same reason he had worn his sword, he supposed – to keep nervous hands occupied. They were both silent until they reached the beach road.

'That is my ship, the *Queen of the Seas* – there, moored in the roadstead. The three-masted one,' he told her, breaking the silence.

She looked where he pointed. 'It's a beautiful ship. Is it really yours?'

'Mine and my father's. We are a family of seafaring traders.'

'From Boston?'

Something else she had remembered. He felt the need to impress her.

'Yes. My family came from England in the *Mayflower*. We prospered in the New World. My father is a very wealthy man.'

She nodded, appearing unsurprised and unimpressed. 'What is it like in Boston?'

'A fine city, set about with great red-brick houses and with a common in the centre. My family home is a little outside the centre, near the sea.'

'Is it cold?'

'In the winter, very. In the summer, hot.'

'Like England?'

'Yes, but colder and hotter.' This conversation was not what he intended. 'Tell me about yourself,' he said abruptly.

She stared out to sea as if she were searching for something on the horizon.

'I am a widow,' she said. 'I have one child.'

His guilty, wicked thought was to thank God that her husband was no longer in the way.

'I would like very much to meet your child, and I am sad to hear of your loss,' he said, not altogether truthfully. 'When did your husband die?'

'Some months ago. Of consumption.' She paused. 'He was living in England. He had left me.' Her voice appeared casual but he was convinced he detected hurt there.

'He must have been insane,' he said forcefully.

She smiled at him and his heart turned over. 'He had his reasons. They were good reasons.'

'I cannot believe it.'

She looked at him, her expression quizzical. 'Captain Darnley, you say you have come to court me, and that you wish to marry me. Is that correct?'

'Totally.'

'Without knowing anything about me? Not even my name?'

'I know it is Tansy.'

'Tansy Henleigh. My maiden name was Quick.'

He stopped walking, turned to face her and took both her hands in his. Her face was tipped up to look at him, and he had to resist the impulse to kiss her full, red mouth.

'I feel I know you, Tansy Henleigh, formerly Quick. I felt I knew you the minute I saw you. I am not a callow youth. I have been at sea for thirteen years now, and captain of my own vessel for five of them. I have seen women in every corner of this world, but I have never seen one who matched you for beauty. I cannot tell you how I felt at the sight of you. It was as if some bond I had not known existed tied me to you. I fell in love at the sight of you. It is a new sensation for me, and one that makes me want to pick you up in my arms and take you away with me and never let you out of my sight again.' The words were pouring from him, until it occurred to him that she might feel he was attracted only by her beauty, and that was not the case at all. 'And it is not just your face,' he explained. 'I watched your smile and your demeanour and saw that there is both merriment and kindness in you. Mistress Henleigh, Tansy, what can I say but that I love you. I do not entirely understand it myself, but it is the most powerful emotion I have ever felt. Forgive me if I seem to rush you, but I shall only be here for ten days while we unload, scrub the holds and take on our new cargo. Then I must sail away again, but I want to win you in those ten days so that when I return we can wed. Do I have the slightest hope? Is there any chance for me?'

'Oh, yes,' she said quietly. 'But the question is, is there is any chance for me?'

He could not think what she meant. 'Such madness,' he said fondly, and finally gave in to the impulse to lift her up into his arms right there on the boardwalk where everyone could see. 'You're so *little*,' he said.

'And you're so large.' She was laughing as she tried to hold on to her hat and her parasol. 'I think you should put me down or my reputation in this town will be lost for ever.'

'And then you would have to marry me.' He kissed the tip of her nose and carefully lowered her to the ground.

She straightened her ruffled clothes, and patted her hair. She was smiling, not angry. It seemed to him that she looked happy.

'Are you always so boisterous?' she asked.

'It is my failing. But I can be romantic, too.'

'As I have seen,' she said dryly. She was standing very still, regarding him, her head to one side. She looked as if she were working something out.

'Captain Darnley, I must return to the tavern now, but if you wish, all of tomorrow shall be yours. But whatever you plan that we should do, first I beg a little time of you. You must be given the opportunity to decide whether or not you wish to continue our friendship. May we please leave it at that for the moment? If you will call for me at seven tomorrow morning we shall see how we go from there.' She then made a funny little wave with her parasol and walked briskly in the direction of the tavern.

He sensed she did not wish him to follow her; sensed she wished to be alone. He stood gazing after her, puzzled by the situation. He was certainly in love, of that there was no doubt, and he was equally certain that she was attracted to him. But what did she mean when she said was there any chance for her? It was as he had thought. She was a woman of some mystery, but he did not care what her secrets were, he was determined that she should be his wife. Shaking his head at the intensity of his feelings, and not a little alarmed by them, be continued to walk along the shore, skimming pebbles at the sea and making them bounce on the rippling water. He would just have to be patient until the morrow.

She was waiting for him the following morning, dressed in street clothes and with a shawl covering her head. She smiled, but gave no greeting except to say, 'We are going on a boat trip, will that suit you?'

'I am familiar with boat trips, mistress,' he told her.

'But this time in a very small boat,' she explained. 'And you will have to sail it.'

'I think I might be able to manage that,' he said with a smile.

The boat was pulled up onto the beach. She motioned for him to climb in and waved for two mulattoes who were dozing in the cool of the morning to push them off. It was a long time since he had handled anything quite so small. It took him a moment to get the measure of the sails and then he began to enjoy himself.

'It reminds me of being a boy again,' he said, 'sailing on the River Charles. Now, where are we going?'

'To the other end of the island,' she said, pointing west. 'Near to Sandy Point. To a plantation called Elsewhere.'

'A strange name.'

'It's really called Ailleurs,' she explained. 'It belonged to a Frenchman once, and he called it that because it was Elsewhere to his home in France.'

'And why are we going there?'

She did not reply immediately. She seemed to be working out an answer. Then all she said was, 'You'll see.'

'A mystery journey?'

'In a way.'

She seemed preoccupied, anxious. Something was troubling her, but he decided he would ask no questions until they reached the plantation. No doubt once they did, all would be revealed.

It was a wonderful morning for a sail; just enough wind to fill the sails and send the boat scudding along, the dark sand of the beach making an artist's slashing line of black to outline the coast. The island from the sea was spectacular, the lower plains of sugar cane a dusty yellow-green against a backdrop of mountains, cloudcapped in the early morning. He could see other islands which he recognised from his navigation, and was surprised how near and clear they looked in the wonderfully fresh light.

She was seated in front of him, the shawl protecting her hair from the wind. She seemed to be enjoying the journey; s small smile turned up the corners of her lips, but she was still silent.

She pointed where he was to beach the boat. This time he had to put his buckled shoes in the water to bring them ashore as no one waited on the deserted stretch of black sand. He had made his hose wet as well.

'We have to walk a little way,' she said apologetically, 'No one is expecting us.'

'It will give me time to dry out.' He had decided not to ask any more questions.

'I'm sorry about your shoes.' She looked as if she meant it.

'No matter.'

It was a long walk, first through sparse forest and then sugar cane. Rounding a corner he saw a house ahead, a long low, wooden building set round with gardens and an orchard. He could hear the chatter of a small stream.

Curiosity was devouring him, but still she offered no explanations. He tried to puzzle it out. He was going to meet her child, that was it. This was obviously her home; she must have been raised here since she walked through the grounds so confidently. But why not just say so?

He followed her down a narrow path and he noticed how straightbacked she walked, more like a black woman than a white. He could imagine her with an amphora balanced on her head like some statue from ancient Greece or Rome. They were not going to the front of the house. She had ignored the wide, palm-lined drive that led to an imposing front door. This path was for servants.

That was it. She was the child of an indentured servant. Irish perhaps, with that black hair. But she had not struck him as a Catholic – too confident by far. Too much of the ruling classes about her.

As they neared a door she turned to him.

'In here,' she said, and there was something in her look he could not fathom. It seemed part fear, part defiance and part resignation. Though perhaps fear was the strongest element.

She opened the door and walked in. He was right behind her and he found himself in a lofty kitchen where a huge fire burned with a spit placed in front of it. There was only one person to be seen, a fat black woman in a vast red turban. She was elderly, her skin fading into grey and cracking into tiny lines. Her thick lips appeared blue.

'Tansy, gal, where you sprung from this early in the morning?' the black woman said, huge arms on square hips. 'You come to see Delilah?'

'In a minute, Grandma.'

Grandma? Grandma! Tansy was looking at him as she spoke, waiting for a reaction. She very nearly had one, but he recovered himself in time. But Grandma? This huge black woman? Then he understood. This would have been the slave who brought her up. Not her real grandma of course.

'I want you to meet Captain Robin Darnley, Grandma,' Tansy was saying. 'He says he wants to marry me.'

The meat-like arms were now folded over the gargantuan chest as Grandma regarded him steadily.

'Glad to meet you, Cap'an Darnley.' She was looking at him with unconcealed disapproval, her suspicious black eyes sliding up and down the long length of him.

Tansy was still watching him intently, still waiting for a reaction. He smiled his pleasant smile at the old black woman and said, 'And I am glad to meet you.'

'It's a shame he can't meet Mama, isn't it, Grandma,' Tansy said, not taking her eyes off his face. 'Unfortunately,' she explained, 'Mama is a slave at another plantation. Windsong. I never see her now.'

He nodded as if she were saying the most normal things imaginable, but it was dawning on him that if Mama was a slave on another plantation, the possibility was that this oversized vision truly was Grandma. But he could hardly ask outright.

'And your papa?' he asked instead, hoping for some verification one way or the other.

'Papa was a slave, too, but he's dead. He died in the war. Our mistress had given him his freedom before he died. My grandma has hers, too. You got it before any of us, didn't you, Grandma?'

'And Tansy here got hers when she married Mr Henleigh,' Grandma said. He had the uneasy feeling that Grandma was playing the same game, whatever it was, that her granddaughter was playing. That they were in cahoots, testing him. 'And 'bout time too, it were. I was beginnin' to think Mistress 'Melia was never gonna get round to it.'

'I suppose you'd like to meet my daughter now?' Tansy said.

'Very much,' he said, trying to make his voice hearty in spite of the confusion he was suffering.

'I'll take him through, Grandma. Mistress Amelia won't mind, will she?'

'She ain't here. She gone over to Macabees. Mistress Isobel havin' her baby any day now. You go'n take Delilah's breakfast up?'

Tansy thought about it and then shook her head.

'Not today,' she said, and put her hand lightly on Robin's arm. 'I got company today.' And suddenly she sounded like a slave.

She beckoned him to follow her again, and keeping far enough ahead of him so that he could not speak to her she led him to what appeared to be servants' quarters off a passage leading from the kitchen. Eventually she opened a door and went in. It was a small room, sparsely furnished but with a window. A child, aged about five, was sound sleep in her cot, thumb in mouth, long lashes on caramel cheeks. A most beautiful child, and one that could have been a model for a cherub for any of the old masters. A black child.

'This is Delilah,' Tansy said proudly, standing aside so that his view of the little girl was unimpeded.

'And she is your—'

Tansy put her finger to her lips and shook her head. 'She does not know that.' She leaned to kiss the child's forehead and, straightening, said, 'Come.'

The child stirred a little as they left the room. Outside Tansy walked ahead again, but this time her direction was the garden.

'We'll sit in the orchard,' she said.

He was in a turmoil on the short walk to where the fruit trees made some welcome shade. He was only thankful that he had managed to keep his equilibrium and show nothing at the series of shocks she had given him. It would have been dreadful if his face had shown one sign

268

of dismay, disgust, horror or any of a dozen reactions that might well have been occasioned by the unexpected knowledge. But the truth was that he felt none of those things. All he felt was pity that this graceful, beautiful woman had been fated to live with such an insoluble problem. He also felt anger that she had chosen to test him in such a way, even though he could understand exactly why she had done it.

Once in the shade, she sank down on the rough grass. She looked white and drained as he settled himself beside her.

'Now you perhaps understand my husband's reasons for leaving me.' Her voice was defiant.

'Not really,' he said coolly. 'Not if you were as honest with him as with me.'

'He always knew. He could cope with my black relations. He was able to convince himself there must be some mistake, that I could not possibly have black blood. He could not cope with proof that I did – the colour of his own daughter. He was a man who believed that all on earth were equal, but that was too much for him. He left me immediately after she was born.'

He realised with admiration that there was no self-pity in her tone. She was merely telling him what had happened and leaving him now to make his own decisions.

'Not a man of honour,' he murmured.

'He was in many ways. We were going back to England. I think maybe it was the thought of presenting his black daughter to his English parents that frightened him.'

'And you think I would do the same thing?' he challenged.

'I don't know. Perhaps not. But at least now you know exactly what you're getting yourself into when you say you wish to marry me.'

'And do you think it was a kind thing to do, to inform me in such a way?' he asked sternly, pulling her so that she was closer to him.

She fidgeted a little. 'Perhaps not. But I needed to see your face when you met them. Your naked face, your unprepared face so that I would know. You see, I'm not ashamed of my black blood. The only problem for me is that I do not understand why I'm so white. Both Bella, whom you just met, and my mother are from Africa. My father was half-white. It was my mistress who persuaded me that it was better I made myself belong to one side or the other. My mistress brought me up as a white girl. She taught me to read, to write, to play, to embroider, to do all the things that a well-brought-up white girl would do. Her argument after my husband left was that I should pass myself off as white as there was no place for me in a black world. And that is why I am Mistress of the tavern, why I wear white women's clothes and use a white woman's voice. You must understand that I am really a fraud.'

He thought his heart would burst with love and pity at the courage she showed and the sadness she hid.

'I knew you were a special woman,' he said huskily, 'and now I am convinced of it.'

'If you wish to return to the *Queen of the Seas*—'

'For God's sake,' he heard himself shout, 'haven't you listened to a word I have said to you? I love you. I loved you the moment I set eyes on you. Do you really think that the fact you have black blood is instantly going to change that?' He could feel his face getting red, he was so annoyed. 'What sort of man do you think I am that I would change my mind and put aside my feelings for that? Besides, you forget, I come from the north of America where there are no slaves and where we believe slavery is wicked. I don't care if you are black, white or sky-blue pink. I love you. All right, there will be more problems than appeared at first, but if we love each other we will overcome them.'

'You don't even know me,' she said, and there was real bewilderment in her voice.

It was the bewilderment that stopped him short; made him think.

'It's true and I don't know why I feel this way,' he said, almost humbly. 'It is really very strange, but I feel we are destined for each other; that we were meant to meet. Don't you feel anything of the same?'

She laughed suddenly. 'I can perhaps let myself feel something now,' she said. 'I thought when you left last year that you were still drunk. I never really expected to see you again – though I had not forgotten you.' She smiled. 'You're really far too large to forget. And then when you came back all I could think of was that I must tell you the truth. I thought at first that I would never mention it, but then if we had children and the same thing happened again, well, I could not have borne it.'

'You thought as far as us having children?'

She nodded, silent.

He picked her up, put her on his lap, and cuddled her like a baby, smothering her face with small kisses.

'You will wed me when I come back, won't you?' he pleaded.

She put her arms round him and hugged him tight. 'I think I just might one day,' she said. 'But please, let's get to know each other first. If I marry again, I want it to be for ever.'

It was, Tansy thought, as she waved her captain goodbye, the best week of her life. He had not been able to be with her all the time since he had his duties to perform on the *Queen of the Seas*, but every minute possible he spent with her. He wanted to get to know the island and they rode together for miles, up into the damp, dripping, mysterious mountains and along the breezy beaches. Finding she had no mount of her own he immediately bought her a charming little chestnut mare and arranged for the stabling until he came back.

More extraordinary, he bought a house. He had been truly dismayed to discover that she lived in one room in Ben's home. She protested that she now had quite sufficient money to buy her own home and had every intention of doing so as soon as her inheritance arrived.

'The husband provides the home,' he informed her, and on the day

270

before he sailed, he took her to see a charming, wood-built house on Pall Mall Square, the most desirable area of the town.

'It was just fortunate it was for sale,' he said, beaming and pleased with himself. 'I have instructed workmen on the renovation that is required, but the decorations are your affair. It will give you something to do while I am away and you may move in whenever you wish.'

They were standing on the latticed veranda on the ground floor of the house, overlooking the green square in front.

'Does this mean that you have decided to make your home in St Kitts?' she asked him. 'Not Boston?'

He took her hand. 'Not Boston,' he said slowly. Suddenly he was serious and as he spoke she could tell that he was choosing his words with care. 'It is too cold in winter by far for a creature of the sun such as you are. But more important, I want nothing that will cause you anxiety. Forgive me, my sweetheart, I think I can understand your husband's concern about his parents. I have been thinking of mine. I have simply no idea how they would face the situation if we should have a child like Delilah. They are old and conventional, and I have no wish to dismay them. We can visit Boston, you and I, for I know they will love you. But I think it wiser if we make our life here and bring up our children here. I have it all planned. I shall buy a warehouse and instead of stinking fish I shall bring in the best and most luxurious goods. Sugar is fetching the highest prices ever known. This island is secure from war − for the time being, at least. The planters have money they do not know what to do with. I intend that they should spend it with me. In the north there is so much that is unknown here. I will provide the best of everything for those who can afford it.'

Mention of children made her say, 'And Delilah?'

'That is entirely up to you. If you want to claim her as your own, I shall be happy for you to do so.'

She looked at him intently. His sea-blue eyes were candid and he gave her a small smile as he said, 'I do mean it, Tansy. I would be proud to bring her up.'

She looked out over Pall Mall Square, a bastion of white supremacy, where he had bought her a home. What he was offering her was too much. She shook her head.

'You don't understand these islands yet, Robin,' she told him sadly. 'It is better if Delilah stays where she is.'

'As you wish,' he said quietly, and she felt an ungrateful pang of disappointment that he did not try to dissuade her.

She still would not set a date for the wedding. She wanted to give him every opportunity to change his mind now that he knew the truth. It was not easy. She understood what he meant when he said he believed they were made for each other. She felt the same way. As he had fallen in love with her, she had fallen in love with him. He was so different from the poetic, pale Mark Henleigh. Robin Darnley was rumbustious, fun, as affectionate and loving as a new puppy. He hugged her and kissed her, loved to lift her off the ground and swing her round like a child. He wanted to make her laugh. Wanted to make her as happy as he was himself. Yet he would surprise her with his knowledge of books and his erudition. He was a cultivated man for all his size and excess energy. And he never once attempted to touch her sexually. She could see and feel that when he held her he longed to go further and she wanted to go further herself, but he always pulled away. He courted her as if she were innocent and a virgin and she respected and loved him for it. And her curiosity about how love with him would be grew.

He had been gone a week or so when Joseph arrived at the tavern with a message from Amelia asking her to go to Elsewhere. Joseph had come by boat and he suggested that he take her back if she could leave right away. He did not seem his usual calm self. He appeared distressed, but when she questioned him, he merely said she must talk to the mistress, that it wasn't his place to tell her these things.

The awful thought struck her that Bella had told Amelia about Robin, and Amelia did not approve. Though why she should not, Tansy could not imagine. But approval or not, she had made up her mind. She no longer belonged to Amelia. She was free. If Robin returned and still wanted her as his bride, she was going to say a wholehearted yes. And no one would stop her.

Grim-faced, Joseph helped her ashore to where two horses were tethered, waiting. In silence they rode to the house.

Amelia was in her drawing room, sitting by the window. She rose as Tansy entered, took both her hands and kissed her. Tansy thought she looked exhausted. Suddenly the forty-five years that Amelia had spent in the heat and damp of the island were stamped on her face.

'Tansy, I wanted to tell you before you heard elsewhere. Something dreadful has happened.' She was speaking hurriedly, her voice low. 'Isobel is dead. She died in childbirth. We tried everything to save her, but it was not to be. The poor child. She had so little of happy life . . .'

Amelia's eyes were brimming with tears and Tansy felt her own moisten. Poor Isobel who had been so brave during the war while never losing the timidity that her monstrous upbringing had bequeathed her. And poor William who loved her so. How bereft he must feel.

'The baby lived.' Amelia was holding Tansy's hands so tightly that it was almost painful. 'It's a little girl. A beautiful little girl. William has decided to call her Precious. The precious life that Isobel gave him, and in doing so lost her own.' She burst into tears. 'William is heartbroken. I don't believe he will ever get over her loss. And I cannot help him.'

Tansy could think of nothing adequate to say. She put her arms round Amelia and held her tight. After a while, Amelia pulled away, wiping her eyes with the back of her fists like a child.

'Tansy, you are such a comfort to me,' she sighed. 'Never leave me. So many go away. So many die . . .'

She visibly shook herself and straightened.

'We must be strong for William's sake,' she said. 'The funeral is tomorrow at the chapel at Macabees. Will you tell Ben? And will you support me? It will be a difficult occasion. I am sure that Zach and Charlotte will come, but it will be the first time I have seen them since they sold Truly and Daniel. Perhaps we can be friends again. The family should not be split in this way though I confess I cannot put aside my anger at what Zach did. Oh dear.' She pushed her hair from her forehead distractedly. 'I'm unburdening myself to you and I brought you here so unexpectedly. We should have some tea, it will help calm us.'

Bella arrived no more than a minute later with the tray. She, too, was sad-eyed.

'Bring another cup and join us, Bella,' Amelia said. 'And let's talk of happier things. Tansy can tell us what has been happening to her.'

'I got another cup already,' Bella said as she busied herself pouring from the big silver teapot. 'I weren't gonna miss this.'

'Bella has told you?' Tansy asked, though it seemed wrong to be speaking of her own happiness when Isobel was dead.

'She said you arrived with the biggest man she has ever seen who announced he wanted to marry you.'

'And did he still want to marry you after he saw me?' Bella asked aggressively.

Tansy couldn't help it. She laughed. 'Astonishingly, yes,' she teased. 'You didn't frighten him away.'

Bella could not control her expression of relief but she was still fractious. 'You hadn' tol' him a thing? He don' know when he got here you got a black grandma?'

'No. I wanted to see how he would react.'

'And supposin' he'd walked out then and there? How you think I'd feel, eh gal? You was cruel to us both, he and me.'

Tansy was downcast. 'I'm sorry, Grandma. I hadn't thought of it like that.'

'Well, you better think more,' Bella said huffily.

'And are you going to marry him?' Amelia asked, breaking up this family argument.

'Yes, if he still wants to marry me when he comes back. I have given him time to change his mind.'

'You love him?'

'Love him! He's wonderful.'

Her reaction was so fervent that the older women both laughed.

'He's bought a house in Pall Mall Square for us to live in and we're going to settle here. He thinks it wiser than going back to Boston, where he comes from, just in case I have another child like Delilah.'

There was a silence.

Tansy went on firmly, 'He said he would bring up Delilah as mine if that was what I wanted, but I said it was better to leave things as they are.'

'That was sensible,' Amelia said quietly.

273

'Sensible! I don' call that sensible. I calls that wicked!' Bella said, clambering to her feet and heading for the door, her tea untouched. 'You white women who's 'shamed of you chil'en, you makes me sick.' She gave the door a hearty slam behind her.

They both stared at the closed door, and then Amelia shut her eyes and shook her head.

'Oh dear,' she said faintly.

'What did she mean, "you white women"?' Tansy asked, puzzled.

Amelia drew a long breath. 'I think, dear Tansy, it is time . . .' She hesitated and Tansy waited, wondering why the mistress looked so agitated and exactly what it was time for. And as Amelia hesitated, there was a discreet knock on the door and Joseph's woolly grey head appeared round the jam.

'Master Zach to see you, mistress. Is it all right if I brings him in?'

Afterwards Amelia did not know whether to be glad or sorry that Zach had appeared when he did. With Tansy so happy over her love affair it would have been the perfect moment to tell her the truth. There was every reason in the world not to burden William with difficult news at such a time, but that could have waited until later. Perhaps waited for ever. Bella, probably deliberately, had given her the perfect lead-in, but Zach's unexpected arrival prevented her from taking advantage of it.

Tansy went off to find Delilah as Zach, in all his usual finery but awkward and uncomfortable, stood stiffly in the middle of the room.

'Pierre brought us the news and I come to offer Charlotte's and my condolences,' he said. 'It is a sad day for the family. We would both like to attend the funeral if you will permit it.' He suddenly stopped speaking, mouth clamped shut, a large, embarrassed man in a situation that was beyond him.

'Oh, Zach!' Amelia flung her arms round him. This was no time to bear grudges. 'It's good to see you. Thank you for coming.'

He hugged her back and she could almost feel the relief spreading through him.

'I would have come sooner, but Charlotte . . .'

'Would not have it.'

'Exactly,' he sighed, perching himself uncomfortably on a too small chair. 'Did Ben tell you what happened?'

'I've not seen Ben since that day.'

'He made up a story. He said you were mistaken because you didn't really know what had happened. He blamed it on Joshua. I didn't know whether to tell you or not, but I made up my mind this morning that I would. Don't be angry, Amelia. If he hadn't done it, my marriage would have been ruined.'

He looked at her, hangdog, as she stood speechless with fury for a moment. Again Ben was blaming it on Joshua. Then common sense prevailed. What did it matter what anyone said about Joshua now? No one could harm him any more. If Ben had been able to reassure Charlotte, well and good.

'I'm sorry I sold Truly,' he said, sounding humble. 'I hadn't realised she meant so much to you.'

'Then tell me where she is.'

'I swear to you I don't know.' He said it earnestly, his blue eyes shining with honesty, but that was how he had looked when he so vehemently denied Justinian's murder. Amelia did not quite believe him. But this was not the moment to pursue the matter. It was enough that they were friends again, although deep in her heart she still could not quite forgive him.

Charlotte was cool with her at the funeral, but Amelia had more on her mind than Charlotte. William was distraught, unable to control his sobs, ashen-faced. She thought at one point he was going to collapse.

When the funeral meats were served in the grand hall of Macabees where Amelia had first seen Isobel, he seemed to recover a little. Tansy sat with Amelia, and Charlotte attempted to comfort William. Zach supervised Julia and James, who behaved with great decorum, a little frightened in the presence of grown-up grief.

'My biggest worry is what to do about the baby,' William said, refusing the food Charlotte was pressing on him. 'We have found a wet nurse, one of the field slaves, but she is surly and I fear she will not give the child the warmth and love of a mother.'

Amelia had been listening without speaking, but suddenly she had a thought. A brilliant one that might just repair fences between her and Charlotte.

'I have an idea,' she said. William turned to look at her hopefully, Charlotte coldly.

'Ask Zach to let you have Ruby. Make her the baby's nurse until you bring someone from England. Ruby has love in her heart for all the world.'

Charlotte's eyes had lit up. Amelia could sense the struggle as she attempted to nourish the anger she felt for her sister-in-law while attempting to suppress the gratitude for this possibility of at last having Ruby removed from her marriage and her life.

'What was that?' asked Zach, whose instincts smelled danger.

'I was just suggesting that William beg Ruby from you to look after Precious,' Amelia said smoothly. 'The baby will be safe and well with her.'

'But—'

'Oh, I know how fond of her you and Charlotte are and what a loss she will be to you – just as I felt about losing Truly. But sometimes one must be selfless.'

Brother and sister knew each other so well that Amelia could tell he did not know whether to burst into rage or laughter at how she had revenged herself on him and won over his wife in one simple move.

He ambled over to her and whispered so that no one else could hear,

'Why is it you always win in the end, you wicked bitch? But don't be too pleased with yourself. I was tiring of her anyway.' Then he turned to William and said, throwing his arms open in a wide, embracing gesture, 'How can I refuse? Ruby is yours.'

Charlotte was standing slightly behind him, and she caught Amelia's eye. 'Thank you,' she mouthed.

Since she was still in view of Zach, Amelia kept her face expressionless, and sensing William was near to breaking, she gently took his hand.

'Show me my grandchild,' she said. 'I want to see again how beautiful she is. And let us talk together.'

'May I come too?' Tansy asked, standing up to join them.

It was obvious that William was grateful for the opportunity to leave. Playing host was becoming too much for him. He nodded, murmured his excuses and left the room. He held Amelia's hand tightly, as if it were a lifeline, as they walked upstairs to the baby's nursery. Tansy followed behind.

Amelia had not seen the baby for some days and as she leaned over her granddaughter's cradle she saw that the child's eyes were wide open – huge, deep blue eyes with extraordinary depth and understanding in them. Curiously adult. Amelia involuntarily drew back at the sight of those eyes. There was something malevolent about the glare this swaddled baby presented to the world. Telling herself not be so stupid, she bent to pick up the child. As she did so, Precious let out a roar of rage, a bellow disproportionate to her age and size. Amelia felt an overwhelming need to get the child out of her arms and hastily handed the child to Tansy. The sound of fury did not abate. With unseemly speed Tansy replaced the baby in her cradle. Neither woman felt any inclination to soothe or pet her. Indeed, it was not necessary. Once laid down, the rage disappeared as quickly at it had begun and the cold, unblinking infant eyes stared upwards again.

'I think she misses her mother,' William said despairingly. 'She does that whenever she is touched. She refuses to let herself be cuddled. It's very difficult to get her to take her milk.'

'How odd,' Amelia said, and she shivered as if a ghost had walked over her grave. 'I think you'd better get Ruby here as fast as possible. Unless you would like me to take her . . .'

It was a relief when William protested that would not be necessary, he could not bear to part with the precious legacy his wife had left him.

'She is all I have,' he said.

'Oh, William,' Amelia protested, 'that is not true. You have all of us.'

'I know, Mama, I know,' he said, contrite that he might have hurt her. 'But she is mine.'

'And very beautiful,' said Amelia, peeping into the cradle again and meeting head on that blue glare. She felt no inclination to pick up the baby again. And neither, it seemed, did Tansy.

* * *

276

March came in like a lion, with the trade winds blustering in a most unseasonal way, tossing the black sand on the beach at Basse-Terre into the air and fighting the powerful wings of the frigate birds. In the grazing fields the egrets kept to the land, hiding behind the cattle, while the wind ruffled their white feathers into snowy down. Tansy did not mind the weather. She had the fancy that the wind would fill the sails of the *Queen of the Seas* and bring Robin back to her more quickly. At least he could not be lying becalmed somewhere while she waited for his return, which should be in a few days' time.

She missed him. She missed him a lot, considering she had only truly known him for one week. And she began to worry, waking in the night in a sweat, that he might change his mind now he knew the truth about her background. She would not blame him if he did decide that to marry her would be a mistake, but it would be hard to bear. Sometimes she rode to the top of the headland that overlooked the roadstead, watching for his ship even though she knew it was too soon for him to return.

She was involving herself less with the tavern, and Ben had promoted Rose, the oldest of the three whores, to serving ale instead of sex. Rose, who must have been nearing forty, was mightily relieved by the promotion. It also suited Ben, who was able to bring in a younger mulatto girl to take her place, which boosted the profits.

Apart from the nagging anxiety that Robin might reject her (she also worried in the small hours that he might be shipwrecked), Tansy was happy. She had not been to Elsewhere for some time as Amelia was at Macabees with the bereaved William. She had taken Delilah with her, something that caused a small twinge of resentment. Amelia had completely taken over the child, just as years before she had taken over Tansy, but Delilah would never pass as white and Tansy doubted the wisdom of the upbringing her daughter was receiving.

She had taken to keeping a diary to show Robin when he returned and she was in her room writing early one morning before the tavern was open when Prissie knocked on her door.

'There's a black man wants to see you, mistress,' she said. 'He looks like a slave on the run. I was going to call the constabulary but he was so set on seeing you I thought I had better ask what you want to do.'

'Did he give you his name? Or say what he wanted?'

'No, only that he wanted to see Mistress Tansy. He looks fierce. Do take care, mistress.'

Perhaps it was someone with a message from Windsong or Macabees, Tansy thought as she went downstairs and into the tavern. A man, not tall, but broad-shouldered with huge arms and strong legs, was standing in the shadows. He was dressed in a torn cheap shirt and breeches; his legs and long feet were bare and covered in scratches. His head appeared round as a cannonball, set close on his shoulders, his hair curled short and tight against the skull. He gave an impression of great physical power.

As she came into the room, he stepped forward and she saw that his skin was blue-black and that he was pouring with sweat.

'Tansy?' he asked.

'Yes,' she said cautiously, surprised at his impertinence at calling her by her given name and then realising this must be someone who had known her when she was a slave. She did not recognise him at all.

'I's Sam,' he said.

'Sam?' For a moment the name meant nothing.

'I's you brother.'

'My brother!'

Suddenly she had total recall of the little boy with whom she had shared Ruby's milk, food, love and attention; the black child, a year younger than her, who had been left behind when she was taken to Elsewhere. She hadn't missed him. He had always been a rough child, pushing and hitting her, but who howled when he was hit in return.

'Sam!' She felt she ought to kiss him, or hug him or do something sisterly, but this broad, aggressive Negro was a complete stranger to her. She tried to find some filial feeling, but none would come.

'I'm runnin',' he said. 'I needs help.' He wiped the sweat off his forehead with an impatient gesture.

She looked around nervously. The penalties for harbouring runaways were severe.

'Come through to the back and we'll go next door and talk in my room,' she said. She was reluctant to take him there but very soon the tavern would be full of people.

He followed her, light-footed. An animal smell of fear emanated from him. She seated him in her chair and sat herself on the chair in front of her desk.

'Where have you run from?' she asked.

'Nevis.'

'Nevis! How did you get across the straits?'

'Swam 'em. Ain't far. Only two miles 'cross the narrows. I went with the tide,' he said, boasting. 'Had to run. I kilt one of the drivers. He whipped me one time too many.'

He was trying to seem unconcerned but the fear was there; he faced the death penalty if he was caught.

'What are you going to do?' she asked, aware that there was no way she could call the constable to arrest her own brother.

He grinned showing strong white teeth. It was not a friendly grin. 'The question is what you gonna do?'

'Me?'

'Seems to me you leadin' a nice white life now. Guess you won' want white folks knowing I's your brother. Well, you half-brother anyway.'

Half-brother? What did he mean? She was transfixed, alarmed by the air of menace about him, menace combined with the blind terror

278

of a trapped animal. And she remembered Amelia's long ago attempt to find him for Ruby and how he had been sold from Macabees as a troublemaker.

'But I guess Mistress 'Melia don' want folk to know that either.' His voice was very deep, powerful like his frame, and she was afraid someone would hear them. He seemed to be gaining confidence. 'Then folk'd know you and me got the same pappy and that Mistress 'Melia you mummy, wouldn'?'

'Mistress Amelia my mother? What are you talking about?' she said bewildered. 'Ruby is my mother.'

He laughed without mirth. 'That what they tol' you? T'ain't true. Ruby be my mama, sure 'nuff. You mammy be Mistress 'Melia. At Macabees when I were there an old woman, Minta, tol' me. She and her mama was there when you was born. "Brought that gal Tansy into the world," she used to say. "Near 'nuff white she be. Near as dam' it." Now I sees with my own eyes she right. You is damn near white. Still, I guess that not su'prisin' if you got a white mammy.'

His black eyes were pinpoints of light, pricking at her. Tansy's head was swimming. She swallowed hard, trying to keep some kind of composure, not to let the shock show. She wanted this man out of her room so she could let what he had said sink in quietly and gently. Amelia her mother? It explained so much. And it explained nothing. But for the moment she had to hang on to herself and her sanity and deal with this brutish man without doing herself or anyone else harm.

'What do you want me to do?' she asked quietly.

He lifted one powerful leg and crossed it negligently over his thigh. For the moment, at least, he was frighteningly in control of the situation.

'Take me to you mammy. You real mammy. I reckons she might just get me out of this mess I seems to be in. Be nice to see my real mammy, too. That Mistress 'Melia she don' care 'bout takin' a boy's mammy away. Where be my mammy now, eh?'

'Macabees,' Tansy said.

'Back with Benson, eh?'

Tansy also thought it best not to mention that Benson was no longer there. The slaves had been afraid of Benson. Maybe this man was, too, though he looked as if he was afraid of nothing.

'It's going to be difficult to hide you,' she said slowly, trying to give herself time to think and wishing that Robin were here to help her. 'And I don't know where Mistress Amelia is at the moment. She travels between the family plantations.' As she said Mistress Amelia, the shock waves rolled again. Mistress Amelia, her mother. Could it really be? 'I'll hide you in the attic while I find out where she is.'

'Ain't goin' in no attic,' he said, suddenly looking around him like a trapped animal. The confidence had gone and fear returned.

'That's up to you,' she said sharply. 'But if you're seen and caught it's not my fault. Do as you please. People are in and out of this room all the time.'

'All right,' he said, getting to his feet. 'But don' you be too long about finding where you mammy be.'

She did not reply, but led the way out of the room and towards the attic stairs. Fortunately no one was about.

'I'm going to lock the door,' she told him as she led him inside. 'Not to keep you in, but to keep others out. It's safer.'

He gave her a suspicious look from under his low brow. 'And then you better slips the key under the door, eh?'

'If you wish,' she said. It didn't make any difference. She wasn't going to call the constable. The ramifications of the knowledge he held were beginning to dawn on her, though she was not sure how he could use the knowledge. Who would he tell? Would he bellow from the gallows, 'Amelia Quick is Tansy's mother? Amelia Quick slept with a slave.' He must have some plan but it was hard to see what.

She ran down the stairs looking for Ben and found him in the cellar, tending his barrels of ale.

'I must talk to you,' she said.

He caught the urgency in her voice and was instantly alert.

'Joshua and Ruby's son is hiding in the attic. He's killed a driver on his plantation in Nevis and he's running. He says he wants to see Amelia, and he says that — ' her voice faltered, 'Amelia is my mother.'

'Jesus!' Ben went white.

'He says he's sure Amelia will help him because of what he knows. What shall we do?'

'Keep him away from Amelia for a start,' Ben said flatly.

'I've told him I don't know exactly where she is.'

'Good girl.' He stood and thought. 'We'll get him to Windsong and let Zach deal with it. We'll tell him she's there.'

'He's no fool, Ben, and he's big, brutish. And he's frightened.'

'Then we'll definitely let Zach deal with it.' He took her hand. 'Are you all right?' He looked troubled. 'Amelia wouldn't have wanted you to find out this way. It's been a shock for you.'

She was trying not to cry. 'Is it true? Amelia is my mother?'

'It's true,' he said sadly. 'But let her tell you about it. It's not my place.'

'But why didn't she tell me before?' Tansy said, her voice anguished. 'All these years . . .'

He put his arm round her and pulled her close to him. 'Why? Oh Tansy, you've lived on this island all your life. You know why she didn't tell you before. How could she?'

' "You white women who are ashamed of your children make me sick," ' Tansy whispered. 'That's what Bella said, and she's right. And I'm as bad.'

'Think about it later,' advised Ben. 'For the moment let's deal with the problem in the attic.'

* * *

280

'We have trouble, Zach.'

Zach was sitting behind his large desk at the chambers in Basse-Terre where he kept an office. He liked to spend his mornings there even though there was little for him to do.

'What sort of trouble?' he asked. Ben had arrived on foot, unannounced, out of breath and without even his frockcoat on his back. He just wore shirt, breeches and boots and Zach noted there were wine stains on the shirt. Most unlike Ben.

'Real trouble. In my attic I have a runaway slave who says he is the son of Joshua and Ruby. He's killed a driver on a plantation in Nevis. And worse . . .'

Ben told him the worst, and at the end of the tale, Zach crashed his fist down on the desk so that his inkpot and quills jumped. 'These ungrateful blacks!' he roared. 'Another of 'em trying to hold us to ransom. Well, he'll learn that the Quicks are not to be threatened.'

'You can't sell this one,' Ben pointed out.

'I can do better,' Zach said. 'The madness, the arrogance of these brutes to think that they can in any way harm the white inhabitants of this island. They have to be taught a lesson. They must be kept in their place.'

'That's all very well,' said Ben, 'but if he starts telling the story of Amelia and Josh—'

'He won't get the chance.' Zach's voice was so flat and grim that it made Ben uneasy.

'What do you want us to do?' he asked.

Zach thought for a good minute. Then he grunted and said, 'Tell him that Amelia is at Windsong and get Tansy to bring him there after dark in a carriage. Dress him up as a coachman and let him drive. Tell Tansy I'm getting Amelia to go there to meet him. Tansy will be more convincing if she thinks she's telling the truth. Don't tell her any more than to get him to Windsong without being seen by anyone. Then leave it to me.'

'You're not going to—'

'Leave it to me, I said.'

Ben looked up into his cousin's face, searching for a clue as to what Zach intended. But Zach's expression was unreadable.

'He can't really do us any harm . . .' Ben said tentatively.

'Of course he can't,' Zach snapped impatiently. 'It's just a desperate ploy and it will not work. I shall see to that. But I will not be held to ransom.'

Ben went back to the tavern preoccupied and troubled. He had an idea what Zach might do and he did not wish to be party to it. Not again. And he was uneasy about leaving Tansy with the slave. But ever the survivor, he decided that perhaps it would be best to do exactly what Zach had demanded. If Tansy took the slave to Windsong, at least he, Ben, could distance himself from events – whatever those events proved to be.

He reported to Tansy what Zach had said.

'What shall I do now then?' she asked.

'Take him up some food and tell him that you'll collect him at nightfall. Better not to mention that I know he is there. Don't go near the tavern. Take him through the other house and go in the carriage. He can drive it. Give him a coachman's hat to wear. In the dark no one will be any the wiser.'

'Then what?'

'Come back here. Leave it all to Zach and Amelia.'

She shivered. 'Why do I feel sorry for him?' she asked quietly.

'Because it's hard not to feel sorry for any poor devil who works in the factory yard or the fields, only to be whipped by his own kind.' He made an impatient gesture as if pushing something or someone away from him. 'The drivers are the worst,' he said. 'It's amazing that more of them aren't murdered. Huh! I'd rather be a tavernkeeper than a slave master any day. Comparatively speaking, getting men dead drunk is a finer occupation.'

He waited while she crept up to the attic with a tray of food.

'How was he?' he asked when she returned, noting she looked flustered.

'All right. He unlocked the door and at first I didn't see him. He was standing behind it, holding a lump of wood he must have found in the attic. He wanted to know if I'd found Amelia so I told him she was at Windsong and how I planned to get him there as soon as it was dark enough. Then he said he wanted a sword. I told him there was no need, but he was insistent. What do you think?'

'A sword?' Ben thought about it. If any kind of justice were about to be done, it would be rough justice. Ben personally believed that justice should be seen to be done but slaves never received a fair trial. Why not give the poor fellow a fighting chance? There were a few anonymous, unclaimed swords in the tavern, left by men who had departed too drunk to remember they had arrived armed. Sam could take one of those. If Zach had murder on his mind, he would not thank him for arming the slave but the fact he was armed might prove fortuitous. At least Zach could plead self-defence if anything should go wrong.

As soon as it was decently dark, Tansy brought Sam down from the attic. They slipped into the stable yard where the carriage was already harnessed up, waiting to go. She climbed inside but he hesitated, the piece of wood still clutched, half-raised, in his hand.

'I don' know whether to trust you,' he muttered, looking about nervously, round head silhouetted against the light.

'Unless you can find your own way to Windsong, you don't have much choice,' she pointed out. 'You'll find the sword you wanted on the box. Let's move before someone sees us. I'll give you directions.'

There was a half-moon sailing in a pale sky and its light helped the carriage lamps split the darkness. Tansy was uneasy and so was her driver. He muttered to himself constantly, holding the sword in one hand and the reins in the other. They skirted the woods round Monkey Hill, no more than a mile from the gates of Windsong; the silence was oppressive.

Suddenly it was shattered by a loud whoop.

From the trees broke a half a dozen militiamen, no doubt from Zach's troup. Tansy watched helpless and horrified as one stopped the horses, four leapt to pull Sam from the box and another stood guard. From the carriage window Tansy saw Sam hit the ground and then leap to his feet, the sword flailing wildly. It took all six men to hold him as he fought desperately. He had nothing to lose. The battle was brief and bloody, but he stood no chance against six. Within minutes he had been cut down, his head almost sliced from his body.

'God blind me!' said one breathless and panting man, clutching at a wound in his shoulder. 'Zach never said he would be armed.'

All six had wounds of varying severity. Sam had not died quietly. Subdued now, they crept back to the horses they had tethered in the woods and took themselves off, presumably to the surgeon in Old Road Town. Tansy was not even certain if they were aware of her presence.

When the sound of the hoofs had died away, she climbed down from the carriage and knelt beside the body of her half-brother. Illuminated by the carriage lamps, he lay in a pool of his own spreading blood. In death his expression was ferocious, big white teeth bared, eyes staring open. The bloodied sword was still clasped in his hand.

'He was my brother and Ruby's son,' she whispered to herself as she looked down at him. 'And I betrayed him.'

She sat by the body for some time, trying to console herself that Sam would have died anyway, swinging from the end of a rope, had he been caught. Slaves who killed received no quarter. At least the sword had given him some dignity, some chance to fight for himself. She tried to tell herself that it was better he had gone the way he did. But the guilt of unwittingly leading him into a trap set by Zach persisted.

Then her mood changed and she became angry. She was angry that she had been kept in ignorance of the circumstances of her birth as if her mother was ashamed of her, angry that Zach could so casually settle matters when someone was in his way or posing any kind of threat to him. Angry that Truly had been so callously sold and Ruby's son brutally killed. And angry with Ben, who for all his refusal to use slave labour, still looked after himself first and who must have been party to the killing tonight. And Amelia? What part had Amelia played in all this?

Amelia had said it was better to be white. The way white people behaved on this island, she was not sure she agreed. It would not be difficult to become ashamed of being white.

While she sat considering what to do next, she heard the sound of hoofs again and into the yellow glow of the carriage lamps two figures on horseback appeared. One, large and looming, was Zach. Beside him rode a constable.

'Tansy,' he was calling. 'Tansy, are you safe?'

'Here,' she called back.

The two figures reined up beside her.

'There you are, Constable,' Zach said, pointing his whip at the dead body, 'a runaway from Nevis. I think you will find he is wanted for the murder of a driver there. Mr Clode from the tavern warned me that he had taken Mistress Henleigh here as hostage. I sent my men out after him. They were forced to kill him in self-defence.' He shook his head mournfully. 'Ah, well, I suppose it has saved the state the price of a trial.' He dismounted and pulled Tansy to her feet. 'Are you all right, my dear?'

She did not want to speak to him. She merely nodded.

'You have been very brave. We are all proud of you and we have come to take you home.'

'I will take myself home, thank you,' she said sharply. 'I am quite capable of driving the carriage. Will you please have the courtesy to move my brother's body. I do not wish to drive over it.'

'Such a God-fearing girl,' she heard Zach whisper to the constable with what was remarkably quick thinking for him. 'She sees even the slaves as her brothers.' He turned again to her. 'We cannot leave you alone. You must be shocked at all that has happened.'

'More than you know,' she said and turning her back on him, climbed up to the box. 'But I prefer to be alone, thank you.'

With difficulty the constable was pulling the body from the road, Zach making no attempt to assist him.

'Tell me,' Tansy called down, 'is Amelia really at Windsong?'

'No,' Zach said. 'She is at Macabees. She knows nothing of this.'

She was surprised at how relieved she felt that Amelia had not been involved. She jerked at the reins and turned the carriage for home, anxious to be away from this place. The horses were restless at the smell of blood; they were as eager to go as she was and set off at a smart pace. She winced as the wheels ground through the dust, obliterating the dark red stain of what had been her brother's lifeblood.

Once back in the stable yard at the tavern, she did not go in. She called the mulatto ostler to unhitch the horses and stable them, and then had her own mare saddled. She had made up her mind to go immediately to see Amelia at Macabees. She could not rest the night without confronting the woman she had just discovered was her mother.

There was a rough track along the shoreline from Basse-Terre that lead to Macabees. It was a difficult ride even in daylight, but she took a lantern and the moon helped light the way. Her mare picked her way carefully and Tansy let her take her time while she thought over the events of the day. Her feelings for Sam were confused. She had not liked him. He was brutish, violent, craven and brave all in one awkward parcel. But then how could he be anything else considering the life he had led? If indeed it could be called a life.

She wasn't sure what she was going to say to Amelia and kept rehearsing different angry, accusing speeches. But her anger was fading;

a deep hurt that Amelia had not acknowledged her was taking its place. Yet behind the hurt common sense nagged. How could Amelia have acknowledged her? For a white woman to sleep with a slave was unthinkable, beyond all belief and decency, and Amelia had done it.

It was late when she arrived at Macabees. The sleepy gateman, recognising her, let her in and walked up to the house with her, just in case all was bolted and barred. Though candlelight still burned in the upstairs rooms, the house was locked. She waited while he went round to the slave quarters to find someone to let her in and to arouse Amelia.

She found she was ridiculously nervous as she went into the huge hall. Amelia's new maid was hurrying towards her, eyes round in her black face.

'Mistress Amelia's a'comin'. She say for you to wait in her sittin' room,' the girl said, her face all curiosity.

Within a few minutes Amelia arrived wearing an emerald green velvet robe which she clutched about her. Her feet were thrust into slippers and her hair flowed loose over her shoulders.

'Tansy dear, is something wrong?' She hurried to hug the girl and finding her unresponsive, drew back. 'What is wrong?' she asked quietly.

'Sam's dead,' Tansy said abruptly.

A frown wrinkled Amelia's brow. 'Sam?'

'Ruby and Joshua's son Sam.'

Amelia's hand flew to cover her mouth. 'But how? And how do you know?'

Both women were standing, Amelia shivering a little in the cool of the night, Tansy upright and accusing.

'He had run. He was on a plantation in Nevis and he killed a driver. He came to me for help. Ben went to Zach and Zach had him killed.'

'But why should he come to you? Zach killed him? But why?'

'Because Sam said he was going to tell everyone that you are my mother.' Tansy said the words quietly, but they seemed to reverberate around the room as if she had shouted them at the top of her lungs. Amelia sank into a chair, ashen-faced.

'Oh dear,' she said faintly.

'Oh dear,' Tansy mocked her. 'Is that all you can say?'

'I was going to tell you.'

'Then why didn't you?' The hurt was firing the anger.

'I was going to tell you,' Amelia repeated, her voice steadier,' when Bella made that remark about white women who were ashamed of their children. And then Zach interrupted. The opportunity has not come since.'

'But that was only a few weeks ago,' Tansy protested. 'I have been your daughter for nearly twenty-seven years. It's all been such a sham, so cruel.' She had to stop to hold back a sob. 'Was Joshua my father?' she asked.

'Yes. I loved him very much. I still do.'

Tansy heard the sadness in her mother's voice. She realised her fists were clenched, her shoulders rigid, and she made herself relax a little.

'Please sit down,' Amelia was saying. 'I've wanted to have this conversation for so long, and I wanted to be the one to tell you the truth. I'm desolate that you had to learn this way.'

'I expect Sam's desolate, too, wherever he is.' Tansy's attitude was still belligerent but she took the seat opposite Amelia.

'You see,' Amelia began,' when I first came to this island I, too, was a slave.'

'A slave!'

Amelia nodded and almost smiled. 'So was Ben and so was Zach. But as you might imagine, Zach does not like us to talk about that now.'

'But why were you a slave?' Tansy's head was bursting with questions, and curiosity had taken over from belligerence.

'That's a long story and one that I'll tell another time. We were meant to be slaves for ten years, but we were pardoned after four. In those four years I lived in the slave cabins at Windsong with the black slaves. I was maid to Elizabeth Oliver and to Charlotte.'

Tansy could not believe her ears. She stared at Amelia, elegant Amelia, and tried to imagine her living in the slave cabins. The picture was impossible to conjure up.

'I was only fifteen when we were brought here from England. Zach was put out for field work while Ben and I stayed in the house. Zach had the hardest time of any of us. He was hated by everyone he worked with. He was friendless, the other slaves did not trust a white working in the same conditions they were. He was bullied and beaten by both the white overseer and the black drivers. It explains the way he is today.'

'And you?' Tansy asked.

'Bella looked after me. She didn't like me much, but I was so young she felt sorry for me. And then Charlotte's father became obsessed by me. He eventually raped me, very brutally, and that changed the attitude of the women slaves. After that they saw me as one of them. By then Joshua and I had fallen in love. Your father was a beautiful man, Tansy. He was good and gentle and he was very, very clever. Had he not been a slave there was so much he could have done with his life. You must always be proud of him.

'When Matthew Oliver raped me, I was pregnant with you and we were terribly afraid you might have been harmed. The other fear was what Oliver would do when you were born. If you were white he would think you were his . . .' She hesitated, choosing her words.

'And if I were black, he would know that you had slept with a slave?' Tansy ventured.

'Exactly,' Amelia said, 'and that slave's life would not have been worth living. So Bella insisted that no one should know you were my baby in order to protect your father. When you were born, you were a little yellow thing. A little yellow flower. That's why I called you Tansy.

286

You could have been pure white, or you could have had black blood, it was difficult to tell. The Olivers were told you belonged to Truly. Just a few weeks after your birth, Matthew Oliver sold Bella, Truly, Joshua and you to Macabees. I never knew why, but thank God Ruby was there to feed you or you would have died.'

'And then you found us and brought us back to Elsewhere,' Tansy said slowly, remembering. 'Why did you leave Papa behind?'

'Zach did. He was afraid of people finding out about us. Zach was very respectable and important by then. He has always worried that one day the truth would come out.'

'And he was prepared to kill Sam to keep it hidden,' Tansy said. 'But what harm could poor Sam really have done? Who would have believed him? It was murder for nothing. Wicked! Wicked!'

'Perhaps. We shall never know now.' Amelia leaned forward in her chair. 'But, Tansy, Sam would have died. If he killed a driver, he had no chance. And if he had not been caught and hung, he would have been a fugitive all his life. And, truthfully, I too would deal ruthlessly with anything that threatened you or your security. You are my only daughter, and I love you, and your life is beginning to be good. I don't want it spoilt. I can understand that you are angry with me for not acknowledging you, but I was never ashamed of you. It just seemed to be the only way to deal with the situation. I did my best for you. If you look at yourself in the glass with honest eyes, you will see that if you were dressed in slave's clothing and spoke as a slave does, moved and acted as a slave does, the world would not question that you have black blood. Of course they would be aware that you are virtually white. They might indeed marvel at how white you appear to be. But it is the fact that you act and sound like a white woman in every way that makes people accept you as white. I did at least that much for you.'

Amelia's head was bent, her face hidden and Tansy thought she might be crying.

'You did as much as anyone could expect from a mother,' she said and moved to kneel in front of Amelia so that she could see her face. 'Please don't cry. I was angry, then hurt. But I do understand – and who I am to be bitter towards you when I myself deny my own child? I realise now that I should have guessed the truth. There were so many clues. I always knew you loved me when I was little. It was you who protected me and spent so much time teaching me. I felt that you were my family. It was you who meant home. But I thought you only did it because I was so pale-skinned.' She laid her head on Amelia's lap, and a tentative hand began to stroke her hair.

'Delilah isn't pale-skinned and I want her to have the same advantages,' Amelia said.

Tansy lifted her head and knelt back on her heels. 'I'm not sure if it's right. What will become of her? She will have no place. She could not . . .'

'Pass as white?'

287

'No. She could not. It will be more difficult for her than it has been for me.'

Amelia sighed. 'Yet I cannot bring myself to neglect her education and how could we let her live out her life in the slave cabins? The choice, Tansy, is to leave her to a black life or give her what advantages we can. She will always be safe here with me, and in time, when I am gone, you will care for her.'

'I would like to care for her now.'

'And what would you do with her?'

'I suppose exactly what you did with me,' Tansy said bitterly. 'There is no way of beating the way things are, is there?'

They were both silent, then Amelia said, 'Leave her with me until you are settled with your sea captain, and then we shall decide what is best to be done.'

She rose and moved to the mantelpiece. Somewhere in the house a clock struck one.

'We have decisions to make,' she said, her back to Tansy, her tone a touch too casual. 'Shall we tell Ruby and Bella what has happened to Sam?'

'No.' Tansy's voice was decisive. 'Better he is lost to them than dead to them, murdered for murdering.'

'You are right,' Amelia said. 'And what are we to tell William?· Do you wish him to know that you are his half-sister? If so, we must tell him immediately.'

Tansy's first reaction was that he should know. But then she thought again.

'I love William so much,' she said slowly, 'I would like him to know that we are brother and sister, but would he not be dismayed to know . . .' She faltered.

'That his mother loved a black slave?' Amelia finished for her. 'Yes, he would,' she went on, answering the question without hesitation.

'I would not wish to dismay William,' Tansy said simply. 'It shall be our secret. But I would like, if you do not object, to tell Robin.'

'And, as your mother, I would like to meet Robin.' Amelia said. 'Will you bring him to see me?'

'The moment he gets home,' Tansy promised. 'But now, tell me please how it was that you became a slave.'

They sat up most of the night, talking. It was well after three when Amelia insisted that they go to bed. They went upstairs, arms round each other's waist, and climbed into Amelia's bed rather than rouse a servant to prepare a room.

The moonlight drifted uncertainly through the long windows as if the gusting wind were fragmenting its beams. Amelia had not drawn the heavy curtains and the light kept Tansy awake. In Basse-Terre there were no trees to disturb the moonlight. She should have slept with ease, it had been a very long day, but her head was awash with memories, small chips of the past that now came together to explain so many things.

More important, for the first time in her life she felt truly at peace, as if every section of the jigsaw that had been her life was at last falling into place. Old mysteries had been solved, old anxieties resolved. She was sure now of who she was, and though to be Tansy Henleigh, white imposter, was not ideal, she was so much more fortunate than many others. So much more fortunate than Delilah, and it was Delilah she was thinking of when she finally slept.

She took a leisurely breakfast with Amelia in the morning before making her way back to Basse-Terre. She arrived at the tavern around noon. The ostler came running to take the reins and hold the mare while she dismounted.

'There be a great big fellow looking for you,' he reported. 'Reckon he's waitin' in the tavern.'

A great big fellow had to be Robin. Tansy broke into a run that precipitated her down the alley and into the street to the front door of the Columbus. Leaning against it, his head resting above the door frame, arms folded, expression aggressive, was Captain Robin Darnley.

'Robin!' she called breathlessly, skidding to a halt in front of him. He looked down at her, arms unfolded, face unsmiling. 'Where have you been?' he demanded.

'At Macabees, with Mistress Amelia. Oh, Robin, I have so much to tell you.'

'You've been out all night,' he accused.

'Yes, at Macabees,' she said impatiently, and then seeing how cross he was, burst out laughing.

'Robin, I have only been with my mother. My mother, do you hear? My real, genuine mother.' She was bouncing up and down on the spot, happy and excited that he was here to share her news. He just looked at her, bewildered.

'You mean Ruby?'

'No, Robin. Not Ruby. Amelia is my mother.'

He pushed back his tricorn to scratch his head. 'Amelia is your mother? The woman who brought you up? The woman who owned you?'

'Yes.' She snatched at his arm. 'We can't talk here. Come to my room. I will explain everything.'

He drew his arm away, mouth pursed. 'What will Ben say if I come to your room?'

'Nothing. We are to be married, aren't we?' She held her breath.

He looked down at her, and his ruddy, cheerful face suddenly became illuminated as if a candle had thrown its light on him. 'You will marry me?'

'Please.'

For a moment he just stood, his jaw dropped. She put up one finger under his chin to close it.

'No man looks his best with his mouth half open,' she informed him demurely.

His bellow of laughter echoed down the street. He threw his hat in the air, picked her off her feet and gave her an ardent kiss, full on the lips.

'When?' he asked when he came up for breath.

'Whenever you wish.' She was breathless herself.

'Today.'

'Make it tomorrow. My mother will want to be there.'

He set her on her feet, looked down at her and she was moved to see that his eyes were bright with tears.

'You have made me the happiest man in the world,' he said huskily. 'And by God, I shall make you the happiest woman.'

'But you already have,' she told him.

Chapter Sixteen

In the event it was a week before the marriage took place. The parson fussed that it could not be done earlier, the house in Pall Mall Square still needed furniture, and they decided that perhaps their wedding guests should be given a little notice of the event even though it meant that their honeymoon would be short. In ten days he must set sail again.

He wanted her to wear a bridal gown, insisting that her previous marriage did not count because her husband could not have been a proper husband if he had deserted her. Tansy rushed around Basse-Terre visiting her dressmaker, making arrangements, sending out invitations and attempting to make their new home habitable for themselves and hospitable for the wedding guests.

All the while she made notes as to what the island lacked when she could not find a fabric or some lace that matched exactly what she had in mind. There was a woeful shortage of fine china, silver and even simple household goods. The island lacked so much; even stones for a doorstep had to be imported, and medical supplies were always in short supply. It was difficult to find something as simple as elegant candles, though plain white wax ones existed in plenty. She realised why Mr Lockett in London was kept so busy buying and shipping items for the Quick family and why the other wealthy plantation owners employed agents in Europe. Robin was right. The islands were going through a period of unprecedented wealth and there was money aplenty to spend on the good things of life, but the good things of life were in short supply. Robin could give up shipping bad fish and end up the richer for it.

What Tansy could not buy, she borrowed from Elsewhere. Amelia had met the tall sea captain and been charmed by him. She had persuaded William to lend Ruby to help prepare the wedding feast, and Bella joined her. Ben offered to supply the wine and ale as his wedding gift, and Zach, who had been startled to meet a man even bigger than he was himself, had sent his house slaves to help with the preparations.

On the day, the groom wore his best uniform and his sword; and he towered over the little parson at St George's who was to wed them. Tansy wore a simple, tight-waisted taffeta gown with a square-cut neckline and a full skirt trimmed with a frill at the hem. Four large bows decorated the front of the dress and her black hair was covered with a veil of muslin. Delilah was flower-maiden, walking ahead of the bride and scattering petals from a woven straw basket; Zach's Julia, solemn in pink, carried Tansy's train. The congregation was motley, sailors from the *Queen of the Seas*, the entire Quick family, members of the town council, the whores and the waitresses from the tavern, slaves and the white family servants from Elsewhere.

The occasion could not have been more different from the small, private ceremony when Mark Henleigh and Tansy married, and the wedding feast was the talk of the town for weeks afterwards. The party spilled out into the green square where three fiddlers and a pipe and tambour played for dancing. By the evening it seemed as if the whole town had come to the celebration, and Robin roared a welcome to them all. It was gone midnight before the last of the guests lurched their way home. Bella had harried the house slaves into leaving the house clean and neat and in the sudden silence after the final guests had said their farewells, Robin led his new bride by the hand up the wide winding staircase to their bedchamber.

Both were afflicted by a sudden shyness and neither spoke as they entered the room. Bella had left candles burning, and the bed was turned down invitingly. Two robes lay over a chair, and a steaming pitcher of hot water stood on the washstand.

'Grandma has made it look so nice,' Tansy murmured, hesitating just inside the doorway.'

'Umm.' He was standing by the bed, not looking at the room but at her. He moved back to where she hovered, and without speaking lifted her into his arms like a baby.

'You are so *little*,' he said and began to kiss her.

He had never kissed her like this before. Tansy realised that previously he had been holding back. These were deep, searching kisses that joined her to him as deeply as if they had been making love. She responded passionately, her arms round his neck, pressing herself against him, trying to get closer as he hugged her to him.

'I love you,' he finally whispered. 'I never realised that it was possible to love in the way I love you.'

He walked towards the bed and set her down on it gently. She lay there, looking up at him, smiling.

'Will you take that pretty dress off or shall I?' he asked.

'We could do it together,' she suggested. He had slipped off his frockcoat and pulled off the waistcoat beneath. He loosened his cravat and dragged his shirt over his head impatiently. His body was browned by the sun and strong and muscular, his chest had a mat of springing dark hair on the breastbone. He was so different from the delicate hairless white of Mark Henleigh, just as the kisses had been different. Mark had kissed her as if he were afraid she might break. Robin's kisses were as robust as the man, but sweet, sweet as honey.

He sat down beside her and she lifted her hand to run it down his bare chest. He shivered.

'How does it come off?' he asked.

She rolled over on to her back, presenting him with a row of small buttons.

'Like that,' she said.

His fingers among the buttons were surprisingly agile, and he grunted to himself as gradually they came undone. Then he peeled back the gown and she felt his lips kissing the nape of her neck and then running down the length of her spine. His big hands slid round under the fabric to cup her breasts and then he gently rolled her over. He pulled her gown from her shoulders and over her stomach and hips until with one hand he lifted her from the bed and pulled the dress from under her, dropping it to the floor.

He watched as she wriggled from her petticoats and stockings until she was naked before him.

'Stand up,' he said, and it was a command.

Obediently she did as she was told, he too stood and walked round her as if surveying a statue. Shy again, she placed her hands over her dark mass of pubic hair, but he pulled her hands away.

'Beautiful,' he murmured, placing a hand under each of her breasts as if he were weighing them. 'Beautiful.'

He had kicked off his buckled shoes while she was removing her petticoats. Now he sat on the bed and pulled off his stockings, his eyes fixed on her.

'Turn round gently and slowly,' he said, 'so I can admire every bit of you.'

She turned, pleasured by the approving sounds he made as he inspected her nakedness, and by the time she was back facing him he, too, was naked. At first the sight of him made her gasp. Robin was a big man in every way and she found herself wondering if she would be able to contain him.

'Don't be afraid,' he said smiling. 'No need to be afraid. Just come here.'

She moved to the bed and sat beside him. He lifted her legs and laid her down again, her head on the pillows.

'You have to be ready,' he whispered. 'I have to make you ready.'

He leaned over her and kissed her lightly on the tip of her nose. Then he turned so that his head was at her feet. He kissed each one of her toes, and then ran his fingers under the soles of her feet, making her jump and giggle a little. Then his hands were tracing her legs, and his mouth was kissing and nibbling at her thighs. Very gently he opened her legs and bent so his head was between, and she felt the wonderful sensation as his tongue found her secret parts, and probed and explored, warm, wet and exciting.

He stayed there for a long time, both tongue and fingers teasing at her until she thought she would explode. And then when she was no longer sure where the wetness was coming from, he turned again to kiss first her breasts and then her mouth, all the while lifting himself ready to lower his body on to hers. As he entered her she gave a cry of joy. She was ready and waiting and welcoming. There was no pain, only pleasure.

When it was over, both of them sweating and hot, a musky smell of lust in the air, she realised that she had had no idea of what love really was. Poor Mark with his guilt and repression had never been able to show her, even though their coupling had improved after that disastrous first time.

Robin continued to show her throughout the night. They slept a little and woke to love again. He lay her on top of him, saying it would be better for her since she was so little and told her she must ride him. He showed her how to lie on her side so that they were scissored together, able to caress and see each other.

Finally he slept, one heavy arm flung over her, the words 'I love you' hanging on his lips, his big body totally relaxed. She lay listening to his quiet breathing, full of wonder at her good fortune that this huge-hearted, loving, generous man was hers and had taken her as his wife, shrugging off all the problems that she presented. She turned her head to kiss the warm flesh of his shoulder where it lay beneath her lips.

'Thank you,' she said quietly so as not to wake him.

Bella was getting thinner, Ruby thought as they jogged out of Basse-Terre after the wedding in the farm cart, driven by Beauboy's successor. Beauboy was long dead, and Ruby, remembering him from her first days at Windsong, found herself in a melancholy mood. She rarely questioned her fate, but the changed fortunes of the little slave girl she had looked after like a daughter made her see how constrained her own circumstances were. And looking at Bella did not raise her spirits. Bella would not last much longer. She had that faint haze of grey on her black skin, and her wrinkles looked almost white. Even her hair seemed thinner and she, too, seemed unhappy.

'You be sad, Bella?' Ruby asked.

'Guess so. Lost my grandchil' today.' She sighed heavily. 'It be better if I tries to forget she ever was my grandchil'. Being at Macabees there, you won' know that she found out that 'Melia's her ma. So she truly in the white world now.'

'She found out?' Ruby was astonished by this news. 'How?'

'Don' rightly know how. 'Melia won' tell me. She hidin' somethin'. But she knows, I be sure of it.'

Ruby considered. 'She been real lucky, but she ain't gonna forget you be her grandma. That Tansy be a real nice gal. It were a real pleasure bein' her mama when she were little. Not like this one I got now. This Precious. I swear to you, that chil' she got the devil in her.' Bella shook her head mournfully. 'She just a baby, but she real bad. I don' know if it be the milk that sourface wetnurse give her, or if she just performin' 'cause she lost her mammy. That chil' she never smile, she cry all the day, and little as she be, she be spiteful. Even Minta with all her potions don' find som'thin' to quiet her. I keeps my finger crossed all times

I have her. I tell you, I'd rather be fucked by Master Zach than look after that chil'. She be bad.'

Bella laughed shortly. 'Guess Master Zach rather you were there for him to fuck, too.'

Ruby grinned. 'Ain't that the truth!'

Bella was slumped at the edge of the cart, her legs swinging over the back. Generally her habits and spirits were still those of a young woman, but her movements had become stiff, and it was that grey powdering of the skin that troubled Ruby.

'How old you, Bella?' she asked.

'Don' know rightly. Guess 'bout sixty.'

'And you still workin'.'

' 'Melia always be tellin' me to stop it, but I don' wanna. What I go'n do if I don' cook? Ain't nothin' else to do.'

Ruby chuckled. 'Anyways, you gets paid for it.'

Bella sighed. 'I been saving that money. 'Melia been helpin' me. I had this thought I could save enough for my Truly to buy her freedom. But it took too long. Master Zach he gone and sold her and Daniel and we don' know where. 'Melia, she that mad when she find what he done, but he won' tell where they be. And it just when 'Melia gonna give them they freedom, too. 'Melia tried everythin' to find 'em, but that Zach he sold 'em to another island. And he won' say which.'

'He won'?'

Bella shook her head. 'My Truly, she know too much 'bout that family, and you know what she like. She a hothead. I reckons she tol' him she'd tell, and that be why he sold her. And that be why he won' tell no one where she gone.' She was silent for a moment, staring at the ground moving beneath her feet. 'All I ever wanted was to have my family 'bout me, but Joshua, he dead, Tansy, she lost as if she be dead, Truly and Daniel they gone. Your Sam he gone missin' too. Ain't got no family left but Juba and I guess maybe you, since you my grandson's ma. T'ain't enough. Ain't no point in gettin' old when you ain't got no family.'

Ruby listened in silence, but her mind was racing. An idea was forming.

'Do you reckon Mistress 'Melia might buy Truly and Daniel if she knew where they be?' she asked.

'She swear to me that she will, but she can' find 'em.'

'If I find 'em, and if they gets back here 'gain, would you give me that money you got saved?'

She was aware of having asked the question crudely, but somehow she didn't think it mattered. If Bella wanted her family back that much, her savings would be a cheap price to pay for their return.

Bella had turned to look at her, her expression a mixture of suspicion and hope. 'What you want that money for?'

'Buy my freedom.'

'You wants to be free?'

'Yes.' She said the word with such force that she silenced Bella for a moment.

'Then what you go'n do when you free?'

'Find me a big black buck of my own. A free big black buck who loves me.'

Bella grunted. 'If they free, they be mulattoes.'

Ruby laughed. 'Never you mind what I go'n do,' she said. 'Does you want me to find where they be?'

'And how you go'n do that?'

'Never you mind 'bout that either. All you got to do is get 'Melia to send me back to Windsong. I can' stand that Precious much longer.'

Bella turned to look her straight in the eye. 'This ain't some trick to get you back to Windsong?'

'No 'tain't.'

Bella pondered. 'You reckons you can do it?'

'I reckons I can.'

Bella's great head was nodding slowly. 'I gotta get 'Melia to send you back to Windsong?'

'That it.'

'And you go'n find out where my Truly be?'

'That what I go'n do.'

'And you wants my savings?'

'Yes.'

'Why don' we try it?' Bella said slowly. 'Why don' we see if it can be done?'

'Mistress 'Melia, can I talk with you?'

Amelia looked up from her embroidery to where Bella stood in the doorway of the sitting room, her hands twisting her apron and looking surprisingly humble. Almost supplicating.

'Of course, Bella. Come in. Sit down. Shall we have a cup of tea?'

'I just tell the girl,' Bella said with alacrity and shouted down the hallway for tea to be brought. Amelia hid a smile.

But as Bella fussed as to where the tray should be put and then poured two cups, Amelia felt a deep pang of sadness. Bella looked ill, but she could not be persuaded to rest. At any suggestion of easing up, she muttered she might as well be in her grave as resting. Time enough for resting then.

'Now, what is it?' Amelia asked when the niceties of the first sips of tea had been observed.

'That Ruby say she can find out where Truly be,' Bella blurted out.

'Oh?' Amelia raised her eyebrows. 'How is she going to do that?'

'She won' tell, but she say she can do it.'

Amelia had a pretty good idea of how Ruby might try to go about such a thing, but was Zach that simple? Would it work? The truth was that Zach could be that simple, and work it might.

'And?'

296

'It mean you got to get she back to Windsong. Anyway, she says she can' stand that baby much longer. She say that baby be bad.'

Slaves were not meant to hold or voice such opinions, but that was not what made Amelia start and slop tea into her saucer. She had believed her own reaction to the child must have been imagination, but for earthy, primitive Ruby, so much closer to nature than the rest of them, to say such a thing was alarming.

'If the baby is bad she needs someone good like Ruby with her,' Amelia said.

'No she don'. That baby need someone who ain't go'n see she bad, otherwise a person can't bear it.' Bella made a dismissive gesture, pushing the subject of Precious away before leaning forward confidingly. 'But if Ruby get back to Windsong . . .'

Amelia sat thinking. If she sent Ruby back, a family rift would develop again. Charlotte would be angry. Zach, on the other hand, would be happy. Ruby was no longer young but whatever it was she had that kindled Zach, it had never gone away. Amelia had noticed his eyes on the black woman throughout yesterday's wedding. He was still hungry for her. But if she sent Ruby back now, she might never get the chance to remove her again.

'Who that Ruby 'long to?' Bella was asking her.

'Technically, me,' Amelia said. 'I have her papers.'

'Then it be up to you to free she?'

'Yes.'

''Cause she and me, we got a deal. If she finds out where my Truly be, and you brings Truly home, I gonna give her my savin's and she gonna buy her freedom.'

'She wants her freedom?'

'All slaves wants their freedom,' Bella retorted.

Giving Ruby her freedom was the key to it all, Amelia realised. It would satisfy Charlotte who would no longer have the woman under her roof. If Zach wanted he could set her up as his mistress privately elsewhere. Or Ruby could take her chances and go her own way. And maybe it wouldn't take too long for Ruby to find where Truly was. Freedom would be the spur.

'You want Truly home enough to give up your savings?'

The corners of the black woman's mouth turned down and her lower lip quivered. Such a sign of weakness in Bella was rare.

' 'Course I give up my savin's,' she said gruffly. 'What I want my savin's for? I wants my family back and Truly and Juba be the only ones left. One day p'haps we find that Sam, but sometimes I think he be dead. I asks every Sunday in the market, but there never no news of he.'

The mention of Sam filled Amelia with gut-wrenching guilt. It also settled the matter. If Bella wanted her daughter that much, it was worth trying anything.

★   ★   ★

297

'You'll have to take her back, Zach.' Amelia paced up and down Zach's small office in Basse-Terre, appearing to be a picture of agitation. 'I know she's my property, but I don't want to sell her. I know you'd never forgive me and, more important, nor would Tansy. But Precious seems to hate her.'

'Little Precious seems to hate everyone,' he remarked.

'And also Ruby is impertinent. She does what she likes and cheeks William's white staff. He, of course, doesn't notice. He has to be protected from himself. I can't have her at Elsewhere. She reminds me of things I would rather try to forget. I'm afraid there's nowhere else but Windsong, though what Charlotte will say I don't know.'

'If it will help you, Amelia, I will have her back.' Zach somehow managed to sound as if he were dubious about doing so, but he could not conceal the light of eagerness in his eyes. 'She was a very good cook and we've missed her in the kitchen.'

'But what will Charlotte say?'

'Why should Charlotte say anything?'

'Come, come, Zach. It's me, Amelia, you're talking to.'

He grinned and she could not contain a giggle.

'Well, she's not going to like it,' he said. 'But I'm very much afraid that she'll have to put up with it.'

Taking herself off to call on Tansy and Robin, Amelia reflected that if Zach was as besotted with Ruby as he appeared, she might just do the trick.

Marianne, who had been promoted from the tavern to become Tansy's housekeeper, informed Amelia, with a perfectly straight face but a Gallic twinkle in her eyes, that Monsieur le Captain and Madame were still in bed.

'As all good honeymooners should be,' Amelia remarked and said, no, not to disturb them, she would come back another day. She went to see Ben. She intended to beg a bite from him before going on to Macabees. Also, no one knew more about Basse-Terre and its inhabitants than he did. He might have an idea of where she could find a nurse to replace Ruby.

He was delighted to see her, coming from behind the long bar to greet her and hurrying her into his own quarters. They hadn't been alone together for some weeks. He called for food and wine, and they chatted at first about the wedding. She told him nothing of her conversation with Bella. She did not trust him sufficiently. He might warn Zach. He was already a little uneasy and she thought she knew why.

'Sam is on your conscience, isn't he,' she asked abruptly.

He blew out his breath in a sort of exasperation. 'Only because it wasn't done right. He should have come to trial but the end result would have been the same. The worst of it was what he told Tansy.'

'He told the truth. I should have done it long before. Perhaps I should be grateful to him.'

'How did she take it when she saw you?'

298

'Quite well, in the end. It was difficult at first. But I think she was glad to know the truth.'

Ben took a long sip of his claret and then put down his glass. 'I have to say,' he announced, 'that your daughter is one of the nicest, happiest, easiest human beings I have ever met. Just like her mother.'

Amelia felt herself blush. 'What a nice thing to say,' she murmured, then, to change the subject, 'Unfortunately her daughter is not as easy. She's beautiful, clever and wild, and what will happen to her, God only knows.'

'She can always come and work here,' he said laughing. 'From what I've seen of her she would be good for business.'

'It might even come to that,' Amelia said gloomily. 'Bella thinks I'm wrong to educate her and bring her up in the same way as I did Tansy.'

'And, of course, she's right,' Ben said. 'But it's too late now.'

'And there's another problem,' Amelia went on. 'I have discovered that Ruby dislikes, truly dislikes poor little Precious. She's a difficult baby and cries a great deal, but it is not good for a child to be tended by one who dislikes her. I fear that Ruby will have to be returned to Windsong and another nurse found. But where?'

Ben was grinning. 'Charlotte will not be pleased.'

'Ruby is a very good cook,' Amelia said firmly.

'I hear she is good at other things, too.'

'Zach did not seem displeased at the idea of her returning,' Amelia said, examining her fingernails. Then she shook her head crossly. 'I am mean and unkind about Charlotte. It's time I forgot what happened long ago, but I can't seem to.'

'Me neither,' he said quietly.

She sighed, an impatient hand movement brushing the subject of Charlotte away. 'Do you know of a nurse here in Basse-Terre who could replace Ruby?'

'Do you want another slave or a white woman?' he asked.

She thought about it. 'A white woman,' she said. 'A sensible one. The blacks are so full of superstition – they think there's something strange about the baby.'

'How do you feel about an ex-whore?' he asked. 'Prissie here is a good girl. She's getting on now, and she's had two kids of her own and brought them up well. She wants to stop whoring. Her family came here a hundred years ago from the West Country as indentured labourers. Same old story – when they'd finished their time, they got paid off in sugar and damn near starved. They had nowhere enough money to buy land. Prissie became a whore like her grandmother and her mother before her. There was no other way they could live. This would be a great opportunity for her. But do you think William would have a fit at the thought of it?'

'For the moment I don't think William will even notice who is there, his grief is still so great. All he cares is that the baby is well looked after.'

'Well, it's nice you don't want another slave,' he said, a touch sarcastically. 'I'll ask Prissie. I'm sure the answer will be yes. You'll have to pay her decently. Whores are used to having money.'

'Of course. And if she agrees, could she leave for Macabees tomorrow?'

He threw up his hands. 'Always in a hurry,' he said. 'But I don't see why not.'

Well pleased with her morning's work, Amelia rode to Macabees. She smiled to herself on the way, thinking how life in the West Indies changed people. The very idea of employing an ex-whore as a nurse to a baby of good family would have been unthinkable in England, but here in the Tropics it was always the devil who drove.

As she had thought, William was happy to leave the arrangements for his daughter's upbringing to her. And it was agreed that when Prissie arrived Ruby would stay for a day or two to show her how things were done before a cart would be sent to take her back to Windsong.

After that, thought Amelia, as she rode along the beach, enjoying the beauty of the sea and the mountains, all they could do was wait and see.

There had been the most frightful scene with Charlotte when he told her that Ruby was coming back to Windsong. Charlotte was convinced that the excuse of Precious was all made up.

'Anyway,' she said, lifting her nose, which with age was regrettably becoming as narrow as her mother's. 'Whoever heard of a slave daring to complain about her charge? How dare she.'

'The worry is for the child, not the slave,' Zach explained patiently.

'Huh! Amelia will have had some hand in this. She has always hated me whereas I have always been charity itself to her.'

'Amelia does not hate you. It is nothing to do with her. It is merely that William is anxious about the child.'

'I do not believe that Ruby even belongs to us,' she hissed.

'Nonsense, of course she does,' Zach said, and scuttled from the room.

It was all worth it to see Ruby back on the plantation again. He made a point of confronting her on her second day back, early, as she arrived in the kitchen. With an impatient and certainly incautious wave of his hand he sent the other kitchen slaves away and stood looking at her.

She was standing behind the table smiling at him, a soft smile, softer than he ever remembered receiving from her before. Could she have missed him?

She confirmed what he longed to believe. 'Well,' she said, black eyes sparkling at him, 'if it ain't that Master Zach come to see me.' Then the eyes dropped so he could not see them. 'It be good to see you, master,' she said, and she sounded almost shy.

He felt ridiculously pleased, and looking at her incredible breasts, forward-thrusting as ever, the gloss on her black skin, the strength of her arms, a series of images assaulted him, of her naked, wide-spread, greedy, sucking him into her, clasping her strong legs round him until

300

he could barely breathe . . . He wanted her again, he could feel himself rising for her like a schoolboy. And he wanted her soon. He kept his face stern. 'I am told you did not please at Macabees.'

She raised her eyes again and shyly tipped her head to one side. 'Weren't home there, master. Home be where you is.'

Only for an instant did he question this extraordinary change in the bold, irreverent Ruby. He wanted the flattery. He wanted to believe her and he let himself do so.

'Nevertheless, you must be chastised for this failure to please. A slave must always please.'

Her hot eyes called to him. 'I tries, master, I tries,' she said demurely.

'Then you must try harder.'

'Yes, master. Very hard, I'll try.'

'I shall expect to see you in your cabin this afternoon. Make sure no one else is there.'

'Just like always, master,' she murmured. 'I be waiting for you.'

He told Charlotte that he was going into Old Road Town to meet his fellow Council members as he had been doing a few afternoons a week since Ruby had been taken from him. Instead, in a lather of impatience, he went to the slave huts. She had always been wonderful to fuck. The old buccaneer's excitement of 'not asking their permission' was there. Their encounters were rough and violent, with her giving as good as she got when it came to pain. He never hurt Charlotte, he didn't want to, but Ruby balanced out his life. With her he had the best of all sexual licence. Yet he had the feeling that this time there might be an added ingredient to their coupling. She had seemed as if, having been without him, she might have come to care for him a little. Though she was only a slave, and it did not matter a toss whether or not she even liked him, he was pleased that she might respond to him as a man instead of just someone with the unalienable right to fuck her whenever he wished.

The foetid smells of cooking, unwashed bodies and hot wood greeted him as he slipped through the cabin door. She would be upstairs waiting. He did not bother with the ladder but stretched to grasp the wood surround of the opening to the floor above and swung himself up in one movement. He was proud of being sufficiently tall to do this and was aware he was showing off a little.

She was stretched on her side, resting on her straw pallet, her eyes gleaming in the gloom. The few thin rays of sunlight that found their way through cracks in the shingled roof bounced off the blackness of her skin. Her legs were together and her breasts rested one on the other. He didn't always bother to undress with Ruby, if time were short, but today he quite deliberately stripped, leaving his clothing tumbled on the grubby floor. He was aroused and when she looked at him she covered her eyes with her hand.

'Oh, master,' she said, 'you gonna punish me with that great big stick?'

'Not yet,' he said. There were other things he wanted to do to her first. He wanted to smack the shining, pert black buttocks and nibble at her breasts, and have her take him in her mouth, all the earthy, lusty, unrestrained things that she seemed so to enjoy. And when his hand landed with a satisfying crack on those buttocks and she shrieked in pretended terror, he found that nothing had changed. She must have been as hungry as he was and he told himself that no one had been there since him.

When he finally collapsed panting away from her hot, slippery body, to his surprise she turned to put her head on his shoulder. Before she had always rolled away from him.

'It been funny without you,' she said softly. 'I missed all this' – and her hand went down to tweak him where he lay flaccid and exhausted. 'It be good to have it again.' She hesitated. 'Did you miss me?' she asked humbly.

'Didn't need to,' he grunted, determined not to let her see how pleased he was. 'Plenty more where you came from.'

'Then why you here with me today?'

'Well,' he said slowly, 'I suppose you are my first choice.'

'Good.' She sounded contented and left her head on his shoulder while they slept.

He visited her every afternoon. He was sure Charlotte knew; her features were pinched and her mouth tight with anger. He did not care. For the moment all he wanted was to get his fill of Ruby. Their relationship had subtly changed. She talked to him, asked him questions about his life. She showed sympathy for his ambitions and listened to him, gave him her full attention in a way that Charlotte rarely did; Charlotte was engrossed in the children. He found Ruby had a sort of basic wisdom and whatever she said to him was helpful. Occasionally he thought with guilt that he was responsible for the death of her son, but he was careful never to mention Sam's name.

One afternoon, when she had been back at Windsong for about ten days, she was like a wild thing in his arms, biting and kissing and licking him, raising him to unbelievable heights of excitement, though even as he wallowed in the sensations he was thinking that he had better not let Charlotte see him unclothed. There would be evidence of this hot afternoon.

Afterwards she began to talk, more volubly than usual, and he found himself dreamily listening to her. She was explaining how happy she had been at Windsong after the dreadful life she had led at Macabees and her misery when she had been snatched away. Subtly in this recital she inferred that all his slaves loved and cared for him and his children.

'I reckons,' she said, her finger stroking his arm, 'that you runs the happiest plantation on this whole island. Ain't no other place as happy.' He could feel the slow nodding of her head as she lay beside him. 'Best thing you ever did,' she said, 'was to get rid of that Truly and Daniel. They was real trouble makers, allus bitchin', allus making bad feelin'.

I tell you I hated them two and the bad tales they told. It be much better now they ain't here no more. One thing troubles me is that one day them two gonna come back again. I know that Bella always pushing for Mistress 'Melia to find 'em for her. But you ought to tell Mistress 'Melia that they bad people, and then perhaps she gonna understand and stop lookin' for 'em. I be afeared that one day she's go'n find 'em and they be back, spoilin' everythin'.'

'Don't you worry,' he said, basking in the glory of having the happiest plantation on the island, 'they'll never be back here again.'

'Ain't that difficult to find someone on this little island,' she said doubtfully. 'That Bella forever at the slave market askin' if anyone seen 'em.'

'They're not on this island,' he told her.

'That don' matter. There be folks from other islands come to the market sometimes. That Bella she always askin'. Sure 'nuff she'll find out one day.'

'They're much too far away,' he said. 'On another group of islands entirely.'

'Well, I declare,' she said, her voice astonished. 'You mean there be more islands than ours? I knows about Nevis, an Anguilla, Antigua and Montserrat, and Stacia, too, but I thought they be the only islands there was. I thought they the whole of the West Indies. You tellin' me there's others?'

He shook his head at her abysmal ignorance. 'There are several other groups,' he explained patiently, 'Truly and Daniel are now in a group called the Windward, on an island there called St Lucia. Our islands are called the Leewards. St Lucia is a long, long way south of here. Even if they ran from their plantation, they'd never find their way back to St Kitts.'

'I be glad 'bout that,' she said solemnly. 'Real glad. This place here much happier without 'em. They grow sugar there on this place, St Lucia?'

'Lots of it,' he told her. 'There are lots of plantations there.'

Her hand was caressing him between his legs, sliding up and down, teasing the sensitive little string, squeezing then sliding, sliding then squeezing.

'So they be on a plantation,' she crooned. 'I hopes they in the fields. Be good punishment for them. What plantation be it?'

'One of them,' he said dismissively. Her hand was having the desired effect. 'Never did know which.' He felt as if he were about to burst under her ministrations. 'You want more?' he asked. 'You greedy bitch. You want more, don't you?'

'I allus wants more,' she said complacently as he rolled her on to her back and wrenched opened her legs again. 'And one thing I can be sure of,' she added as he humped his body to cover hers, 'is that you allus gonna give me more, ain't you?'

She was guiding him in, her big, confident hand wrapped round him, making sure he was in just the right place. He began to ride her, and as he plunged deeper and deeper into the black dark well of her he was saying, 'Yes, yes, yes, yes.'

She met Bella at the Sunday market in Basse-Terre near the jail. The market had grown in the last few years, though some plantation owners were uneasy that it created an opportunity for the blacks to plan an insurrection. The slaves lived in fear that these gatherings where they could meet slaves from other plantations and learn news of friends and relatives would be banned, but for the time being the market continued. The clergy could hardly object and demand that the slaves attended church, for religion was forbidden them.

It had been agreed that both Bella and Ruby would attend the market each Sunday morning so that Ruby could report any news. This Sunday Ruby came bearing a couple of pies made from pumpkins grown in the Windsong gardens, and Amelia had sent Bella off with a batch of homemade bread.

Ruby loved the market. It was, she thought, the only happy place for most slaves on the island. Only on Sundays were the slaves not roused by the rising bell or the mournful sound of a blown conch shell. The market was the one place where they could play drums and hear tribal music, prohibited by the whites on the plantations in case the drums carried messages to rise up. As the time for the market to close neared, groups formed to sing the old songs from Africa that had survived the horrors of the middle passage and the drums rolled with a free touch. At the market they could wear what best they had, mostly their masters' and mistresses' cast-offs, but finery for all that. Bella wore her red gown, a present from Amelia at Christmas, with a brilliant yellow shawl and a huge, startling green silk turban. Amelia had laughed as she left Elsewhere. 'Ruby won't have any trouble finding you anyway,' she teased. 'You'll stand out in any crowd.'

Even so, it was not easy to find any one person in the Sunday market. There was no form or structure to it. People laid out their wares wherever there was space. A few had rough tables to hold their goods, but these were packed up and put away as the produce was sold. Poor whites and white tradesfolk sometimes came to the market to buy cheaply, and there was always a good sprinkling of freed mulattos The area was dirty, smelly, the prevailing odour that of pigs, but it blazed with colour from the piled fruit and vegetables and the slaves' clothing. It was also extremely noisy. Ruby enjoyed every minute of her Sunday mornings there.

Bella had sold her bread when she saw Ruby pushing through the crowds towards her. She looked resplendent in a blue bodice with short sleeves and a low, round neck which was amply filled by the curve of her breasts. She wore a blue kirtle over a darker skirt and a bright pink kerchief tied round her head.

304

She was smiling, and it was a triumphant smile. Bella hurried towards her.

'You heard somethin'?' she asked eagerly.

'They be on the Windward Islands,' Ruby said immediately. 'St Lucia. On a plantation.'

'What plantation?' breathed Bella, her hands clasped in delight.

'He don' know. And I believes him.'

'You think 'Melia will find 'em?'

Ruby laughed shortly. 'She better. I wants my freedom. I wants to be able to spit on that Zach Quick if I've a mind to. I hates that man, Bella.'

But Bella was not concentrating on Ruby's troubles. Bella had never looked happier. 'How'd you do it, Ruby?' she asked.

'Same way any black gal gets anythin' out of a white man. On my back and on my belly and on my knees – every which way he wanted to fuck me, that's how I did it.'

'At least you got somethin' for it.'

'Let's hope we both gets somethin' for it,' Ruby said grimly and then burst out laughing. 'I'd sure hate all that effort to go to waste.'

Bella offered to buy them a ripe melon and, content with their achievements, they settled themselves, backs to a wall in the shade to share the fruit which the trader had cut into slices for them.

'It be nice of you to buy this melon,' Ruby said with a chuckle, 'but I don' wants you being too free with that money of yourn that's gonna be my money.'

'They don' be home yet,' Bella pointed out.

They were wiping the sticky juice from their mouths when a man neither of them recognised sauntered over.

'Ain't you Ruby?' he asked.

'Sure am.' Ruby was eyeing him for possibilities. He was big, black and handsome. She gave him her most beguiling smile.

'And you got a son called Sam?'

'Sure do.'

The man looked uneasy. 'You ain't heard the news?'

'What news?'

'Your boy be dead.'

'For a moment Ruby felt her heart stop, then she began to tremble. 'How he be dead?'

'I don' know the all of it, but word at the plantation—'

'Which plantation?' she asked fiercely.

'Windsong. Word be at the plantation your Sam ran, from Nevis. He kilt a driver . . .'

She shut her eyes. Killed a driver. He was only a baby when she had seen him last.

'Don' rightly know what happened then, 'cept he got stopped by militiamen. They kilt him, but he got a sword from somewhere, and he fought hard. Them militiamen got hurt real bad.

That Sam, he fought, he fought like six men, and he be a hero.'

'A dead hero.' It was Bella speaking, her voice full of disgust. 'How they know where to find him? Who sent for the militiamen?'

'Word be it were Master Quick. It were Master Quick sent for the gravediggers after he dead. That boy's head weren't barely on his body. They put him in the plantation, and the field women, they puts flowers on his grave 'cause he a brave man. Ain't many stand up to them militia.'

'Why no one tell me?' Ruby's voice was anguished.

'Seems only the field folk knows,' the man said apologetically.

Bella was rocking backwards and forward in grief. 'That boy be my grandchil',' she said, 'and I ain't never seen him since he were little. If he kilt a driver, don' be no hope for him. They gonna kill him anyways. Better he dies like a man than on a rope. Better he dies a hero.'

Ruby could not speak. She buried her face in her hands. All she could think was that she had pleasured the man who had ordered the death of her son. Her only consolation was that she had tricked him, but she knew she could never let him touch her again. If he did, she might just kill him.

Amelia always let Bella take the cart into Basse-Terre for the market. Slaves walked miles from the outlying districts, sometimes starting before dawn, in order to enjoy their day of pleasure only to have to walk back again. Bella was spared this, and she was able to take the stunned and shocked Ruby as far as the drive of Windsong before setting off for Elsewhere. There she found Amelia waiting under the shade of the tamarind tree in the garden in front of the house.

'Well?' she asked even while Bella was still climbing down from the cart.

'That Ruby done it. Truly be in the Windward Islands on St Lucia. But no one knows what the plantation called.'

Amelia flung her arms round Bella. 'We'll find them! We'll find them now,' she said. 'No doubt. It might take a while, but we'll do it.'

'Better be quick,' Bella warned. 'I reckons that Ruby not gonna take much more of that brother of yours.'

'It's a long way to St Lucia, Bella. I'll have to send an agent to search. It could take a month or two.'

'That bad news for Ruby,' Bella said, pulling a face, 'but I guess it been so long now, bit longer won' matter. As long as that Truly come home in the end. Problem be that Ruby found out Master Zach he fixed for her Sam to be kilt by the militia. I tells you, 'Melia, she fair set to kill Master Zach herself.'

Amelia felt the blood drain from her face. 'Oh, my God,' she said. 'What happened?'

Bella gave her a suspicious look. 'You don' know?'

Amelia could not bring herself to lie out loud. She merely shook her head. Bella headed for the kitchen. After a few paces she turned and said, 'Well, you better ask your brother then. He be the one who know

306

what happened. And you better do somethin' quick or you gonna get you a dead brother.' She stumped into the house, leaving Amelia to worry whether or not anyone knew of Tansy's involvement in Sam's death. One thing was sure. It was never going to be possible to explain what had happened. The only hope was to let the blame rest on Zach.

It was early the next morning when Amelia received an unexpected visit that left her thinking that perhaps there was an active God up there somewhere. A distressed and tearful Charlotte arrived with a request. She had come to beg Amelia to remove Ruby from her home.

'I don't think I can stand it much longer,' she sniffed dismally, clutching a small linen handkerchief to her face. 'He visits her in the cabins every afternoon, and when he comes back he barely speaks to me. I've tried everything to interest him in me again, but he seems totally besotted by her. And she is so smug, so full of herself around the house that I could bring myself to kill her. It's got so bad I searched out the penalty for killing a slave and found there is no penalty unless the Crown can prove malice. Well, I'm so full of malice for that black harlot I could swing for it, providing,of course, I had the courage to do it. What can I do? Zach denies it, but I'm sure Ruby is legally yours.'

'That's true,' Amelia told her.

'Please take her back for everyone's sake. Zach and I were so happy when she went away. She has been a thorn in my flesh all my married life. I cannot bear her under my roof a moment longer, or I swear I will snap and do something I might regret.'

Charlotte's distress was stamped all over her. Her hair was unkempt, her gown spotted, her face blotchy with crying.

'I'm certain,' she whispered, 'that the harlot has laid some African spell on him. Perhaps fed him some herb to bind him to her. It's as if he's in some kind of trance. I know at night as he tosses and turns beside me that it's her he wishes he was with. There's some evil there.'

Listening, Amelia wondered if it could be true. Did Ruby have knowledge of old ways to ensnare, or was it just her smouldering sexuality that had so entranced Zach? Whatever the cause, there was no need for this enchantment to continue. Ruby had done her job and done it well.

'I will take her back,' she said. To her embarrassment Charlotte collapsed onto her knees and buried her head in her sister-in-law's lap, sobbing with relief.

After thinking long and hard, Amelia rode to Basse-Terre that afternoon. She went to persuade Ben to talk to Zach and to make him see that if Ruby were not removed, his marriage would be ruined. At first Ben was reluctant to interfere. But Amelia had thought about that eventuality as well.

'Listen, Ben,' she said, 'I've been thinking. If you will do this for me – well, really for Zach since it is not right for him to be so enamoured of a slave – I will sell you the tavern.'

'You will?' She could see that he could not believe what she was saying. His brown eyes narrowed and he stared at her suspiciously. 'You're telling me that after all these years of my asking you'll sell it to me now? Do you really want Ruby back that badly? It can't be out of affection for Charlotte.'

'That's true,' Amelia said ruefully. 'What also is true is that I've been thinking of letting you have it for a long time now. I no longer require it for security. William has no need of it and no money worries. He will inherit Elsewhere, and Macabees is already his. When I die he will be the largest landowner on the island. And I don't think he's cut out to be a tavernkeeper. But, even so, in return for the tavern I want you to speak to Zach. It is not, as you so rightly guessed, for Charlotte's sake, though I do feel pity for her. It is more for Ruby. Ruby is a good woman. I no longer have any animosity towards her and she has helped me and my family in ways I would rather not discuss. I want to give her her freedom. Will you get her back for me?'

Ben turned down the corners of his mouth and nodded. 'If you're going to give her her freedom, yes.' Then he added, 'You don't think she'd like work at the tavern?'

'What sort of work?' Amelia asked cautiously.

He threw back his head and laughed. 'As a whore, of course. It's what she's been all her life. She's a natural.'

Amelia found herself bridling at the masculine assumption that a woman would want to continue whoring when it was no longer necessary.

'Once she is free what she does with her life is her own affair,' she said stiffly. 'And you would, of course, have to pay for the tavern.'

He was grinning again. 'Not too much, I trust. After all, it was I who made it a success.'

'Not too much. I shall settle the money on Delilah. Money gives more liberty than declarations of freedom from plantation owners.'

'Consider it done,' he said cheerfully. 'You shall have your Ruby, Delilah shall have her dowry, and Charlotte will get her husband back. Poor old Zach will be the only one to suffer.'

'He'll recover,' Amelia said. 'Just as I did.'

'And as I never have,' Ben told her, reaching to take her hand.

PART IV

Chapter Seventeen

'She gone off again, mistress.' Juba was standing in front of her, his black face a picture of misery, eyes rolling and hands clasped in front of him.

'Oh dear.' Amelia looked helplessly at her granddaughter's man and wished he wasn't quite so feeble. Delilah made his life a misery and he had no idea how to deal with the girl. She was twenty now, as exotic as a bird of paradise and wild with it. Juba had fallen in love with her when she was fifteen, by which time Delilah had already had several sexual encounters with various of the factory slaves. So besotted with her was Juba that he had turned a blind eye to these adventures.

Delilah was a problem. At the age of thirteen she had flatly refused to continue with her lessons from Amelia. Arms akimbo, black eyes scornful, thick hair Medusa-like round her head, she had demanded to know what good learning to read music and speaking French was ever going to be to her? She was asking the same questions that both Tansy and Bella had asked on her behalf long ago. Bella had not lived to see how right she had been. She died quietly in her sleep in 1719 and Amelia missed her still. Delilah had been inconsolable at her great-grandmother's death, and deeply affected by it. The loss seemed to cause a crisis of identity in the girl. She had always been more African than European in attitudes and manner, and Bella had encouraged her to recognise the African aspect of her heritage, recounting how life was on the Guinea Coast and the misfortunes that had brought her people to these beautiful but cruel islands. Amelia had not liked it but she said nothing, telling herself that Bella had the right.

When Bella died, it seemed that Delilah had made a decision to be all black. It was not so much that she ignored the existence of her white blood as despised its presence in her. Amelia was forced to accept that the girl had good reason and reluctantly let her slip back into a black way of life. She could talk, walk, dress and behave like a white lady of quality, but she chose not to. She was happier dressed in the rough clothing of slave women and chatting in their patois.

When Juba came to Amelia a few months after Bella's death and asked humbly if he could take Delilah for his woman, Amelia agreed, providing Delilah was happy with the arrangement. Juba was then twenty-eight years old and had been sharing a cabin with Truly and Daniel since they had been brought back from St Lucia in 1715. It was time he broke

311

away from his parents and had a woman of his own. Technically, he was still a slave, though without any of the usual restrictions. His parents had been given their freedom but decided to stay on at the plantation. Truly was forty-five and tired of life. The fire in her had been beaten out by a cruel slave master in St Lucia. Her health was destroyed. She moved and breathed with difficulty. All she wanted now was somewhere safe and peaceful, and Daniel, always the gentler of the two, had been happy to go along with that.

Juba was like his father, steady as a rock; a big gentle man who made himself useful around the plantation and liked nothing better than to look after children. Zach's Julia and James loved him but they were grown up now and did not need him. He was never happier than when Tansy's children, Mark and Melanie, came to stay at the plantation. They were boisterous youngsters, aged eleven and nine, with the happy disposition of their parents, and they were both white of skin. Unlike their rebellious half-sister, neither showed the slightest trace of their African ancestry.

Delilah needed someone steady and patient, someone who loved her. Juba seemed the answer. He was a cut above the other slaves. Truly had taught him to read and write in the same way that Amelia had taught her. He was intelligent enough, but lacked strength of character. He was by no means what Amelia had hoped for her granddaughter, but what she had hoped for was an impossible dream. Tentatively she put the proposition to the girl.

'Will we have our own cabin?' was Delilah's first question, 'or do I have to go on living in your house?'

There was an unattractive accent on the word 'your' and Amelia hesitated before replying. The money she had received for the tavern was put away for Delilah; there was enough and more to buy a proper home for her either in Basse-Terre or Old Road Town. That, though, did not conform with Delilah's determination to live like a slave, albeit a privileged slave. Her preference for the slave life did not include the slave's labour. Amelia was aware that the offer of a house or even the money would probably be scornfully turned down.

'You can have your own cabin if you wish,' Amelia said.

'All right then.' Delilah's tone was flatly indifferent, and it was with considerable misgivings that Amelia told Juba she had agreed.

It had gone well for a while. Delilah became pregnant within weeks and had two children in three years. Both were boys and improbably called Broderic and Bradley. Then came a series of miscarriages, and though she was not sure of it, Amelia had the impression from Juba's doleful demeanour that Delilah was refusing to sleep with him.

And then Delilah started to disappear. Sometimes she would go off to the Sunday market alone and not reappear for days. Other times she would go into Basse-Terre for just a few hours and visit either Tansy or Ben and then return. When she left the plantation, she always managed to leave secretly and Juba had no idea where she was or when she would reappear.

'How long has she been gone this time?' Amelia asked him.

'It be nearly a week. She went off on Sunday and I ain't seen her since.'

'Who is looking after the children?'

'Me and Mammy, like we allus does when Delilah goes. I don' think I can bear with it much longer, Mistress 'Melia. I loves that gal and she makin' me real unhappy. What she do when she goes? That's what troubles me real bad. Can' you make her stay home? Other slaves don' be 'lowed to do these things.'

Amelia sighed. Like Juba, Delilah was technically a slave though she had never been treated as one; she had always owned a *laissez passer* that allowed her to move around. No one had quite known how to describe her position, and she herself had assumed that she was a slave. Juba knew it was not quite that simple. He knew, as did his parents and the older members of the household, that Delilah was Tansy's daughter even though Delilah did not know it herself. This was never spoken of, but the knowledge hung above all their heads and made dealing with the wilful young woman almost impossible.

'Have you ever told her who her mother is, Juba?' Amelia asked abruptly, thinking that there were few secrets between lovers.

Juba drew himself up and the hangdog look vanished. 'Why'd I do that?' he asked, almost belligerently for him. 'If she knowed that, she wouldn't be with the likes of me.'

He might not be very good at coping with Delilah, but he obviously knew where his best interests lay, Amelia thought. Nevertheless, something had to be done.

'I will see if I can find her and talk to her,' she said. 'But whether it will do any good . . .'

Juba was profuse in his thanks, but Amelia seriously doubted if anything she said would have the slightest impact on the girl. And she groaned at the thought of a trip to Basse-Terre. These days she felt the heat and tired quickly. When her lack of energy annoyed her she had to remind herself that she was fifty-six years old. No longer young. She tried to ignore her pains and aches, telling herself they were normal, but the weather bothered her and sometimes she found herself dreaming of cool Devon. It had been heavy and oppressive for days lately; the breeze seemed to have deserted the island, and people speculated uneasily whether or not this was hurricane weather. But there was a bright side to a trip to Basse-Terre; it could include a visit to Macabees to see William, and then perhaps she would stay the night with Tansy in Pall Mall Square, a part of town now grown more grand than ever.

Though she would never have said so to Juba, Amelia was pretty certain where her granddaughter went when she vanished. She had little doubt that she would find Delilah at the Columbus Tavern, being sheltered by Ben. If she was not there, she would be with Ruby at her little pie and cake shop. She was closer to Ruby than anyone else.

Like Ruby before her, Delilah was a natural whore. But whether she was being paid for it, and how deeply Ben was involved, Amelia didn't know. She hoped Ben was not employing her, but she wouldn't put it past him.

She arrived at Macabees to a warm welcome from William. He had become middle-aged before his time, weighed down by the cares of running the plantation, his involvement, along with Zach, in the running of the island, and, most taxing, the problem of his daughter.

Precious was not a normal child. She had inherited her mother's fine blonde hair, delicate features and blue eyes. She was a remarkably pretty girl, but the eyes seemed dead. There was no one at home behind that blue stare. Her manner was both timid and menacing, as if her mother had bequeathed her her own childhood terrors. She rarely spoke. No one was entirely certain just how much speech she had. Occasionally she would make a pertinent statement so clearly and directly that all who heard were astonished. Other times, she would not speak for days.

She came alive before a harpsichord. Her gift for music was remarkable. Sometimes she would sped the day at the instrument, playing Bach endlessly and other compositions that could only have been her own. Her music was wild, strong and alarming and she begged her father to buy her an organ. Mr Lockett had been instructed to ship one from London, and it had arrived in time for her thirteenth birthday. The house resounded to her violent music until the slaves put their hands over their ears to blot it out and her father built her a music house in the grounds to spare the household. The slaves were all in fear of her, believing that she harboured bad spirits. She disliked them in turn. As a tiny child she had screamed whenever anyone black came near her – as Ruby had discovered. Now she was older, all she had to do was fix them with her dead eyes to make them scuttle from the room clutching the chicken's foot they carried against evil. Prissie, who still remained in the household, had managed to achieve some kind of relationship with the girl. After a lifetime of dealing with lonely, violent, unbalanced, inadequate men, Prissie had taken the problems of Precious in her stride. She had never feared her, never liked her much, perhaps no more than she had liked her customers, but she dealt with the child as she had dealt with them – kindly and justly. When Precious became violent, Prissie had an arrangement with Bessie's daughter, Minta, who had taken over her mother's role of witch doctor/nurse to the slaves. Minta's medicine calmed the girl more effectively than anything the white doctors could prescribe and Prissie thought it better not to enquire too closely what was in the potion.

Precious was a puzzle. She was no idiot and she was perfectly content when her father took her around the plantation with him. It was a bizarre father-daughter relationship. He was the only one she had any kind

314

of intelligible conversation with, but the subject was always the mathematical logistics of the plantation. She could look at a field of cane and calculate with astonishing accuracy how many tons of sugar it would yield and how many barrels of molasses. She could do the most complicated sums with hardly a thought. At fourteen her father had given her control of the plantation accounts and stock, and her abilities had considerably increased his profits. She could deal with figures and write down music, but a coherent sentence in a letter was beyond her. It was no wonder that the blacks whispered that she was a witch.

She did not appear for luncheon and Amelia was relieved. She tried hard to love her grandchild, but she found the cold stare disturbing. And the child's table manners could have been improved. For one so brilliant with a keyboard, she was oddly unco-ordinated with a knife and fork.

William was full of the news of the capital's change from Old Road Town to Basse-Terre.

'Oh, there are so many developments,' he said. 'The last of the French are finally going — such a time it has taken to get rid of them. I thought they would never part with their lands. Now we will be able to sell that fertile ground around Basse-Terre to our own people. There are twenty thousand hectares of French land for sale, and three commissioners from England will sell them to the highest bidders in lots of two hundred acres. There are plans to build a new court house in Basse-Terre, though we shall have to levy a tax on Negroes to raise money to pay for it. We shall also establish a public market. It is absurd that the slaves have their own market and we do not.'

'Will they let anyone buy the land?' Amelia asked thoughtfully.

'What do you mean?'

'Well, freed slaves, for example.'

'If they have the money, I don't see why not. Though it might not be a popular thing to do. Why?'

'I was thinking it might be something for Juba and Delilah.'

William laughed condescendingly. 'They could never afford it. Really, Mama, you are always thinking about the slaves. I have never known anyone like you. It is simply not the done thing, you know. You are far too kind and tolerant with them. They will only reward you with ingratitude. I don't understand why you do it. It really should stop, you know.'

She hated it when he was smug, and he often was. She did not want a smug son and there was one sure way to puncture his smugness once and for all. It was time, she thought.

'Perhaps,' she murmured, mouth smiling sweetly while the eyes were green ice, 'that's because I was once a slave myself.'

'Don't be ridiculous, Mother,' he said patting his lips with his napkin.

'It's true,' she said calmly, and in a few pithy, brief sentences told him of her life adding, 'I think you are perhaps old enough to know now that Tansy is your half-sister and that Joshua was her father and

315

that I loved him very much.' She watched the colour drain from his face and then returned to her syllabub

'God!' he gasped. 'It explains so much. Delilah . . .'

'Does not know Tansy is her mother and I would be obliged if you did not mention it.'

His hands were shaking and he leaned towards her almost threateningly. 'Do many people know about this?'

'I've no idea. Why?' She stared at him challengingly. 'Does it matter?'

'Well . . .'

'William, I was a slave. I lived as your housemaids live for four years of my life. In a slave cabin. I *know*, as few white people could ever know, that blacks are no different to us. I loved a black man. I had the pain of never being able to admit to it. I loved your own father dearly but he came after. I could not even tell Louis I had a child and that perhaps is the saddest thing that ever happened to me. I am telling you about my life so that you can understand why I am careful of the slaves, and all you say is do many people know of this. I ask you again, does it matter?'

'I suppose not,' he muttered but there was no conviction in it.

She sighed deeply. 'Oh, William, I'm sad to see you become so pompous.'

'Mama, I'm sorry. I do not mean to be,' and suddenly he sounded humble.

'Then don't.' She tapped him on the arm with her fan and said, 'We will talk about it no more. Tell me instead your own news. How is Precious?'

He was eager to change the subject, but she knew he would brood on what she had told him and come back to it on another occasion. Guilt began to prick at her for dealing him such a profound shock. William found it difficult to cope with anything even remotely unpleasant. He was the last person on earth who should have had such an unconventional parent and strange daughter, but somehow he had managed to cope with Precious. Perhaps in time he would come to terms with his mother.

'Precious is well,' he said, his face brightening, 'and Mama, such an extraordinary thing has happened. She has a suitor.'

'Ah!' said Amelia, trying to hide her surprise.

'And you will never guess who.' He was beaming.

'Who? Tell me.'

'James.'

'Zach's James?'

'No other. Zach came visiting with the family when they were on their way to see you in the spring, do you remember? Precious was much taken with James. She could not take her eyes off him and she followed him around the entire time he was here. He is of course most handsome. She did not speak much, but she listened to him and responded and she played her harpsichord for him. But different music, gentle, loving music. It was most extraordinary and he seemed to like her. Since then he has been back many times, paying court. It would not be fair to say that this has changed her. She is still a problem and,' he raised his eyes to the ceiling, 'so spiteful with the staff. I have had to keep her from the kitchen since she tried to attack the cook with a kitchen knife, but when James is about she is softer and easier to deal with.'

'Well!' Amelia said, not sure what else to say.

William sounded almost shy. 'I think he may ask for her hand.'

'William, she's barely fourteen.'

'She has the body and the bearing of a much older woman. I think my Precious was born adult. There has never been anything childish about her. In my reckoning she is ready for marriage and it seems that James believes the same.'

James must be mad! was Amelia's first thought, and then she saw the hand of Zach in this. He had always wanted Macabees and lost it when William married Isobel. If James married Precious, as crazy as she was, Macabees would be firmly within Zach's family when William died. But could Zach, would Zach, sacrifice his son in such a way? Yes, he would, she thought.

'And what will you say if he does ask for her hand?'

'I shall give him my permission.'

'You think that is a good idea?' Amelia could not look her son in the face. She busied herself with her claret.

'What else can I do?' His voice was anguished. 'If it would make her happy I must allow it. I know what you are thinking. Uncle Zach will be persuading James to consider her. I know how he longs for his family to own Macabees, and one day, this way, it will be theirs. But does it matter? I would like more freedom to devote to my work on the Council. The boy can run the plantation. What does anything matter after you and I are gone? If she wants him for a husband, and he is prepared to take her, I cannot refuse her.' He lowered his voice. 'Poor bereft child, I cannot refuse her anything.'

'You should marry again and have other children,' she urged.

He was affronted. 'There will never be any woman for me but Isobel. I love her only and always will.'

She sighed. William had inherited her own single-mindedness. 'Then we shall just have to wait and see how it all works out,' she said. 'Perhaps, as you believe, it will all be for the best.'

But her heart bled for James as her carriage rocked over the rough road to Basse-Terre. James was handsome, strong, and above all kind. Were they being unfair to Zach? Was it James's good heart that was causing him to court Precious? Precious was certainly remarkably pretty, her rare smiles dazzling, but she was not normal. Nothing about her was normal. What kind of life could James possibly share with her?

She voiced her fears to Tansy as they sat taking tea on the veranda

317

overlooking Pall Mall Square, watching the small world of Basse-Terre drift by.

'Ruby has always been convinced Precious is evil,' Tansy said. 'She prays to her dark gods for her, but she hates to be in the girl's presence. She is truly afraid of her. Poor James. Sacrificed for Zach's ambitions.'

'You don't think it's his own kind heart?'

'I think Zach is using James's kind heart. Can you not stop it, Mama?'

It was some years now since Tansy had begun calling her 'Mama' and every time she did Amelia felt a small dart of happiness.

'I don't think I should interfere.'

'Maybe not. And we have our own problems, have we not? Delilah is in town. She's been here since Sunday. Robin saw her at the tavern.'

'I came looking for her. I thought she might be there. Tansy, is she . . .' She could not bring herself to put the question.

'Whoring? I think so. I don't know. Ben doesn't say, nor does Ruby, but then they wouldn't. Robin offered Delilah work. He would be glad of some help at the warehouse. The business is going well, but the work bores him. He's reluctant to go back to sea. He enjoys family life and the children and doesn't want to miss them growing up. But she laughed in his face. She said she didn't believe in work. Work was for slaves. It breaks my heart, Mama. I so long to tell her the truth, but I fear it's too late.'

'Well yes,' Amelia murmured.

Tansy threw up her hands. 'History repeats itself,' she said ruefully.

'It seems to.'

'But I don't think there will be the same happy ending between her and me as you and I share,' Tansy said sadly. 'I fear she is lost to us both.'

Delilah had been staying with Ruby since she arrived in Basse-Terre. They had met up at the Sunday market and gone back to Ruby's little house in Irishtown together. Irishtown was a slum, but that did not bother either of them; Delilah because she had no interest in her surroundings, and Ruby because it was her own little house, bought with Bella's money.

When Truly and Daniel came home, Bella handed over her savings to Ruby, as promised. Ruby then offered the money to Amelia in return for her freedom. Amelia refused to take it but gave Ruby her freedom anyway. She left Elsewhere instantly and went to Basse-Terre where she started a pie and cake shop. Ruby was a good cook, and the shop did well. In the thirteen years she had been free, she had become comfortably off. In the beginning she had found all the black bucks she wanted, but now, in her mid-fifties, men were no longer a priority. She said if she never had another she wouldn't care.

Food had taken the place of men. Ruby was fat. Her bottom and her bust were enormous, two great curves turning her into a mobile S. Way back, just after she left Elsewhere, Zach had come calling as soon as he found out where she was. It gave her the greatest pleasure of her life to send him on his way. She had imagined herself spitting on him, telling him he was the worst lover she had ever had. She meant to hurt him, accuse him of murdering her son, but when it came to the crunch she could not bring herself to do or say any of it. Ruby was a realist. She accepted that Sam had been doomed the moment he murdered the driver. So she let Zach no further than her doorstep and merely informed him that she didn't have to fuck with him any more.

'But I thought you wanted to,' he cried, bewildered.

The big, silly, vain man standing before her looked like a hurt child. She relented.

'Well, maybe I did at the time,' she soothed.

She had seen him on the street just a couple of months previously. It took him a minute, but he recognised her through all the blubber and his face crumpled as if someone had stolen his dreams. She often wondered if he guessed that his indiscretions with her had led Amelia to find Truly and Daniel. She toyed with the idea of telling him how he had been tricked, but guessed she would probably never get round to it.

She had told the story to Delilah who thought it the most wonderful joke. Ruby was Delilah's best friend, recipient of all her confidences. It was Ruby she told of her boredom with Juba.

'Beats me how that man ever made one baby, let 'lone two,' she said scornfully. 'He like that,' she waggled her middle finger dismissively. 'Not like them men at the factory, now they know how to fill a gal. And he don' even know how to kiss.'

'At least he be black,' Ruby said.

'But he ain't no buck.' The middle finger waggled again. 'And he that humble all the time it drive me crazy. Yes, mistress 'Melia, no, mistress 'Melia, anything you says, mistress 'Melia. It make me sick.'

'Why you hate Mistress 'Melia so much?' Ruby asked her.

' 'Cos she wanted to make me somethin' I don' be.' Delilah said flatly. Ruby couldn't argue with that and dropped the subject. She herself had good feelings about Mistress Amelia and she didn't want to fall out with Delilah over them. Best to stay quiet.

She was aware that Delilah was an alley cat. Each night the girl went out in the dark looking to be fucked. And she didn't want paying for it. She just wanted fucking. Ruby had been hot herself in her day, but she did not understand this indiscriminate need for a man. She didn't want to judge, however, and mentally shrugged. People were people and nothing would change them.

This time Delilah had stayed in Basse-Terre longer than usual. She had spent two nights at the tavern where Ben would have given her (and whoever she had picked up) a room. Ben saw it as a matter of business. As long as the room was paid for, he figured that whatever Delilah did was none of his affair. Not that a room was imperative for Delilah. A hay loft, the back of a cart, pretty much anywhere would do. Delilah's couplings were rarely long drawn out. But Ruby had made it clear that she could not bring back strange men to the little house in Irishtown, and Delilah accepted that.

They were having a bite of breakfast together when Delilah suddenly said, 'I not goin' back to Elsewhere.'

Ruby's first thought was a selfish one. What was she going to say if the girl wanted to stay with her permanently? Ruby liked her home to herself.

'Why not?' she asked cautiously.

' 'Cos I can' stand it. Can' stand that Juba slobberin' over me. Can' stand seeing them slaves in the fields and the factory while I got no work. Can' stand bein' tied down by them runny-nosed kids he put on me. Can' stand any of it. I wants to be free.'

'Delilah, considering you be a slave, you be the freest person I ever knowed,' Ruby told her.

'Don' mean slave-style freedom. I means,' she hesitated, and her voice changed to that of a white woman as if she could not express herself any other way. 'I mean freedom of the spirit. Freedom of the heart. Freedom to be my own person.'

'But you b'long to Mistress 'Melia.'

'So they tell me, but she has never told me. She has never once in my whole life treated me as if I were a slave. Explain that to me.'

Ruby rapidly considered whether or not she should tell the girl the truth. And then decided against it. This one would never forgive as Tansy had done.

'Don' think I can do that. Guess p'haps she just need a pet and you got chosen.'

'I'd rather be a slave. I don't want to be anyone's pet.'

'So what you gonna do?'

Delilah shrugged her slim shoulders. 'Suppose I could whore. Might as well get paid for it.'

Ruby chuckled. 'It be a living, but s'pose 'Melia wants her pet back at Elsewhere? You don' have freedom of the spirit or anythin' else. She can do with you 'xactly what she want.'

'I think she'll let me go,' Delilah said slowly. 'If Tansy asks her to.'

'And why you think Tansy gonna do that?'

Delilah thought about the question and in answering reverted to being black. 'Don' rightly know,' she said. 'It just a feelin' I be havin'. But I reckons she will.'

Ruby wasn't altogether surprised when she found Amelia on her doorstep. It had been more than a year since the two women had met and Ruby was shaken by how thin her former mistress had become. Amelia was as pretty as ever, her face fine-drawn, the leaf-green eyes smiling, and the curly hair still with all the bounce and life it had ever had. But there were lines round her mouth, and she was thin. Really thin.

'Looks like you needs some o' my meat,' Ruby said, patting her thighs as she ushered Amelia into her small parlour. 'I gonna feed you my honey cakes. You needs fattenin' up.'

'I find I'm not interested in food these days,' Amelia said. 'But I am always interested in your honey cakes.'

'Then you shall have some.' She made sure Amelia was comfortably seated and then left her while she prepared tea and cakes.

'Them fine friends o' yourn gonna be wondering what you doin' visitin' with me,' Ruby said as she poured. 'But I knows why you be here. You be lookin' for Delilah, ain't that it?'

'That's it.' Amelia nodded her head. 'And you know where she is, don't you?'

'Not at this actual minute. But yes. I knows where she is.'

'And are you going to tell me?'

'Sure.' Ruby grimaced. 'But you got troubles. She say she not goin' back to Elsewhere.'

Amelia put down her teacup rather too gently. 'I wondered when she would make that decision. But what about her babies?'

'Seems to me,' Ruby said slowly, 'they don' be her first concern. She talkin' about freedom of the spirit and the soul. Guess she just mean freedom.'

'From responsibility,' Amelia suggested.

'Come on now, mistress, when did a slave have any responsibility 'cept to do what she told?' Ruby knew she was mocking, but sometimes these white folk were too much to bear.

'What does she want?' Amelia asked.

'Tol' you. Freedom of the spirit and the soul. She talkin' about goin' whorin',' Amelia winced, 'says she might as well get paid for it, and there's truth in that. But maybe she won'. She thinks that Tansy will give her money.'

'I'll give her money.' Amelia's voice was angry.

'But she don' want you' money. She don' want nothin' from you.'

Amelia's head dropped into her hands.

'Listen, Mistress 'Melia,' Ruby said gently, 'why don' you let her go? You won with Tansy. You ain't gonna with this one. In time, maybe, she'll come home again. Most times, most folks do.'

'Oh, Ruby, I pray to God you're right. If not what will become of her?'

Ruby considered the matter. 'Guess she'll become the best whore this town's ever seen,' she said, and then gave a deep rumbling chuckle. She was pleased when Amelia's face cracked into a reluctant grin.

'Well, as long as she's good at something . . .'

Amelia finished her tea and rose to go. She put her arms round Ruby who hugged her tight, noting again the frailness of the woman who had been her mistress.

'God bless you, Ruby,' Amelia said.

*   *   *

James Quick was nervous as he rode up the long driveway to the grim, grey pile of Macabees. It was unlike him not to be fully at ease. He was a cheerful young fellow of twenty-two, brought up with every advantage and with all the confidence that money can give. He was perhaps not as bright as his sister, Julia. More like his father in that it took him a while to work things out, and like his mother in that he enjoyed the pleasures of life. In spite of being something of a dandy himself, Zach complained that James thought more of fine clothes and social gatherings than matters of business.

This was the eighth time in six weeks that he had called on Precious Quick. He was not entirely sure why except that his father kept urging it. But if it had just been his father's interest in Macabees, he would not have been riding on this sullen hot day when he could have been cool in the shade somewhere.

Precious Quick was the reason he was nervous. She both fascinated and troubled him. She was extraordinarily good-looking with white-blonde hair, eyes so pale blue that they looked as if they had been washed and left in the sun. Her mouth was a neat, small, pale pink bow. Her chin was perhaps a mite too square, but it was balanced by a long, straight nose with nostrils that flared. Her face was too strong for prettiness and, he thought, all the better for it. She was also mysterious; intriguing. He knew people said her silence was caused by the fact that she was touched in the head but he could not believe there was anything truly wrong with her. The way she played the harpsichord, and the business brain, which he himself so lacked, surely proved that her odd manner was brought about by finding the world around her lacking her own perceptions. She was, he believed, too strong, too sensitive, too clever to suffer the many fools who surrounded her.

And yet there was something frightening about her. That cold blue stare which she turned on others was chilling. But she never turned the hostile glare on him. There was a different light in her eyes when she looked at him. At first he had thought the look to be rapacious, but now he had convinced himself it was not that at all. It was, he believed, a look of passion. He just wished she would talk to him a little more, tell him her feelings, but it was as if she closed a door on him when he asked her questions. She just half-smiled, a secret smile that did no more than turn up the corners of her lips. He wanted to find the key to her. He wanted to learn what lay behind that strange smile. But he was certain of one thing. She was attracted to him.

His cousin William greeted him with much back-slapping and hearty urging that he make himself at home. His effusive manner rather surprised James. Normally his cousin was a reserved man.

'Come to see Precious, have you?' William was all uncharacteristic joviality. 'She'll be pleased you're here.' He mopped a high forehead that was beaded with perspiration. 'She has not been well for the past few days.'

James was alarmed by this news. 'Nothing serious, I trust?'

'No, no. Not at all. She's much calmer today. You'll find her in the music room. You know the way, don't you?'

The music room was silent as James knocked and then opened the door. As he did so a blast of noise came from the organ, making him jump and leap back. Precious was at the keyboard and for the first time he experienced that dead, menacing look. Then she saw who it was and her expression changed. The eyes took on a feverish glitter and the music became gentle and sentimental, though underlying it there was still a throbbing, sinister bass note.

He sat quietly and listened until she stopped playing, her blonde head bowed over the keyboard. He rose to his feet and lightly touched her on the shoulder. She whirled round on the stool, and to his dismay he saw that her teeth were bared. Again, her expression changed as she looked into his face. She had forgotten he was there.

'Your papa tells me you have been unwell,' he said gently.

She nodded, and her eyes filled with tears.

'They are angry with me,' she whispered.

'Who is angry with you?' he asked, his hand on the pommel of his sword. 'Who dares to be angry with you?'

'Prissie. Papa. Everyone.'

'But why?'

Her mouth closed into a tight thin line, and she stared at him without speaking.

'Why?' he asked again.

'Mustn't,' was all she said, moving her hands as if she was about to push him away. But it seemed to him she was pleading with him; that she needed his help. He felt the fascination drawing him towards her again. Soon, very soon, he was sure she would reveal herself to him, all reserve gone.

'Will you walk with me in the gardens?' he asked her.

She looked at him, considering, mouth drawn into a tight bud. She was a tall girl with a full bosom and narrow waist, perfectly built for the fashion. She wore an ice-blue dress, cut low to reveal the curve of her fully developed breasts and laced lightly at the front. The skirt was very full, stiffened with whalebone to stand away from her body. He found it hard to believe that she was not yet fifteen.

He held out his hand and she took it and rose to her feet. As her hand closed almost too tightly over his, he felt a frisson run through him, a frisson communicated from her. He gasped and her eyes met his with a look of query and something else he could not read.

'You are very beautiful,' he said, his voice low.

She smiled without speaking and dropped an awkward curtsy. Her clumsiness touched him. He had noticed that there were times when she was unsteady on her feet and when they walked together she held onto his arm on rough ground. At the balls which were now so popular in Basse-Terre she would never dance, but sat alone, eyes glittering, watching others. She would not even dance with him and he believed

323

it was because she knew that she was ungraceful and did not wish to make a display of it.

From the music room they only had to step through long doors to be in the open air. It was still hot and sullen, but the path that led down to the stream was well-shaded. They walked in silence, Precious still holding his hand. James could not understand his own emotions. His feelings towards this girl were so complex. He was half repelled by her, half drawn to her. He found it exciting, perhaps because her temperament was so different from his own easy-going, cheerful personality. He felt a compulsion to make her happier since he had persuaded himself that her strangeness was caused by deep unhappiness. Poor girl, to have lost her mother at birth – a mother who had suffered so badly in her own childhood. James believed that he could make up to her for all these misfortunes.

He also dreamed of kissing her, and wondered what it would be like to lie with her. James had already experimented with the slave girls, but they merely assuaged importunate urges. It would be different with a white girl. If he were to lie with Precious he would be gentle and kind, there would be spirituality in their joining. He would show her, innocent that she was, the greatest pleasure of life, and he was certain that instead of feeling simply relief, as he did with the slave girls, with her he would find paradise.

They reached a wooden seat which William had placed by the stream. Misty Stacia jutted from the sea ahead and looked close enough to touch. To their left was the bulk of Brimstone Hill where slaves, reduced by distance to ants, hewed the rock as they carved out the ramifications of the fortress being constructed there. But James had eyes only for Precious.

In his many visits he had discovered that conversation was difficult and he had become used to being silent with her; she seemed to prefer it that way. When he did speak, she would nod and sometimes briefly respond.

'It saddens me to know that you have been unwell,' he said. Her hand was still clutching his and she turned to look him full in the face.

'You would not be angry with me?' she asked, startling him by the clarity and forcefulness of the question.

'Never!' he said stoutly. 'I cannot imagine such a thing.'

She gave a long, quavering sigh, and then to his astonishment she took her hand from his, placed her arms round him, almost squeezing the breath from his body, and kissed him. It was no child's kiss. Her damp mouth, slightly parted so that he could feel the tip of her tongue, stirred him into instant life. He had never experienced such a kiss. The slave girls stoically permitted whatever he chose to do, but they did not kiss, and he had no desire to kiss them.

It was a long kiss. She clung to him for a full minute, pressing her mouth and body into his. Then she drew back, leapt to her feet and without speaking turned and ran back to the house.

324

Stunned, James stared after her retreating figure, trying to quell the ardour she had aroused. The kiss was not a ladylike thing to do, but then Precious could not be judged by ordinary standards. Precious did nothing that conformed. If she had kissed him, he reasoned, it was because she loved him and it was her way of telling him so. Did he love her? he asked himself and after consideration told himself that he did. His erection also told him he did. In time, when they were married, his love would break through all her reserves. He thought of the unexpected kiss again, and again the fire rose in his belly. Marriage was the answer. When they were alone together in the deepest intimacy permitted to man and woman, she would open to him like a flower. He must marry her, and soon. The thought struck him that they were cousins, but with so few white women to choose from on these islands, if cousins did not marry no one would wed.

He resolved that he would speak to Uncle William this very minute and ask for Precious's hand. He had no doubts that she would accept him and that they would live happily ever after.

He hurried back to the house and found William just climbing into the saddle.

'Are you off to town?' James shouted.

William leaned to pat the restless horse's neck. 'Only to the factory yard.'

'I wanted to see you. May I ride with you?' His own horse was tethered near the door of the house.

'If you wish,' said William. 'I have to see the overseer. There has been some unrest among the slaves.'

'Is it serious?' James asked as he mounted.

His cousin hesitated and then uttered a flat 'No.' James had the impression he did not wish to discuss the matter.

'Your mama is well?' William asked, changing the subject as they set off down the path.

'In fine health,' James said politely, 'but I wanted to speak to you about Precious.'

William turned to give him a sharp look. 'Oh?'

There seemed to be no point in beating about the bush. 'I would like to ask for her hand in marriage, William.'

William reined in his horse, his face troubled. 'You love her?' he asked.

'I do.'

'This is not your father's doing?'

James was offended. 'I have told you, sir, I love your daughter. It has nothing to do with my father.'

'Have you mentioned this to her?'

'No, sir. I thought since she is so young I should speak to you first.'

William shook his head and stared down at where his hands held the reins. 'She is not easy,' he muttered.

'I know. But I think I understand her.'

325

William turned to look him full in the face. 'I must say to you, James, that nothing would make me happier than for you and my daughter to be wed. But I must also warn you that no one, *no one* understands Precious.'

'I believe that I do,' James said firmly, and convinced himself of it. The older man sighed. 'Perhaps,' he said. 'Perhaps it is possible.'

'Then I have your permission?'

William nodded reluctantly and kicked his horse into moving again. 'Why don't you go and ask her?' he said and spurred the horse into a gallop. James, suddenly left behind, stared after him, his head full of questions. Then he turned and rode back towards the house, looking for Precious.

'You be comin' to the market?'

Delilah was wearing a full, brilliant-red skirt with a tightly laced, low-necked white bodice. A kerchief was tied round her wild hair, not hiding but enhancing its luxuriant mass. She knew she looked good. She knew she looked like a gypsy with her dark eyes and skin but near-European features. Her glass told her that she would have no trouble finding herself a man in the market today.

Ruby was watching her quizzically and Delilah wondered if perhaps she was outstaying her welcome. She had been at the Irishtown house for nearly two weeks. Juba had come looking for her but she had sent him on his way back to Elsewhere, telling him she was never going back, and that if Amelia wanted her, Amelia could come and get her.

'Guess you be nothin' but a runaway slave,' Ruby told her.

' 'Melia ain't gonna do nothin',' she said defiantly.

'Why you think that?'

The question stopped Delilah. Why did she think that? There wasn't any answer except that a gut feeling told her that Amelia would not report her to the constabulary. She tossed her head. 'Don' know, but she ain't,' she retorted.

It was time she did something positive. She could not continue to live off Ruby indefinitely, but the only things she could do, like speak French, play the harpsichord and sing, weren't going to earn her a living and she was damned if she would be maid to any white woman. It wouldn't be wise to let it be known she could read and write. There was still the prospect of whoring at the tavern, but Delilah couldn't quite bring herself to be paid for it. She slept with many men, but she chose them for herself. They did not choose her. Delilah only fucked with men she wanted.

She was hungry for sex again now. It was two nights since a British sailor off a man o' war had taken her to bed at the tavern. The experience had not been particularly satisfactory. He was a handsome, curly-headed fellow, not unlike a young Robin Darnley, but once in bed he did not smell right. And his buttocks were too white and pallid. It was better than nothing but Delilah was more comfortable with black men. Black

326

men did not patronise her; some of them even liked her for what was white in her looks. White men treated her as though she were a black whore.

She and Ruby set off for the market together through the lively streets of the small town. Basse-Terre was expanding and a growing population of poor whites and freed mulattos lived there. The whites were mostly in the victualling trades or had bought slaves to hire out as jobbers. Many of them lived in Irishtown, and most were Catholic, though they were forbidden to worship in public. They had no right to vote or hold public office either. The coloureds earned modest livings as shopkeepers, fishermen, boatmen, drivers and porters if they had no real skills, though it was hard to get a licence to operate even the simplest jobs. The whites did not make it easy.

The market was as busy as ever, colourful, smelly and noisy. Delilah walked ahead of Ruby whose bulk was causing her to huff and puff in the heat. Delilah did not wish to be too closely connected with Ruby in public. People might think she was Ruby's daughter and suspect that she would grow to the same size one day.

She swayed through the market, shoulders back, breasts forward and hips grinding, knowing that folk were looking at her, the women with pursed lips, the men with lust in their eyes. She had no money to spend, but there was nothing she needed. She had come here to see and be seen.

They had been perambulating for only about five minutes when a man caught her eye. Most times the people who came to market were the same ones. It was not possible to know them all, but faces became familiar. This man she had never seen. He was tall and block-like in build with a huge head on square shoulders. His hair, like her own, was black and fuzzy but long for a Negro. He was definitely not all African. His skin was not white, not black, but like a burnished sheet of copper. And in his shining face was a large mouth and a pair of big pale-brown eyes set aside a long, narrow nose that slid upwards at the end. The narrow face was almost cruel, but the nose gave it a comical aspect. He was laughing out loud when she first saw him, a great roaring laugh that turned heads. He was not young. She judged around forty.

Perhaps the most unusual thing about him was his clothes. They were obviously not cast-offs. His stockings were silk, pale pink silk, his shoes were silver-buckled, his shirt fine linen. The deep maroon breeches were well-cut. He wore the clothes of a gentleman and he looked like a gentleman.

He would do, she decided.

At that moment he saw her. The laugh abruptly stopped as he looked at her, his face serious, and it dawned on her that they belonged to the same species, neither black nor white, not peasants like the others in the market and with unmistakable signs of money and education about them both. Their glances caught and fixed, then slowly, his face serious, he began to walk towards her. As they came face to face he bowed.

'Noname Benson, at your service, madam,' he said.

327

She blinked, then laughed. 'Noname?'

'The story told is that my black mother was so disgusted by the whiteness of my skin that she would not name me. My white father, on the other hand, found me white enough to acknowledge as his son. And you?'

It was an explanation he had obviously made before but listening to it she had the most extraordinary feeling that she had known him once, perhaps in another life and at another time. She sensed that this meeting was important and that their destinies were entwined in some way. For once, there was nothing sexual in the feeling. Only the knowledge of having, in some curious and inexplicable way, come home.

'And you?' he repeated.

Ruby, who had been hovering just behind Delilah spoke for her. 'She be Delilah Quick.' Ruby's face was amused as her sharp eyes scrutinised them. 'Guess I gonna leave you folk to get to know each other. See you tomorrow, 'Lila.' In spite of her bulk she managed to melt into the crowd, leaving Delilah still standing silent and staring.

'Delilah?' he said thoughtfully, and his voice was smooth, a white man's voice. 'A perfect name for the perfect woman.'

Recovering herself, she tossed her head. 'How do you know I'm the perfect woman? We haven't even spoken yet.' Her tone was cool, but she was furious with herself for speaking like a white woman.

He smiled. 'I just know,' he said simply, and offered her his hand. Without fuss, she took it; it was warm and dry. He stood looking down at her for a moment before saying, 'Where can we go to talk?'

'Talk?' she asked. Men did not normally wish to talk her.

'Talk,' he said firmly.

Without speaking she led him towards the Columbus Tavern. It took five minutes to reach the doors, and in that time neither of them said a word, nor did their hands unclasp. Inside the busy room, Ben was behind his bar. He looked up as they came in, grinned, and then raised his eyebrows at the splendour of her escort.

'This is Noname Benson, Master Clode,' Delilah said. 'We want to talk. May we use your parlour?'

Ben's rusty eyebrows rose further in his forehead. 'Talk?' he asked.

'Talk,' Noname Benson said even more firmly.

'My parlour?'

'Parlour,' Delilah's voice was patient, as if speaking to an idiot child.

Ben shrugged. 'Make yourself at home,' he said.

She led Noname behind the bar and into the small sitting room beyond, a room that Ben had made cosy for his own use when the tavern was quiet. She motioned Noname to seat himself in one of the high-backed chairs and settled herself in another.

'Are you a whore?' he asked, but his tone was interested rather than aggressive.

She was not offended. 'No,' she said. 'I choose my own men. I do not get paid for it.'

He nodded as if that was what he had expected to hear. 'And I do not pay,' he said.

She laughed, and with a gesture that took in all his finery said, 'I believe you. Now tell me who you are.'

He rose again, and bowed. 'Noname Benson—'

'I know that,' she interrupted. 'But who are you really?'

He understood what she meant.

'No name and no one,' he said. 'An appendage of my father, Richard Benson. Lucky? Yes, lucky. For some strange reason my father acknowledged me. Others he didn't. He was the overseer of a plantation on this island. Macabees.'

'*That* Benson,' Delilah breathed. 'He's legendary on this island.'

'For cruelty?'

She hesitated, and then nodded. 'I know about him,' she said. 'My mistress's son owns Macabees now. He married the Ramillies daughter.'

'The one that threw my father out?'

'I don't know. I was only small when it happened.'

'Isobel she was called,' Noname said, remembering. 'She called my father to her drawing room and told him he was not needed any more. She told him she wanted no more cruelty on her plantation, and that it would be better for him if he left the island. So that's what he did, taking me with him. I was twenty-four years old.'

'Where did you go?' Delilah asked.

'St Barthelemy, a tiny island north of here. Only eight miles long. It's barely fertile.' Suddenly he grinned. 'There's no sugar cane worth speaking of there, praise be. It won't grow. In fact, not much in the way of crops grows at all and so there are hardly any blacks. The folk who live there are French and dirt poor. They can't afford many slaves. And they work side by side with those they do have.'

'Why did you go there?'

Noname shrugged. 'We were heading for Anguilla where my father had an overseer's job arranged on a sugar plantation. We got blown off course. When he saw St Barth's, my father thought there were business opportunities there. The local French, he said, were peasants, with no judgement, no initiative. Primitive people. So we stayed. And we got rich. We're about the richest people on the island. My father supplies rum to the seamen who pull in and out of the harbour all the time. He has his own distillery. He owns a small shipyard, repairing boats and building them. He sells locally-grown timber all over the West Indies. It's tough timber used in shipbuilding and it's one of the few things that grows well on St Barthelemy. The two of us built the business up together. It's true my father is a cruel and ruthless man, though he never has been towards me. I sometimes wondered if he stayed on that island because life was going to be better there for me. Black people aren't despised on St Barth's and mulattos are accepted.'

'But your mother?'

'Benson was mother and father to me.'

329

'But you must have had a mother.'

He laughed again. 'Of course,' he said. 'She was called Truly, but she hated me and I hated her.'

Shaken, Delilah took a deep breath. 'I have a sort of aunt called Truly.'

'Everyone has a sort of aunt or uncle on these islands,' he said, suddenly abrupt. He seemed to want to change the subject. He said, 'Would that innkeeper friend of yours give us a drink?'

'Claret, ale or rum?' she asked.

He considered. 'A tankard of ale, please.'

She slipped out and came back with a tankard for him and a glass of claret for herself. He took a long draught and said, 'Now you. You're free?'

'I don' be free,' she said defiantly, lapsing into patois. 'I be a slave.'

He didn't believe her. 'Then tell to me how it be you don' be free,' he drawled. He was mocking her. 'And tell us for why you talk like that when you don' need to?'

Embarrassed she reverted to speaking properly. 'I am a slave,' she said, 'but mistress doesn't treat me like one.'

'Why not?'

'I don't know. No one seems to know who my father is, and my mother died when I was born. My mistress sort of took me over. My friend, Ruby, you met out there—'

'The huge woman?'

'Yes. She says I'm Mistress Amelia's pet. But I don't want to be anyone's pet.'

'Better to be a pet than a dog. Dogs get whipped. I bet you've never been whipped in your life.'

'No.'

'Me neither.' He grinned. 'Great, ain't it? We've got a lot in common, you and I. Bet your missing dad was white. We're just a pair of spoilt mulatto kids and ain't we the lucky ones.'

'I don't feel like that,' she muttered.

'Don't tell me,' he said. 'You feel you don't belong no place.' Again he was mocking.

'Yes.' Her tone was defiant.

'Listen, lady, you can belong any place you choose. Why don't you ask that mistress of yours for your freedom?'

'I wouldn't ask her for the time.'

He wrinkled his wide brow. 'Why? Is she bad to you?'

'No.' The word came out reluctantly.

'Don't you like her?'

'No.' This time the accent was positive.

'What did she do wrong?'

Delilah hesitated. What did Amelia do wrong? It was a difficult question to answer. Finally she said slowly, 'She confused me.'

'That's really terrible.' His voice was brisk, dismissing such nonsense.

Stung, she began to explain herself and as the tale of her childhood, her life with Juba, her disinterest in her two children poured out, she began to see herself more clearly. She was right in saying that Amelia had confused her with tantalising glimpses of a life and a style that would never be permitted to her. But it was her own stubbornness that had rejected any opportunities her upbringing might have offered her.

'I never felt I was lovable,' she finished dismally. 'I felt that my colour must be such a disappointment to Miss Amelia who tried so hard to make me white.'

'So you have had a lot of men?' he asked, his voice matter-of-fact. 'Looking for love?'

That was it, of course. She nodded.

He drained his glass and smiled at her. 'So what are you and I going to do now, Delilah Quick?'

She looked at him thoughtfully. She had never felt so comfortable with anyone in all her life. This man was an equal. They talked the same language except that he was more of a realist, and perhaps he was right. With just a few words he had made her face her own problems. He was also extremely handsome, though she had always preferred her men blacker in the past. But as his amber eyes twinkled at her over the big, promising mouth, that stirring began in her gut, that hot hunger and the sudden suspicion of damp juices gathering.

'What you wanna do?' She spun the patois out, rolling her eyes and mocking herself.

'Fuck?' he suggested. 'Best way I knows to get them preliminaries over and if you've been lookin' for love maybe this time you gonna find you've found it.'

Precious was not in the music room. James had been confident that he would find her there, and was momentarily nonplussed when there was no sign of her. He made his way back towards the great house, suddenly uneasy about what he was doing. It was the unexpected kiss and his reaction to it that had caused him to act so hastily. He realised gloomily that even Precious's father seemed to be offering him a warning, but he was painfully aware that, having chosen to ignore the warning, he had little choice short of behaving in an ungallant fashion but to propose to the girl.

In an attempt to rationalise what he had done, he told himself that all men briefly regretted the loss of their freedom and that his doubts were perfectly natural. But the sense of foreboding had not gone away when a house slave opened the front doors and let him into the great stone hallway. As the door closed behind him, the library door to the right opened, and to his relief Prissie appeared.

'Well, if it isn't James,' she said and hurried to take his hands in hers. 'What a pleasure to see you. Though,' and a small frown flitted across her brow, 'we have seen rather much of you lately. To what do we owe the honour?'

Surely she knew he was courting Precious. He had the impression that everyone knew it. But he liked Prissie and he knew she liked him. They were old friends. When they were all younger she had always accompanied Precious to family gatherings where she spent her time, along with Juba, amusing the children. Seeing her made him recall how difficult Precious had been at those gatherings and how only Prissie's firm common sense had been able to quieten her. Prissie had authority. She never behaved like a servant, and therefore all treated her as an equal.

'I was looking for Precious,' he blurted out.

'Ah. She is in her room. She was over-excited so I sent her to rest.'

He was silent for a moment. 'That will be my fault,' he finally confessed. 'I kissed her.'

Prissie's shrewd grey eyes regarded him. 'Did you kiss her or did she kiss you?'

'Well.' He did not know how to answer.

'Exactly,' she said briskly. 'Why did you want to see her?'

'I have just asked William for her hand in marriage,' he said, trying to sound enthusiastic. 'He has sent me to ask if she will have me.'

Prissie's face was, for a moment, a picture of dismay before she quickly recovered her normal composure.

'James,' she said slowly, 'You are both very young to wed. And Precious—'

'Needs me,' he said eagerly, convincing himself. 'I know what you are going to say, but she is different with me. She loves me. I'm sure of it.'

'And do you love her?'

'Yes,' he said stoutly. It was true. He did. The fact that he was a little afraid of her did not alter that.

Prissie sighed. 'Well, seeing the errand you are on, I suppose the master will not object if you visit her in her room. It is the fourth on the left at the top of the staircase.'

'Thank you, Prissie,' he said and, grateful to be ending this conversation, leapt towards the stairs. He was halfway up when he heard her call and turned back.

'Be careful, James. Please be careful,' she said, and her expression was troubled.

There was silence when he knocked on the fourth door to the left, and after three tries, he gently opened it. Precious was lying on the bed, on her back, her head on the pillows, eyes closed, breathing heavily. Her skirts were up across her chest. She still wore her stockings, but her white thighs, bare white belly and a bush of blonde pubic hair were visible. One hand was between her half-opened legs, and to his horror he saw that her moving hand held a slender glass vase, the bottom half of which was buried inside her.

She heard his gasp, turned her head, eyes open, the pale blue irises blurred as if in smoke. Staring at him, her hand moved faster and faster

332

as he stood helplessly watching, trying to control his own excitement at what he was seeing. He knew he should have been repelled, disgusted, but instead he had to restrain himself from joining her there on the bed and replacing the glass with himself. Then her body heaved and shuddered into stillness. The glass snapped in two and there was a stain of blood on her hand where she had been cut. She flung the remains of the ornament across the room and then regarded the red blood on her white skin with satisfaction. Her pink tongue came from between her thin lips to lick it away. She spread her legs wider and with a drop of blood brightening her bottom lip, stared at him challengingly.

'Now you do it to me,' she said, and there was no way he could have denied her or, indeed, himself.

Chapter Eighteen

Zach was at his desk in the court house in Old Road Town where he now sat as judge. He was pleased with himself. He had just managed to persuade the Governor that William Rosier-Quick should also sit on the bench. Despite lack of legal training most of the rich planters were judges, and he was anxious that the Quick family should be fully represented. He was also pleased with his son James, who was to marry Precious at the end of March, a month after her fifteenth birthday. Macabees would one day belong to the Quick family. After arriving as slaves only forty-two years ago, his family would be proprietors of three of the most important estates on the island. Zach had every reason to be satisfied with life.

He was somewhat put out when his clerk informed him that a Miss Prissie Tucker wished to see him. He had never approved of the arrangement whereby an ex-whore from Ben's tavern had brought up Precious and had promised himself that when he was Precious's father-in-law, Prissie would have to go.

He told the clerk to send her in. He was surprised by her dress and her demeanour. Prissie had become a handsome, well-dressed woman of certain age, most respectable in her grey gown and bonnet. She seated herself at his invitation, carefully smoothing her full skirts down over her shins. There was no trace of the whore. She looked what she now was, a middle-aged, responsible lady's maid.

'What can I do for you?' he asked.

'You must forgive me for visiting you unannounced,' she said, her voice composed. 'But I am very fond of your son James and would wish to save him from harm.'

What was the woman on about? 'Indeed,' he said disdainfully.

'I felt that I should speak to you regarding Precious Quick.'

He felt his face redden at the woman's impertinence.

'I beg you, sir, please do not let your son marry her.'

Zach began to bluster. 'Madam, this is intol—'

'She has always been strange and difficult, as you know,' she continued as if he had not spoken, 'but since she reached late puberty a year ago she has become not only difficult but dangerous. I fear for your son if he marries her.'

She was so earnest, so calm and convincing that Zach sat back in his seat.

'She cannot help it,' Prissie said, her voice sombre. 'It is as if her mind was locked at birth and someone threw away the key. She cannot escape from herself and this makes her angry with the world. She finds release from some of her anger through music, but unfortunately it can also take the form of cruelty. Precious likes nothing more than to see the slaves being flogged.' She nodded her head slowly to emphasise the point. She had his full attention now. 'It is her greatest pleasure. I accept, sir, that there are many women who enjoy the spectacle, but Precious takes it further. She likes to be permitted to flog the younger slaves herself. If your son should ever see her do this, I think he would no longer love her. Master William, understandably, has not informed your son of this side of her character, nor has he told him that she loves to watch the cock fights that the male slaves organise. Precious likes the sight of blood.'

Zach shivered at the thought but said defensively, 'It is not unknown for women to flog their slaves.'

'True.' Prissie nodded gravely. 'But over the past few weeks, since James has been calling on her, we have had serious trouble with Precious. She was found trying to murder a slave baby. She had twisted cord round its neck when the mother fortunately interrupted her. The slaves were already frightened of her and now they are even more restless. The master has given orders that she is not to be allowed near the slave compounds, but it is difficult to keep her away. You see, sir, she has these violent rages – not often, perhaps every four weeks or so – when she is almost uncontrollable. She is very strong and the rages make her stronger. Last week we found that she had cut off the heads of the house slaves' chickens with a kitchen knife. She explained she wanted to see them run headless. We found her splattered from head to foot with their blood. So you can understand, sir, that she is not suited to being a gentleman's wife.'

'She is different with my son,' he heard himself saying, knowing it sounded feeble and wishing he had never let the woman in. He did not wish to hear this. He did not wish to know.

'At the moment she may be different. But she has not the mental strength to stay that way. I myself have feared her when I have had cause to correct her. She has no sense of right and wrong and it seems impossible to instil this into her.'

He had heard enough. He rose to his feet placing his hands on his desk and leaning towards the woman sitting opposite.

'I do not wish to hear any more,' he hissed. 'I thank you for telling me, but I would be grateful if you would speak of it to no one else. I must now decide what is to be done. My son is in love. He can be stubborn. It may prove to be his decision.'

'But you will warn him, sir? No one else will. The master deludes himself that marriage will end all her problems.'

'He believes that?' Zach muttered.

'He persuades himself of it. But I know that marriage will change nothing.' Prissie had risen, tweaking her clothes back into order. 'One day, sir, something terrible will happen. It would be sad if it were to happen to your son.'

Zach felt the hairs on the back of his neck rise. He came round his desk and took her arm, leading her towards the door.

'You do not believe me, sir?'

'I think you exaggerate,' he said roughly.

'I am afraid,' she said composedly, 'that your ambition outweighs what should be concern for your son's happiness.'

'Madam, mind your own affairs. You are impertinent!' he thundered.

She looked at him coolly. 'And you, sir, are a fool.'

Puce with anger, he bundled her through the door, slamming it on her back. He wanted her gone so that he could think. But in his heart he already knew what he would do. And that was nothing.

Prissie was not prepared to leave it at that. She liked James. He had been quite the nicest of the children in the Quick family, a warm-hearted lad who could not bring himself even to tread on a beetle. James was a little helper to all the world. He wanted everyone to be happy and did all in his power to make them so. Even as a small boy he had had incredible patience. She could understand exactly why he was so drawn to the pathetic, pretty Precious and why he should delude himself that with him Precious would become a normal young woman. She was one of his lame dogs. But Prissie knew better than anyone that there was no possibility of Precious ever becoming normal and she did not see why James should be sacrificed on the twin altars of his father's greed and his own good nature.

She would speak to Amelia. Amelia was the one in the family with common sense and the only person that Zach ever listened to. She had to return to Macabees now before she was missed, but her plan was to go into Basse-Terre the following morning and enlist Ben's assistance for a meeting with Amelia. Maybe Ben would go to Elsewhere with her; being with him would make what she had to say easier.

Precious had been calmer for the past two months, and maybe it was true that the thought of marriage was helping her. Then a terrible thought struck Prissie. It was her habit to monitor carefully Precious's menstrual pattern. She had noticed early on that Precious was at her most difficult around twelve days after she had bled. It was at these times that, with help from Minta, she fed the girl calming potions. With all the excitement of the engagement, Prissie had not been keeping such a careful eye on her charge's cycle. As her horse picked his way over the rough track, she remembered that James had gone to Precious's room and made his proposal in that period when she was being given Minta's calming medicine. That was nearly three months ago and to her horror Prissie realised that Precious had not had a show of blood since.

'Oh my God,' she groaned. 'Oh my God!' and dug her heels into her ambling horse's side.

Back at the estate she went looking for Minta who would be busy somewhere in the great house. Minta and her mother had worked in the fields at Macabees after Matthew Oliver had sold her and Bessie all those years ago. Vincent Ramillies did not permit women slaves indoors and Bessie had soon died. Field work had been too heavy for her after a lifetime as a house slave. Minta, though not young, was tougher and had survived, to be brought back indoors after William's marriage to Isobel. In spite of what Minta knew of the Quick family's past, Amelia had urged that she be employed as a maid. Minta, long and stringy with oddly bowed legs, had a surfeit of energy. She never stopped cleaning, insisting that in a house the size of Macabees there was always something that needed cleaning or polishing or what she called a 'little bit o' love.'

It made her hard to track down in the rambling house, but she had her own reasons for keeping busy. No one ever worried about keeping an eye on where she was or what she was doing, it was assumed she was working, and that gave her the opportunity to gather herbs and plants and concoct her potions without interference. Her mother had been a gifted herbalist. Minta had all Bessie's knowledge and more that she had discovered for herself.

Prissie found her in the ballroom where she was on her hands and knees washing the wooden floor, singing to herself. The slave was in her fifties but looked older, her heavy face deeply lined, her hands like work-hardened claws.

'Minta,' Prissie hissed. 'I must talk to you.'

The black woman leaned back on her bony knees and wiped the sweat from her forehead with the back of her hand. She methodically wrung out her floor cloth and hung it over the side of the wooden bucket before scrambling to her feet and following Prissie up the stairs to what had been the nursery.

The two women were not exactly friends, but they were comfortable together. They shared both the burden of Precious and a few secrets. When James had begun calling on Precious, Minta had confided in Prissie that her father had been Matthew Oliver.

'My mammy were a handsome woman when she were young,' she explained, 'and for a while there the master fucked her most nights. Folks thought she'd put a spell on him on account of her bein' a med'cine woman. Then Bella come to Windsong, and it be her turn. He never did take much heed o' me. I were too black.' She gave a great cackle of laughter. 'Strange, ain't it. That stuck-up Charlotte be my half-sister. 'Magine her face if she knowed. And I be auntie to Master James.'

'Another good reason why we should do something to help him,' Prissie said grimly.

With the nursery door firmly shut, Prissie poured them both a neat rum from the bottle she kept in her room.

'We're going to need this,' she said. 'I have bad news. I think Precious is pregnant.'

Minta did not seem overly surprised. 'How long she gone?' she asked.

'Guessing, about three months. Since the day I let James go up to her room.' She shook her head, exasperated. 'He said he was going to propose to her, not consummate the wedding before it took place.'

'Don' 'spect he had much chance if she was in one of her states. She like a hot bitch dog those times,' Minta said. 'Might not even be him.'

This awful thought turned Prissie white. 'But who else?'

Minta chuckled. 'Ain't gonna be anyone black, for sure. That gal hates the slaves jus' about as much as I hates her.' Minta always made it clear that her help with Precious was given for Prissie's sake only.

'But there isn't anyone else white possible. It has to be James,' Prissie said.

Minta shrugged. 'Don' be no cause for upset. They gonna marry, ain't they?'

'I want to try and stop the wedding,' Prissie said firmly. 'It's not right. But if she's pregnant . . . Minta, can you stop it?'

'The baby?'

'Yes.'

The woman considered. 'Don' know. Time gettin' on. It be dangerous. P'haps she die.'

Minta's face as she offered this possibility was inscrutable.

Prissie was silent. Was Minta suggesting she could end the problem once and for all? Guiltily, she could not help thinking that perhaps that would be no bad thing. But there was Master William to consider. He had had too much tragedy already, and for all her strangeness, he dearly loved his daughter. Prissie shook herself.

'I'm going to have to talk to Mistress Amelia,' she muttered, half to herself.

'Now that do be a good idea,' Minta said.

Prissie slept badly and in one of her many waking moments decided that she would go straight to Elsewhere without Ben, otherwise the journey would take too long and she would be missed. She did not want Master William to find out what she was planning. She was not even sure herself why she was so anxious to prevent this marriage except that there was no one, no one at all, who really understood the full complexity of Precious. The girl had been Prissie's unrewarding charge for a long time. She was demanding, violent, cruel, talented yet vacant, and sometimes heartbreakingly sad and pathetic. All Precious's emotions were on the surface, but the one emotion she did not seem to possess, the great void in her, was affection. Prissie was paid well for her work, and in order to keep herself sane she insisted that she had some free time. She did not believe that anybody could stand twenty-four hours a day of Precious, and certainly not as a labour of love, for the truth was that Precious was unlovable.

The rough track between Macabees and Elsewhere was well worn and easy to follow. Behind loomed Brimstone Hill and the strange smell of sulphur that came from the land beneath the fortress, ahead rose the mass of cloud-capped Mount Misery. Prissie enjoyed the ride. It was always a relief, a little holiday, to be away from Precious. This morning Minta was keeping an eye out for her – discreetly. The slaves did their best to keep out of Precious's way. She had a habit of spitting at them and, if they were close enough, clawing at their faces.

Amelia greeted her warmly at Elsewhere, but Prissie was shocked at how fragile she had become. As they settled themselves in a small sitting room, she thought that Amelia looked as if a strong wind would carry her away. The green eyes were as bright and smiling as ever but there was an alarming pallor to the skin.

'Are you ill?' Prissie heard herself blurt out.

Amelia shook her head. 'I do have some pain occasionally, but it's not significant. I have little interest in food, though. As I become older the heat of the island troubles me. It's strange, but after all these years I find myself thinking of Devon. The winters were so cold and crisp in Devon.' She sounded wistful.

'You should take a trip home,' Prissie said.

'Too late for that. My life and family are here. Tell me, how is William?'

'He is well.'

'And Precious? Is she looking forward to her wedding?'

Prissie hesitated, then found her courage. 'That's what I've come to talk to you about, Mistress Amelia. I've already been to see Master Zach, but he would not listen. This marriage is the most terrible mistake.'

'I know.'

Amelia had spoken so quietly that at first Prissie thought she had misheard.

'You know?'

The greying russet head nodded. 'But tell me, why do you think so?'

Prissie recounted what she had said to Zach. 'But there is more,' she said, 'things I could not bring myself to say to him. She is so strange' – she hesitated, not knowing exactly how to explain – 'with her body. Sometimes she takes off all her clothes and tries to walk naked about the house. And she does, well,' she hesitated again, uneasy speaking of such matters to a lady, 'things to herself. Things that are not decent and she does not care who sees. Minta makes potions that calm her, but at certain times of the month we dare not leave her alone. Her instincts are primitive, like those of an animal.'

Amelia's head was bent as she listened. 'Then perhaps,' she suggested, 'married life will help her.' But there was no conviction in her voice.

'No. Nothing will help her. It is beyond any human power that I know of. This marriage is cruel and wicked for James. His young life will be despoiled.' She struggled for words. 'No one knows, no one understands what she is truly like. But remember, I've known her all her life; if she and James marry, it will end in tragedy, I'm sure of it. Please, I beg of you, speak to your brother. He listens to you.'

'The day is so near . . .'

'I know. I should have spoken before, but I was afraid to interfere. And there is more. I'm sure she's pregnant.'

Amelia's hand flew to cover her mouth. 'By James?' she whispered.

'I think so. She hates the slaves and there are no other white men on the plantation who would interest her. Though at those times . . .'

'Anyone?' Amelia asked quietly.

'Maybe.'

The two women sat in silence, and then Amelia sighed.

'It would be as much a waste of my breath as it was yours to talk to my brother,' she said finally. 'He won't listen to me, not any more. But maybe James's mother would have some influence. I will speak to her, and we must find out if this coming child is James's. If it is, I fear the lad has cooked his own goose. He'll have to go through with the marriage.'

'Unless . . .'

Amelia's eyebrows rose in query.

'She lost the child,' Prissie finished, and then added tentatively, 'Minta . . .'

Amelia lifted an admonitory hand. 'No. It's too dangerous. Whatever happens, the pregnancy must take its course.'

Reproved, Prissie dropped her head. Amelia climbed painfully to her feet and moved to put her hand on the other woman's head.

'I have never said to you, Prissie, how grateful I am for all you have done for my granddaughter over the years. It cannot have been easy. You have been more loyal than anyone could have expected, and you were right to come to me. This marriage is wrong, but I fear it may be out of our hands. I will do my best, as you have done, but if it goes through, all we can do is hope. And pray.'

After Prissie left, Amelia had Pierre send someone to Windsong to inform them that she would be visiting the day after tomorrow unless this was inconvenient. She was not looking forward to the journey, but it would have to be done. She had told Prissie that the pains she suffered were insignificant, but this was not true. Sometimes she could barely move for pain in her gut, and what the doctor provided for her ease was of little use. Perhaps, she thought, Minta might be of more help. She should have asked Prissie, but then that would have been making a fuss.

She was taking the afternoon rest she could no longer do without when a disapproving Pierre came to inform her that she had yet another unexpected visitor.

'I was uncertain whether or not to send him away, madam,' he said, 'but he was so persistent, and so . . .'

'So?' she prompted.

Pierre seemed lost for words. 'You will see, madam,' he finally said.

She did see. The man waiting in her hallway was big, copper-coloured, and most beautifully dressed. His clothes and the panache with which he wore them could have given instruction to Zach. As she appeared, he bowed.

'Have I the pleasure of meeting Mistress Rosier-Quick?' he asked.

'You have.'

'Noname Benson, at your service.'

Amelia froze. Her mind went back over the years to the kitchen here at Elsewhere and a distraught Truly telling her rape at the hands of Benson, the Macabees overseer. And the results of that rape – a near-white child she would not name. Noname Benson.

What had he come for? To torment Truly? She would not have it.

'What can I do for you?' she asked icily.

'One small thing,' he said, smiling, and she noted how well he spoke and how pleasant the timbre of his voice was.

'And what is that?'

'Give Delilah her freedom so we can marry.'

She was stunned. 'Delilah?'

'Yes, Delilah. Your slave Delilah.'

She was about to protest that Delilah was not a slave and then stopped herself. Instead she said that he had better come into her sitting room where they could talk.

She seated him so that the light was full on his face. She did not want to miss a flicker of expression in this man. She placed herself in the shadows.

'How do you know Delilah?' she asked.

'I met her in Basse-Terre – you know, the way one does.'

There was a twinkle in his amber-flecked eyes that said it was not a question of their having been introduced and she felt a reluctant smile twitch her lips.

'And where is she now?'

'At this moment? In the kitchen of your home, talking to your slaves.'

'Ah,' said Amelia. 'She has come home.'

'Not for good,' he said gently.

She found herself liking this man. 'And what if I insist she stays here?'

'You won't.' His voice was full of confidence.

'You sound very certain.'

'I am. Because you love her. It is obvious you love her, though why you should . . .'

Pain sliced through Amelia, taking her breath away for a moment. The pain made many things that had troubled her seem much, much less important. She waited for a moment until she could breathe again and then sighed.

'I love her because she is my granddaughter.'

He nodded. 'I thought it might be something like that. Who is her mother? Tansy?'

Amelia nodded.

'Do you want her to know?'

'Of course I want her to know,' she said harshly. 'Tansy and I have always wanted her to know. But . . .'

'You were afraid for your own white skins?'

'Yes.'

'And yet my father, my cruel, hated, despised father had no such fears for himself. He accepted me completely.'

'Your father has the advantage of being a man and therefore is not judged,' Amelia said, suddenly sharp.

'True.' He rose to his feet and strode about the room, picking up an ornament here and there and inspecting it. Amelia watched him patiently.

'Will you give her her freedom?' he said eventually.

'Of course. She has always been free. It was just that I wanted to keep her with me, but she made her own decision and left.'

'And you will not object if we marry even though I am so much older than she is?'

'No. Not if you can find someone to marry you.' She relaxed in her chair. The pain had lifted and she found she was suddenly happy. This man, this well-spoken mulatto with his charming manners and knowing eyes would have been the answer to her prayers for Delilah had she known he existed. And exist he did. She began to hope that some happiness might be possible for her difficult granddaughter after all.

He sat down again and smiled at her. 'Our wedding will not take place here. I shall take her to my home. On St Barthelemy. There, folk would look askance if we were not wed.'

She felt a pang at the thought of the girl being so far away, but merely said, 'It is a Catholic island, is it not?'

'It is. Now,' he leaned towards her, 'I am not going to tell her what you have told me. It is not the time. But the day will come when she is assured and content in her own skin, when we have our own family and she learns what it is to be truly free and to be whoever she wants to be. Then she will appreciate what you have done for her, and only then will I tell her.' He was smiling, and she found herself smiling back.

'And if I am no longer here, you will see that she makes her peace with her mother?'

He looked at her with questioning eyes, taking in her pallor and her thinness, but making no attempt at soothing noises. 'Of course,' he said.

'Then thank you,' she said quietly. 'You have done me a great service.'

He nodded gravely. 'And you also for me. Delilah and I were made for each other, and you made Delilah.'

She laughed out loud. 'I'm so glad it was worth all the effort,' she said cheerfully.

He nodded, taking her remark with a seriousness she had not intended. 'Will you do me another service?' he asked, still grave-faced.

'If I can.'

'May I see my mother?'

It was Amelia's turn to be solemn. This was dangerous ground.

'Your mother is a wonderful woman,' she said slowly, searching for the right words. 'She is strong, brave and not one to waver or to change her mind. She is prouder of her ancestry than anyone else I know. She does not compromise. I doubt if she has ever forgiven your father, and I am afraid that means she may never accept you. She is old and tired and in ill health now, but you have much to be proud of in her. She may have rejected you and will probably continue to do so, but she has always been true to her race, and more particularly to herself. So,' Amelia drew a long breath, 'the answer to your request is that yes, you may see your mother if that is what you wish, but it might be less painful for you if you did not.'

'Nevertheless . . .'

She smiled. 'I thought that was how you would feel. Ask Delilah to take you to her, and then please bring Delilah to me.'

She waited quietly in her room. It did not take long. In quarter of an hour he was back, Delilah anxiously hovering behind. She thought she detected tears in his eyes.

'You were right,' he said quietly, 'but I am still glad I met her.'

Amelia decided to make her journey to see Charlotte in two stages rather than face the bone-shaking carriage ride from her end of the island to Windsong at the other in one go. The day after Prissie's visit, one of the male slaves sailed her from the jetty near Sandy Point to Basse-Terre where she begged a bed for the night from Tansy.

She wanted to see Tansy. She wanted to tell her about her encounter with Noname Benson and, more important, about the remarkable difference in Delilah. She also wanted to know if Tansy had met this amazing man who seemed to have tamed her fiery daughter.

'Oh, yes, I've met him,' Tansy said as they sat in the shade of her veranda. 'In fact I told him to go and see you. I hope that was the right thing to do. Delilah was still declaring that she would never ever beg you for her freedom, and I said in that case why didn't he ask you.'

'And he did.' Amelia raised her eyes skywards. 'I gave her the documents right there and then. It was extraordinary. Her eyes lit up, she held the papers to her chest and she said, "How can I thank you!" Fervently. Gratefully. I hadn't realised how important it was to her. I can't remember that it was ever that important to you. There was no surliness, no resentment. She was speaking normally, not in that damned patois, and it was obvious that she was happy and in love. I cannot believe our good fortune that she and Noname Benson discovered each other.'

'I feel the same.' Tansy put down the needlepoint embroidery she had been working at and stared into space. 'I wondered, just wondered, if it would be safe to tell her the truth.'

'I half did,' Amelia confessed. 'I told him.'

'Mama! Was that wise?'

'I think so.' She repeated the conversation she had had with Noname. 'I think he speaks good sense. Handled his way I believe it will all come right in the end.'

'I trust so,' Tansy said, and sighed, picking up her work again. 'But then I must face the problem of what to tell Mark and Melanie.'

'If Delilah settles in St Barthelemy it may never be necessary,' Amelia said. 'We have to let her go. It will probably prove best for all of us.'

'Perhaps.'

The two women were silent with their own thoughts for a long moment, then Tansy giggled and said, 'It is the most remarkable thing that he is Truly's son. How he came to be such a polished fellow sired by the wicked Benson and born of prickly old Truly is hard to believe.'

'He wanted to meet Truly.'

'Oh dear.'

'Yes, oh dear indeed.'

'And did he?'

'Yes. She wouldn't speak to him. She barely even looked at him. Daniel was apparently dreadfully embarrassed and did his best to be hospitable. Truly just turned her back and walked away. Then after he had gone, she stormed into my sitting room and gave me a most uncomfortable ten minutes for having the temerity to let him near her.' Amelia shook her head and smiled. 'And yet I couldn't help feeling that she was pleased to have seen him grow so fine. I think she was relieved there was no obvious trace of Benson in his temperament. And I suspect she was not unhappy that poor Juba was relieved of the problem of Delilah. I said she should be proud of this remarkable man and she tossed her head in that way of hers and asked me why. Then I got a lecture on how good and gentle her own father had been and how Noname had obviously inherited these fine qualities from him, therefore she proposed to go on being proud of her father and certainly not of this usurper of her father's temperament. Or words to that effect.'

Tansy was laughing. 'She doesn't change,'

'And never will now.'

The air was cooling as evening drew on, and Tansy suggested that they go inside. She called for the candles to be lit and both women went to their rooms to prepare themselves for dinner. The stairs were not easy for Amelia. She had to stop several times to get her breath.

'Mama,' Tansy said, concerned. 'You're not well. Should you not see the surgeon?'

'Of course not,' Amelia said lightly. 'You forget I'm getting old.'

But sitting in the quiet of her daughter's prettiest guest room, she

345

told herself that she really should see the surgeon. But she knew what he would tell her, and she knew what he would want to do. She was certain that the end result would be the same and she had no intention of putting herself through unnecessary pain and suffering. She was not afraid, her life had been full, she had done all she wanted to do. But she might just get Minta to make her some pain-relieving draughts. She had more faith in Minta than in the island doctors.

At dinner that night, with her grandchildren paying her court, Robin beaming at the head of the table, and Tansy smiling and happy and prettier every day, she felt a deep contentment. If only she could help poor, sweet William; if only there were some way to cure Precious, how perfect life would be. But life, she reflected, was never going to be that perfect.

She and Tansy were at Windsong just before ten the following morning. Charlotte was waiting to greet them. In her usual fussy way she took them to the veranda at the back of the house and ordered coffee to be brought. That same settle where Amelia had fought with Matthew Oliver was still there, and she plonked herself down on it with a certain defiance. After all, it was such a long time ago.

'It's so good to see you both,' Charlotte was twittering, though Amelia knew that she was never quite at her ease with either of them. Poor Charlotte, she thought, forced to entertain two ex-slaves. But Charlotte was doing her best, and when she had handed them their cups, she enquired politely whether there was a reason for this unexpected visit.

'Well, yes, there is,' Amelia said. 'Charlotte, tell me, are you happy about James's marriage?'

Unexpectedly Charlotte's blue eyes filled with tears. 'Oh no,' she said, searching in her sleeve for her handkerchief. 'Not at all. My heart bleeds for my son, but what can I do? His father will not listen. I know she is your granddaughter, Amelia, and I'm sorry to have to say it, but she is both mad and wicked. And for my James to wed her.' She sank her head in her hands and broke into quiet sobs.

'Have you spoken to James?' Amelia asked gently.

Charlotte looked up, her eyes already red. 'His father has forbidden it.'

'Is James at home?'

'He is in his room, preparing to visit Precious.'

'Can we send for him?'

Charlotte's eyes grew round and she looked about her nervously. 'His father . . .'

'Has not forbidden me, nor can he,' Amelia said firmly. 'James is now the only person who can stop this marriage if he wishes, and we must make him see that we will support him if he is persuaded that that is what he should do.'

'Oh my!' Charlotte moaned, but she rose to her feet. 'I will go and find him myself,' she said.

As James came in to kiss her cheek and greet her with warmth, it

346

seemed to Amelia that the lad was visibly less happy-go-lucky than he had been all his young life. He looked as if he had not slept and his eyes were anxious. Amelia did not believe in beating about the bush and as soon as he was seated she plunged in.

'James, I want to talk to you about your marriage to Precious. I know it is late, but are you certain that it is what you want to do?'

He turned scarlet. 'Of course,' he said stoutly.

'James, forgive me for interfering in your life, but Precious is my granddaughter. Perhaps I know more about her than you do. She is not right—'

James leapt to his feet. 'I know she's not right. People keep telling me she's not right, but none of you understand the poor girl. She needs me, she loves me . . .'

'You are sure it's love she feels?'

He stared at her. 'I don't understand.'

'Precious has strong sexual feelings, but I do not believe she is capable of love. Not as we know it.'

Again his cheeks flamed scarlet. 'I am marrying her,' he said flatly. 'I will not change my mind. I cannot change my mind.'

Amelia considered and then said, 'Because she is pregnant?'

Charlotte gasped and fell back in her chair, her fan waving desperately as if to push Amelia's words into extinction. The scarlet in James's face turned greeny-white. His hands clutched at air. His voice a croak, he said, 'Pregnant?'

'Yes, I'm afraid so,' Amelia said gently. 'Are you responsible?'

He almost collapsed onto the settle beside her. 'Yes,' he said. The small, significant word hung on the air until Charlotte gave a tiny shriek and appeared to faint. Amelia ignored her; Tansy picked up the fallen fan and waved it briskly over her aunt's face.

'Then there's nothing more to be said, is there?' Amelia looked down at her lap, not wanting to see James's face. 'You will have to go through with it.'

Charlotte recovered with amazing speed. She stood up abruptly, her stance almost threatening.

'James! How could you? The disgrace!'

'I don't suppose it was entirely his fault,' Amelia said wearily, 'was it, James?'

'Perhaps not entirely,' he muttered. 'But I should not have done it. And I did not know she was pregnant.' He suddenly squared his shoulders. 'Mama, Tansy, do you mind if I talk to Aunt Amelia alone for a moment?'

Charlotte looked affronted, but Tansy gently took her arm. 'Come, Aunt Charlotte,' she said. 'We'll take a turn in the fresh air.'

Thin nose high, her back stiff with indignation, Charlotte permitted herself to be led into the garden, leaving James and Amelia looking at each other.

'I feel I must explain myself,' he began slowly. 'I do love her; I find

347

myself most enormously attracted by her. She is so pretty, so fascinating. I want to help her; I long to help her. And she *is* different with me. But I do realise that perhaps I have made a mistake and one that will affect me as much as her. Aunt, I am sometimes afraid of her – a grown man afraid of a slip of a girl, imagine it! Now that we are lovers she frightens me in a different way. It's as if she wants to devour me. And, as you say, there is no love there, no tenderness. Worse, she brings out things in me that I hate and despise. I wanted to be her knight, her troubadour. I wanted to rescue her from her own prison, but I begin to see that is not possible. I have even agreed with William that we will live at Macabees; strange places confuse Precious. I shall be isolated from my own family, and now there is this baby to consider. Suppose, poor thing, it is like sad Precious? Aunt Amelia, what am I to do?'

She held out her hand and he clutched it gratefully.

'I was hopeful that the baby was not yours,' she said quietly.

'You did not think such a thing of me?' His voice was sad.

She laughed ruefully. 'James, believe me, we are all capable of such things. I was hopeful merely because then you might have been saved from this marriage. Now I fear there is nothing to be done. You could not desert her with your baby on the way but you will have to endeavour not to let yourself be smothered. William could do with help running the plantation. Busy yourself with that. Make your own freedom. Prissie can handle Precious better than anyone, and Prissie has your interests at heart. She tried to stop this marriage. She went to see your father, and then me. She will help you all she can. You must make yourself a life apart from your marriage. And who knows, perhaps marriage will help Precious. Perhaps she will become less, well, strange.'

'My poor Precious,' he said with such sadness. 'If only that could be.'

'And you will be a father, James. There is no reason why the child should not be normal. Think how different most children are from their parents. You are nothing like either your mother or your father. You are your own person, and this baby will be the same.'

'I pray you are right.' He sounded doubtful.

'Of course I'm right,' she said, outwardly confident, but in her heart she felt no confidence at all.

'She went for me with a knife today.'

'Dear God. How did she get it?'

'Kitchen.'

'We must get a lock on the drawer.'

'Ain't no point. She'll find the key. She allus does. Cunning. We's afeared she go'n try and kill my Ella's baby 'gain. That gal hates black folk but she sure hates black folk babies more.'

'She has to be watched.'

'Ain't possible. Not all the time. She be like a ghost at night. Walks like something from the graveyard.'

'We must try. She has to be stopped before she does kill someone.'
'There be only one way to stop her prop'ly.'
'No.'
'Be the right thing to do.'
'No.'
'If t'ain't her it'll be some other body.'
'No.'
'You be sorry,' the black voice warned.

Chapter Nineteen

Everyone agreed it was a lovely spring wedding with the March weather at its breezy best, the young, handsome groom so attentive to his bride, the pale-eyed, pale-skinned bride ethereal in her white satin gown, sent specially from London. She looked so slim that Amelia wondered if the girl really was pregnant. Perhaps Prissie and Minta were wrong. The whole church held its breath when the time came for Precious to make her vows. The 'I do,' was clear as a bell, though she stumbled through the rest of it, and in places was barely audible. The words 'I plight thee my troth . . .' she never did manage to say and she clung to James's hand throughout as if she would fall if she let go.

William, soft-hearted as always, cried with joy. Charlotte also, though her tears were more of grief. Zach looked remarkably pleased with himself, Ben inscrutable and Amelia had great difficulty keeping a smile on her face.

James was only relieved that it all went without too much embarrassment. Precious was well-behaved enough at the wedding ball though she said nothing and stared about her as if she were not entirely sure what was going on. James helped her through the first dance and once the floor of the Macabees ballroom was full of swirling couples he sat with her quietly, holding her hand while they both watched the glittering scene before them until, at midnight, he quietly took her to their new bedchamber.

He settled down at Macabees quickly and found life more tolerable than he had expected. William took much of his time, explaining the workings of the plantation. Sometimes Precious would ride with them, and James was amazed at her grasp of the financial side of the estate. When dealing with figures, she seemed like a normal woman.

Macabees was a pleasant place to live, a wealthy and wonderfully comfortable house. It was cooler than Windsong with the breeze blowing in from the sea. From his bedroom James could hear the waves pounding on the black sand beaches near the house. The slaves were well-trained and everything ran smoothly. William might have been a sentimental man, but he was not sentimental about those who worked for him. They were expected to perform their duties to a high standard and he was not above having them whipped if they did not. Like all planters he had a deep distrust of his slaves and believed they must be kept in their place. And even the kind-hearted James had to admit that now the white population was so heavily outnumbered, too much laxity was unwise.

351

James took Amelia's advice and rationed the time he spent with Precious, and she did not seem to mind his absences. He sometimes thought she had forgotten she had a husband when she shut herself in her music room and played for hours at a time. They were together only for meals and in the evenings, and for his own sake he made a great effort to improve her table manners and managed to delude himself that he was making some headway. They shared a master bedroom but he had his own small dressing room with a day bed next door. He used this when Precious's demands on him became too pressing. He had quickly learned that when he was out of her sight he was out of her mind, and this gave him unexpected freedom.

As her pregnancy progressed, she became fractious and it troubled him that he wasn't sure whether or not she knew what was happening to her.

'Do you think she knows she is having a baby?' he asked Prissie.

'I don't know,' Prissie said with her usual frankness. 'I keep telling her, but I don't know if she understands. It's possible she does not wish to understand.'

When he talked to her about what they would do when the baby came, Precious just stared at him blankly. Then one day she said with devastating clarity, 'I do not want a baby. Take it away.'

'Of course you want a baby,' he heard himself gabbling. 'It will be our baby to love and bring up together.'

'I do not want a baby.' Her face was implacable. He did not know what to say. 'You'll feel different once it's born,' he ventured hopefully, his tone almost pleading.

'I do not want a baby.' Then she added conversationally, 'I shall kill it.'

He felt as if the hair on his head was standing upright. He was suddenly cold. 'Precious!'

'They wouldn't let me kill the black baby. I shall kill this one. Where is it?'

'What do you mean?' he stammered.

'Where is the baby? I want to kill it.'

He had never felt so frightened or confused in his life. How could he explain that the child was growing in her? And if he did, what horror would she perform?

'There isn't any baby. Not yet.' He was backing towards the door. He needed Prissie. 'Not for a long time. You'll feel different. You'll feel . . .' The door handle was behind him. He pushed it and escaped, leaving her sitting at the table, her food smeared over her mouth.

Prissie heard his frantic calls and came from her room. White-faced he recounted the conversation.

'It's terrible, Prissie,' he said. 'Surely she's not capable of killing. She said something about not being allowed to kill a black baby.'

The fleeting expression he caught on Prissie's face scared him almost as much as what Precious had said.

352

'She is capable of killing?' he asked fearfully.

Prissie looked at him with compassionate eyes. 'Yes. The mother, Ella – she's Minta's niece – caught her with the baby and stopped it. She has done other things . . .' her voice trailed away.

'Prissie, I have a right to know.'

She sighed. 'Before you were married she cut off the heads of the slaves chickens. All of them. Last week, while you were out with William, she had one of her rages. The kitchen cat has had kittens. She got hold of one of them. She cut its throat. James, she is dangerous, and is getting worse. Perhaps the pregnancy is causing it, but I beg you to be careful.'

He felt overwhelmed by horror, but said, trying to convince himself, 'I don't believe she would harm me.'

'I pray you are right.'

'But the baby?'

'We will have to wait and see. Only a month left now.'

He shivered. 'This is a nightmare.'

'I know,' she said. 'But have courage. Nightmares end.'

'I don't see how this one can,' he muttered.

He slept in his dressing room that night. Precious went up to bed before him, and she was sound asleep when he came into the room. Very quietly he undressed, blew out the candles and climbed into the uncomfortable day bed. Sleep did not come easily. He kept imagining Precious cutting a kitten's throat, and in his half-asleep state, the kitten changed to a baby. He sat up, sweating, listening to the noise of the night insects to assure himself all was well.

He had slept fitfully for an hour before finally falling exhausted into deep slumber. He was dreaming; dreaming that he could not breathe and that he was in a deep, black hole underground from which there was no exit. Then somehow he realised that he really could not breathe, that it was no dream. He fought for consciousness. Something was on his chest, something heavy; then it was at his throat, growling. It hurt. Terrified, he heaved the weight off him, fear giving him strength. He heard a crash as a body hit the floor. He leapt out of bed and onto his feet, fumbling for tinderbox and candle. The candle spluttered into life. Curled on the floor, eyes glinting, was his wife. The candlelight gleamed off a small kitchen knife which she had dropped. She looked up, her teeth bared, and then she saw his face. Her eyes widened, her mouth fell open and the thin mouth quivered.

'Sorry sorry sorry sorry sorry sorry . . .' she began to whimper.

Appalled, he pulled her to her feet. His throat hurt and he could feel blood trickling. She had been trying to kill him, but her remorse made him realise that she had not even known that he was her victim. He was trembling. She was unsteady on her feet and he had to support her pregnant weight. The mournful 'sorry sorry sorry' continued until he heard himself bellow, 'Be quiet!' Startled, she was silent, looking at him, ice-blue eyes feverish with tears, her face pathetically pretty.

353

'Oh my God,' he said, torn with pity and dismay. 'Oh God, help us both.'

She began nuzzling him, licking the blood from his neck, trying to make amends. He felt sick as he pushed her away and sat her on the day bed. He took one of the lighted candles to the glass over the dressing table. She had made a small cut on his throat. It was bleeding heavily though she had done no real damage. But had the baby been harmed in her fall to the ground? He turned to look at her where she sat. She showed no signs of pain, but tears were trickling down her pale cheeks.

'Oh, Precious,' he said despairingly.

'You said you would never be angry with me.' The words were crystal clear, her hands stretched out to him, supplicating.

He sank down beside her. 'I'm not angry,' he told her, and it was true. He was full of love and pity and a need to help her. He was also deeply sad. He would never feel safe with her again.

'I won't kill the baby if you don't want me to,' she whispered.

'I don't want you to,' he said firmly. 'If you do, then I shall be very angry indeed.'

'All right then, I won't.'

And she gave him a smile of such dazzling sweetness that he thought his heart would break. He wanted to kiss her but hesitated. Sometimes he only had to touch her and she was clawing at him, kissing him, pressing herself against him like a hot little animal. He did not want to make love but he did want to comfort her. Cautiously he kissed her and to his relief she responded like a child, offering up a puckered mouth. He led her into their bedroom and helped her settle herself in bed.

'Now go back to sleep,' he said gently. 'We don't want to hurt the baby.'

There was an unexpected flash of ice in the blue stare she turned on him, and then it vanished and the feverish look of love returned. 'Sorry sorry sorry sorry,' she began again.

He put his fingers over her lips and said sternly, 'Go to sleep.'

She shut her eyes obediently and he went back to the glass to deal with the cut on his neck. It was still trickling blood over his nightshirt. He staunched it with cold water from the filled jug Minta had left for the morning. Then found a large white kerchief which he tied round his neck. He decided to discard the soiled nightshirt, and climbed naked into bed beside Precious. She was very still and he thought she was asleep. He lay for a while miserably wondering what could be done to help her, and then, exhausted, fell into a deep sleep.

Precious could not sleep. Her attack on James had brought about one of those rare moments of lucidity when her brain seemed clear of fog, though it raced on different planes. Her head was too full for comfort. On one level she could hear music and was mentally translating the sounds into written notes that matched those on her harpsichord. On another level she was aware of James slumbering beside her. The sound of his breathing was comforting. She had become accustomed to his presence. His smell, the small snuffles he made in his sleep, were all familiar. She was sure it had happened a long time ago but she could remember with blazing clarity that she had tried to hurt him. The memory filled her with dread that she might do it again. James's gentleness, his patience with her, gave her a tiny measure of security in the confusion of her life. She sensed that he loved her as her father loved her. They were the only two people who made her feel safe and she never wanted to upset either of them. Her problem was finding sufficient control not to do so.

In another section of her brain she was terrified. At this precise moment she realised that her body was uncomfortable because of something to do with a baby but that understanding wavered, coming and going, confusing her. She could not grasp the concept that a baby was the reason why her shape had changed. Was this baby they all talked about inside her? The thought was worse than any of her nightmares. She imagined it feeding from her, growing secretly, bloating her, robbing her. Sometimes it felt as if there was indeed something in there kicking to get out. Would it burst her open at the end? And would she die? The thought was horrible; she wanted to smash the bulge to kill whatever lurked inside. But she had promised James she would not do that.

She was also aware of a general malaise. She seemed to feel pain she could not pinpoint. She knew that her left side ached and she had a dim recollection of falling but other things were wrong. What with the aches and pains and the weight of her belly in the heat of the night, sleep was impossible. James stirred uneasily as she shifted, trying without success to get more comfortable. Eventually, careful not to wake him, she crept out of bed. She stood still in the darkness, holding her breath to make sure he had not heard her, and as she listened she spotted something glinting in the moonlight. It was the small kitchen knife that James had put on the mantelshelf. She picked it up like an old friend and ran her finger along the blade, so gently it could have been a caress. Then moving like a cat in the darkness she slipped out of the bedroom and down the stairs into the great stone hallway. With James out of her sight she immediately forgot his existence.

Precious liked the night and the darkness. She was less clumsy, more sure-footed in the dark, using instincts rather than eyes. As a child she had prowled the house and the grounds almost every night, returning to her room just before dawn, but since her marriage this habit had been curtailed by the presence of James in her bed.

She needed little sleep and for her the nights were too long. Now, as she slipped along the passage through to the back doors out of the house, she felt a kind of happiness and freedom. The dark covered her, hid her. She could do as she wished. *They* were not watching. They could not see.

In the garden she stood with her arms folded over her swollen stomach

355

looking up at the mass of stars in the deep velvet blue above her head. She stood for some time counting them, wondering what their purpose was. The full moon was obscured by a cloud and as a gentle wind blew the patch of grey on its way a blaze of cold, silver light dimmed the stars.

Who had put out the stars? She had not finished her counting. She looked around for the culprit, but the night hid its secrets. The habitual anger welled and the midnight noises of a million insects roared in her ears. She pointed the knife threateningly at nothing.

Anger blotted out the last fluttering remnants of lucidity. She looked around for something to hurt to relieve and revenge the rage and confusion. Fury was a fireball in her head, waiting to explode. *They* became angry with her when she was angry and she could never explain why. The words would not come to order and that made her angrier still. She thought to scream at the sky, but some deep cunning told her *they* would find her and catch her if she did and take her and imprison her in the house again while the darkness called to her.

She began to prowl towards the slaves' cabins, but suddenly she halted, the knife dropping to the ground. A long groan was forced from her and she clasped both hands over her stomach. Something, it must be the horrible lump, was creating waves of tearing agony; a great hand was squeezing at her. Pain rolled, leaving her breathless, but it was gone as abruptly as it had arrived. Stunned by the ferocity of the attack, she stood still for a full minute, trying to think. Then, shakily, she bent to pick up the knife. She lost her balance and toppled onto the damp ground. She lay there, trying to work out what was happening to her.

Whatever had caused the agony seemed to have gone away. Cautiously, fearful of waking whatever was now sleeping inside her, she clambered clumsily to her feet, grateful for the gentle breeze on her hot face. She looked up at the sky. The stars had reappeared and again she began her counting. They twinkled down at her cheerfully like jewels. An emotion that she barely recognised as pleasure took her as if by the hand. She smiled at the stars until, again without warning, the pleasure was banished by another explosion of pain.

She sank to her knees, groaning but somehow holding back the scream that waited in her throat. As before, the pain roared in her ears, rolling over her like a huge, vicious wave, and then it was gone.

Kneeling, the knife clutched in her hand, useless protection against this hidden attacker, she stared about her wildly. The cabins were in sight, silent and still; she could smell them. She looked back up at the stars but they had dimmed again. One seemed to fall, a burning silver knife in the dark. She thought it had come to pierce her and whimpered as she covered her eyes. When she looked again, it had gone. Slowly she got to her feet and moved on.

She was almost at the slave cabins when the pain struck again. Totally bewildered, she fell to the ground and curled herself into a tight ball. It did not help. She uncurled and instinctively stretched and strained against the pain until it faded away, leaving her exhausted. She had no sooner recovered when the pain returned. And again. And again.

A voice was telling her it was the baby they all wanted her to have that was doing it. She was certain the voice was right. It was all the fault of the baby. But where was the baby?

She tried to clear her head of the swirling mists to think where the baby was. There had been a baby, and she had nearly killed it. A black baby. But *they* had stopped her. They wouldn't let her do it. A black woman had stopped her and *they* had been angry with her. The mists were clearing and her head felt calm. She remembered exactly which cabin the baby had been in. She remembered exactly where it lay in the darkness. This time she had to kill it and then she would be safe. She would creep into the cabin, cut its throat as she had cut the throat of the kitten and then without waiting to see the blood she would hurry back to her bed and lie beside James so that he would never know what she had done.

Another surge of pain convinced her that this was the right course of action. Once it had passed, she crept to the cabin she wanted. Its wooden door had been left open to let in air. On hands and knees she crawled through the doorway like some silent night creature; she did not want her shadow to change the density of the light so that someone woke up. Safe in the shadows, she stood for a moment, wrinkling her nose against the smell and letting her eyes and senses adjust to a deeper darkness. She sniffed delicately. Precious remembered people's personal smells and she had not forgotten that of the black child. It was there in the corner, near its sleeping mother. Her tread was so light she could have been floating, her hand like a butterfly as she covered the baby's mouth. With the knife between her teeth she lifted the child, one-handed, from the rags in which it lay. It was heavy and she had to struggle not to breathe noisily as she carried it back towards the door. She crouched to re-enter the insect music of the night and the merciless glare of the moon.

The baby was wriggling in her arms, its black eyes round in its black face. She could both see it and sense it. Her left hand remained clamped firmly over its mouth as she looked down at the cause of all her troubles, hating this baby they plagued her with night and day. She laid it on the ground and with her right hand took the knife from her mouth. This time she would not be stopped.

Then the enemy struck again; a crippling bout of pain caused her to double up. Her left hand went to clutch at her stomach and the child instantly uttered a mighty wail. Frightened, Precious was back in the mists of her confusion again, not sure where she was or what she was doing. The sound of the child crying mingled with shouts of her own name. It was James calling her. She was sure of it. He would stop her killing this baby. She fumbled for the knife but someone grabbed her from behind. Like a trapped animal she spun round, teeth bared. A black, contorted face was thrust near to hers. Minta's face. Instinctively she spat, and instinctively Minta backed away. 'Precious! Precious!'

She could hear her name on the wind and the sound brought about a revelation. At last she understood that it was not the black baby who was causing her this pain, it was a baby secreted inside her, eating her, robbing her, hurting her.

She gave a high, thin cry of despair, and although she knew that James would be angry with her and she would never be able to explain, she plunged the knife towards her stomach. The baby had to die. But Minta's strong, skinny hand was over hers, forcing her arm upwards. She could see the veins standing out on Minta's neck and the hate in her face, until, guided by Minta, her own hand plunged the wicked little knife into her own heart.

It was not long after dawn when Amelia was woken with the news that she was needed at Macabees as soon as possible. She had slept well; Minta's potions gave her sleep without pain. Instantly alert she rose and quickly dressed. The message had not said why she was needed but she assumed that even though it was nearly a month early, Precious's time must have come. The baby would be arriving.

The quickest way to Macabees was on horseback, and though it was painful for her to ride, for a first sight of her great-grandchild she was willing to put up with the discomfort. As she rode, with Pierre grey-haired and puffing at her side, she said a silent prayer that the terrible fate that had befallen Precious had not befallen this child.

As soon as she entered the huge hallway of Macabees she heard the high, thin wail of a newborn baby. Pleased and excited, she flung her cloak, hat and whip to a slave and hurried towards the great stairway only to find Prissie running down, her hand stretched out in a warning to wait.

'Thank God you are here, Mistress Amelia.' Prissie's voice was breathless. 'Don't go up. Not yet. Come into the library.' She looked white and exhausted. Her clothes were untidy and her normal composed demeanour was absent. It was obvious she had been crying.

'What is it, Prissie?' Amelia asked as the door closed behind them. 'What's wrong?'

'Precious. She's dead.' Prissie burst into tears. 'The poor child,' she cried, 'the poor unhappy child.'

Amelia seemed to have lost the support of her legs. Shocked, she sank into a chair. 'She died in childbirth? Like her mother?' she asked in a whisper.

Prissie, groping for her handkerchief, shook her head. 'No. No. It was terrible. She killed herself. Minta found her outside the slave huts. She was in labour. She had taken Ella's baby again and we think she had been trying to kill him but instead she plunged the knife into her own heart.' She stopped speaking to blow her nose hard. 'Perhaps she could not understand the pain she was suffering. But her hand is still holding the knife, thank God, so no other can be blamed. Master William sent for the constable so he could see for himself how it

358

happened. The baby was near to birth. Minta was able to deliver it. She saved its life.'

Amelia listened appalled. She felt she should cry, but somehow the death seemed a blessed relief. She wanted to ask if the baby were normal, but the question seemed callous. Instead she asked, 'is it a boy or a girl?'

'A boy.' Then Prissie answered the unasked question. 'And seemingly normal, but then Precious appeared normal at birth . . .'

The women looked at each other in thoughtful silence, and then Amelia sighed, rose to her feet, and said, 'I must go to William and James.'

'That is why I sent for you. They are distraught. I have not informed Master and Mistress Quick. I thought Master James would need to gain strength before seeing his mama. He is having sufficient difficulty with his own grief without carrying hers.'

'Where are they?'

'Guarding the body, down near the slave cabins, with the constable.'

Amelia did not want to see the body, but this was no time to be squeamish. Resolute, she shook her skirts into place and went to join them.

It was nearly eleven o'clock and the sun was high as she went out into the gardens but it had not yet burn off Mount Misery's usual cap of clouds. Here, so much lower, the sky was clear and the sea glittered turquoise, green and blue on the horizon. It was not a morning for death, she thought.

As she neared the slave cabins she saw William, James and the constable, all with their backs turned to her, a tableau frozen in the bright sunlight. Beside them lay something covered in white, long but with a small sinister raised area; the handle of the knife disturbed the symmetry of the sheet that covered Precious. The men had not seen or heard Amelia, and not wishing to interrupt, she hovered behind the group.

'Are you content, Constable?' William was saying, courteous as ever, though his voice was unsteady.

He received a ponderous nod.

'It would seem that the young lady killed herself. Madness, no doubt brought on by the pains of giving birth.'

That was not quite right, Amelia thought sadly. It was madness brought on by the long and difficult birth that killed her mother.

'That is what we believe,' James was saying distractedly. 'The baby came early. It was not due for almost another month.'

'So you said, sir.' The constable sounded patient, as if James had imparted this information several times already. 'Perhaps you should now get your people to bring her into the house, ready for burial. Of course, she cannot be buried in hallowed ground, poor girl, though if you have suspicions about the slaves . . .'

'We have none,' William said harshly. 'Perhaps you could see your way to removing the knife.' He turned his head. 'I cannot.'

'As you wish.' The constable pulled back the white shroud. Amelia shut her eyes. 'There you are, sir,' she heard him say.

'Please take it with you.' James's voice was strangled.

The constable turned the bloodstained knife over in his hand. 'Sharp that,' he said almost admiringly. 'Are you sure you don't want it, sir?'

James put his hand up as if to ward off a blow. 'Positive. Now, if you will excuse us . . .'

She could see the two men were close to breaking. It was time to intervene.

'I am Mistress Rosier-Quick, Constable,' she said, lightly touching the man's arm to gain his attention. 'We thank you for coming so promptly. Should you require some refreshment before your return, Prissie, our – ' She hesitated, what was Prissie? 'Our housekeeper, will look after you. Please ask for her in the kitchen. Now, we have much to do. I am sure you will not object if I take my son and my nephew away from here. As you can imagine, the sight is a painful one for them.'

She did not wait for a reply but took William and James's arms and purposefully led them back towards the house.

In the cool of the big drawing room James hid his face by looking out of the window while William lowered himself with exaggerated care into a wing-backed chair. It seemed to her that he had aged. Grief had hollowed out his eyes and painted a pallor of grey on his normally ruddy skin. It had been the same when Isobel died. William was no stoic in grief.

'Thank you for coming, Mama,' he said, dabbing at his eyes with a large handkerchief. 'I am grateful.'

She brushed thanks aside and spoke to James. 'Come and sit down. I want both of you to tell me exactly what happened. It's better to talk about it.'

James did not move from the window. William sank his head in his hands. 'First Isobel, now Precious.' She could hardly hear what he was saying. 'Am I never to be permitted to love? Now what shall I do? Why does God take those I love? Where is happiness now?'

'Perhaps upstairs with your grandson,' Amelia said gently. 'Now come, tell me.'

He looked at her with tragic eyes. 'I knew nothing until James woke me and told me she was dead.' He broke into noisy sobs. 'James will tell you.'

'It was all my fault.' James's voice was too calm as he stood silhouetted against the light, his face still towards the window. 'I should never have slept. I should never have left the knife within her reach. I keep asking myself if I did it deliberately, but that cannot be for she could have used it on me again.' He stopped speaking.

'Again?'

He turned round and moved the blue cravat he wore away from his neck. His throat looked as if someone had drawn a thin, red line round it.

'Precious did that?' Amelia asked, trying to control the revulsion she felt.

He nodded. 'In the middle of the night. She did not realise it was me. I flung her off me to the floor. Oh, Aunt Amelia, is that why the baby came too soon? I loved her. How could I have hurt her?' He had turned his back again in order to keep his tears private. 'And then I slept and she went out. I woke to find she had gone. By the time I had dressed and run to find her it was too late. Minta was busy saving the baby. There was nothing to be done for Precious.'

There was a heavy silence. Amelia tried to suppress the thought that it was better that she was dead. Better than someone else dead at her hands. Better for James, for William and probably even for the baby. It was not a thought to voice. She felt a sudden surge of pity for Precious. How could any of them judge her since none of what had happened had been her fault? She had come into the world angry and confused and left it in the same mind. And yet it was too easy to say that life was a burden for Precious. None of them knew what life was for her. No one had ever come close to finding out.

'It is not your fault,' Amelia said firmly. 'It's no one's fault. Not even Precious's. We have to face the fact that she was not right and never has been. And now we have to think of her child.'

William looked up, his expression haunted. 'But suppose . . .'

There was no point in burying their fears. 'That the child has Precious's problems?' she finished for him.

He nodded.

'Why don't we go and see?' she suggested.

William stirred uneasily in his seat. 'I cannot, not yet,' he muttered. 'I'm not ready. The child killed her,' he added in a burst of unreasonable resentment.

'Nonsense!' Amelia said sharply. 'Don't be fanciful, William. Life killed her. Thank God she has left you a legacy. Hopefully a good legacy. Stay if you wish, but James and I are going to the nursery.'

James turned and looked around him wildly, as if seeking escape, but she was waiting, implacable. Reluctantly he joined her and followed her out of the room.

They climbed the stairs in silence. Aware that Amelia was short of breath, James gave her his arm. The crying had stopped. Was the child safe? Amelia wondered in a sudden panic and found herself hesitating outside the nursery door. It was James, finding courage, who opened it. Inside, Prissie and Minta were gathered round the seated stubby frame of Minta's niece, Ella. Her bodice was pulled up and she was feeding a tiny white baby with a fluff of blond hair and sleepy blue eyes. One tiny pink hand rested on the deep brown of Ella's swollen breast, the miniature mouth sucked contentedly. All three women were smiling as they looked at James and Amelia framed in the doorway.

'Isn't he beautiful?' Prissie said. 'Oh, Mister James, you have a fine son.'

James took a tentative step further into the room.

'He hungry, but he be happy,' Ella volunteered.

'Ain't nothing scary 'bout this baby,' Minta informed them. 'This baby don' got no devils in he heart.'

'You're sure?' James sounded like a child craving reassurance.

'I's sure as I ever bin 'bout anythin' in this world.'

His gaze moved to Prissie for confirmation.

'Minta is right,' Prissie told him, and repeated, 'He's beautiful. A bit small as yet, but Ella will soon mend that.'

James stood still for a moment, watching. The child released the nipple and suddenly yawned, clenching tiny fists. Minta's face crinkled into a smile.

'He go'n sleep now,' she predicted.

James walked across the room as if he were approaching something that might be frightened and run. He drew level with Ella's chair, bent, peered, and then slowly and gently picked up his son. No one moved, and Amelia felt her eyes begin to smart.

As if he was seeing a miracle, James looked down at the baby. Then he looked at Amelia, his honest young face alight with pleasure.

'I shall call him Peregrine,' he said.

Chapter Twenty

September 1728

'My Dear Delilah.'

Amelia contemplated the three words and then tore up the sheet of paper on which they were written. It was still too soon to be over-affectionate towards her granddaughter. Delilah, in spite of her new life on St Barthelemy, had not entirely lost her prickles. Since she had left St Kitts she had written a few stiff and formal letters to Amelia, warmer ones to Tansy. The last to arrive had given news of her pregnancy, news she had already given some weeks earlier to Tansy who had promptly taken herself off to Elsewhere to impart the information to Amelia.

And what colour in the lucky dip of Caribbean life would this child be? Amelia wondered. Would Delilah reject the baby if it proved too white? Perhaps it would not matter. St Barthelemy seemed less colour conscious than the other islands and Delilah herself was more relaxed, less angry about her own mixed blood.

'Dear Delilah,' Amelia began again, 'I am so delighted to hear about the baby. I am sure that you and Noname must be very happy and I hope that you have an easy pregnancy and birth. Tansy is already plotting to visit St Barthelemy to see the baby when it is born and if my health permits I may come with her. In the meantime she is planning to sail to Boston in New England to take Mark and Melanie to meet their grandparents. There is much excitement about the trip and she and Robin are even discussing whether they should sail on to England itself to visit Upottery, the tiny village in Devon where I lived when I was a girl.

'It seems that much has happened since you left. I know Tansy has told you of Precious's death. We are not yet over the period of mourning, but I am happy to say that William and James are beginning to get over their grief. The new baby, Peregrine, has helped. He is now coming up to four months old and is to be christened next week. Robin will be one of his godfathers and most pleased to be asked. Peregrine is the most enchanting baby in spite of his difficult start in life, so cheerful and alert all the time. He hardly ever cries, does not mind who cuddles him, and is beginning to grow apace. Everyone spoils him for it is impossible not to do so. Apparently he smiles whenever he sees his father and James is so proud of him, as indeed are William and I.

'He is still small for his age and it is astonishing how much happiness this little scrap has brought to the Quick family. Even William who suffered greatly from melancholy since the death of his wife has responded to this grandson, and he is so much more content I sometimes think that maybe he will be persuaded to make a new life with a new lady. James has fully recovered from the shock and there are whispers that he is friendly with one of the Wyatt girls on the Beverly Plantation. I am hopeful this is true. He is too young to remain single.

'The other news I have for you is that I have persuaded my brother Zach to let me buy a piece of the Fortland property at the limits of Basse-Terre. It has just come on to the market now that the quarrels with the French owners have finally been resolved. There has been much controversy over this fertile land. The lots have been made at 200 acres and are therefore far too expensive for anyone but the planters to buy. The council have managed it all very neatly, leaving no chance for the poorer whites or mulattos to acquire even a small patch of land by which they can support themselves. In my view this is unwise for it gives no chance to those who need help to help themselves.

'Ben has acquired a large holding which he will have managed. He says he likes the life of a tavernkeeper too well to leave it. My brother, of course, also has a holding. I am not interested for myself. Elsewhere is too far away from Basse-Terre to make the running of a new plantation there simple. I have bought the land for Truly, Daniel and Juba.

'We have chosen a plot at the extremity of the land where they have few neighbours and hopefully will not suffer any harassment. For the present it will be said that Daniel and Juba are managing it for the Quick family, but in reality it will be their own. I tell you this because one day your sons, Broderick and Bradley, will inherit the land. If you should wish for your child by Noname to have a share you must inform me as I am engaged at the present in putting my affairs in order.'

She paused to think whether it was wise to write more about the two boys. They were six and five now, handsome lads, though it was obvious that, young as he was, Broderick had inherited Truly's uncompromising, sometimes surly, nature. She decided to say no more. It was possible that Delilah would dislike mention of the children she had left behind her.

'There is much excitement in the town,' she continued, 'for the day after the christening the new Governor, the Earl of Londonderry, arrives. There is to be a reception for him at Windsong with Zach as host. You can imagine my brother's delight in having been chosen for this honour. The whole family are to be on parade for the occasion as well as all the other planters, members of the Council and what society we have. I must allow I am looking forward to it myself. All family members are to stay at Windsong with our own personal slaves for the christening and the ball the following night. Heaven knows where Charlotte will put us all. Such a too-ing and a fro-ing you cannot imagine, with every lady in the town ordering a new and splendid gown intended to eclipse all other gowns. Robin, who has by far the best fabrics to offer, is delighted, business is so good.

'I think of you often,' she concluded, 'and Ben of course is always asking after you. If you could find a moment to write to him it would make him happy. Like Zach and me, he is getting old and he has such a soft spot for you.

'I cannot tell you what pleasure it gives me to know that you are content with your husband. I am only sad that our two islands are too far apart to make visiting easy. I was much impressed with Noname and would have liked to know him better. I am so glad that you both met.

'And for now, my dear, I wish you farewell and great happiness with your new family. Your friend, Amelia Rosier-Quick.'

She put down her quill and quickly skimmed the letter for errors then folded it for posting. It would be some weeks before she received a reply but she had almost made up her mind to include the new baby in her will regardless of what Delilah said. After all, he was one of her great-grandsons, as were Broderick and Bradley, though the white blood in Juba's pair was dissipated. They were to all intents and purposes African, and Truly had made it clear she wanted no interference from Amelia in their upbringing.

Not that she had ever had any intention of interfering. She had learned by experience that education and white manners were a burden for those who must live in a black world.

Would it ever be thus? she wondered. As the whites on the island became increasingly outnumbered by blacks she could not believe that one day those oppressed people would not rise up in spite of all the planters' vigilance. The day must come when by sheer weight of numbers they would own the land – without bloodshed, she prayed. But would there be black and white by then? She smiled at the thought of her own white blood tumbling down through the ages via Delilah, Broderick and Bradley and now this new baby, who would also have the white blood of Benson. One part of the Quick family was no longer pure-blooded, and she had no doubt that Zach and William, and perhaps even James, had fathered children by their slaves. How complicated it was and what a fuss people made. She felt she was fortunate to have shared the lives of those few black people who had never ceased to be part of her life. Those four years had given her an understanding denied to most white people.

For a moment she sat thinking of Joshua, of how much she had loved him, and how the outcome of that love was perhaps a small landmark in the slow evolution of the Caribbean.

The thought made her cheerful. Perhaps the legacy she was leaving behind was an important one – more important than the land and the riches that the Quick family had acquired. It had not been a bad life, she thought, not a bad life at all. And turning her mind to next week's festivities, she told herself that she was going to enjoy what was left of it.

*　　*　　*

365

The morning of the christening dawned threatening, with gusting wind rattling the windowpanes of Tansy's bedroom, accompanied by the drumbeat patter of heavy rain. For some days the weather had been unsettled with a sultry heaviness about it that made people lethargic and bad-tempered. The winds were strong and she had been woken in the night by its howling and the bangs and crashes of slamming doors, falling trees and flying roofs that the gale swirled along in its wake.

Robin was out of bed, bending to peer out of the window, big and broad in his nightshirt. The sight of him still turned her heart over; she found it impossible to take for granted how much happiness he had given her. Now, something about the way his solid male feet and legs planted themselves before her lacy curtains and the way his hair curled over his neck created a sudden, urgent need in her.

'What's it like out there?' she asked, snuggling back into her pillows.

'Bad.' He turned back. 'I think we're in for a hurricane.'

Her dark eyes glowed at him over the edge of the sheet. 'Then it's not worth getting up, is it?' she said provocatively.

He grinned. 'I've got work to do,' he told her. Nevertheless he took off his nightshirt and she stretched out a hand to take hold of his half-erect penis.

'Come here,' she said, using it as a guide to lead him back into bed.

'You're a shameless hussy,' he said as he enveloped her in a bear hug, 'and I love you.'

There was something peculiarly satisfying about making love while the elements raged outside, Tansy thought later as, the urge assuaged, she dozed behind the curtains of her bed. She was alone. He had made love to her, and then he had kissed her, asked if that would keep her content for the moment, and left to check on his warehouses before returning for the christening.

They were to gather at St George's Church in Basse-Terre at three o'clock for the occasion and then go on to Windsong for the feast. Amelia was already at Zach's and would travel with him and the rest of the family to the church. The journey from Elsewhere was too much for her in one day. Not for the first time Tansy wished that she could persuade her mother to come and live in Basse-Terre. Elsewhere was so far away, and it was obvious that there was something seriously wrong with Amelia's health, but she would not discuss it. Nor would she countenance the thought of leaving the plantation.

'It's my home. It holds all my memories,' she would say when Tansy pressed her.

But the zest for life had not left Amelia. She had been overjoyed at the birth of Peregrine and was equally pleased with Delilah's news.

'If only we could acknowledge the baby,' Tansy had said to her. 'I can acknowledge none of my grandchildren.'

'There is little we can do about it,' Amelia said. 'Do you blame me?'

'Oh, no! Never!' Tansy assured her fervently. 'Your sins were responsible for me.'

366

'At least my sins were not responsible for Precious's troubles,' Amelia said sadly. 'But I can say to you as I can say to no one else that I am relieved that poor Precious has gone from us. Much of what I told you about what happened has never been revealed to Zach and Charlotte. I felt it best for them not to know just how mad she was at the end in case it made them fear for Peregrine's sanity. But so far he, sweet soul, seems to have nothing of his mother in him. I believe her sickness was an accident of birth. It's terrible that she should die by her own hand and in such misery, but better than if she had lived to kill someone else.'

Tansy treasured these confidences and with a lurching sense of dread wondered what she would do when her mother had gone. The thought of her dying was terrifying. She could not envisage a world without 'Melia. Her mother was the one person, other than Robin, from whom Tansy had no secrets. It was the same for Amelia. They could talk to each other with complete honesty.

Tansy pushed sad thoughts aside and climbed from her bed to look out of the window. The trees in the square below were bending low under the fierce wind. Rubbish from the market flew like confetti in the air and the sky was grey and leaden with no glimpse of sun. The rain thundered down from clouds that blotted out the mountains, creating puddles and streams in the stone pavements and rough roads. The ghauts in the hills and in the town would be full, transformed into rushing rivers. Tansy wondered how on earth she would keep her christening hat on in all this wind, and if the Earl of Londonderry could possibly arrive in time for the ball being given in his honour. It was no day to be at sea.

She sang to herself, an old song from the plantation, as she laid out the clothing she was taking to Windsong for herself and Melanie. Later the maid would pack it all and that afternoon it would be taken to Windsong by wagon, along with Robin and Mark's finery, ready for the feast after Peregrine's christening and the ball. She was looking forward to the events and had spent considerable time and money on the gowns she would wear.

Tansy had lived up to her promise to herself to become a queen of society in Basse-Terre. Robin was one of the richest men in the community and it still amused her to see how the wives of the planters fawned upon them and shamelessly angled for invitations to the extravagant soirees that she gave both in the Pall Mall Square house and the old French mansion that Robin had restored outside the town on Monkey Hill.

Since Robin imported fine furniture and household goods, wines and spirits and fabrics, she had the pick of all that came into St Kitts. Her homes were exquisitely furnished; she was the best dressed woman on the island, and any rumours that were whispered about her early background were brushed aside for a place in her magic circle. Tansy enjoyed it all hugely.

She smoothed a hand over the cherry-red silk of the dress she would wear tomorrow. Would Bella regard her as a traitor if she had lived to see this day? Or would she be glad for her? She would never know the answer, but one thing was sure. She was glad for herself.

Though the wind never faltered in its fury, dementedly howling through the church, gusts battering the tower and knocking at the great wooden doors, at least the sun came out briefly for Peregrine's christening. It saved the guests' finery from a soaking, though the gale still whipped up skirts and tried to snatch hats. Amelia had to be helped into the church by Ben and James; she was too slight to fight alone against such a violent wind.

Peregrine gurgled cheerfully throughout the ceremony, sounding like running water and putting a collective grin on the face of the entire congregation. As she smiled, Amelia said a little private prayer of thanks that this new addition to the family seemed set to be one of its happiest members. She was certain, totally and completely certain, that whatever devils had plagued Precious, they would not plague Peregrine. Mark and Melanie had been happy babies and had grown to be happy young people; children to be proud of. Why should this baby not be the same?

The sun capitulated to cloud, the rain plunged down again just before the congregation left the church and there was a great rush to gain the shelter of the waiting carriages. With one hand the women hitched up their skirts to an indecorous height to save them from the mud, while with the other they held on to their hats. The men jammed their tricorns in place and helped the women into the carriages which looked set to blow away until the weight of their occupants steadied them. The horses were uneasy, the coachmen wet through and it was a slow and cautious procession that made its way to Windsong.

The guests were family with a sprinkling of Council and Assembly members and a few of the other planters. Zach's carriage had left first and Charlotte and Amelia were already in place to greet arrivals as the others arrived.

'It's as well that we are all to stay,' Robin said to Zach once all were safe in the hallway of the house. 'We are in the teeth of a hurricane. By tonight it will not be safe to be out of the house. Believe me, there is worse to come. Your guests may have to remain another day before it is over.'

Zach accepted the word of the sea captain without question. 'We shall be safe here,' he said.

Robin nodded. 'Let us hope that the Earl is also safe or your ball tomorrow will be for naught.'

'My God, you think he may be in danger?' Zach's face was a picture of comic dismay. He was afraid his great moment would be lost, thought Amelia with affection, smiling to herself.

'Well,' said Robin with a great bellow of mirth, 'I'd wager he's seasick right now.'

368

The feast was to be served at six thirty and the ladies hurried to their rooms to change their damp, limp dresses and to repair hair and toilette. Amelia took the opportunity to rest. Minta's draughts helped, but they were inclined to make her sleepy. She had been put in the room Charlotte had used when she was a girl, and as Amelia stretched comfortably on the bed the memories returned. Memories of crimping Charlotte's hair, of Charlotte crying, 'But no one does my hair like you.' She thought of the time she had slept in this bed when the Olivers fled to Nevis and she was free again to do as she wished. It was all such a long time ago.

She slept soundly for an hour and then, waking with difficulty, called for her maid to help her dress. She and Tansy had a friendly rivalry when it came to their gowns, both liked to outshine the other and were secretive about what they wore to gatherings they both attended. Amelia rarely went to the balls that were given by the plantation owners any more, but all vanity had not gone. She had chosen a dinner gown in her favourite emerald green for this evening. For tomorrow's ball, she would be in silver. She was pleased that as thin as she had become, her breasts were still full and firm and filled the décolletage, and though her skin was a touch yellow, the brilliant green of her eyes dimmed the dark circles beneath them. She no longer looked young, but age and illness had not totally eclipsed her beauty. Her hair, now quite grey, was coiled high on her head and set about with jewels, revealing a slender neck and a face of small bones and full mouth. But it was the eyes, as it had always been the eyes, that retained all the allure that she had had as a girl. She was pleased with herself in the glass, but unaccountably weary. The familiar pain was stubbornly in place but she steeled herself to ignore it as she went from her room.

Before she went down the staircase to the drawing room where the other guests were already being served champagne, she wanted to see Peregrine. She slipped along the corridor to James and Julia's old nursery and knocked gently on the door before popping her head in. Prissie was sitting by the cradle, sewing. She looked up and smiled when she saw it was Amelia.

'How fine you look,' she said admiringly.

'Thank you.' Amelia managed to drop a small curtsy. 'I wanted to see the object of all this excitement. Is he asleep?'

'No, merely inspecting his fingers,' Prissie said. 'He has just discovered them and is enthralled.'

Amelia leaned to peep into the crib and received a chirrup for her pains.

'Is he always so happy?' she asked.

'Always. A pleasure to nurse. Ella, who has no cause to care for him, is besotted and he thrives on her milk.'

'So very different . . .' Amelia murmured.

'Indeed.'

'So very fortunate.'

369

'Indeed.'

The two women smiled at each other.

'May I hold him for a moment or will it disturb him?'

'Nothing disturbs him, but he may be wet on your gown. Let me find something to protect you.' She bustled to the linen chest, took a napkin and wrapped it round the baby then handed him to Amelia. The child stared at her with interested eyes as she rocked him.

'He is the heir to a great fortune,' Prissie remarked.

'More importantly, it seems he is the heir to good health and a sound mind,' Amelia said. 'He is a blessing.' She kissed him lightly on the forehead and handed him back to Prissie. 'I must go down,' she said. 'Will you tell Minta when you see her that I would like some more of her potion? Stronger if it is possible.'

'No better?' The look Prissie gave her was a mixture of worry and sympathy that also held a touch of fear.

'It will never be better,' Amelia said with a dismissive gesture. 'But tonight I intend to enjoy myself.'

Ben was to lead her into dinner and the admiration in his eyes told her that her efforts with her toilette had been worth while. Tansy rushed to kiss her.

'You have done it again, Mama,' she whispered. Amelia stood back to inspect her daughter, dramatic as ever in cherry red, black hair cascading unfashionably but beautifully.

'No,' she whispered back. 'You win.'

'You are the two most beautiful women in the room,' Ben said solemnly, and Tansy tapped him with her fan before giving him a kiss.

Amelia took her cousin's arm with both relief and pleasure. He, too, had aged. The red wig he wore seemed to emphasise the fact. He was plump, his waistcoat stretched over his belly, but he had not lost his Puckish quality. She had known him for so long that it felt good to be with him and she found herself wondering if perhaps it had been a mistake to say no to him so often. Maybe they would have been content together, but he would have had only half-measure. He should have married Marianne who adored him still. But then she would have had half-measure. Perhaps things were better as they were.

The dining room looked magnificent. The long linen-covered table was laid with the finest silver and crystal. Charlotte's china was specially imported from Chelsea in London, and her superb silver candelabra marched the length of the table, blazing with light and warming the room. The light glittered on jewels, and reflected off the shining fabric of rich gowns and the gold buttons and buckles of the men. Amelia settled herself in her place with Zach on her right and Ben on her left and looked about her with pleasure. Even had she married the Earl her father promised her so long ago, he could have given her no grander life than this.

The food was her only problem. She could not eat. She felt as if there was some internal locked door that prevented her from swallowing. Her

370

mouth and tongue welcomed the tender slices of lamb, her throat was ready to accept the food, but she had a conviction that after her throat it would not pass the door and that there was nowhere for it to go. She could manage the soft vegetables and the wine. The meat she dare not touch. Ben, seeing her dilemma, slid some of slices onto his own plate.

'Pig!' she said, giving him a mischievous grin. He gazed at her sadly. It was the same look she had seen on Prissie's face, the look that all those who loved her wore when they saw her afresh. This look of love and pity, with its intimations of mankind's mortality, made her realise just how ill she was.

'I'm all right,' she said gently. 'Don't look like that.'

He turned his head and she saw a muscle in his throat move as if he were trying to hold back tears.

After the posset was served, the house slaves refilled the glasses and Zach rose to his feet. The buzz of noise and wine-induced laughter died away. He stood with his head bent for a moment and Amelia realised that her ambitious, ruthless brother was overcome by emotion. He looked up and began speaking and his eyes were bright with tears.

'Ladies and gentlemen, family and friends,' he began, his voice strangled, 'I am happy to welcome you all here today on what is the happiest day of my life.

'My beloved son has given me a grandchild, a healthy, bonny lad who can only bring happiness to the Quick family. And he could not be more a part of our family since his other grandfather is William Rosier-Quick, the son of my dearly beloved sister Amelia who sits here beside me.

'Tonight I am going to ask you to forgive the sin of pride for I wish to indulge myself in it. I am proud of my sister and my cousin Ben, I am proud of my wife and children, and especially proud of my new grandson. And it is a matter of pride to me that one day this new member of the Quick clan will inherit three of the largest and most beautiful plantations on St Christopher. He is the heir to all that my sister and I have achieved since we arrived on this island nearly forty-two years ago.

'I think the time has come to tell you of our beginnings, of how we arrived here dirty, hungry and afraid, branded as felons.' He nodded solemnly as a murmur ran round the table. 'For most of the years of my life since that January morning when my sister, my cousin, and I found ourselves in the slave market at Old Town Road I have striven to hide that beginning, but today I understand that my shame was unwarranted. Today I am proud of what we have done.

'Of all of you here only my sister, cousin and my wife know what I am about to tell you. Our troubles began when our father died in the battle of Sedgemoor fighting for Monmouth in that long ago English rebellion. His gently-born children were sentenced to ten years' slave labour in the West Indies . . .'

He paused and Amelia stared at him open-mouthed. She could not believe her ears. All the years of concealment gone in this amazing burst

371

of revelation. She turned to look at Ben who had a half-smile on his face. 'What is he going to say about his buccaneering, I wonder?' he whispered in her ear.

The room was transfixed. No one moved as Zach continued his story.

'It was to this very plantation, Windsong, that we were sold. I worked the fields with the other slaves, my sister and Ben were employed in the house. We slept in the slave cabins, we had no privileges. None at all.'

He paused again, and Amelia noted that Charlotte was fidgeting with her fan. Her family might not come well out of this.

'But as some of you may remember, that fearful ten-year sentence was repealed when good King William came to the throne. We were free. Alone, penniless, but free. Of course, much else happened to us. But we survived and we won through. And there is romance in this story . . .' He bent to take his Charlotte's hand and drew her to her feet.

'No buccaneering, no tavern, no Joshua,' Ben whispered.

'. . . My dear wife, who I am proud to have standing beside me tonight, found it in her heart to love this "felon", found it in her heart to give me her hand in spite of the past that was forced on me.

'And it was her father, a true English gentleman, who helped me onto the road that has led to my years of service to this island that has become my home. My son James continues that service, as does my nephew, William, and I pledge to you that my grandson, Peregrine, will also continue the tradition.' He half raised his glass, and added, 'You may wonder why I tell you this. I tell you out of pride, not just in my own achievements, but in those of every man and woman sitting at this table.

'We exiles are strong people. We work and we survive. Consider what we have done on this little island. We have built a thriving economy, a prosperous town, fine homes; we have created great wealth from small beginnings. Our plantations provide great wealth for the mother country. Yet each and every one of us is far from home, living in a cruel climate, surrounded by alien people.

'My beginnings here were not as yours, but each one of us has taken charge of our own destiny. Your ancestors came to a land of opportunity, perhaps with trepidation in their hearts, and turned it to their own and England's ends. We continue the tradition. England should be proud of us all.' He raised his glass higher. 'And therefore I ask you to drink to the future of St Kitts and to my grandson who is the future. Long may they both prosper.'

He sat down to a burst of cheering. Men were on their feet raising their glasses, faces red in the candlelight. William looked as if he were having difficulty hiding an expression of dismay and Charlotte 's smile appeared painted on.

'Now why did you do that?' Amelia asked her brother under cover of the cheering.

He straightened his shoulders and lifted his head. 'It was time the truth was told,' he informed her.

'You pompous old thing,' she teased. 'I know what you're up to. You're turning yourself into a legend, aren't you? But you did leave rather a lot out.'

He opened his mouth to protest, saw the laughter in her eyes and looked skywards before laughing, a touch sheepishly, himself.

'Oh, Amelia,' he sighed. 'You don't change, do you?'

It was Ben who saw that all was not well. It must have been no more than a minute after her exchange with Zach that Amelia began to feel unwell. Though she felt queasy, the pain was no worse and no better, but the lethargy she had suffered all day overcame her. She felt as if she just wanted to lie down and sleep for ever. Breathing had become difficult and she was blazing hot. She could feel sweat trickling between her breasts and the small curls on her forehead were clinging to her skin. As she struggled for composure, Ben took her hand and turned her to face him.

'Is something wrong?' he asked anxiously.

'It's just the heat in here,' she said. 'I need some air. I'm going to slip away for a moment.'

'Let me come with you.'

She seemed to be burning up but smiled at him coquettishly, asking herself why she did so.

'It's not necessary. I'll be better alone. I shall be back in ten minutes.' He looked hurt and disappointed. 'If I'm not,' she said lightly, 'you can come and find me. But I will be back. Oh yes, I will be back and perhaps I'll fill in the gaps in Zach's story for his guests.'

She heard herself giggle and caught Ben's worried look.

'I am all right,' she assured him, not believing her own words, she felt so peculiar.

As brandy and claret glasses were refilled, the noise in the room was like a blow to the ears. Desperate to get out, she rose to her feet, steadied herself by clinging to the table, and began to make her way to the door. Zach, who was shouting a conversation across the room, did not notice her go. Tansy did, but Amelia gave her a little reassuring wave as she walked carefully out of the room.

In the hallway, she leaned her back against the closed door of the dining room, catching her breath. She drew her bare forearm across her forehead to wipe away the sweat. It seemed to her that the constant ache she suffered had stilled; perhaps the claret had helped. But she could not understand why she felt so desperately tired and yet light-headed. Could she have a fever? The candles seemed so bright, wavering points of searing light, troubling her eyes. Light of the world; candles were the light of the world, banishing darkness, holding fear at bay.

She shook her head to recall her wandering mind and stood listening. Here in the hallway, away from the noise of the feast, the howl of the wind reigned, ferociously screaming down the chimney and drowning out the sounds of revelry. It battered the sturdy walls of the house and rattled the front door as if demanding entrance, a million banshees rushing through the night. She had heard the extraordinary voice of a hurricane before, but never one as violent as this. 'Windsong, Windsong,' she said out loud. 'Such a wild and savage song. Such a song for these islands.'

Slowly, exasperated by her own weakness, she dragged herself towards the front door of the house. She wanted to be out in the wind and the rain, she needed to be part of the song. Somewhere in that relentless roar something was calling to her. It did not frighten her to hear her name on the wind; she realised she had been waiting for this summons to follow the elements for a long, long time. She had escaped once when the sea nearly took her. Now she had a fancy that nature had been biding her time to snatch at her again, and now the moment had come.

The slave who acted as porter and doorman had emerged from his cubbyhole and was watching her, puzzled. She thought it was Daniel standing there, Truly's Daniel. She smiled at him.

'Open the door for me, Daniel,' she said.

The slave looked alarmed. 'It's Joseph, mistress, and I don' dare open that door. If I opens that door this house it go'n blow away.'

She shook her head impatiently. 'It won't blow away. Not this house. This is the wind's home. Windsong. The wind is singing to Windsong. Open the door, Daniel. I wish to go out. And shut it after me.' Her voice was imperious.

'I'll try, Mistress 'Melia,' he said unhappily and she was aware that she was frightening him.

He turned the great key and pulled the heavy bolts. He began to pull and the wind pushed at the wood, blowing the door open and into the house with what seemed like a whoop of delight. Amelia laughed out loud at the impertinence. Skirting the edges of the gale and clinging to the door jam, she managed to propel herself onto the steps of the house. She stood there clinging to the rail while Joseph fought to shut the door as she had ordered. The wind in her face stretched the skin back, baring her teeth. She turned sideways against it and pulled herself down the steps, feeling her hair whip about her head, shedding jewels and pins. She held her face up to the rain, letting it cool her. Already she was drenched, her emerald gown clinging to her. Exhilarated, she laughed at the sky. Then, with no warning, the wind calmed. There was a sudden silence. She stopped, listened, her head to one side, the sense of exhilaration lost.

An understanding of what she was doing came with the sudden silence. The rain had cooled her fever; her head was clear. She walked into the garden, intending to find the pool where she and Joshua had first made love. Something told her that there was no time left and that was the place she wanted to be. It was all over, neatly and tidily, perfectly. Her life and the lives of those she loved were in order. For her there was nothing left to do except wait for the enemy inside to take her over. But maybe she could forestall the enemy, cheat him of his prey. She began to walk but the wind returned, whipping itself into a fury. She fought against it, but for each step she took forward it hurled her back two. Then an almighty gust lifted her, threw her frail frame into the air and carelessly dropped her down. She could not get up again. Each time she tried, the wind pushed her back as if chiding her for even trying.

'You win!' she said for the second time that night and lay in the cool, sodden grass, considering and accepting that she really did not wish to get up. She had merely been obeying a lifetime's instinct of refusing to be beaten. There was no longer any purpose in the fight. It was time to give in, time to rest, time to be peaceful.

Her eyes were closed and she was very still when Ben found her. He called her name, anguished, and for one last time she turned her green gaze upon him.

'I knew you'd come,' she said and sought for his hand. 'Oh, Ben, hasn't it all been wonderful!'

And as her eyes closed again, she was smiling.